ECHOES OF THE WELL OF SOULS

A WELL WORLD NOVEL

PT-CDP-674

BY JACK L. CHALKER
PUBLISHED BY BALLANTINE BOOKS

AND THE DEVIL WILL DRAG YOU UNDER

DANCE BAND ON THE TITANIC

DANCERS IN THE AFTERGLOW

A JUNGLE OF STARS

THE WEB OF THE CHOSEN

THE SAGA OF THE WELL WORLD

Volume 1: *Midnight at the Well of Souls*

Volume 2: *Exiles at the Well of Souls*

Volume 3: *Quest for the Well of Souls*

Volume 4: *The Return of Nathan Brazil*

Volume 5: *Twilight at the Well of Souls: The Legacy of Nathan Brazil*

THE FOUR LORDS OF THE DIAMOND

Book One: *Lilith: A Snake in the Grass*

Book Two: *Cerberus: A Wolf in the Fold*

Book Three: *Charon: A Dragon at the Gate*

Book Four: *Medusa: A Tiger by the Tail*

THE DANCING GODS

Book One: *The River of the Dancing Gods*

Book Two: *Demons of the Dancing Gods*

Book Three: *Vengeance of the Dancing Gods*

Book Four: *Songs of the Dancing Gods*

THE RINGS OF THE MASTER

Book One: *Lords of the Middle Dark*

Book Two: *Pirates of the Thunder*

Book Three: *Warriors of the Storm*

Book Four: *Masks of the Martyrs*

THE WATCHERS AT THE WELL

Book One: *Echoes of the Well of Souls*

ECHOES OF
THE WELL
OF SOULS

A WELL WORLD NOVEL

JACK L. CHALKER

A DEL REY BOOK

BALLANTINE BOOKS • NEW YORK

A Del Rey Book

Published by Ballantine Books
Copyright © 1993 by Jack L. Chalker

All rights reserved under International and Pan-American Copyright Conventions. Published in the United States by Ballantine Books, a division of Random House, Inc., New York, and simultaneously in Canada by Random House of Canada Limited, Toronto.

Library of Congress Catalog Card Number: 92-90404
ISBN: 0-345-36201-2

Manufactured in the United States of America
First Edition: May 1993
10 9 8 7 6 5 4 3 2 1

This one's for my family:
For my father and mother, Lloyd Allen Chalker and
Nancy Hopkins Chalker,
who lived to see their son "make it" but not
to see this book, but whose strength and support
continue with me;
For David Whitley Chalker,
the unknown Super Mario Brother
who wasn't even born when the last one appeared;
For Steven Lloyd Chalker,
whose birth was another delaying factor in getting
this one finished;
And for Eva, as always.

A FEW WORDS
FROM THE AUTHOR

During a trip to the North Cascades up Lake Chelan in Washington State back in 1976, the Well World was born. This account has been published elsewhere (*Dance Band on the Titanic,* Del Rey, 1988) and won't be repeated here, but if you missed it, it gives as fully as I can explain it the creative processes which led, later that year, to the writing of *Midnight at the Well of Souls* (Del Rey, 1977 and ever after).

Midnight became my big hit, all the more so because it did it without any prior successes (my first novel, *A Jungle of Stars,* published the preceding year, sold okay but wasn't exactly a massive hit). Its fate was that it became, through means that no one can explain, a "campus cult classic" of the period—that is, a book everybody just *had* to read. Its sales, not only in the U.S. but in Britain, Germany, Denmark, and many other countries, have continued strong in the sixteen years since it was written, and it essentially made my career as a professional novelist.

It also brought me to a kind of personal fork in the road where I either jumped one way and risked everything or took the other and played my life safe. I was thirty-three years old and teaching history, and I had tenure at a time when history positions were few and far between. The safe road was to keep teaching until retirement and write, perhaps, a book every year or two when I had the time as a kind of profitable hobby. The other route was to go for broke and see if I could make it as a professional writer—even though it would mean giving up all that security, even tenure, at a time and age where I might not be able to get any of it back. I had the insight to realize that this was a once-in-a-lifetime opening and, ultimately, the ego to think I could make it.

To be practical, though, I'd need some real money, and fast. My publishers were paying me more than most beginning writers made, but it certainly wasn't enough to provide any security, and while I had ego and guts, I was practical enough and selfish enough not to want to starve in a garret someplace. Contrary to popular myth, starving in garrets has nothing to do with art; it has to do with your ability to recognize that after you do the art, it's a business. Shakespeare, Dickens, Twain, and Melville never starved in garrets, and I'd already gone through a sufficient number of life traumas that I didn't need to wallow in any more.

My publishers wouldn't pay enough to make me feel secure for other projects, but they would if I did a Well World sequel.

Now, understand, *Midnight* was never intended to be the start of a series. If it had been, I would have laid out things a lot differently. And I hadn't intended to write more, because what in the world do you do when you have already established that your hero is, at least in a science-fictional context, a god? The answer had to be to make him a peripheral character while featuring someone else, someone quite different. *Exiles at the Well of Souls* involved some of the same characters and time line but featured someone new and not godlike, the space pilot and high-tech thief Mavra Chang, and a mostly new supporting cast who went much farther afield geographically and otherwise.

I found I *liked* Mavra and the expanded Well, and on the manuscript page when I had ended *Midnight,* a fairly big book, I instead was introducing a new character into *Exiles.* Since the publisher had some length limitations (because of cost—buyer resistance to a much higher price for a gigantic volume meant they couldn't price it profitably), we split the book in two, with the second half published as *Quest for the Well of Souls.*

Doing a few independent novels as well during that period with totally different plots, settings, ideas, and objectives kept everything in at least creative perspective for me. Thus, when I finished *Quest,* I discovered I had enough unused notes to actually do another book. I had always wanted, for example, to go to the northern hemisphere of the Well World, and that was enough of a challenge (and had few of the layout problems compared to the south), so I wrote what my publisher titled *The Return of Nathan Brazil,* and then, in a big finish, I destroyed and re-created the entire universe, killed countless trillions of people, destroyed most civilizations, and had an upbeat ending in *Twilight at the Well of Souls.* It was a good ending, and I had no intention of ever writing another fictional word about the Well World.

Twilight was written in 1979 and published in 1980. The three novels in five volumes created a tight and, I thought, satisfactory epic. In spite of pleas from very large numbers of readers, I resolved that I was done, finished. I started work on *Four Lords of the Diamond.*

Now, I *did* have a couple of smart-ass lines I got used to giving at autographings, appearances, speeches, and SF conventions when I would inevitably be asked to do more Well World material, the most common of which was naming a dollar figure so impossibly high compared to what even the best in the field were getting paid at the time and saying that if somebody offered me *that* much, *and* if I had an idea I thought would not cheapen, and might possibly enhance, the existing books, I *might* consider it.

I have found that when you *are* actually offered *that much,* good ideas somehow pop out of the woodwork.

This book, and two more to follow, comprising the single work titled *The Watchers at the Well,* are the result. I have better titles than the ones we use, but the old experience with *The Return of Nathan Brazil* showed that some folks out there don't realize it's a Well World book unless it says Well of Souls in the title. While the story eventually caught up to the huge total of sales made by the other books in the series, it was a much slower starter. Don't blame me— blame yourselves.

And this brings up a last question. If you're too young or new to this literary form of ours or you're reading this because your wife/husband/brother/sister or whatever said you should, and you haven't read even *one,* let alone all five, of the previous books, what should you do?

The *correct* thing to do is to go and buy them. The friendly folks at Del Rey assure me that they will all be readily available at your nearest bookstore when this title comes out. They've never been out of print in any event, so if by chance they *aren't* there, either find a better, more aware bookstore or have them ordered.

But if you're not sure, or maybe cannot afford to invest twenty bucks, and want to just start reading this book, could you?

The answer is yes. This one, with the two that follow, has been constructed in such a way that while it contains two main characters from the earlier books and takes a few elements from them to move the plot along, everything here is explained and opened up as new. It will be quite a while before you actually get *on* the Well World, anyway, and by then the new characters who are partially the focus of this work will have to find out what you must know. Longtime readers will find it something of a refresher course, although I hope the information is what you need and not an encumbrance.

I enjoyed going back after such a long time, although I nearly went crazy trying to keep the Well World straight myself. The original books were done at a time when I was still using a (gasp!) *typewriter,* and so I didn't have my usual computer files to check and had to do it all the hard way. I have tried very hard to do justice to my own concept and my own convictions about my art, and I think I have. I haven't just dashed this off; indeed, this novel has taken the longest period I have ever used to write a book, and it's been among my most difficult to do as well. Over the period, too, I've thought that God or at least a great supernatural power was against me. Everything happened from my computer breaking down to having to undergo not one but two eye operations during this period. Well, the Powers lost. Here it is, and I wouldn't be offering it to you unless I thought it was as good as I could make it.

As I say, there are two more to come. Will I write others beyond that one? Well, I'm not going to say a flat "No," just as I didn't in 1980. And I'm not about to name another dollar figure, either. Maybe I will sometime, though—if this or its companion makes the *Times* bestseller lists . . .

Hey—naming a goal worked the *last* time, didn't it?

> Jack L. Chalker
> Uniontown, Maryland
> February 29, 1992

ECHOES OF THE WELL OF SOULS

A WELL WORLD NOVEL

PROLOGUE:

NEAR AN UNNAMED NEUTRON
STAR IN THE GALAXY M-22

In the nearly one billion years it had been in its lonely imprisonment, it had never lost its conviction that this universe required a god.

For eons beyond countless eons it had traveled through space in its crystalline cocoon, imprisoned until the end of time, or so those who'd fashioned the cage had boasted, yet what was time to it? And could any prison hold one such as it? Not entirely. They could hold the body, but the mind was beyond imprisonment.

The universe had been re-created, not once but many times, since it had been cast adrift by the only ones who could achieve such a feat, those of its own kind. It had been startled at the first re-creation, for it had been separated and walled off from the master control lest even in its eternal damnation it should somehow get inside once again. The Watchman had done it, the Watchman had reset all, but even the Watchman could not reset its own existence or alter its imprisonment, for it was of the First Matter.

Indeed, each time the system had been reset, its own power had increased; each re-creation required so much energy drawn from dimensions beyond the puny universe of its birth that for moments, for brief moments, there was no control at all, no chains, nothing to bind or hold, and its mind had been able to contact more and more of the control centers.

The jailers had not counted on that. They had not counted on a reset of their grand experiment in any way touching it, in any way influencing it; indeed, there had been much debate about whether to have a reset mechanism at all, and even those who argued in favor of it never dreamed it would actually be used, let alone more than once. Nothing was supposed to influence the prisoner in its eternal wanderings, but even gods can make mistakes; their mistakes, however, were of the sort that no one but another god could ever know of them.

But then, of course, freed of time, they nonetheless could never free themselves of its frame of reference; it was too ingrained in their genes and psyches. Unbound by instrumentalities, they had created their own boundaries in their less than limitless minds—minds indeed so limited that they could never accept the fact that absolute power was an end and not a means.

The last reset had done it. Intended to repair some sort of rip in the fabric of space-time itself, apparently wrought by *artificial* means, the reset had proved the need for a cosmic governor beyond doubt. The shift had been subtle, as they all had been subtle, yet the mathematics of its own prison were absolute, while that of the rest of the universe was not. At the crucial moment of the massive power drain, the one tiny fraction of a nanosecond when energy was not being equally applied as parts of the universe were selectively re-created, it was subject to the absolutes of physics without an interfering probability regulator.

It had been enough, *just* enough so that when the regulator kicked back in, it hadn't allowed for that most infinitesimal of lapses.

A neutron star grabbed at its prison, pulled it with ever-increasing speed, not enough to crash into the terribly dense surface but enough to create massive acceleration, to eventually propel it, like a missile in a sling, to speeds approaching that of light, bending time and space, catching it in the eddies and currents of space and punching it right through a tunnel, a hole in space-time created by the series of massive bodies here.

As usual, the prisoner did not know where or when it would emerge, but it also knew that for the first time the regulator didn't know either and would be slow to attempt adjustment. In that period it would be free of the regulator; in that period there might be a chance.

Then only the Watchman would stand between it and ultimate power. It was a being that even space and time could never fully contain, a being that had spent long eons planning its rule and reign. It would have to meet the Watchman eventually; it knew that and welcomed it, for the Watchman was in a way very much a prisoner as well, doomed to wander forever until needed yet always alone.

It looked forward to that meeting. In a billion years it had never been able to imagine who they'd gotten that was stupid enough to volunteer for the job and yet so slavishly loyal that, in all this time, it had never once taken advantage of the position.

A SMALL TOWN
IN GEORGIA

It had been a shock opening the door to the apartment and seeing just how much was missing.

Have I accumulated so little in my life as this? she wondered, oddly disturbed as much by the thought as by the emptiness.

Even most of the furniture had been his. He'd been nice, of course, offering to leave some of it, but she wanted everything of his, everything that might bring her back into contact with him, removed.

The effect was as if thieves had broken in and stolen anything that could be carried but had gotten scared off just before finishing the job. The drapes were hers, and the small stereo, the TV and its cheap stand, the six bookcases made of screw-it-together-yourself particleboard that sagged and groaned under the weight of her books, and the plants in the window. But only the big beanbag chair with the half dozen patches afforded a place to sit.

She went over to the sliding glass door that led to the tiny balcony and saw that the two cheap aluminum and plastic patio chairs and the little table she'd picked up at a garage sale were still there. So, too, were the worn chairs at the built-in kitchenette. He'd been sparing of the cutlery and glassware and had taken nothing save his abominable Captain Crunch cereal.

Feeling hollow and empty yet still distanced from the emotional shock, she put the small kettle on for tea and continued the inventory.

All her clothes were still there, of course, but even though they took up the vast majority of the closet space, there was an emptiness. The dresser and makeup table were just where they always were, but the room looked grotesque without the water bed, just the impression of where it had rested on the discolored and dirty carpet. She would have to tend to that right off the bat. She wondered if she could get a bed in four hours and doubted it; she'd have to either go to a motel tonight or sleep on the floor with just a pillow and sheets until it was delivered. There was no way in heaven that she could get as much as a twin mattress in the little Colt she was driving.

A sudden wave of insecurity washed over her, almost overwhelming her, and she dashed into the bathroom and then grabbed the sink as if to steady herself.

Funny how the bathroom had a calming effect. Maybe it was because, other than being minus his toiletries, it was intact. Then she looked at herself in the mirror, and some of the fear, the emptiness, returned.

She was thirty-six years old and, thanks to the two years she'd spent working at various odd jobs while waiting for an assistantship to open up so she could afford grad school, only seven years out of college. All that time she'd been a single-minded workaholic—push, push, push, drive, drive, drive. Two years teaching gut courses at junior college because even in an age when they were crying for scientists to teach, she'd discovered, there was a lot of resistance from the older male-dominated science faculties to hiring a young woman. All the research and academic excellence counted for little. Oh, they'd never come right out and said anything, but she knew the routine by now; at first she had been merely frustrated but was quickly clued in by her female colleagues at the junior college. *"They never take you serious unless you're well over forty because they think you're going to teach for a while and then quit and have babies"* and *"They still believe deep down that old saw about women not being as good as men in math and science."*

But they also, she had to admit, credited experience. Not that she hadn't tried that route, but the big openings for her were in the oil industry, and that meant both swallowing a lot of her principles and old ideals and also facing the probability of going off to Third World countries where women had no rights at all and trying to do a job there.

Finally she got *this* job, one she really loved, thanks to an old professor of hers who had become department head. As an instructor, teaching undergrads basic courses, it hadn't been the fun it should have been, but it allowed her to work as an assistant on the real research, even if it wasn't *her* grant and wouldn't merit more than a "thanks" in the articles that might be published out of it. Still, she'd done more work in the lab than the professors who *would* get the credit, trying to show them, prove to them that she was in their league and on their level.

And now she was thirty-six going on thirty-seven, not yet tenured, teaching elementary courses to humanities students who didn't give a damn but needed these few basic science courses so they could get B.S. instead of B.A. degrees. And she was alone in this mostly stripped apartment, going nowhere as usual and doing it alone.

Not that *he'd* dropped *her*. She had been the one to break it off, the one to give the ultimatum. It was always understood that they had an "open" relationship, that they were free to see others and not be tied down. They even laughed at the start about making sure they both had safe sex and got regular tests for any nasties that might be picked up. And she'd meant it at the time. The problem was she'd never fooled around with anybody else after he'd moved in, even though she'd had the chance. She simply didn't need anybody else. But he'd kept doing it and kept doing it and kept doing it until he'd done it with a regularity that finally showed that he was not about to slow down or become monogamous.

She felt guilty, even now, for being jealous. Worse, it wasn't based on morality but on her ego. She'd never expected to be so wounded, and it bothered her. *What do they have that I don't? What do they give him that I can't? Am I that bad in bed?*

Best not to dwell on it now. Best to pick up the pieces and go on to something else. She was good at that, she thought ruefully. It seemed like all her life she was picking up the pieces and going on to something else.

She slipped out of her clothes, removed her glasses, grabbed some towels, and went in to take a shower. The mirror on the shower wall reflected her back to herself with no illusions. She stepped very close to the glass so that she could see it clearly, her vision without the glasses being perfectly clear for only a foot or so in front of her, then stared at the reflection as if it were someone else, someone she hardly knew.

Her black hair was cut very short, in a boyish cut; it was easy to wash and easy to manage, and it had fewer gray hairs to pluck that way. Her face was a basic oval shape with brown eyes, thin lashes, a somewhat too large nose, and a mouth maybe a bit too wide, but not much. Not an unattractive face, neither cute nor beautiful, but with maturity creeping into its features, hardening them a bit—or was that her imagination?

Average. That's what she was: average. Not a bad figure but no bathing beauty type, either. Breasts a little too small, hips too wide. With the right clothes she could be very attractive, but this way, unadorned, her body would win no prizes, no envious gazes, no second looks. She looked like a million other women. *Generic, that's me,* she thought glumly. *I ought to have a little black bar code tattooed on my forehead.*

That was the trouble, really, in academia as well. There *were* women at the top of most scientific disciplines, including hers, none of whom would have any problems being wooed from one major chair to another, writing their own tickets their own way, but they were very few in number because the deck was still stacked. Those women were the geniuses, the intellects who could not be denied. As "attractive" was to "knockout," so "smart" was to "brilliant." Intellectually, she knew that the vast majority of people, male or female, could not have attained a doctorate in a field like hers, but it just wasn't *quite* enough. Enough to finally teach at a great university, but only as "Instructor in the Physical Sciences"—not just Physics 101, which was bad enough, but, God help her, "Introduction to the Sciences for Humanities Students"—and a lowly assistant on research projects whose grants and control were held by middle-aged male professors.

The shower helped a little, but not much, since it left time for more brooding. Was it the fates that struck her where she was, or was it rather lapses in herself? Was she demanding too much of a guy and maybe too much of herself? With people starving around the world and the working poor standing with their families in soup kitchen lines, did she have any right to complain about a dead-end life if it was such a comfortable, yuppified dead end? Was she being just daddy's spoiled little girl, in a situation many would envy, depressed because she couldn't have it all?

A line from one of her undergraduate seminars came to her, fairly or not, and tried to give her some relief from those hard questions. The professor had been a leading feminist and sociologist, and she'd said, *"It's not tough enough being a woman in this day and age, we also have to be saddled with some kind of constant guilt trip, too."*

She was, she knew, at a crisis point in her own life, no

matter how miserable other lives might be. She was at an age when biological clocks ticked loudly, at an age when ease of career change was fading fast with each passing page on the calendar, when any move that could be made had to be made or the status quo would become unbreakable. At some point in nearly everybody's life there came the time when one came to a cliff's edge and saw a monstrous gap between oneself and the other side, a side that was nearly impossible to make out. She was up for tenure and possible promotion next year, and she'd not heard anything to indicate she wouldn't get it, although one could never be sure. It was something she wanted, yet it also meant being here, on this side of the chasm, for the rest of her life.

Or she could break away and take real risks and, like most people who did so, fall into the chasm. But all the people who got what and where they wanted, the satisfied movers and shakers, had taken that same risk and made it to the other side. Not all of *those* people were happier than they'd been before, but many were. The trouble was, she was on the old side for making that leap. She was, after all, in this situation now because she craved stability, not earthquakes. Taking a risk in her personal life would mean saying yes to the first guy who proposed who wasn't a geek or a pervert. And professionally, to take a risk would mean first having someplace to jump to, and the offers weren't exactly pouring in, nor did risky opportunity just fall from the sky.

The vortex was never black; rather, it revealed the underside, the sinews, the crisscrossing lines of mathematical force that sustained and essentially stabilized the relevant parts of the universe. The Kraang examined those lines, noted the symmetry and precision, and, this time, noted the relay and junction points. Now, after all those millennia, the slight deviation the Kraang had been able to induce in the last reset had paid off; a line was being followed, not avoided as always before. The

Watchman's line, the focal point for probability itself, the emergency signal and warning beacon for the physics of the governable portions of the cosmos . . .

The emergence, as always, was like suddenly being catapulted out of a great tunnel; there, ahead, a solar system, a governed construct in a pattern the Kraang understood well, although it had no knowledge of what sort of creatures might live there or their current stage of development. It did not matter. The Kraang was not supposed to be in this sort of proximity, and already the signal of an aberration would be flowing back to Control, but it was a very long way, and even at the sort of speed such messages could travel Underside, it would be several seconds before it reached Control, and then Control would react.

By now the Kraang knew how it would react.

Control was not self-aware, for if it were, it would be a living god of the universe with no limits and no governor. Automatic maintenance meant automatic response; the experiments were supposed to be controlled, not supervised.

The Kraang's great mind searched frantically for the now-invisible termination of the force line. *Great Shia! Where was it?* A world incredibly ancient, a world with an artificial yet living core . . .

For a moment the Kraang experienced panic. No such world existed in this system! The nine planets and dozens of assorted larger moons were all dead save the experiment itself! A billion years the lords of chance had made the Kraang wait for this moment! A billion years, and now to be faced with failure . . . ! It would be too much for even the Kraang to bear.

And then, suddenly, it found what it was looking for. A planet once but no more, pulled apart by the strains of gravity and catastrophe, broken into impossibly small fragments that still worked together, trapped into sufficient cohesion by Control's grasp of the energy of probability. Although in a million million pieces, the living heart still somehow functioned in what remained, two tiny steering moons and a vast additional ring . . .

Its mind reached out. Success! Connection! *I give a small part of myself to you!*

A sudden and violent bump, a wrenching jar—its container had been struck head on! An asteroid, small yet effective, had slammed into the container, altering its trajectory. It began to move quickly away, toward the still-distant inner gas giant. The Kraang relaxed and understood. Control was correcting. At this speed and trajectory the Kraang would rush headlong toward the giant world beyond, well away from the active matrix, and the giant's great gravity would slingshot the container around, accelerate it to tremendous speed, sufficient to generate a space-time ripple, to take it out of this system, perhaps out of this entire galaxy.

But it would take two years, as time was counted here, for it to reach the giant and the better part of a third to achieve the desired effect. Out here, in the real universe, Control was constrained by its own laws and the basic laws of physics. Corruption of the system had now occurred; the experiment was now invalidated. It would have no choice but to use whatever mechanism it created to call the Watchman, down there, somewhere, on the experiment itself, the blue and white world third from the sun . . .

"Lori, could you step into my office for a minute?"

It was symptomatic of the problems in her professional life and of her feelings of hitting brick walls. Whiz kid Roger Samms, Ph.D. at twenty-four, was always "Dr. Samms," but Lori Sutton, Ph.D., age thirty-six, was almost always "Lori" to Professor George Virdon Hicks, the department head and her boss. Hicks was basically a nice guy, but he belonged to a far older generation and was beyond even comprehending the problem.

She entered, somewhat puzzled. "Yes, sir?"

"Sit down, sit down!" He sighed and sank into his own chair. "I've got an interesting and fast-developing situation here that's causing us some problems and may be opening up some opportunities for you. Uh—pardon me for asking, but I'm given to understand that you're living alone here now, no particular personal ties or local family?"

She was puzzled and a little irritated at the speed of campus gossip. "That's true."

"And you did some of your doctoral research at the big observatories in Chile?"

She nodded. "Yes, under Don Mankowicz and Jorje Paz. It was the most fun I've had in science to date."

"Did you get over the mountains and into the Amazon basin at all?"

It was hard to see where this was going. "Yes, I took a kind of back-country trip into the rain forests with the Salazars—they finance their fight against the destruction of the rain forest and its cultures by taking folks like me on such trips. It was fascinating but a little rugged."

Hicks leaned forward a little and picked up a packet in a folder on his desk and shoved it toward her. She opened it up and saw it was full of faxes, some showing grainy photographs, others trajectory charts, star charts, and the like. She looked them over and read the covering letter from the MIT team down in Chile who'd sent them. And she was suddenly very interested.

"About nine days ago, during some routine calibration sweeps for the eighty-incher that's just been overhauled, they picked this up. We're not sure, but we think it's a known asteroid—at least, a small one discovered about a dozen years ago should have been in that vicinity at about that time. It should have cleared the orbit of the moon by a good two hundred thousand kilometers, but something, some collision or force unknown, seems to have jarred it just so. It's big—maybe as big as eight hundred meters— and it's just brushing by the moon right now."

She shrugged. "Fascinating, but we've had ones as big as or bigger than this come in between us and the moon."

"Yes, but they missed."

She felt a cold, eerie chill go through her, and she looked

at the computer readouts again. "It's going to hit? This is—this could be Meteor Crater or Tunguska!"

He nodded. "Yes, on page three, there, you see that the current estimate based on angle, trajectory, and spectrum analysis of the composition estimates that possibly a third of it will survive to impact, possibly as a single unit. The explosion and crater are going to be enormous."

"And it's going to hit land? In South America?"

"We can't be completely certain, not for another ten to twelve hours, maybe not even then. There are a lot of questions as to the exact angle of entry, how much true mass it represents, whether it will fragment, and so on. They're now giving better than even odds that it'll impact off the Chilean or Ecuadorian coast in the Pacific, but if it's very heavy and hard inside and if the mass is great enough, it'll come down short, possibly in the Andes, more likely in the Brazilian rain forest short of there. Fortunes are being wagered in every observatory and physics department in the world, or will be. It'll hit the news shortly; there's much debate, I understand, on how early to release it, since we'll inevitably get special media coverage with experts talking about global warming and a new ice age from the dust and you name it and people living in both the wrong hemispheres panicking anyway. It'll be out regardless by the evening news tonight."

She nodded, fascinated but still puzzled. "So what has this to do with me?"

"There'll be scientists from all over and news organizations as well gearing up to go in, but the Brazilian government is very concerned about possible injuries or deaths and wants nobody in the area. They have troops already up there trying to get the few settlements evacuated in time, and that, plus the usual red tape, is putting the brakes on most efforts. The exception is Cable News, which has some contacts there and a good relationship with the Brazilian press and government. They've used us before for science pieces and are mounting a team to cover it. To the frustration of the others, they'll probably be the pool. They need somebody with them to tell them what the devil it is they're seeing, or not seeing, and they've called us."

She sat for a moment, not quite wanting to believe the implications of the conversation. Finally, worried that she *had* misunderstood, she asked, "Are you asking if I would go?"

He nodded. "Very short notice." He looked at his watch. "You'd have to leave for home now. Pack in an hour or so. Your passport is current?"

"Yes, but—"

"Don't forget it. They've got the visas. They'll send a helicopter here for you and your stuff. You'll be on a private charter with their team leaving Hartsfield at seven tonight."

"But—but . . . Why me?"

He looked almost apologetic. "Grad assistants can cover your courses with no sweat, but Doctor Samms is in a rush to get his research organized for a presentation at the AAS next week, and both Kelly and I are, frankly, too old for this sort of thing, as much as I'd love to see that sucker come down—pardon the expression. Nobody else is qualified to observe the event and free enough to go who also wouldn't be stiff as a board and look like an ass on television. So it's either you or they call another university. And I'm afraid I have to call them back in less than ten minutes or they're going to do that anyway."

"I—I hardly know what to say. Yes, of *course* I'll go. I—oh, my God! I better get packing!" The fact that he was being fairly left-handed about it all, that she'd gotten the job only because she was the only one so unimportant that she could be easily spared, didn't bother her. This was the kind of luck she dreamed about, the one break upon which she might be able to stake out a scientific position that would be so unique that it would ensure her stature and prominence.

"We'll make sure you're covered," Hicks assured her. "Five o'clock this afternoon they'll land to pick you up at the medical center heliport. Don't forget your passport!"

She wanted to kiss the old boy, who now could call her "Lori" any time he wanted, but she was in too much of a hurry. Jeez—she'd have to get the suitcases out of the storage locker, haul them up. What to take? She had little clothing or equipment for this kind of trip. And makeup— this was television! And the laptop, of course, and . . . How the *hell* was she going to pack and make it in just three hours?

It was tough, but she managed, knowing she'd forgotten many vital things and hoping that she would have a chance to pick them up in Brazil before going into the wild. The mere hauling of the suitcases and the packing had her gasping for breath, and she began to wonder if she was up to the coming job. She began to feel both her age and the effects of letting the spa membership lapse about a year earlier. She also worried about how much of that clothing, particularly the jeans, would fit. In the months since she'd thrown Harry out, she'd found solace for her dark mood in large quantities of chocolate and other sugary things and generally letting herself go.

Well, the hell with it. If they were going to give her this kind of notice, they could damned well buy her appropriate jungle clothing.

She locked up and hauled the suitcases to the car, discovering for the first time that one wheel on the big suitcase was missing. She just wasn't *ready* for this, not with this kind of deadline—but she knew she needed it, needed it bad.

The helicopter was just about on time. It was, she saw, amused, the one Atlanta's pop radio station used for traffic reports and had that big logo on the side. She wondered how the commuters were going to get home tonight.

The pilot got out, bending slightly under the rotors, and put out his hand. "Hello! I'm Jim Syzmanski," he said in a shouted Georgia-accented voice. "You're Doctor Sutton?"

"Yes. I'm sorry for the bulk, but they didn't give me much notice on this."

He looked at the two suitcases. "No sweat. You ought to see what some of 'em take to a mere accident." He picked them up as if they weighed nothing and stored them in back of the seats. "Get in, and we'll get you goin'."

Although not new to helicopters, she'd never been in one of these small, light types with two seats and a bubble, and it was a little unnerving for a while. Still, the pilot knew his business; it was smooth and comfortable, and they were approaching the airport in a mere twenty minutes, about two hours less than it would have taken to drive and park.

"Sorry to rush you here so you could wait," the pilot told her, "but they need the chopper back over the highways, and this was the only slot I had to get you. Your bags will be okay here. Not many facilities in this area, but unless you want to hike a bunch to the terminal and back, I'd say just head for that waiting room over there. It's pretty basic, but it'll do. I'll radio in once I'm up and tell them that you're here and waiting. It shouldn't be long."

She thanked him, and he was off as soon as he got clearance, leaving her alone in the hangar area. There was a sleek-looking twin-engine Learjet just beyond the barrier with the news organization's corporate logo; she assumed that it was the plane they were going to use.

She turned and walked toward the indicated lounge area, which wasn't much more than a prefabricated unit sitting on the tarmac. A few official-looking people were around beyond the fence, but she suddenly felt nervous about being there without some kind of pass or badge. What if she got arrested for possible hijacking or something?

The lounge proved to have a few padded seats, one of those portable desks so common at airport check-ins, a single rest room, a soft drink machine, two candy machines, a dollar changer, and an empty coffee service. Suddenly conscious that she hadn't taken the time to eat anything since breakfast, she looked at the machines and sighed. The cuisine in this place wasn't exactly what she needed, but it would have to do. Hartsfield was such an enormous airport that getting to a point where she could even catch a shuttle to a terminal was beyond her current energy level, and she was afraid to leave. If they showed up and didn't find her here, they might just leave without her. One of Murphy's ancient laws—if you stay, they'll be late. If you go, they'll show up almost immediately. This wasn't exactly scheduled service, and any rules beyond that weren't very clear.

She fumbled through her bag. At least she had some ones and what felt like a ton of change at the bottom.

Nothing brought on depression faster or made time crawl more than having rushed like mad only to wind up stuck in an empty building, she reflected. The adrenaline rush was wearing off, replaced by a sense of weariness. If the pace had continued, it wouldn't have been so bad, but to be dropped suddenly into lonely silence was murder.

It also gave her time to worry. Had she packed everything that she needed? Was she dressed right for this? Thinking of utility, she'd pulled on some stretch pants, a Hubble telescope T-shirt because it was the only thing she could find that would mark her as perhaps a scientist, and some low-top sneakers. Her old hiking boots were packed, at least, but she doubted that she had a pair of jeans that still fit. Prescription sunglasses, check. But her spare pair of regular glasses were still in her desk in her office. Damn! *That's one,* she thought glumly. The pair she had on and the sunglasses would have to do.

She also hadn't stopped the mail or papers or arranged for her car to be picked up. It was too late to call anybody who could do much tonight; she'd have to call Hester, the department secretary, from Brazil tomorrow.

She went over to the window and looked out on the field. The sun was getting low, and the tinted windows reflected her image back through the view. *God! I look awful!* she thought, worried now about first impressions. She hadn't really realized how much she'd let herself go. She was becoming a real chubette, even in the face, and the very short haircut that had proved so convenient and would also be best for the tropics somehow looked very masculine against that face. *I look like a middle-aged bull dyke,* she thought unhappily. She was supposed to go on TV looking like *this*?

She was suddenly struck with a twinge of panic. What if the television people saw her and decided that there was no way somebody looking like her could go on? What if they told her at the last minute that they were getting somebody from the observatories in Chile? There had to be quite a scientific team assembling there for this event.

It was the deserted civil aviation terminal, she told herself. Rushing around from a standing start and then being dropped into this lonely silence. She wasn't very convincing, however. She was getting old and fat and unattractive at an accelerating rate, and it scared the living hell out of her.

She kept going to the windows and peering out at the Learjet, wondering if she shouldn't be outside, even in the dark. They might miss her, might not even know she was there.

Suddenly she heard voices approaching. The door opened, and two people walked in. The first was maybe the thinnest woman she'd ever seen short of Ethiopian famine pictures on TV; the woman almost redefined the term "tiny." Maybe five feet tall, weighing less than some people's birth weights, dressed in jeans and a matching denim jacket, she was perhaps in her mid-thirties, although it was hard to tell for sure, with a creamy brown complexion and one of those Afro-American hairstyles that looked like the hair was exploding around the head.

The other was a tall, lanky man in jeans and cowboy boots with disheveled sandy brown hair and a ruddy complexion who needed only a stalk of wheat in his hand to be the perfect picture of somebody who'd just stepped off the farm.

"So, anyway, I told George—" the thin woman was saying in one of those big, too-full voices small people seemed to have or develop, when she saw the stranger and paused. "Oh! Hi! You must be Doctor Sutton!"

"Uh—yes. I—I was beginning to think I was forgotten."

The tiny woman sank into a chair. "Sorry about that. When stories happen this fast it's always a mess, and this won't be the last of it. I'm Theresa Perez—'Terry' to all— and this is, believe it or not, Gustav Olafsson, always 'Gus.' I'm what they euphemistically call a 'producer,' which means I'm supposed to make sure everything's there that needs to be there and that the story gets done and gets back. It sounds important, but in the news biz it's a glorified executive secretary to the reporter. Gus is that peculiar breed of creature—we're not sure if they're human or not— known as the 'news photographer.' The kind of fanatic who'll insist on taping his own execution if it'll get a good picture."

" 'Lo," said the taciturn photographer.

"They tell us it'll be five or ten minutes and then we'll board, taxi out, and wait two hours to get out of this damned mess," Perez continued. "The traffic in this place is abominable. You know the saying, 'A wicked man died, and the devil came and took him straight to hell—after, of course, changing in Atlanta.' "

Lori smiled, although it was an old joke. "I know. Is that our plane out there?"

"Yeah. Don't let it fool you. The boss has a *real* fancy one just for his own use. The rest of them are corporate jets. We almost always fly commercial, but if we took Varig down, with all the changes and schedule problems, we'd never be sure of getting where we need to get in time. When you have a schedule problem, the Powers That Be unfreeze their rusted-shut purses and spring for a special. You have bags?"

"Two. They're still in the hangar over there—I hope."

"We'll get them."

"I hope I'm going to be able to pick up something before we go into the bush," Lori told her. "I'm not even sure my old stuff fits."

"I know what you mean. Well, we've got about seventy hours total, and it'll be tight, but we should have a little time in Manaus to get *something*, anyway. It's a decent city for being out there in the middle of nowhere, particularly since it became a main port of entry for airplanes. I was down a year or so ago when we did a rain forest depletion story. One of these times I'm going to be able to see something of these places we get sent. It's always hurry, hurry in this business, and after being ying-yanged around the world, when you get some time off, you want to spend it home in bed."

Lori nodded and smiled, but deep down she envied somebody with that kind of life.

"She never stops talking," Gus commented in a dry Minnesota accent that fit him well. "Ain't gonna get no sleep at all on this trip."

Perez looked up at him with a wry expression. "Gloomy Gus, always the soul of tact. No wonder you can't keep a job."

Lori looked puzzled, and Perez said, "Gus is a free lance. Half the foreign photographers, sound men, and technicians are, even for the broadcast networks. Nobody can afford to keep on a staff so large that it can be all the places with all the personnel it needs to cover the world. I have a list of hundreds in different categories. This time Gus was the first one I called who was available."

"What she really means is that they don't want to pay top dollar to the best in the business during the long times when there's nothin' happening," Gus retorted.

"I gather you two have worked together before."

Perez nodded. "Twice. Once on the Mexican earthquake and again on one of those stock 'volcano blows its top' stories from Hawaii. Beats me why folks still have houses around that thing to begin with. Gus specializes in natural disasters. That's how he got tagged 'Gloomy' as much as his shining personality."

The door opened again, and a middle-aged man in a pilot's uniform came in. "We're ready when you are," he told Perez.

"Let's go, then," the producer responded, getting up, and they all filed out after the pilot.

"My bags!" Lori said suddenly.

"Need help?" the pilot asked her.

"No, not if they're still there, thanks. Just bring them out to the plane?"

He nodded, and she dashed into the hangar. Somebody had moved them to one side, but they were still there and apparently otherwise untouched. She picked them both up and walked toward the jet. The pilot—actually the copilot as it turned out—took them and stowed them in an external baggage compartment, along with Perez's overnight bag and Gus's small suitcase and huge mass of formidable-looking cases containing, she supposed, his camera, lenses, and the like.

The Lear *was* the way to fly, she decided almost instantly. It was like the first-class cabin of the finest airliner but no coach section behind. Just four extralarge and comfortable swivel airline seats with extended backrests and two pairs of standard seats against the aft bulkhead between which was access to the rest room. There was a small table in the center of the four swivel chairs that looked like a junior version of a corporate boardroom conference table. There were compartments overhead and other places to stow gear. There were also ashtrays, something she hadn't seen on many planes for a while. Not that she needed one, but clearly the regulations didn't apply if one owned the plane.

"Turn forward and you'll feel the seat lock into place," the copilot instructed them. "Everybody fasten your belts and keep your seats in the forward locked position until we have altitude. Once we're up, I'll come back and show you the rest. We've got a window coming up, though, and we don't want to miss it. You get bumped to the back of the line here, you may sit for hours."

They still sat for a little while, but finally the small jet taxied out to the starting position and in a very short time was rolling down the runway at what seemed breakneck speed, although it probably wasn't any faster than the 767 that had gone before them.

The flight was surprisingly smooth and comfortable once they were airborne; more so, she thought, than a bigger plane, although it had been much bumpier taxiing. She had been surprised to see the "Fasten Seat Belt" and "No Smoking" signs just like on a commercial jet. In a few minutes, the panorama of Atlanta at night was obscured by clouds and there was nothing to do but wait until those magic lights vanished, signaling freedom. Not that she wanted to get up right at the moment; the angle of climb was pretty steep and seemed to go on forever.

Finally they leveled off, and the seat belt lights went out. Almost immediately the copilot came back to the cabin. "Anybody hungry?" he asked.

"Starved," Lori responded.

"We get our meals from the same caterer as the big boys on flights like this. The executives have their own food specially prepared, but this is cuisine à la Dobbs House, I'm afraid. No better or worse than the usual airline fare. I'll stick them in the microwave, and we'll at least be full up until breakfast." The small kitchen was cleverly concealed and easy to manage. He put the dinners in, set the controls, then came back and pressed a large square button on one of the bulkheads. A section opened outward, cleverly revealing an impressive-looking bar.

"It's more or less serve yourself," the copilot told them. "Anything you might want is here. Hard stuff, soft stuff, beer, wine—good wine—as well as coffee, which I'll start when we reach altitude. Ice is in the hopper there, glasses in the bin. Trash goes in here, and dirty glasses go in this other bin over here."

A bell went off, and he went back to the small kitchen. "Let's see . . . we've got Delta fish, United Salisbury steak, and USAir lasagna. I'll just put them on the cold trays and set them on the table, and you can fight over which one you want."

"What about you and the pilot?" Lori asked him.

"Oh, we have to eat yet different meals, but that's later. Both of us ate before we came."

He showed them how to unlock the seats so they would swivel once more and also demonstrated that they were nearly full recliners with a nice footrest emerging when the backrest was lowered. Pillows and blankets were above.

Lori didn't care which meal she got and wound up with the Salisbury steak. She couldn't help noticing that Terry had the fish and a diet Pepsi. Only the congenitally thin acted like they were obese all the time.

"So—is this it?" she asked the two newspeople. "I mean—no reporter?"

Terry chuckled. "Oh, there'll be a reporter, all right. Himself." She lowered her voice as deep as she could. "John Maklovitch, CNN news," she intoned solemnly. "He'll meet up with us in Manaus. Flying in from God Only Knows, as usual. In fact, he should beat us there if his connections work out right. We'll use local free-lancers. I've already set up with my counterpart from TV Brasil. Right now they think it's fifty-fifty that the meteor will come down before dawn, so we're going to try and catch its act as it comes in, from the air. It would be neat if we could catch it hitting the earth, but they still can't predict exactly where within a couple of hundred miles last I heard, and it'll be traveling a lot faster than we can."

"Might be for the best we're not that close when it hits, if it hits land," Lori noted. "A big one like this could have the force of a decent-sized atomic bomb, in which case you'd get everything you might expect from a bomb, maybe including radiation—the great mystery explosion at Tunguska in Siberia in 1908 was radioactive, although that might not have been a meteor. The estimates I saw in the papers I read today indicate that this might be the largest one in modern times. The shock wave alone will be enormous, and the crater will be fantastic, like a volcanic caldera, very hot and possibly molten."

"Sounds like fun," Gus commented. "No chance this thing isn't a meteor, though, is there?"

"Huh? What do you mean? Little green men?"

"Well, I saw *War of the Worlds* on TBS last week. Good timing."

She laughed. "I seriously doubt it. The only danger, and it's very remote, is that this is going to be something like the Tunguska explosion I just talked about. Massive blast damage for hundreds of miles with no evidence of what caused it. Many people think it might have been antimatter."

"Auntie what?"

"Antimatter. Matter just like regular matter only with opposite electrical charge and polarity. When antimatter hits matter, they both blow up. Cancel out. Don't let that worry you, though. I never bought the antimatter Siberian explosion. Nobody ever explained to me why it didn't cancel out when it hit the atmosphere if it was. Others say it was a comet, although there's no sign of the meteorite fall that would accompany one. At least one major Russian physicist thinks it was a crashed alien spaceship, but I don't think we have to take that one seriously. Don't worry—it'll be plenty big enough if it's the size they predict even after losing the bulk of its mass in friction with the atmosphere. I *hope* it lands either in the jungle or in the sea. The track prediction I saw takes it over some fairly populous parts of Peru if it clears the Andes. There's no way they could evacuate all that region, not in three days."

"Don't get Gus hoping," Terry cautioned. "If it came down in downtown Lima, he'd be so ecstatic about the photo ops, he wouldn't even *think* of the misery. And no matter what he says, he'd *love* it to be an invasion from Mars. As I said, news photographers aren't quite human."

Gus looked sheepish. "Well, it ain't like this happens every day."

"In fact, it *does* happen every day," Lori told him. "Meteor strikes, that is. It's just that the particles hitting the Earth are usually small enough that they burn up before they reach the ground and just give pretty shooting stars for folks to look at. The ones that *do* reach the ground are often the size of peas or so, and most land in the ocean, in any case. It's just the size of this monster that makes it so unusual."

"Well, wherever it hits and no matter what damage it does, we'll be the first on the scene," Gus told her. "That's our job."

"Actually, we're praying for Brazil," Terry added. "The other organizations will be forced to use our pool in that region. If it goes into Peru, well, there's a ton of broadcast teams in there now from dozens of countries and more arriving every day. We want to be first and exclusive. If we're not, we're not doing our job."

"If it *does* land up in the upper Amazon, at or near the Peruvian border, it'll be hell to get to on the ground," Lori pointed out. "No roads or airstrips up there, and what natives there are will be primitive and not very friendly. But I'm mostly worried about the idea of covering it from the air."

"Huh? Why?"

"While it's huge, it's not going to come down in one piece. As it comes through the atmosphere, it'll fragment. Some decent-sized chunks and a huge number of little ones will come off. Some will be large enough to fall on their own over a wide swath and cause enormous damage. Even so, on the ground you can take advantage of some cover, and the odds of being hit by a fragment in the open are still pretty low. In the atmosphere, though, it will be extremely turbulent, and if even a very tiny fragment hits the plane, it could be disaster. And when it hits, like I said, it'll be like an atomic bomb."

"It's what we get paid for, Doc," Gus commented, sounding singularly unconcerned. "Can't cover a war without gettin' in the line of fire once in a while."

"I'm afraid he's right," Terry agreed. "Listen, Doctor, if you feel it's ridiculous to risk your life being with us, we can rig up something on the ground for you to join in the comments, but we have to be where the action is, risk or not. In this business you have to develop a kind of insanity, sort of like being a permanent teenager, taking risks and never thinking about the consequences. If not, we might as well stay in Atlanta and just cover the aftermath. We're good at what we do, which is why so few of us get killed, but reporters *do* get hurt sometimes, even killed sometimes, in the pursuit of a story, and this is a major one. I thought that was understood. We'll have a ton of very famous scientists back in Atlanta and around the country feeding stuff to the anchors from their safe offices in the States. *You're* the one who'll be on site. You have to think about that, and now."

It was a sobering thought she hadn't considered up to that point. There was risk in this, not the career risks and romantic risks she'd thought about before—those suddenly seemed very minor—but *real* risk to life and limb. As the meteor came in over the coast of west Africa, it would begin to burn and shatter, and pieces would begin to break off. Most would fall in the Atlantic, but by the time it reached the Brazilian coast, it would be quite low and quite hot and coming in incredibly fast. Those pieces would be raining down over an area perhaps hundreds of miles wide. Parts of the country would look as if they had been bombed by an enemy air force. Fortunately, the region was in the main lightly populated, although there would be some towns that would suffer. But if it cleared the Andes, it would rain over populous portions of Peru like a carpet bomb attack. And there was nowhere that was totally unpopulated anymore except most of Antarctica.

This could be a major disaster, and she was being taken right into the middle of it, as dangerously close as possible to get the right pictures.

She could die.

My God! No wonder they passed the buck to me! That probably was unfair, she told herself, but she still wouldn't put it past them.

Of course, a lot of science was achieved at great risk. The geomorphologists who worked with exploding volcanoes took risks as a matter of routine; medicine and biology since well before the days of Madame Curie took risks as well. It could be a dangerous business, but it usually wasn't. The last astronomer to take a risk greater than pneumonia from spending a long, cold night at the telescope was probably Galileo before the ecclesiastical court in Rome.

Of course, it would be easier if she really *were* here doing science, but she wasn't. There were teams of top scientists all over the region doing that kind of work; with the level of prediction achieved by the computers on this event, it would probably be the most studied and viewed happening in contemporary science. She had no equipment, no labs waiting back home for her findings and samplings, no support at all. She was a mouthpiece, a witness for the cable TV audience.

Terry was getting a bunch of papers out of her briefcase. "Unless you want to bug out in Manaus, you'll have to sign these," the producer told her, shoving the papers over. "I have to fax signed copies back when I arrive and then Fedex the originals. It's mostly standard stuff."

She took the papers and started to look through them. The first was the personal release—she agreed that she had been told there was risk to this job and that she accepted the risk and wouldn't sue the company if something happened, in exchange for which they'd cover all medical expenses from on-the-assignment injuries. The second was the general waiver and promise to abide by the rules of the corporation and do what she was asked to do, etc., etc. The third covered her under the group lawsuit insurance policy in case she said something on the air that somebody else didn't like. The usual.

The fourth, however, was of more positive interest. It was basically a set of rules for an expense account for a foreign assignment, how to prepare one, what they would and would not cover, and the like. The list of what they covered was pretty damned extensive, but the rule apparently was to receipt everything and give it to Terry before a certain cutoff date. And finally, there was an agreement that she would work for up to seven days on this assignment as their exclusive agent and on-camera representative as a free-lance commentator, and licensed unlimited use of any and all footage and commentary given during that period for the onetime fee of—my heavens! That was hundreds of dollars *per day*!

"You look surprised," Terry noted.

"I—I never expected to be paid for this."

"You aren't plugging a book, you haven't got a forth-coming PBS series or whatever, so you're hired as a free-lancer. Just remember that your fee is based on doing satisfactory work and I'm the one who decides if you do."

Lori sighed. She knew at that point that even if she wasn't being paid a dime she'd have to see it through, grit her teeth and go through with the whole thing. Very dangerous or not, this was the chance of a lifetime, the potential turning point in her life she'd abandoned all hope of ever getting.

"I'm in," she told the producer.

AMAZONIA:
ROCKFALL MINUS ONE

Manaus lay so far into the Amazonian interior of Brazil that since its founding, its major connection to the rest of Brazil and the world as well had been just the Amazon River. Although now it was possible to reach the city by road, the river and the airplane were the primary twin connectors of the city to the rest of civilization.

Still, Manaus was a very large city, born during the boom in gold and other treasures of the Amazon discovered and developed in the nineteenth century. Great old houses and a magnificent if now rundown center city, with its old-world buildings defiant against the jungle, looking more like Lisbon at its finest, displayed Manaus's past, and with the development of the interior in full swing, it was something of a boomtown again. Its airport, always vital since the founding of the national airline decades before, was as grand and modern as any in the western world and was the main port of entry for foreign airliners, almost as if Brazil were intent on reminding all its visitors that there was more to the country than Rio and São Paulo. There were first-class hotels here once more, with all the amenities of modern civilization, and in its bustling streets one could buy almost anything.

With a corporate credit card, it wasn't hard for the two women to pick up what they needed, although it was a hardship to do so in the couple of hours allotted to the task. Terry had to be back at the hotel in a hurry; she'd been on the phone and fax in the hotel's business center almost since arriving, and she still had much to do. By the time they returned, messages had piled up, and before heading back down to the business center, Terry told Lori to order from room service and unpack and repack as needed.

A bellman came up a few minutes later with a folder full of papers, and Lori looked them over after being told they were from Terry. They turned out to be faxes of the latest computer summaries, including maps and tracking data. It was now felt that the angle and velocity would not take the approaching meteor over the Andes, which was a relief to Peru and Ecuador, of course, but the projections also indicated it would track a bit north of the original estimates.

She grabbed a map of Brazil and did a plot. If the projections held up, it would luckily hit in one of the remotest and least populated areas left in the country, but that would also present new dangers. If anything happened and the news crew went down in that region, they might never be found.

She decided to talk to the concierge. He was an old man with more Indian in him than anything else, and it took little imagination to imagine him in the midst of the jungle in some primitive tribe.

"*Sí, senhora.* The region, it is very, very wild. The natives there, they still live in the old ways and would not think too well of strangers. Strangers have cut, burned, destroyed much forest, many animals. Ruin the land and ways of the peoples. Those tribes, they will know of this. They will think anyone who come is come to steal their forest. Best you no go there."

"We'll try not to land if we can avoid it," she assured him. "What do you think the effect will be of the meteor hitting there?" She knew he'd heard all about it. Everybody had, and it was all anybody was talking about.

"They will think it a god, or a demon, or both. They will be very afraid."

She nodded. "Good. They will avoid the impact area, then. It might actually be safe to at least inspect the area afterward."

"What you say is true of the natives, senhora, but I still would not land there or even fly a small plane there."

"Oh? Why not?"

"Ah—how to put? There are certain people just over the border there who also do not like strangers."

He would say no more, but she got the idea. What a place to be heading for! One of the wildest jungles left in the western hemisphere, with snakes and dangerous insects, fierce natives who would see any stranger as a despoiler of their land, and not far away revolutionaries, drug lords, or worse seeing strangers as spies or narcs.

She went on down to the business center to see if any new information had come through. Terry was on two phones at once but looked up when she saw the scientist walk in.

"Hold on a minute," she said into both phones, then said to Lori, "Pick up that line over there—three, I think. You can get more than I can from him."

She wanted to ask who "him" was, but the producer was back on the phones again, so she went over, punched line three, and said, "Hello, this is Dr. Sutton."

"Ah! Somebody who speaks English, not telebabble!" responded a gruff voice at the other end, a voice with just a trace of a central European accent.

"And who am I speaking to?" she asked.

"Hendrik van Horne."

She knew him at once by reputation. Van Horne was something of a living legend among near-object astronomers. "Dr. van Horne! It's an honor. Where are you? Chile?"

"Yes. Things are going quite crazy here. We've had to get the army up to protect us."

"You're under attack?"

"From the world press, yes! It's insane! Those people—they think they own you! I am told you are going to try to track it down by air."

"If we can, more or less. I doubt if we can be there when it hits, but we should be first over it after it does, I would think."

"Ah! I envy you! No one in living memory has seen such a sight! Your account will be very important, Doctor, since you will be first on the scene. By the time that bureaucracy over there gets things set up, the trail will be days or weeks old. You must record everything—*everything*. Get a dictating recorder."

She hadn't thought of that. "I will. I think I can get one here in the hotel. But—I have no instruments. I'm with that same press, you know, and they're only interested in the story for the television."

"Yes, yes. They said they didn't have room for such things since they had to have all their own equipment," he responded with total disgust in his voice. "Nevertheless, the Institute for Advanced Science in Brazil is sending over a basic kit. Get it on board if you can and use it. Tell them it's a condition of their permission to go. Lie, cheat, steal. They deserve it, anyway. Do whatever you can."

"I will," she promised. "Do you have any hard data on the meteor, so I can know a bit more what to expect?"

"Not a lot. It is crazy. The spectrum changes almost as you watch. Whatever it is made of defies any sort of remote analysis. It drives our instruments crazy! That is why we cannot even estimate its true mass. Assuming it is very hard mineral, though, we estimate that the object when it hits will be at least a hundred or more meters across. A hundred-plus *meters*! Think of it! There will be no doubt when *this* one strikes. It will shake every seismograph in the world. The impact site should be at least the size of Meteor Crater in Arizona, perhaps larger and deeper. There will be a tremendous mass expended into the atmosphere by its impact, so be very cautious. It will also be quite some time cooling, which is just as well. We are all dying to know what its composition is that can give these insane readings."

"What do you mean by 'insane readings'?" she asked him, curious.

"I mean that from scan to scan, from moment to moment, the instruments start acting like there are shorts in the systems. They'll give you any result and any reading you want if you just wait. It is almost as if the object is, well, broadcasting interference along a tremendous range. Satellite photos, radar, and laser positioning seem to be the only reliable things we can use. We know what it looks like, more or less—and it's unexceptional in that regard—and its size, speed, trajectory, and so on, but as to its composition— forget it."

That *was* weird. "What's the estimated impact time?"

"If it acts like a conventional meteor and stays true, and if our best guess on mass is correct, and if it remains relatively intact, it is likely to impact at about four-forty tomorrow morning."

She nodded. Still in the darkness. If the sky was even partially clear, it should be one of the most spectacular sights in astronomy.

She thanked van Horne and hung up, then turned to Terry. "What's the weather supposed to be over that area in the early morning hours?"

"Hold on," Terry said into the single phone she was now using. "What?"

"The weather over the region we're going to. They say impact before dawn, about four-forty."

"Scattered clouds, no solid overcast at that hour."

"Good. Then we should be in for quite a show."

Lori was really getting into it now, the excitement of the event overtaking her fear. This, after all, was the kind of thing that had brought her into the sciences to begin with. Unlike some of the small number of other women in her field who'd studied with her, she hadn't gone into physics to prove any points. She had gone into it because, as a child, she'd stared up at the Milky Way on cloudless summer nights and imagined and wondered. She had glued herself to televisions during every space shot and had dreamed of becoming an astronaut. She had even applied for the program, but competition was very stiff, and so far NASA hadn't called.

NASA and the U.S. Air Force, of course, were tracking the meteor with satellite monitors and airborne laboratories with all the most advanced instruments, but they wouldn't be allowed in until well after the impact. Lori's news crew was going to be close, the first ones in, and they would, as van Horne reminded her, have the all-important first impressions. A grandstand seat for the cosmic event of the century.

Terry hung up the last of the phones. "That's it," she said flatly. "Let's get this show on the road."

"We're leaving *now*?"

"Take your smallest suitcase and just pack three days worth, including some tough clothes just in case we can get down near it." She looked at her watch. "My God! Three o'clock! Let's go! We've got to be in the air in an hour!"

They went back up to the room quickly. "What's the rush? It's still thirteen hours away," Lori pointed out.

"We're shifting our base for the evening to a private ranch closer to the fun. Took one *hell* of a lot of work to get permission from them, but they've got the only airstrip in the entire region."

"I didn't think *anybody* civilized lived up there."

"Well, 'civilized' is a matter of opinion. Francisco Campos isn't exactly a great humanitarian. More like a cross between the Mafia and the PLO."

Lori gave a low whistle. "How'd you ever get him to agree to help us?"

Terry grinned. "You'd be surprised at the contacts you

have to develop in this business. Truth is, he's so afraid of the inevitable army of media and scientists and government officials, he's allowed us to be the initial pool while he treads water and tries to figure out how to handle what might be coming. It's one reason why we're exclusive in the area. He's been known to shoot down jet planes with surface-to-air missiles."

"And they let him just *stay* there?"

"He's inches over the border. He's worth more than the entire Peruvian treasury and has better arms and maybe a larger army than the government. The Peruvians also have enough trouble with their own revolutionaries, the Shining Path. Sort of a Latin American version of the Khmer Rouge. Compared to them, Campos is a model citizen."

In the lobby Lori met the man Terry always referred to as Himself for the first time. He looked tall and handsome and very much the network type; in his khaki outfit, tailored by Brooks Brothers, he looked as if he'd just stepped off a movie set.

"Hello, I'm John Maklovitch," he said in a deep, resonant voice that made Terry's parody seem right on target. "You must be Doctor Sutton."

"Yes. Pleased to meet you at last."

"Had a problem getting in," he explained to them. "I wound up having to get here from Monrovia via England, Miami, and Caracas." He turned to Terry. "Everything set with Campos?"

She nodded. "As much as can be."

"Let's get cracking, then. It's going to be one of those long, sleepless nights, I'm afraid."

Once up in the air, it was easy to see why the natives would hate strangers. What once had been a solid, nearly impenetrable jungle now had vast cleared areas, and other huge tracts were on fire, spilling smoke into the air like some gigantic forest fire. It was as if the jungle had leprosy, the healthy green skin peeling away, revealing huge ugly blotches that were growing steadily. It was hard to watch, and after a while she turned away.

Maklovitch was going over his game plan with Terry and working over some basic introductory script ideas. "The equipment already there?" he asked worriedly.

"They flew it in this morning before coming back for us," Terry told him. "We have a couple of local technicians from RTB in place and checking it out. When we get there, we'll do as many standups as they want us to, time permitting, but then we fly. We'll tape from the plane if we can and do live commentary—audio is firm and direct, and they can pick up the NASA pictures until they get our feeds. It's the best we could do with the equipment we had available. Plan is to take off about two and take a position on the track of the meteor about four hundred miles out—that'll be sufficient for us to link via Manaus. Then we follow it in. Plan is, if it comes down anywhere in our area, we'll find it, circle and shoot what we can, then get back to the ranch and raw feed whatever Gus has along with your standups. Then, if it's within a couple of hundred miles, we'll use one of Campos's helicopters to get in to the site. If it flattens as much of the jungle as they say it will, we might be able to land for a standup. If not, we'll be able to get some pretty spectacular close-in pictures."

"I hope this won't be like Matatowa," the reporter sighed. "Everything set up for it to blow, half a million bucks spent, and the damned earthquake hits three hundred miles south. I'd hate like hell to have this thing drop into the lap of ABC."

Their attitude was reassuring to the novice scientist. No talk of danger, no talk of risks, no reservations—just how to get the story. It may have been foolish to dismiss those thoughts, but it was also infectious. Maybe one *did* have to be crazy to do many of the things others took for granted; maybe those who took the risks were the ones who knew how to live, too.

"You're going to have to be on your best behavior and bite your tongue at this ranch, Doc," Terry said to her.

"Huh?"

"These are *extremely* dangerous guys," she explained. "Nobody knows how many people they've killed or what they're capable of, but no matter how macho or weird they are, go with the flow. I haven't dealt with these guys face to face before, but I've dealt with their type in Colombia. The Nazis must have been like these guys—smart, articulate, well educated mostly, often charming and cultured, but nutty as fruitcakes in the most psychopathic way. No comments, questions, or moral judgments. We're not here to do their story this time. Let's just do *our* job, okay?"

She nodded. "I'll try and just stay out of their way if I can. We won't exactly have a lot of time, anyway."

"We'll probably have one of them with us," Maklovitch noted. "I seriously doubt if they're going to like a lot of low-level photography of that region without some controls on their part. They'll have a man with us and another with the ground station just to make sure that nothing they don't want seen gets out. Don't worry too much about it, though; satellites can take better pictures of the region than Gus can."

"Like hell," the photographer growled. "Give me an altitude of just a few hundred feet and I'll tell you what's real and what's camouflage. Besides, we don't have a lot of satellite coverage in the southern hemisphere. They'll be on their toes with us. Bet on it."

"Yeah, well, don't you go trying to get away with shots you know are taboo," Maklovitch warned. "This thing's dangerous enough as it is. It wouldn't take much convincing if we were to wind up dead and burned from what they'll say is a tragic accident with the debris from this meteor. There're too many of these crackpots down here for us to cause trouble with Campos. Let the powers that be handle that. You just get the shots you're being paid for and not the kind in the back of the head."

The "Seat Belt" sign went on, and they heard the engines slowing; they were coming in on the Campos airstrip.

Darkness fell fast in the tropics, and it was difficult to see much. It was clear that the strip wasn't commercial caliber; it was bumpy as hell, and they could hear cinders hitting the wings and underside of the plane as they taxied in and slowed to a stop.

It was almost seven-thirty; seven and a half hours to go.

The door opened, and the heat and humidity streamed in. If anything, it seemed far worse than even Manaus, although climatologically there wasn't a lot of difference. A beat-up old station wagon, a full-sized American model not seen on U.S. roads in a decade, bounced up, and several men got out. They carried submachine guns and looked incredibly menacing.

One of the men shouted something to them in rapid Spanish, and Terry responded in kind. She turned to them and said, "Everybody's supposed to get into the wagon and go up to the main house. Air crew, too. They say they'll unload the rest of the gear and bring it along. I think they're supposed to search the plane—and the gear—although they don't say that."

"No problem," responded the voice of the pilot behind them. "They did this earlier today, although Joel and I just had to stand behind the wagon."

Terry said something sharply to the men in Spanish, then explained, "I just told them not to touch the communications equipment and relays. If they get out of whack, we might as well not be here."

The Americans all squeezed into the wagon, and the driver slid in, put his Uzi between his legs, and roared off. Lori was glad to see that she wasn't the only one suddenly holding on for dear life.

The ride was mercifully short, and soon they were in front of an imposing Spanish-style structure that seemed out of place in the middle of nowhere. Three men were waiting, two of whom had weapons and looked like bodyguards; the third was a tall, dignified man who seemed to have stepped out of the pages of some Latin novel. White-haired, including a thick but extremely well-groomed mustache, his skin almost blackened by the tropical sun, he nonetheless was more Spanish than South American and a far cry from the Brazilians they'd been with the past day. He was also the sort of man who clearly had not only been handsome when young but had remained so into advancing age.

So help me, he's even wearing a white suit! Lori thought, somewhat amused in spite of her nervousness at being around so many guns.

John Maklovitch got out first, followed by the others. He approached the man in the white suit casually and nodded. *"Buenas noches,"* he said in a friendly and seemingly unconcerned tone.

"And good evening to you, my friend," responded the older man in a deep, rich baritone with only a trace of an accent. "I am Francisco Campos, at your service. I must apologize for all the guns and procedures, but this is a very dangerous area. To the west, we have some of the most ruthless revolutionaries on this continent; to the east, some of the most savage tribes remaining on Earth. We have a rigid set of precautions, and although some really are not appropriate for your visit, it is easier for my men to maintain their routine. The sort of men who are willing to live out here are not always the most intelligent, but they are good people."

"We understand perfectly," the newsman responded smoothly. "We were a bit concerned that they might disturb our transmitting equipment. It's delicate and needs to be calibrated as it was in Manaus this afternoon. If it's thrown out of whack, we will have disturbed you for nothing."

"They have been alerted by your technical staff here as to what to look for and what not to touch," Campos responded. "Please be assured that none of my men will harm your equipment in any way. Of *that* I can assure you. But come, you will be eaten alive by the insects out here. Come inside and relax. I can get you drinks and perhaps a light supper."

"Thank you. Your hospitality is most gracious. Uh—may I present my companions? The air crew you have seen, but this young lady is my producer, Theresa Perez, and this other lady is Doctor Lori Sutton, our science adviser for this story. The tall one here is Gus Olafsson, our cameraman."

"Delighted to meet you all," he responded, bowing slightly. "Perez?" he said quizzically. "You are from a Latin country?"

"Some say that," she responded. "Miami, actually."

"Cubano?"

"Partly. My father was—a *Marielito*. My mother was from Grenada. But I was born in Florida." She paused. "I apologize and mean no insult, but we have to get set up and in communication with Atlanta. We'll have to do one or two standups before we take off. They're already running nearly continuous coverage, and they'll be expecting us. Perhaps when we are done we can avail ourselves of your generous hospitality, but it *is* our job."

He paused, and for a moment they weren't sure if he was going to take this as an insult, but then he smiled and said, "Of course! I apologize for my stupidity! You see, we are very remote here, and schedules, time clocks, and such are as foreign as snow to us. *Mañana* is our watchword here, I fear. But there is but one meteor, *sí*? And it will not wait. I understand." He turned to one of the other men and barked some crisp orders in Spanish quite different in tone from the one he was using with them, then turned back to them.

"I have asked Juan, my son, to accompany you. With him along, you will find few barriers. His English is fairly good, so you should not need the lovely Señorita Perez to translate, and Juan is a very good helicopter pilot who can assist when you need it." He paused again and for the first time seemed slightly nervous. "This meteor—it is huge, yes?"

"Very large," Maklovitch acknowledged. "Maybe the biggest thing to hit the Earth in thousands of years."

"What will happen when it hits, if I may ask? Here, for example."

Lori decided it was time to take over. "Señor, I don't think we should mince words. Perhaps nothing, although the last track I saw takes it within 150 kilometers of here. There will be debris, some of it possibly as large as heavy rocks and some of it extremely hot. The explosion itself when it lands will be gigantic, like an exploding volcano or worse. How much of the effect you'll get here, whether fallout of rocks or blast damage, will depend on how close it hits. Make no mistake—if it does not clear the Andes, and we do not believe it will, it will hit within a 150-kilometer radius of this estate. Within fifty, you will suffer some strong damage. Within a hundred, some minor damage analogous to an earthquake about that far away. I would certainly take some precautions to secure things, tie them down, get breakables off shelves, that sort of thing, but I wouldn't panic. The odds are very good you won't be in the direct path—but you will know when it comes."

Campos seemed impressed by this. "I thank you. I will do what I can to 'batten the hatches,' as they say, then watch you and pray."

"They hooked up a relay to the house?" Maklovitch asked, impressed.

"No, no. I will watch you on my satellite television. On CNN."

The reporter seemed momentarily taken aback. "Good heavens!" he muttered, more to himself than to the others. "I wonder if the ratings people know about places like this?"

Just then a figure emerged from the house, summoned apparently by one of the bodyguards.

There was no question that Juan Campos was the son of Francisco, but there was a difference far greater between them. What was handsome and cultured on the older man seemed somehow raw and violent in the younger, almost as if the veneer of civilization had been stripped off with the years. His hair was long and black, his mustache was large and bushy, and the eyes were—well, *mean*. He wore green military fatigues that showed custom tailoring and combat boots, and the leather gun belt around his waist held a holster with a mean-looking automatic pistol sticking out of it.

Lori thought, but didn't dare say, that the younger man looked almost like the generic poster of a Latin American revolutionary.

Francisco introduced them around, and the younger man nodded to each in turn, giving each of the news team a penetrating stare, as if he were trying to memorize every detail he could see about them.

Finally he said, in a voice both deeper and more gruff than his father's as well as more heavily accented, "All right. We go."

Terry gave Lori a sudden look that was understood almost instantly; this wasn't their guide but their keeper, and no matter what kind of bastard he was, he was in charge.

They walked around the very large hacienda toward some large outbuildings in the rear, and almost instantly they could see where the crew had set up. A small area against a nondescript green-painted barn was being test lit by some very bright portable lights, and a generator rumbled to give the whole thing power. Gus was happy to see that they'd brought his gear around, and the crew, almost all Brazilians, had already unpacked some of it and set up for the spot.

Terry looked around in the darkness. "Too bad we couldn't get a better backdrop," she commented. "This could just as well be Macon County with that barn."

"No photographs of the ranch," Juan Campos growled. "Your plane or this barn only."

She shrugged. "Too bad. John will have to carry the remoteness with his personality."

The reporter chuckled, but then he turned to Juan Campos to get the other ground rules straight. "What do you want me to say about where we are?" he asked. "Just that we're on a remote airstrip well inside the jungle, or can I say more?"

"You may mention my father and his hospitality," the man in green responded. "In fact, we want you to do so. But do not mention me or what you have seen here."

"Fair enough. Uh—for the record, what does your father officially grow and export from here?"

"Bananas," Juan Campos responded flatly. Terry rolled her eyes, and Lori had a hard time not laughing in spite of the danger. It was all too, well, *comic book,* real as it might be.

"Doc, you and John stand over there against the barn," Terry instructed. "We want to play with the lighting, and Gus wants a camera test. We'll have to adjust to get rid of some of the shadows. John, I'm going to talk to base and see what they want and when."

They were already getting bitten by all sorts of small insects—a medical crew had met them at the airport in Manaus and had filled them with shots, but in spite of that and liberal doses of industrial-strength bug repellent on the plane, Lori was still not sure what was biting her or how hard it would be to look into a camera and not keep scratching and swatting. Thoughts of assassin bugs and malaria mosquitoes came to her unbidden. Once in the lights, though, the little bastards seemed to gang up in swarms. It was going to be a very tough few minutes with those lights on.

Almost as surreal was the little Brazilian man with the pancake and small kit of makeup who actually came in and touched both of them up while Gus took his own sweet time doing his tests and also rearranging the lighting. Finally the main lights went off, leaving them with enough electric light to see but still giving an almost eerie sense of darkness after that brightness.

"Can't do with available light and get a decent shot here," Gus told them, "but I think we can manage with just the one portable light there."

He seemed oblivious to the bugs. "Aren't you getting eaten alive, Gus?" Lori asked him. "How can you keep that steady?"

"Aw, shucks, this ain't no worse than a Minnesota lakes summer," he responded casually. "Up there the bugs got to get in all their eating in a real short time. You catch 'skeeters in little teeny bear traps."

"Yeah. Sure." She remembered an old boyfriend once saying that anybody who started something with the words "Aw, shucks" should be closely watched and never totally trusted. Gus wanted everybody to think of him as just a country hick from the Minnesota backwoods, but this was a man who made a living as a free-lance cameraman for foreign correspondents. She couldn't help but wonder what that country hick act concealed. Perhaps he was the type of person nobody could *ever* really know.

It was amusing to watch Maklovitch at work. He'd stand there with his scribbled notes, lights on, camera running, and go through the shorthand script several times, often stopping and looking disgusted and then starting all over again. Occasionally he'd examine himself in the tiny monitor and call for somebody to adjust his hair or put a little makeup here or there, and then he'd also go back and forth with someone on the microphone as if he were on the telephone. It was a moment before she realized that he *was* sort of on the telephone; he had an earpiece connected to the large apparatus beneath the satellite dish just beyond and was clearly in direct communication with Atlanta.

Suddenly he looked around. "Doctor Sutton!" he called.
"Yes?"

"Get over here! We want to introduce you and go over
the initial spot."

She hurried over, suddenly as self-conscious of her appearance as Maklovitch was of his, but it was too late to do
much about it.

Terry came up to her and handed her an earpiece similar
to the reporter's. She stuck it in her ear. A small microphone
was clipped to the front of her blouse.

"Hello? Doctor Sutton? You reading us?" a man's voice
came to her.

She was suddenly panicked, unsure of how to reply. Maklovitch was an old hand at this sort of thing and said, "Just
talk. That little mike you have on will pick you up. Just use
a normal tone. It's pretty sensitive."

"Uh—yes, I hear you fine," she responded, feeling sudden panic and stage fright.

"All right. We'll be coming to your location after the next
commercial spot."

"That can take twenty minutes," Maklovitch commented
dryly. Then he said to her, "It's going to be easy. Just relax,
I'll make some introductory remarks, introduce you, then
ask you the same kind of questions we've asked all along.
They might have a few extra questions as well, but don't
expect anything complex or anything you might not be
ready for. This isn't brain surgery, and the audience aren't
physicists. Okay?"

She nodded nervously. Up until now this was the one
thing she'd thought the least about; now, oddly, it was the
thing that was making her the most nervous, and she tried
desperately to calm down.

"All I want to do is not make a fool of myself," she told
him honestly.

"Don't worry. You'll do fine. The one problem is the
audio. You'll be hearing two channels at once sometimes—

the director or supervising producer in Atlanta and the anchors. Just don't let it confuse you."

The next few minutes were something of a blur, but all thoughts of the discomfort, the lights, the bugs, and the heat and humidity faded. She remembered being asked, "Is there any danger that this asteroid is large enough to cause world-wide problems?" and answering reflexively.

"If you mean the sort of thing that wiped out the dinosaurs, a nuclear winter, no," she told them. "At least not from the figures I've seen so far. We *did* have a near miss with an asteroid that might have done us in a few years back, but this isn't in that league. Still, it is a very large object, relatively speaking, and there will be some very nasty aftereffects. We might well have some global cooling for a period of years, much as if a couple of very big volcanoes erupted at the same time, and, depending on the upper-level winds here, an even more dramatic effect on the South American and possibly African continents for some time. It will be impossible to say anything for sure until we see it hit."

"Then we don't have to find a survivalist with a fallout shelter," one of the distant anchors said jokingly.

"No. Although if you're living in the western Amazon basin and know somebody with one, it might not be a bad idea," she responded.

There was more of that sort of question and answer, but considering she wasn't even going on current data, there was, she reflected, nothing she could say that any nonscientist might not have said from somewhere in the States.

Still, when the light went down and somebody, probably Terry, said, "Okay, that's enough for now," Lori felt almost stunned, not quite remembering what had gone on. Almost everything—their questions, her replies, even her annoyances—seemed distant and unfocused, beyond remembering clearly. She was suddenly afraid that she'd just made an absolute fool of herself on national television.

Terry came up to her and asked, "Well, what do you think about the new data?"

"Huh? Oh—sorry. It's all something of a blur. New data?"

"Yeah. Impact point ninety kilometers west southwest of here in—" She looked at her watch. "—about three hours, give or take."

"They're that certain? There are so many variables . . ."

"NORAD's computers are pretty good these days, I hear, since they got into such hot water over muffing even the *continent* Skylab was gonna hit some years back. If this asteroid hadn't gone into unstable low Earth orbit, they might be guessing still, but it's deteriorating now right on schedule. They fed in the wobble and decay characteristics, and their computers came up with the predicted mass, and that was the missing element. They say they're ninety-plus percent sure. Didn't you hear *anything*?"

"I—I *heard* it, but it just didn't register. I guess I was just too nervous."

The producer grinned. "You did fine. Look, we'll keep getting data for the next hour or so, and if this prediction continues to hold, we'll do one more standup and then it's off to the plane. Take it easy, relax. Don Francisco's men brought out some sandwiches and drinks. Take the coffee, go easy on the beer, and don't touch that sangria—it's like a hundred and fifty proof."

She looked over at the small but elegant-looking spread. "I see Gus isn't taking your advice on the sangria," she noted.

"Aw! He's a cameraman. He has a reputation to uphold."

Lori was much too excited and nervous at that point to think about putting anything in her stomach, so she wandered over to where the technicians were monitoring the steady satellite feed and listened to the program.

It appeared that there would be no fewer than a dozen instrument-laden airplanes aloft at rockfall, after all, although Lori's group would be the on-site news pool. If nothing else, this would be the most covered impact in history, witnessed and monitored by more people around the world than any other. And even though they would have a ringside seat, the best view would be from the big tracking telescopes in Chile, which could lock on to the meteor while it was still coming in. She only prayed this wouldn't be another one of those overhyped duds astronomical science was famous for. If the thing *did* break up as it entered the atmosphere, or if the resistance was stronger and the angle less steep than projected, it might be nothing more than an anticlimactic meteor shower with very little reaching the ground. Still, this rock was so large that *something* would hit, and it would be bigger than a baseball, that was for sure.

If it did hit with real force, it would be very dangerous, but then they'd be in the perfect position to view the impact. The newspeople were concerned only with their pictures and an event opportunity which allowed them to build audience and sell diet plans and commemorative plates and such via commercials; *she* wanted to be in the neighborhood when a big one hit and see it just afterward. It was the chance of a lifetime.

Terry was preoccupied with her clipboard, which was constantly being updated to the point where it resembled the tracks of drunken worms more than a comprehensible schedule, listening to cues and the remote director's queries and commands from the tiny transceiver she wore like a hearing aid in her left ear. Oblivious to anything beyond the moment, she was startled to the point of near shock when somebody grabbed her rump and squeezed.

"How *dare* you!" she spit, whirling around, only to see the leering grin of Juan Campos. He was obviously high, possibly from drink—he smelled like it, anyway—but also, possibly, from something more. "You touch me again and I will grab your balls and twist them off!" she snapped in Spanish.

He just grinned and gave a low chuckle. "Spirit. I like a pretty girl with spunk."

"You are a pig!" she snapped. "Would you dishonor your father's hospitality in his own home?"

"My father is an old man," Juan Campos responded. "In his time he did as much and more, but now he remembers himself only as a gentleman. He sits here in his palace and acts the *patrón,* Don Francisco, the great benefactor of his people. It is I who now make it all possible, not him."

"Shall we tell him that? He is not far."

Campos stiffened. "You will not *approach* my father!"

"Then we will approach him together and ask him what he thinks of his son's behavior to his guest!" She started toward the house, and he suddenly reached out, grabbed her arm, and pulled her violently back. High or not, there was a homicidal, lunatic look in his eyes and manner, the kind of dark malevolence that would give anyone chills.

"All right, bitch! For now! But you will not always be in this place and so—*protected.* You forget where you are and how long a journey you have to get anywhere else!"

And with that, he faded back into the shadows.

Terry put on a good, tough front, and she *was* tough after all she'd been through in her job, but she was badly shaken by the encounter. It was a sudden mental free-fall back to Earth, a reminder of just how dangerous this place and these people were and how vulnerable she and her people were, too.

She hoped that one of those damned meteors would strike the bastard or perhaps wipe out this whole sordid place, but she knew that there would be no such luck. Her father's caution years ago, when she'd first gone out on her own, floated back to her. "Always remember that God reigns in heaven," he'd told her, "but Satan rules the Earth."

Perhaps, she thought sourly, she'd seen so much of the latter's evil, she just took it for granted.

John Maklovitch came over to her. "We've got one quick standup in five minutes, then we'd better get to the plane," he told her. "It's coming in." He was suddenly aware that she was hardly listening. "Something wrong?"

"The pig of a son just made a move on me and threatened me," she told him.

The newsman nodded. "I figured as much. Think you can handle him?"

"Alone? Sure. I've got a black belt, remember? But against him and some cronies with their big guns—well, I'm not so sure. Besides, what would the old man do if I broke his son's neck? We've got to get *out* of here, you know."

He thought a moment. "Maybe, but I'll report it in to the studio so they'll know to check up if something happens after the story. Nobody is dumb enough to do anything until we're breaking down. Tell you what . . . You remember the massacre in Chad? Why don't we just try the same gimmick? I'll have sound rig a trigger switch on the remote mike for me. Stick close to me, and if he pulls anything, at least he'll be broadcasting it back to the studio. You can imagine what the old man would be like if he heard *that* on his satellite TV!"

She gave him a weak smile. "Thanks, John. Let's get this show on the road!"

He hesitated a moment. "What about the doc? Think she'll get the same treatment?"

"I dunno. Maybe. She's kinda old and frumpy for Juan, but some of these other guys—you haven't seen many women around here." She sighed. "We'll *all* stick close."

The second spot went smoothly, and then everybody started to move fast. Gus and an assistant from the Brazilian network gathered their material and headed for the front of the big house; the sound man, also Brazilian, stuck with the newsman and the two women, his portable pack energized. Neither Maklovitch nor Terry said anything about Juan to Lori; no sense in alarming her unnecessarily and then possibly having to spill the backup plans where other ears could hear.

"We'll be on almost continuously from about five or ten minutes before anything shows up right through the strike and aftermath," the newsman warned the scientist. "Just comment on what you see and don't worry about what's going out. Just remember to watch your language."

"I'll try," she assured him. "I'm getting used to it now. I think once I'm away from this place, well, it'll be more relaxing."

"I know what you mean. We have to return and drop off the backup tape and the like for uplink, but we'll have to play it by ear from that point. If the main body hits anywhere within 150 or so miles of here, as it's supposed to, we'll probably have to use Don Francisco's helicopter to get in close. I, for one, want to see it close up after it hits if conditions permit and before the military and scientific teams get in and start blocking everything off. Still, if the thing looks like a nuclear blast, it might be too dangerous."

"It still depends on how much burns away and whether it fragments," Lori told him. "But if it's a good size, it's going to be a very nasty sight."

They took the station wagon back to the plane with guards and the technical crew riding in a truck behind. The pilot and copilot were there, looking a little uncomfortable and anxious to be off, but they helped the crew stow its gear.

"Wait a minute and let me and Hector here check the remote exterior cameras," Gus asked them. He and his Brazilian associate climbed aboard, and in a couple of minutes Gus stuck his head back out and said, "Come on in! Gonna be kinda crowded, though."

Terry walked up to the plane and went inside and saw immediately what Gus meant.

Sitting in the last row were Juan Campos and a big smelly bodyguard.

Campos grinned when he saw Terry. "Come in, come in! We are all one big happy family here, no?"

It was fifty-nine minutes to rockfall.

THE BEACH AT IPANEMA,
BEFORE SUNRISE

It was nearly deserted before dawn, this beach that was famous in song and story but would, before the morning was run, be crowded almost to bursting with bodies craving the sun and wind and waves. He liked the waves, the warm bodies wearing nothing or nearly so, the fun and general *life* of it all, and he came here often to watch, often entertained most by the reactions of puritanical American tourists seeing their first nude and topless bathers in what was basically an urban resort, but he liked this time, too, when he could still hear the waves, smell the salt air, and see that, indeed, there was sand on the beach.

The homeless, particularly the bands of pitiful, roving children, were also pretty much absent now, huddled away in corrugated cartons, abandoned buildings, and other hideaways, away from those who might prey even on them. Also absent for the moment were the hustlers, con men, pickpockets and petty thieves who roamed the area near the beach.

Not that he was alone, nor did he particularly want to be. Here and there, walking along the waves, barely visible in the beginnings of false dawn, were occasional couples and a determined jogger, and, up on the walk, a big man in a colorful shirt was either walking two enormous dogs on leashes or they were walking him. In the small cafés within sight of the beach there was already activity as they prepared for the morning onslaught of tourists and urban escapees, and as always in Brazil, the overpowering aroma of brewing coffee was beyond even the abilities of the morning breezes to completely dissipate.

This, in fact, was his favorite period of any year or season, when he was not working, and had nowhere to go, and could just walk around and enjoy the sights, sounds, smells, and, yes, people.

That would surprise those who'd known him over the long course of his life or even the few who currently knew him more than casually. He liked people; he genuinely liked them, else he'd never be here and certainly wouldn't be stuck in this rut. He just couldn't, wouldn't get *close* to individual people, not if he could help it. No matter how good or how wonderful or fascinating they were, they had a fatal flaw, all of them, that would eventually break his heart.

People grew old. People *died.*

That was why he particularly relished times like this. A few weeks in a town far from his normal haunts, an anonymous stranger to everybody he might meet. And they in turn were here temporarily from, usually, very mundane pursuits, here to have a good time and be convivial and then go home.

So long as he didn't stay very long or they remained an even shorter time, all was equal. The people he'd met, the experiences he'd had while on these faraway holidays, were golden; they were, in fact, what kept him going. No matter who he met, they were equals, and, at least in his mind, they would always stay that way, for he could be close and friendly or cold and distant as it suited him to be, and those people with whom he interacted would be forever young, forever alive, because he would never see or hear of them again.

He liked this age, too, or at least he liked things more

from this age onward. Those who idealized the past, whether recent or ancient, should have had to live through and endure it. Then, perhaps, they would appreciate what they now had and just how far things had come.

It also continued to astonish him how much of history duplicated itself, sometimes in the smallest details. It would have astonished even great Caesar to know that he, or one nearly his twin, had crossed the Rubicon before, and what measure of futile toil had been done on a Great Wall for inner China long before the first brick was laid for that wall in this world; to know that Michelangelo could accomplish more than one David—and more than one Sistine Chapel; that Great Zimbabwe had stood before, almost but not quite on the same exact spot, and that Alexander had marched and Aristotle had thought not once but over again on more ancient ground. That Cyril, whom they would make a saint, would again and again commit the atrocity of burning the great library at Alexandria, and, once again, what remained of Greco-Roman writings would be preserved for Europe against Europe's best efforts by black Songhai at its library in great Timbuktu. Only the Hindus seemed to know, as they always did, that the cosmic wheel eternally came back again and again to the same place.

He understood why this was so, that the first natural development of Earth had been recorded through him in a vast data base so distant that none here could comprehend such a gulf and that "reset" meant just that, not a random restart, lest the experiment be spoiled.

He knew more or less what he was and had his own dim memories of before, but even now he found it more and more difficult to recall specific details, to remember all that much. The human brain could manage only so much. It was not a factor with these mortals, who died before they approached a fraction of their capacity, but for such as him it was . . . spooled off.

Still, there *were* differences; there were always differences, but until now, through the countless centuries that preceded it, they were relatively minor ones. Even major changes tended to rectify themselves over time, allowing history to rejoin the original flow. Still, he hadn't remembered the collapse of the Soviet Union at any point in this age, nor the creeping fascism edging out idealistic if no less abhorrent communism. It was so hard to remember, but that change had jolted him as nothing else he could remember with its sense of wrongness. If such a major departure was somehow allowed, did that mean that the experiment was inevitably corrupted or that perhaps this time history was running true? Certainly it would delay space exploration and colonization, perhaps for a century or two. He recalled fleeting snippets of time spent in the Soviet Mars colony. It was so long ago, and the thought was so fragmented, he could not be certain if it was a true memory or not, but he felt that it was. It sure wouldn't be now. It would be interesting to see which *would* be the nation to get out to the stars. Or was there still some "rectification" to come?

It bothered him, not so much in principle—he didn't really care if things went differently or not, let alone who did what—but the mere fact that the difference existed at all. It seemed far too big to "rectify." Something just as bad or worse might well come out of it all, but it seemed far too huge a departure for correction, and, lost memories or not, he was certain that a change this major had never happened before.

Could it be some new glitch in the system? He hoped not. He *prayed* not. He wanted no more of that sort of thing, and anyway, if it was a glitch, the emergency program should call him and provide a means for him to come and fix things. That hadn't happened. And it wasn't as if, at this stage of technological development, he could just hop aboard an interstellar spacecraft and steer for one of the old portals. These people had barely made it to the moon the old-fashioned way, and when they had, they'd lost interest.

He could never comprehend that; it seemed like social devolution. Oh, well . . .

His thoughts were suddenly broken by the sight of a couple standing on the walk above looking out at the sea. There seemed something decidedly odd about them, but he couldn't figure out what it was. Curiosity and the lack of anything better to do took him toward them. He saw that the woman was in a wheelchair—one of the elaborate, expensive, motorized kinds. There was something odd about the man, more than the fact that he was overdressed for the area and the occasion, something in the way he stood, in the carriage of his head, and in the sunglasses he was wearing.

It was enough to draw him closer to them. One did not often see a blind man and a wheelchair-bound woman out on these streets at *any* time, particularly on their own. Perhaps they were merely naive—thieves and muggers were not at all uncommon near the beach, and this couple was in no position to either defend themselves or give chase should they be threatened with violence. But he admired their courage and their obvious insistence that just because they were both handicapped did not mean that they were going to shut themselves away for the rest of their lives.

The woman sat oddly in the wheelchair, a position no one would naturally assume. A quadriplegic, most likely, with some limited control of at least one hand and arm sufficient to move the power joystick but not much else. She looked to be in her early to mid-forties, an attractive woman with short brown hair and lively eyes that seemed to pick up everything in a glance. She saw the stranger approaching and said something to her companion, who nodded.

The man had on a white business suit and a well-knotted dark tie and wore a broad-brimmed Panama hat. He was a handsome man, too, perhaps a shade older than the woman, with signs of gray in the black hair that emerged beneath the hat, and he was fairly tall, almost a head taller than the man who was now walking toward him. He also had a look about him one saw only in this country—a curious mixture of nationalities, part Amerind, part European, part black, that had merged over the past four centuries into a unique and distinct new race, the Atlantic Brazilian.

"Good morning, sir and madam," the small man greeted them in an oddly accented but still very good Brazilian Portuguese dialect. He could see them both tense, as if they both had also just realized their vulnerability. "Please rest easy. I was simply walking along and could not help noticing you here. This is not a terribly safe place, you know."

"I was born only two kilometers from here," the man responded in a deep, elegant baritone. "I have no more fear of this place or these people than would you."

"What is he saying, Tony?" the woman asked in English with a clipped British Midlands accent. "I'm afraid I can't make out more than a word or two."

The stranger immediately switched to English. "I'm sorry, I hadn't realized that you both weren't locals." His accent was still odd, but the words were clear.

"Just small talk, my dear," the blind man assured her.

"I distinctly got the impression of a warning," she persisted.

"I was just saying that this is a dangerous area these days, what with so many homeless youth gangs, thieves, and the like around," the small man explained.

"And I told him I was very familiar with the area," her companion added.

"Well, I said much the same," the woman noted. "Your memories of this beach are about twenty years out of date."

"You do not live here, then?" the small man asked.

"No," responded the Brazilian, "we live in Salisbury, in England, actually. But I have been promising myself that I would return home someday no matter what, and after passing up previous opportunities, I decided that this was the time."

"You are staying with family, then?" The small man hesitated, feeling suddenly a bit embarrassed. "I'm sorry. My name is David Solomon—Captain David Solomon."

"Air force?"

"No. Merchant. My ship is the *Sumatra Shell* out of Bahrain. One of those huge supertankers filled with oil. I live aboard her for four months at a time, going back and forth from wherever there is crude oil to where they want me to unload it, seldom getting off for more than a few hours or a day at a time. When I'm rotated off, I like to come to places I either have never been or haven't been to in a very long time."

"I shouldn't think that someone with a name like yours would be too welcome in Bahrain," the man responded. "I, by the way, am Joao Antonio Guzman, and this is my wife, Anne Marie. I generally use 'Tony' as a first name because, frankly, the British do a terrible job on 'Joao.' They still pronounce Don Juan as Don Jew-an, you know."

"I can imagine," the captain replied. "And you're right. I'm Jewish, and that's neither popular nor even particularly legal in the Gulf, but nobody really minds so long as I stay out of Saudi Arabia. Besides, I am also Egyptian, which helps a great deal in such things. In fact, for practical reasons I'm listed on my documents as a Coptic Christian. Nobody ever cares or checks, and frankly, as religiously observant as I am, one faith is as good as another. In any event, I'm not there long when I'm there, and quite often I'm nowhere near Moslem territory. I've been running from Brunei to Sydney most recently, and neither of them gives a damn what religion I might be. Certainly my Dutch employers don't."

"And you're here on holiday, then?" Tony Guzman asked him. "First time?"

"First time in—a very long time. I've rented a small cottage at outrageous rates a few kilometers south but still near the beach. I just started walking and wound up here this morning. I like to watch the sun rise."

"As do we," Anne Marie told him. "It's such a huge, warm sun at this latitude. Tony, of course, can't see it come up except in his mind's eye, but he can feel it, and of course he has many more of these in his memories than I do, growing up here. We did this yesterday, too, taking a taxi from the hotel."

"Then you're not staying with family?"

"I have little family left here now. None close," the man told him. "The few that are left tend to be uncomfortable either with my condition or with the fact that I married an Englishwoman and am now a British citizen."

"And one that makes them *more* uncomfortable," Anne Marie put in.

"Well, I don't find either of you uncomfortable," he said with a casual honesty they instantly knew was real. "In fact, I find you very interesting people, and I salute you for not letting anything get in the way of your enjoyment."

"Do you have a wife? Children?" Anne Marie asked him.

He shook his head. "No, no one, I'm afraid. The kind of life I lead, the kind of job, just doesn't lend itself to marriage, and I'm unable to have children, so that point is moot."

She sighed. "That's one thing we have in common. I used to be able, it's true, but going through it would have killed me, they said."

"Your accident was early, then? Sorry—again, I don't mean to pry. If you'd rather not discuss it, we'll drop it."

"Oh, I don't mind a bit. I minded the *accident,* and I'd much rather be walking about and feel something below the armpits, but I certainly don't mind talking about it. I just wish it were more spectacular than it was, really, so I'd have a story to tell. An IRA bomb perhaps, or an aircraft accident, or perhaps a sport injury, but it was nothing so dramatic. Truth is, I don't even remember it. It was winter, I was sound asleep in the family car coming home from some Christmas visit to relatives, we hit a patch of ice, slid off, and rolled down an embankment. I was always a sound sleeper, so all I remember is tumbling and some very sharp pain in my neck and back, and that's it. I woke up unable to move anything below the neck. Years of therapy got me to this point, where I stuck. There're just no more connections to make."

"Mine was a bit more exotic," her husband added. "I was a pilot for Varig, and we had fuel and mechanical problems coming into Gatwick. We came in all right, but the nose wheel collapsed on landing, and we slid off the side of the runway and into a ground control radar hut. The base was concrete. All the passengers survived with only minor injuries, but we hit the small building head on. It shattered the windscreen, which is very hard to do, and crumpled in a part of the nose around the cockpit. My copilot had eleven broken bones and eventually lost his leg. I, on the other hand, had a piece of metal driven right into my skull. I have a *very* large metal plate in my head that makes it impossible for me to withstand airport security today—you should see their expressions when they use the hand scanner!—and although there is nothing wrong with the eyes themselves that we know of, there was internal bleeding and damage, and I've been unable to see since. I spent three years in British hospitals of one sort or another and remained there, partly because I had little to come home to and partly because, with the military government in power here and Brazil in such a bad shape economically, I could get much better care in the English system. Besides, I had to relearn even the basics of balance and get my confidence as a sightless man, and the therapy was quite good. I met Anne Marie while I was still in therapy."

"You shared hospitals?"

She laughed. "No, by that time I'd been this way for years. But I found I could sit and rot at home, watching the telly and being spoon-fed by doting relatives and nurses, or I could get out and do something. When an old friend of Father's who'd been working in the physical therapy wards voiced frustration that many people with relatively minor disabilities compared, say, to my own were so depressed and suicidal that they put themselves beyond help, I thought I might be able to do something. After all, if you've lost an arm, or legs, or even your eyes but you are confronted with someone with a more serious disability, like me, actually *doing* something, what sort of excuse do you have?"

The captain liked them more and more as he heard their stories.

"In truth, we are one person," Tony Guzman noted. "Most of me works all right, except my eyes, and Anne Marie's eyes work quite well. So she guides me and describes the world to me, and I do for her what she cannot do for herself. You would be surprised at how one could get used to almost anything."

"No," the captain responded, thoughtful. "No, I wouldn't. We all have crosses to bear. Some are just more obvious than others."

"But what of you?" Anne Marie said. "No wife . . . Do you have family of any sort?"

"No, not really. Well, there is one person, but I have no idea now where she is or what she is doing."

"A sister?"

"Not exactly. The relationship is rather—*complex*. Hard to describe. It's been so long, though, that I find it difficult now to even remember what she looked like. We had some sort of fight. I can't remember what it was about or even if I understood it then. She walked out, I thought for a little while, but she never returned, not even for her things. I never saw her again, even though I half tore that city apart looking."

"You speak of it as long ago, but you are not that old, surely," Tony noted.

He returned a grim smile the man could not see. "I am much older than I look." *Much* older. The city, after all, had been Nineveh at the time of its glories.

"I hesitate to say it, but from your account I would say that she met with foul play," Tony noted.

"Foul play possibly," he agreed, "although she's not dead. Once or twice I've run across someone who had known her, but never did I learn of it in time to track her. Like me, she is a survivor. If I had a clue as to where she might be, I'd still drop everything and go hunting for her, but, again like me, she could be anywhere in the world."

"You still think of her like that, even though you say you can hardly remember her looks?" Anne Marie asked, amazed. "Surely there must be someone else for you out there."

"I'm afraid not. We are bound in a way. Two of a kind. It's no use going into details, but trust me on that." He turned. "Ah! Here comes the sun!"

The three of them grew silent and let the great orb appear from the ocean depths, seeming huge enough to swallow the whole world. Finally Solomon said, "Have you two had breakfast yet? There is a café just a couple of blocks inland from here that is excellent. I would be honored if you would join me. My treat."

Tony said nothing but seemed to wait for his wife to speak. She mulled it over, then said, "Thank you, I believe we will. But then we must get back. I have to keep to something of a schedule, and I have some medications to take. But right now I feel all energy. We shall do some things this morning and go to sleep early."

"What? With all the nightlife here?"

She laughed. "Not tonight. Haven't you heard? They say there's some huge meteor that's going to come in tonight and crash in the western jungle. Some of these bloody locals are panicking and moving out for the night or staying in church or whatever, afraid that God is going to smite them or something. They say, though, that it might be visible here in the early morning hours. Between one and three A.M. Atlantic time. They say it might fragment and give us all a

spectacular natural fireworks show. I shouldn't like to miss that, with the luck of being here when it comes."

"I had to pull every string I know just to get into our room," Tony told him. "There is not a vacant room anywhere in the area or farther inland, either. All the scientists and *touristas,* the sort of people who go on eclipse cruises, are all here for it, as are the newspeople from a hundred countries."

"I haven't paid much attention to the news," the captain admitted. "I *did* hear something about it when I noticed the shops selling lucky charms and meteor repellent in the last week or so. I thought it was far away and inland, though."

Anne Marie roared with laughter. "Meteor repellent! That's wonderful!"

"Don't laugh," the captain responded in a serious tone. "I will be willing to wager a good amount of money that nobody who uses it has ever been hit by a meteor."

They all laughed at his little joke, and then Tony said, "It is supposed to be visible from here—if it is clear. Of course, it is rarely clear here."

The captain thought a moment. "Look, I've got a minivan. If you're really keen to see it, we might manage the wheelchair and drive up into the inland mountains for a while, maybe above some of the coastal weather. That's if you feel up to it."

"Oh! That would be *delightful*!" Anne Marie exclaimed excitedly. "Sir, I will *ensure* that I am up to it. It is only one night, and we *are* on holiday, after all!"

Tony frowned and started to say something, then thought better of it, but it didn't escape the captain's notice. He had the distinct impression, though, that Tony was not all that thrilled by her being out on an expedition, however conservative. It made the captain wonder if there was something else important he didn't know but should.

They had an excellent breakfast, and Anne Marie couldn't stop talking about their good fortune in meeting

the captain and how excited she was to be going somewhere where she was *sure* to see the big show.

After eating, Solomon accompanied them back to their hotel, one of the better ones in the area, as it turned out, with some handicapped-equipped rooms. Tony took his wife from the wheelchair with well-practiced motions and found the bathroom, acting as if he could see very well, indeed. He was certainly well adjusted to his blindness and had the room memorized.

He took some time with her in the bathroom. Finally they were done, and he brought her out and laid her on one of the beds.

"Thank you, Captain, for a *delightful* morning," she said, sounding suddenly very tired. "I can hardly wait until tonight!"

Tony pulled up the covers on the still unmade bed, then made his way back to the door. The captain went outside, and Guzman followed, keeping the door slightly ajar.

"Captain, I think there is something you should know," the blind man whispered, switching to Portuguese.

Solomon responded in kind. "I thought there was something."

"We are here, at grave expense, because it is the last chance we will have. She has been growing weaker and weaker, and eventually even the automatic organs like the heart and lungs will fail. It is only a matter of time. This is, most likely, our last holiday."

"I suspected as much. How long do they give her?"

"God knows. The doctors argued against this trip. I asked them how long she might last if she went into a hospital or was under constant home monitoring. They said a few weeks to no more than six months. Then I asked them how long it would be if she made the trip. They responded that it might be a few weeks to no more than six months but that it would certainly shorten her time. You have been with her this morning. I think you have seen why I fell in love with her. If she were to die today, here, it would be as she

would want it, still out, still active, still doing new things. I
think the doctors are wrong. I believe she would have died
far sooner rotting at home. Certainly she would have died
in misery instead of here, in my homeland, about which I
have spoken all too much, watching the sun rise and smelling the smells and meeting the people. You see?"

He nodded. "But even you think this kind of silly trip
tonight might be too much for her, is that it? Shall I make
some excuse and call it off?"

"No! Not now. Had this been suggested only to me, I
would have refused, but—well, you saw her. Perhaps it *will*
kill her, but not before she sees the meteor. I just—wanted
you to know."

The captain nodded. "I'll keep it an easy drive. And I
suspect you might be underestimating the power of her will.
She may die within the period the doctors say, but I think
she'll pick her own time and place." He patted the blind
man on the shoulder. "I'll see you at six."

There seemed to be only three kinds of people in metropoli-
tan Rio that night: those who were terrified of the meteors,
those who were profiteering from it, and those who were
anxious to see what they could of the big show. Bars served
meteor cocktails—which differed from bar to bar, but who
cared?—and one main hotel advertised an Asteroid Ball in
its rooftop club.

The captain found his new friends waiting for him, and
once he was shown how the wheelchair collapsed, they
managed to get everybody in the Volkswagen minivan. Getting out of town wasn't difficult, but though traffic normally
thinned out going farther inland, the two-lane road through
the mountains that formed the natural barrier between the
city region and the dense jungle beyond was almost bumper
to bumper.

"It looks like everybody else had the same idea we did,"
the captain noted sourly.

"Well, there are not many roads back here, and even

those give out not far beyond the mountains," Tony noted. "I do know a few places that might be less traveled, but the road may not be paved."

"I'm willing, but I don't want too rough a road, not only for Anne Marie's sake but also because even though this is a good, solid Brazilian-made car, it doesn't have four-wheel drive," Solomon responded.

"These would be service and old military roads no longer in use. I do not know how rough they might be, but you should not need four-wheel drive for them. At any rate, we can take a look and you can make a decision from there."

The captain shrugged. "If your memory can get me to them, by all means," he said. He was a bit surprised. It had been Tony, after all, who had worried so much about Anne Marie's fragility that he hadn't been enthusiastic about the more civilized trip they had planned.

For a blind man who hadn't been in the area in twenty years, though, Tony was proving remarkably accurate.

"There should be a dirt road going up the side of the mountain on your right about two kilometers after that intersection," Tony told him. "It will have a sign marked DO NOT ENTER—MILITARY DISTRICT ROAD. Ignore it and go on up. It has not been used as more than a lover's rendezvous in more than a decade."

The captain was a bit suspicious at Tony's detailed recall. "How do you know all that?"

Tony smiled knowingly. "Well, I will tell you the secret. For a thousand cruzeiros the head porter was more than willing to suggest this and to write out the directions for Anne Marie. He has used the spot himself, you see. It is not likely, however, that there will be many up there tonight, or so he said, although he doubted we would be alone and suggested we use discretion with our lights."

"All right, I'll do what I can," the captain responded, chuckling. "Yep. There it is. Pretty imposing sign and the remains of a gate and gatehouse." He pulled off, slowed to a crawl, then went into second gear for the climb. It was steep, and he would not have liked to have met someone traveling in the opposite direction, but it was manageable. The climb also seemed interminable, and he kept a wary eye on the temperature gauge, which was climbing precipitously, but just as he wondered what was going to happen when he boiled over before reaching the top, the road swung around and there was a pulloff. He took it and waited for the temperature to come down. "Hard to say how much farther the top is and how many switchbacks we might face," he explained. "I think we want to not only get up there but be able to get back down without having to coast." He looked at the dashboard clock. "It's a little after midnight. What time did they say the big show was?"

"Sometime after two," Anne Marie told him.

"We'll make it," he assured them. "Plenty of time. How are you holding up?"

"I'll be all right. I had hoped to nap partway, but I was too excited earlier, and at the moment this drive is a bit too unnerving and too steep for any such thing. I'm afraid to close my eyes."

"Don't blame me," Solomon responded. "I'm not the one that came up with this place. All I can say is that there better be a nice view of a clear sky up there or I'm gonna be mightily pissed off. Uh—pardon the language."

"Take no mind of me," Anne Marie responded. "I'm feeling a bit, well, you know, myself."

He started up again and, three switchbacks later, reached a level, debris-filled area that went back quite a ways. The headlights revealed it to be deserted.

The captain looked at the crumbling remains of buildings and gates and fences and frowned. "Did your porter tell you just what this place used to be for?" he asked.

"No," Tony admitted. "It would have to be either something very secretive or something very mundane, such as a storage area for road-grading equipment—there are many rock slides through here, or there were in my day."

The captain took the minivan on a very slow circuit and stopped when the headlights illuminated a large concrete pad. "A helipad. That's what that is," he told them. "Either this provided a quick getaway for VIPs or it was used to spirit people out of the city in secret. You could take somebody out from a rooftop in Rio, bring him here, then transfer him to just about anywhere. The buildings seem too small for a real jail but perfectly adequate for some quiet interrogation with no prying eyes around."

"Oh, dear," muttered Anne Marie.

Tony just nodded. "As military governments go, the one that ruled here for more than a decade wasn't all that horrible, but particularly in the early days, they went after communists, labor union people, vocal opponents of the regime . . . It wasn't as bad as Argentina or even Uruguay, but the military mind is rather consistent, and security is always the most zealous and secretive, particularly at the start of a military regime. It was because they were not totally fascist that the army is still held in some esteem here, and they were not overthrown—they finally admitted they hadn't the slightest idea how to run a large country and essentially quit. Still, there was probably much sadness here, and now it has become a lover's hideaway and a refuge for would-be stargazers. There is something very Brazilian in that."

"Well, we've got a fairly clear view from here except in the direction of the city," Solomon noted. "We still have a lot of light pollution but if there's anything to see in this area, we should see it."

"Try the radio," Tony suggested. "There is most certainly some coverage of it somewhere."

From the evidence of a slow turning of the dial, the "coverage" was mostly Brazilian music, the only obvious tie-in being a classical station playing *The Planets*. At the half hour, though, after the general world news headlines and local stories, the announcer said, "And finally, throughout the region, thousands of people are up in the hills or on rooftops or out at sea awaiting the arrival of what scientists say will be the most spectacular meteor display in centuries. If you are still up and listening to me, you should delay going to sleep another three-quarters of an hour and go outside and find a clear view to the northeast. Scientists tracking the meteor state that it should land somewhere in the remote upper Amazon basin, possibly near the Peruvian border, but it should be quite low over Rio when it arrives at approximately two-fifteen local time. Authorities state that the meteor will probably look much like a huge burning moon, but traveling very fast. Nothing is expected to strike Rio or anywhere within a thousand kilometers of the city, but as a precaution, police and fire teams are on the alert. Remain tuned to this station for updates."

"I'm not at all sure I like that last business," Anne Marie commented. "It sounds like they aren't bloody well sure of anything."

"Hundreds of meteors strike the Earth every single day," the captain reminded her. "Most are very small, and most fall into the ocean, but getting hit by one is not exactly the sort of thing sane people worry about. This one is unusual because it's so large, because it's going to strike land, and most of all because it was spotted early, so we know it's coming. But your odds of winning the Irish Sweepstakes three years in a row are far greater than the odds that even a splinter of this meteor will strike where you are. All that was, as he said, just precaution. You can never predict these things a hundred percent, and if it breaks up, pieces of it might fall in the region. Even then, it'll just make a more spectacular show for us to see—but it'll also mean even less damage to the world when the main body hits."

"Is that true?" Anne Marie asked. "Can the thing really do damage to the world? I realize I shouldn't like to be under it when it crashes, but—the world?"

"One of them killed the dinosaurs," Solomon said. "The

whole climate of the planet was changed because so much dust and debris was kicked up high enough that it gave us twilight for several years. The plants died, the swamps dried up, things grew too cold, and the giant creatures couldn't eat or adapt to it."

"But that is just a theory, is it not?" Tony put in.

The captain was silent for a moment, staring off into space. "Yes, just a theory," he responded. "But the right one."

Anne Marie stared at the strange little man in the darkness and frowned. "Indeed? And how can you know that?"

Because it was a pain in the ass, even with the greatest computers in creation, to figure out just the exact spot to aim it where it would do exactly that, he thought to himself. Aloud, in a lighter tone, he said, "Well, I *told* you I was older than I looked."

They weren't sure whether to laugh or edge away from him at that, but since he had the car and the keys, a nervous laugh seemed the most prudent choice.

The captain got a blanket out of the car and spread it on the ground, then went back and got out a small hamper and a cooler. He then helped Tony get Anne Marie's wheelchair set up and her into it.

"Some light snacks, sinful sweets," the captain told them. "And some good wine, although in case you couldn't or wouldn't drink, some fruit punch as well."

The stars were out, not as many as would be visible farther out from the city but far more than could be seen in Rio itself. There was a quarter moon at this season, but it was a late moonrise and had not yet shown itself, nor would it until almost an hour after the meteor arrived. That much luck was with them.

The captain amazed them with his knowledge of the stars and constellations. There didn't seem to be a single one he couldn't name, or tell its distance from Earth and details about its composition.

"You know more than most astronomers could keep in their heads, I think," Tony noted, unable to see the stars but nonetheless fascinated by the tour. "This is from navigating a ship?"

"From navigating a *lot* of ships, and of different types," the captain responded.

"Do you think there is other life out there?" Anne Marie asked him. "Strange creatures, alien civilizations, all that sort of thing?"

"Oh, yes," he answered confidently. "A vast number. The hugeness of the cosmos is beyond anyone's comprehension. Some of them may already have spaceships and be in contact or even commerce with one another."

"You mean in this solar system?" Tony responded. "I would doubt it."

"No, no, there's nothing else in our solar system worth mentioning. I mean beyond. *Far* beyond. Thousands and millions of light-years, in this galaxy and many others."

"You are a romantic, Captain," Tony said skeptically. "What you say about other creatures and civilizations might well be true, but those same distances would prohibit contact. The speed of light alone says no."

"Well, that *is* something of a stopper," Solomon admitted, "but not as much as you'd think. Gravity bends space, light, even time itself, and it's but one of a great many forces at work. If a ship could be built to withstand those forces and make use of them, both space and time might be bent, reducing a journey of many centuries to a matter of days or weeks. They once said that heavier-than-air craft could never fly under their own power, and for many years it was believed that the sound barrier was so absolute, its vibrations would tear an airplane apart. *Nothing* is impossible— absolutely nothing. It just takes a lot of time, work, ingenuity, and guts to eventually figure a way to cheat."

Tony shook his head. "My education was as an engineer, and I know about solving such things, but I believe that practical interstellar flight is just outside the rules of God."

"Well said, sir! You sound like a medieval pope!"

"Oh, stop arguing, you two!" Anne Marie scolded. "I don't care if it's possible or not, since even if it is, none of us will live to see it, but it is fun to imagine. I wonder what sort of creatures there *are* out there."

Captain Solomon looked at the stars. "Oz, and Olympus, and Fairyland, and a hundred other lands not quite imagined here on Earth. If you like, play a game. Suppose you could wish yourself up there, become one of those other creatures—what sort of creature might you like to be?"

She laughed. "I'm not much good at imagining *creatures,* and most of the ones on the telly are pretty slimy."

"Well, there'll be slimy ones, of course. But, if you can't think of some creature out of whole cloth, pick one out of mythology or classical fantasy."

"Umph! It's so difficult to do! I suppose I should fall back on the obvious, as my therapists would say in the old days. Lying there, unable to move for so long, I used to dream of being a racehorse. Isn't *that* a silly thought, even if an obvious fantasy for me? Anne Marie, interplanetary racehorse!"

"Well, be a centaur, then, or is that 'centauress'?" the captain responded in a light mood. *I knew another centauress once, but I can't even remember her name* . . .

"What about you, Tony?" Anne Marie prompted. "What sort of creature would *you* be? How about an eagle? Flying about, and with remarkable eyesight as well."

"Possibly," Tony responded, sounding a bit irritated with the game but nonetheless going along for Anne Marie's sake since she was getting such a kick out of it. "But, and I am being fully honest here, if such a thing were possible, then I should like to be whatever you were." And he meant it, too. The captain could feel the love that was there and was almost consumed with envy for this unfortunate blind and crippled pair of mortals.

"How sweet, my darling," she said with a smile. "But what of you, Captain? We haven't heard your own choice."

"I'm afraid I have grave limits on that part of my imagination," he answered seriously. "I can think of myself only as Gilgamesh, or the Wandering Jew. Always the same, never changing, walking through the world but unable to fully become a part of it."

"I believe I'd like that," Tony said. "Never changing, never aging, and never beyond repair, as it were. Watching the ages come and go, empires rise and fall, and great events as they occur. Yes, I might find that quite enticing."

"No, you wouldn't," the captain came back a bit sharply. "Suppose you had to do it without Anne Marie? Without *anybody* to share it with? Watching everyone you knew or liked grow old and sick and then die, watching as many horrors as great things and being unable to do more than bear witness to them? Always alone, without even anyone to talk about it with or share experiences with on an equal basis? Is that a blessing or the worst of curses? You tell me."

"Without Anne Marie? Hmmm . . . I think I see what you mean. But I would insist on Anne Marie as well!"

"I'm not so certain of that myself," she put in. "I mean, after centuries together I'd expect even the most loving of people to get rather sick of one another."

Both men were startled by her comment, Tony because he could not conceive of such a thing and the captain for far different reasons.

Was that ultimately what it was? Did I need her so much that I failed to realize that I could be a pretty boring and predictable stick-in-the-mud that might eventually drive anybody nuts? Could it be as simple as that?

"You might grow sick of *me*?" Tony asked her, genuinely a little upset.

"Don't worry, darling, I'll give you a few thousand years or so," she answered playfully. She paused for a moment, sensing that her response had really bothered him. "Oh, come off it, Latin lover! It's just a silly game to pass the time!"

The captain turned and looked back toward the northeast. "Sorry I caused any problems. As Anne Marie said, it's just a ga— *Holy smoke!*"

Anne Marie suddenly looked up in the same direction and gasped. "Tony! *The whole sky is lighting up!* It's like the sun's about to rise!"

But it was thirteen minutes after two in the morning.

In spite of many predictions to the contrary, it was quite clear to astronomers that as the meteor dug into the atmosphere, it was coming apart. Not enough to keep a large mass from striking fairly close to where they had predicted but enough so that pieces, some fairly large, would shower down along the route inland. This had been feared but was not completely unexpected.

It began while still well over the Atlantic, a brilliant, shining fireball that turned darkness into eerie twilight while providing a surprisingly multicolored display in its wake for those watching openmouthed on ships at sea and from monitoring aircraft. This caused a lot of attention but little concern; the ocean was vast and swallowed whole the splinters that managed to make it all the way to the surface.

As the meteor approached the continent, however, it was lower in the sky and slowing slightly, although its speed was still so great that observers on the ground saw the fireball flash past in the space of but a few seconds.

To the captain and Anne Marie, sitting atop the hill not many kilometers from Rio, it was an eerie, awesome sight nonetheless. The meteor approached from over the horizon, illuminating the eastern sky like the coming of dawn, slowly obliterating the stars, and overwhelming even the glow of the city lights. When it suddenly appeared, much lower on the horizon than they had expected, it was a miniature sun, a massive fireball that seemed several times the size of a full moon. Even the captain had to admit that he'd never in his incredibly long life seen anything quite like it before.

It came with blinding speed almost directly over them, and at just about that moment the captain, who'd gotten to his feet without even realizing it as he gaped at the sight, suddenly reeled, cried out, and dropped to his knees.

The sensation was momentary but powerful: a sudden loss of orientation and a pervasive, cold, desolate emptiness that struck to the core of his soul, as if someone had just walked across his grave . . .

At the same moment there was a series of thunderous explosions that echoed all around them and a brief but violent wind that came out of nowhere and struck with surprising force.

"Wha—what's happening?" Tony cried. *"What's happening! Anne Marie!"*

"I'm all right!" she shouted to him, although already the wind and explosions seemed to be dying down, vanishing into pale echoes as if they had never been there. "Oh, good lord! There are streamers—sparkling things, hundreds—no, thousands of them, falling all over. Reds, yellows, greens, golds, pure white—incredible! Captain, can you—" For the first time she looked over and saw Solomon bent over double, looking agonized. *"Captain!* Are you all right?"

The captain gulped down several deep breaths. "Yes, yes! I'm all right. It was—strange. I've never felt anything like that before. Never. It's fading now. Did you feel it?"

"Only the wind."

He was getting some self-control back but was clearly still shaken. "That was just the fireball sucking up some of the air in its wake. It must have come almost directly over us. The explosions were sonic booms. It's still going *very* fast, unless it's already crashed by now." He looked out at the spectacular fireworks display still raining down all around them. "Some of those are *big*! I think I can see smoke in the direction of the city!"

There was a sudden, jarring explosion very close by, an explosion so near that the ground trembled and Anne Marie's wheelchair began to vibrate, almost tipping over. The captain again fell, this time from the tremors.

"What now? Earthquake?" Tony asked, frustrated that he could see nothing.

"I don't think so," the captain responded. "I think a big chunk came down pretty damned close to us." He picked himself up off the ground and wiped off some dirt. "Everybody okay?"

"Yes—I think so," Anne Marie responded. "Oh, my! This was quite the adventure, after all. I doubt if I will ever forget this. I'm *so* glad we came!"

The captain began looking around and immediately saw a reddish-orange glow from the direction of the road below—the road they'd used to get there.

"You two stay here and try to relax," he told them. "I'm going to walk over and see just what hit and where." He had visions of landslides that might possibly trap them atop the mountain, but he didn't want to alarm his companions until he knew just what the situation was.

He was also still somewhat shaken by that terrible paralyzing sensation he'd had as the meteor had passed overhead. Nothing, but nothing, had ever felt like that before.

It had felt like death.

Not the warm, dark cessation of life he'd imagined but cold, terribly lonely, empty, corrupt—the cold of decomposition and the grave.

He reached the point where the road started down, but he didn't have to walk far along it to discover what had hit and where. No *wonder* the earth had shaken! He couldn't imagine why it hadn't knocked them off the hilltop and toppled the car, for all the good the car was going to do now.

Below, near the point at which the dirt road met the main paved highway, was a large glowing object. There was a lot of steam and a hot, acrid smell as if the area had suddenly gone volcanic and melted rock and road. It was impossible to see much detail without going down quite a ways and it wasn't terribly clear how much of the dirt road remained intact, but he didn't dare leave his two companions to go down to check.

He started back toward them, reaching into his pocket and taking out a large cigar, which he stopped to light. He had refrained from smoking near Anne Marie, but this was the kind of situation that called for a good cigar. The hilltop was dark again, and all the debris made it a tricky walk, but he made it back to them without falling or twisting an ankle.

"We've got a real problem," he told them straight out. "Our friend that just passed over left us a present right at the base of the hill, and it's none too clear if we're going to be able to get down very easily."

"Oh, dear!" Anne Marie exclaimed. "What will we do, Captain?"

"There's a good-sized meteor chunk that came in and hit right down there. That was the earthquake we felt. It's still glowing hot—probably will be for days—and I'm not sure how much of that road is still there or whether there are any rock slides or other obstacles. The only thing we can do is try very carefully to make it down in the car. If it's impossible, then we'll have to go as far as we can, get out, and manage on our own. I'm pretty sure that if we can get down to the main road one way or another, people will be along fairly soon who might help. But the plain fact is, we have to get down there, since nobody knows we're up here and neither of you is exactly in condition to climb down the side of this hill even if we had ropes and such to do it with."

"I don't like it," Tony told him. "The whole road might be undermined, and there might well be rather narrow passages. Not only would that cause me obvious problems, but Anne Marie's chair would never make it."

"Couldn't we build a signal fire or something from all this junk?" Anne Marie asked. "I mean, there are sure to be all sorts of folks out here sooner or later, right? If it's big enough, possibly helicopters. You *did* say that this was once a helicopter landing pad, didn't you?"

Solomon nodded. "The trouble is, I think this is only one of a *lot* of fragment strikes, and it's pretty far out. I would expect people along the main road any time now, particularly others who came out here like us to get a better look, but in terms of the authorities and helicopters and the like—possibly sometime. The glow toward Rio has increased, I think, and I suspect that there are a number of fires and possibly worse."

"Check the radio," Tony suggested. "At least we'll know where we stand."

The captain nodded, went over to the minivan, and, after discovering he had to start the engine to power the radio, flicked it on.

There was mostly static.

"I think Jesus may have lost his power," the captain said a bit sarcastically. The great statue that sat on the mountain that directly overlooked Rio was the symbol of the city, but that same mountain and two others nearby were where the transmitting towers for radio, television, and other telecommunications were located. If power was out up there, it wouldn't matter what was going on below.

He slowly turned the dial, finally getting a low-powered broadcast heavy with static.

". . . out in two-thirds of the city, and there are numerous fires from sparks and cinders all over. Because we have managed to keep our power and remain on the air, we will keep broadcasting information as we know it. Civil authorities have asked that no one attempt to use the telephones and that they remain in their homes and remain calm. Fire brigades are out all over the city, and police are trying to free people trapped in buildings and cope with dozens of accidents as most of the traffic signals are out. A declaration of martial law is expected and may be in force now; we have no way of knowing from here . . ."

Solomon got out but left the radio on. "Sounds pretty bad. Martial law, fires, power outages, you name it. They didn't expect this. Not knowing anybody in particular is up here, I seriously doubt if anyone's going to be out this way for some time—maybe a day or two. Even if they knew we were here, I think we'd be a pretty damned low priority. We've got the remains of the little picnic I packed, but that's it, and there doesn't appear to be any water or other facilities up here. If you're too nervous to make the attempt down, my next inclination would be to go myself and see if I could find help—but, again, that might take a very long time, and I really wouldn't like leaving you two up here for an extended period."

"Ordinarily I would agree on getting down, but I am afraid that Anne Marie might get stuck halfway and then what do we do?" Tony asked.

"This is one of those 'there's no good solution' problems," the captain replied. "Anne Marie, you said you had medicine you had to take religiously, and you've been fairly weak as it is. How much of an extra supply of that medication did you bring?"

"Oh, my! Yes, I see what you mean," she said thoughtfully. "I'm afraid, dear, that he's right—we have no real choice in this."

Tony sighed. "I don't like it, but all right. Let us get packed up."

The captain helped, then, as they got settled in the van, he tried the radio again. One of the big stations at least had gotten back on the air, albeit with lower power than usual, and the details of what had happened in the city and beyond were soon clear.

Possibly hundreds of pieces from the meteor had come down, ranging from fingernail-size to a few as large as soccer balls. A number of homes and buildings had been hit; there was a crater in the center of the financial district about ten meters wide that had, among other things, severed the main electrical and phone cables to and from the city center; and many other fragments had been large enough and hot enough to touch off fires. A few, in poorer and rundown areas, had quickly become conflagrations. Although only two people were known to be dead and perhaps a dozen others had injuries serious enough to need hospitalization, the massive fires in the densely populated poor areas gave an unspoken but implicit promise of a much higher toll.

The swath cut by the shedding meteor was twenty to twenty-five kilometers wide, and reports of isolated rockfalls in other areas were still coming in. A large segment, larger than any that had struck the city, was seen to have fallen somewhere in the mountains beyond the city, but at the moment it wasn't known where it had fallen or if it had caused any major damage.

The main body had landed, perhaps only seconds later, in the remote upper Amazon basin, still within the country and inside of one of the new native reserve areas designed to protect the rain forest and the habitat of primitive tribes who lived there. Early reports said that there was massive damage at the main site, with the forest knocked down and ablaze, like the aftermath of an atomic bomb. The Archbishop of Rio had announced a special mass of thanks and salvation for tomorrow, noting that if the impact had come sooner, along the coast, there would have been massive loss of life.

The announcer then paused to gather more information, and the station began playing Jobim's *Quiet Night and Quiet Stars* . . .

The captain switched off the radio and drove slowly over to the road.

"Well, that big one in the mountain must have been the one that hit below," Tony noted.

The captain frowned. "Maybe. But I can't understand—if it was that big, and much smaller pieces caused so much damage, why we didn't have a minibomb effect here as well."

"That was quite a jolt when it hit," Anne Marie pointed out.

"Exactly. The jolt, yes, but something that hot, hitting with that kind of force, should have done far more if it's anywhere close, and I think it is. I'm beginning to have a very bad feeling about this."

"What do you expect? Martian invaders?" Tony joked.

"No. Nothing like that." He took a deep breath. "Well, here we go."

Solomon was surprised at how far they managed to get before fallen rocks and other debris stopped them. They were actually at the lower turnout of the last switchback before the main road and could see down the steep kilometer or more to the paved road below even though they couldn't reach it.

Anne Marie gasped at the sight on that main road. "What is it?" Tony pressed her.

"The meteor! Or at least the big piece of it! It's *huge*! It's stuck half in the road and half in the opposite hillside. It looks mostly buried in the hill and there's a lot of bubbling and hissing around the edges, but you can see a big part of it! It's *glowing*—a dull, almost golden yellow, and it looks like some huge gemstone, kind of like stained glass. Good heavens! I'd almost swear it *was* something artificial!"

The captain stared at it. *Just my imagination?* he wondered. *Or is that huge flat area facing outward the shape I'm afraid it is?*

He got out and surveyed the path, dully illuminated by the glow of the strange object. Surveying the scene, he went back to them and said, "I think I can angle the car so it'll give us light from the headlights the first part of the way down, after which, if that thing keeps glowing, we won't need any more light. It might be a tight fit, but I think we can get the wheelchair down, though we might have to lift it over at one or two places. Are you willing?"

"I think better down than back up at this point," Anne Marie replied.

It was not an easy task, but it was manageable. At one point dirt and rock had covered much of the road, making it difficult to get the wheelchair around without going off the side, but the captain managed, then, bracing her on the other side, got Tony around as well. Several times the blind man stumbled, but he was game all the way, and in about thirty minutes they made it down to the road.

The meteor had taken out much of the paved area, and between its own extrusion and the landslides the impact had caused, it would clearly be some time before any vehicle could get past. Still, there was more than enough room for them to manage, if no more slides occurred, and once on the other side, they would at least be well positioned when the first cars driven by the curious or investigators made it to the scene.

"I'm surprised there aren't a lot of people on both sides already here," Anne Marie said. "I know we were hardly the only ones to come up this route."

"We don't know how bad some of the slides are elsewhere, and perhaps other pieces fell as well, doing damage," Tony pointed out. "It might well be a while, but at least I believe we have more of a chance down here than up there. What do you think, Captain? What should we do now?"

Solomon was staring at the meteor. "Huh? Oh, sorry, I wasn't paying attention." He paused a moment, then said, "You two stay right here. I've got to get something off my mind one way or the other. I won't be but a moment."

With that, he walked down toward the still-glowing object. As he approached, the thing seemed to change somehow; the glassy surface took on a duller sheen, and then other forms seemed to appear just underneath.

Anne Marie gasped. "It looks like—something *alive*!" she said. "Like a network of arteries and veins or fluids going through pulsing tubes. I've seen this sort of thing under microscopes!"

"Your imagination is getting the best of you," her husband responded. "You've been through a lot tonight."

"No, no! I'm serious! I swear it! And it seems to be getting more and more detailed as the captain goes nearer to it. Captain!" she called out worriedly. "Don't go any closer! Watch out!"

The captain gestured confidently with his right hand. He walked around to the left, where the shoulder of the road still allowed passage, and as he did, a single gemlike "face" in the center seemed to darken on its own, becoming in a moment jet black, while the rest of the object remained unchanged.

"Son of a bitch! I *knew* it!" the captain grumbled. "A damned *hexagon*!" He stood there staring at it and said, louder, "You coulda been a little more *subtle,* damn it!"

The object didn't respond. He knew it wouldn't. Although so advanced that it would be incomprehensible to Earth science, it was just a machine.

"I don't want to go through it all again!" he told it, knowing he was talking only to himself. "I didn't even want to do it the *last* time, and you forced me. What do you want me to do? Wipe out everything again? Just when they've gotten to the start of the fun part? Before I've even completely forgotten who and what I am? Screw up thousands of civilizations because one damned thing went refreshingly wrong in history? Well, I won't do it! Get *her* to do it! *She* knows how! I encoded her and linked her to the Well!"

He stopped for a moment, trying to calm down. Maybe it *had* gone for her as well. It would be ironic if she, too, were in Brazil, although what she'd be doing in the Amazon basin was beyond him. Still, he knew the machine wouldn't let him stay here while somebody else did the reset. He hadn't taken himself out of the core matrix. If somehow it allowed him to get around the embedded fragment without taking him in, swallowing him up, it wouldn't matter. It would send more of these, and more, until he would feel under constant bombardment. Either that or it would figure some other way. When one had the power to manipulate probability, one could be staved off for a while, but eventually one would get one's way. Besides, suppose he walked away and this gate stayed open? An invasion of people at this stage would not exactly be in anybody's best interest.

He sighed. Perhaps this time he could minimize the damage. Perhaps this time he could opt himself out. Still, it was pretty clear that he had no choice at this point, not until he was there, inside, at the controls. There simply weren't any options left open to him.

He had to go to the Well one more time.

But he also had certain other, more immediate responsibilities. He turned and walked back to the waiting couple.

"Don't ask me questions," he said to them, "but I know what this is. You remember that game we played up top? What would you like to become if you could?"

"Yes," Anne Marie responded nervously, suddenly not certain of the captain's sanity.

"Tony?"

"Yes, but what's the point of this?"

"That thing's a door. Now, you've *got* to trust me on this, and no, I'm not losing my mind. I once spent a lot of time and effort trying to avoid going through such a door before and failed. I'm not going to make *that* mistake again. The result is, I'm going to go through it. When I do, I think it will close behind me. If the two of you go with me, I can promise you that Anne Marie will walk again and that you, Tony, will see again. It's no heaven where that door leads. Remember, even Oz had wicked witches and the land of

Jason was filled with dangerous people and more dangerous creatures. But it's not a bad place. It will heal you."

"You're raving mad," Tony responded, shaking his head.

"Look, I'm offering you a single chance. If there's no door there, then we go on by and we wait for help. If there *is* a door, you walk through it with me. Understand?"

"This is ridiculous!" Tony fumed. "I won't stand for any more of this! We'll wait right here!"

But Anne Marie, while more in tune with Tony's viewpoint than the captain's strange comments, nonetheless felt that something within the man was not lunacy but sincerity. "Just who *are* you that someone would send such a thing for you?" she asked him.

"I'm not going to tell you that, for your own protection and mine," he replied. "And if you decide to come with me, not a word that I knew anything about it to begin with. Not one word. We were just three people who went to see a meteor and found this curiosity and walked through. Understand?"

"I'm not going to listen to any more of this rot," Tony fumed.

The captain stared at him. "I understand how you feel and what it sounds like. But when I leave, you'll be stuck here alone, the two of you. I'm not certain *when* help will arrive. And the best way to reach the most likely source of help is around that thing over there. The door is that blackness that opened when I approached. You saw it, didn't you, Anne Marie? I can see that you did. It'll open again. What do you have to lose?"

She almost believed him. She *wanted* to believe him. "If— just granting your point for argument's sake—if what you say is true, would Tony and I still be together?"

He shrugged. "I can't promise that. I can only promise that he will see and you will walk and be strong again." He looked at Tony. "I remember our conversation. Is it worth it to take a chance, considering the alternative? We don't have much time. Sooner or later there will be hundreds, maybe thousands of people up here. Sightseers, rescuers, newspeople, scientists, road crews—you name it. I can't have them accidentally going through. I'm going now. You can go with me and what I have said will come to pass, or you can go on past and wait and hope that rescue comes quickly for Anne Marie's sake and enjoy your few weeks or months or whatever."

It was Tony's turn to sigh. "Captain, I will allow you to lead us past that thing. Beyond that I will not go."

"We love each other, Captain," Anne Marie said simply. "I'm not at all certain I would wish to live without Tony, healthy or not."

The captain gave them a humorless smile. "However, that option's not open to you, is it, Tony?"

"Haven't you understood, Captain?" the Brazilian asked him. "That is not the option you believe. We shall not wait for the inevitable, or survive each other."

The comment stunned Solomon. "Now there are two ways I envy you," he told him. "The kind of love you show is rare, and the ability to end your lives by your own decision is something I have always wished to be able to do."

"What? Do you believe you are a vampire or some such, too?" Tony asked derisively.

"No. But I told you all along that I am a lot older than I look. The same thing that sent *that* and knew just where and when to drop it insulates and protects me." *And controls me,* he thought to himself. *Walk this way in the early morning. Meet these two. Go up into the hills to a remote area . . .*

He sighed. "Well," the captain added, "we might as well get on with it. You have a great choice at this moment that I wish I had but do not. You can choose life or death for the both of you. Anne Marie in particular hasn't had that choice before, so it was an easy decision. Now your choice has a complication. Do you both *want* to die? Or are you merely reconciled to it? I'm giving you another choice." He paused a moment. "Let's go and get this over with."

He walked slowly forward, and Tony began pushing the wheelchair as Anne Marie gave short instructions that kept them going in the right direction. Still, beneath the automatic commands she was giving, she was also thinking, wondering if this strange little man was telling the truth and, in the impossible event that perhaps he was, whether the price was worth it.

She saw the activity just beneath the surface of the fragment speed up as they approached, and as they moved to the right, she saw the big facet, more than two meters high even though slightly buried in the ground at its bottom edge, open to an impossible, impenetrable darkness.

The captain stopped dead center of the opening. "Well, here is where we possibly part company," he told them. "I have enjoyed meeting you, and I am happy that at least some of the good that is within this race of humankind shines so brightly in you. It knows you're here. It won't close until you go on past. In any event, spending this evening with you has made it somehow easier for me." And with that, he walked straight into the blackness and vanished.

Anne Marie's heart leapt at the sight. The captain hadn't gone into the darkness or been enveloped by it, he had simply touched it and vanished.

"Captain?" Tony asked, frowning.

"He's gone, dear, just like he said," Anne Marie told him. "He went into it, and that was that. Strange. I think we've just had a close encounter, as they call it."

"Gone? What do you mean, 'gone'? Is there an opening in the thing? Did he crawl inside? What?"

"No, dear. He just walked into it and vanished. *Poof!* One moment he was there, the next he wasn't."

"An illusion of some kind. Or he was burned up or this thing has some sort of radiation. What he said just *can't* be true! It's not *possible!*"

"Perhaps. But it looked awfully quick and painless, you know, and there's no trace of him. I am feeling very, very exhausted, my darling, and I am in a great deal of pain. I am not at all certain I can stand it at this altitude until someone comes."

He swallowed hard, his emotions in turmoil. He wasn't *ready* for this! Not yet! It wasn't anything like what they'd planned! "What do you want me to do?" he asked in anguish. "Go into that thing? Now?"

"You don't have to if you don't want to. You know that."

"I go where you go!" he snapped. "But—"

"But what? It's quick, painless, no bodies, no traces, no one to grieve over and no mess left for others to deal with. They'll find the car, the porter will remember us, and we'll be listed as victims of the meteor. I *know* it's not what we wanted, but it is here, and there will not be a better time. I *know* I shall not survive to get even to hospital, and I do not want to die in hospital or be kept alive on machines. Do it for me. You may make your own decision afterward."

He neither moved nor spoke to her. The blackness on the face of the object remained unchanged.

"Come! Why do you fear the moment when it's at hand? We've discussed this over and over. Do it for me."

He was almost in tears, but he knew he had to give her the truth of his deepest fears.

"I—I am afraid that what the captain said might be true."

"Then we will be healed, isn't that right?"

"And separated in some strange, unknown place!"

"If I am healed, I will find you. Come. My pain grows with each moment, and no matter what he said, this thing could close at any moment. Go right and just walk ahead."

She suddenly pushed the joystick. The wheelchair lunged forward and lurched to the right, and both chair and occupant vanished into the darkness, leaving only silence.

"Anne Marie? *Anne Marie!*" His fear of losing her overcame all other thoughts. He turned right and walked straight ahead.

And without warning, he felt a sensation of falling.

Back on the paved mountain road above Rio, the dark hexagon winked out and the meteor began to undergo a dramatic transformation. The other facets, which had pulsed with an analog of a living circulatory system, began to fade; circulation failed, patches of decay began to appear, finally spreading over the surface of the object.

Its purpose accomplished, the Watchman and all others evidencing a desire to do so having passed through, the device had no other reason to exist, and very quickly it died.

By the time the first of the curious and investigators reached it, shortly after dawn, it resembled a huge, irregular lump of granite or gneiss laced with enormous veins of obsidian.

ROCKFALL:
UPPER AMAZON

Theresa Perez was not amused. "What in hell are *you* doing here?" she asked Juan Campos acidly. "There is no room on this plane for you two. We have to work."

Campos grinned evilly at her. "So? We give you our hospitality and you would then deny me seeing this great sight? Even my father thought that we were owed this."

"What's the problem?" Maklovitch called, squeezing into the plane. He saw Campos and the bodyguard. "This wasn't part of the agreement," he noted with irritation. "We're on a tight schedule here and even tighter quarters."

"The agreement has been changed," Campos responded. "We are staying right here. If you choose not to take off, then sit. My father believes one of the family should be aboard."

Maklovitch thought fast. Right now the deadline outweighed all else, and in this plane Campos was as much at their mercy as they were at his. "All right—you come. *He* goes, and now!" the newsman added, pointing to the bodyguard.

"Ramón goes where I go."

The newsman thought a moment, then decided to call the bluff. "Very well. Terry, get on the horn and tell them that

Don Campos has insisted on placing two armed men aboard. Because this exceeds our weight and room limits, we cannot go. Tell them the Campos file is to air rather than be sent to Don Campos. Understood?"

The gangster jumped. "Now, wait one minute. *What* file? You—bitch! You radio *nothing* without my permission!"

"Too late," she told him with a smile. "We're already live to the studio. They're hearing every single word we say. Are you ordering me to switch us out, knowing that it means that here, on live audio, you are forcibly kidnapping us?"

This was getting a little too complicated too quickly for Juan Campos. *"What file?"*

"Your father knows," the newsman responded. "Why do you think we were offered his hospitality? I thought you told us that you really ran things around here." He paused a moment. "Now, since we're going nowhere, shall we all go see your father and explain the situation?"

Campos suddenly didn't know what to do. His first impulse was to take them all out and shoot them, but he was in fact acting on his own and he was not at all certain how his father would react when word of that came down. Nobody had said anything about a deal, but it explained much.

"All right. He goes, I stay."

"And you give him your pistol and stay in that seat as long as we're in the air," the newsman said firmly. He looked at his watch. "Better make up your mind right now or it won't make any difference. That meteor won't wait."

Campos threw up his hands in disgust, then handed a pistol over to the bodyguard and told him to get off and wait. The bodyguard, hesitant and not without some protest, complied.

None of them were fools enough to believe that Campos didn't still have various weapons on him, but at least it was one less. Now, with the bodyguard out, Lori climbed on, looking confused, and they took their seats.

The technicians had been working steadily since they'd arrived. Gus now had a console bolted in the center rear of the plane through which he could control several exterior cameras and see what each showed on small black-and-white monitors. The pictures were being recorded in a compartment beneath the cabin and also being sent by a computer-controlled *ku*-band satellite uplink mounted atop the aircraft that would relay them back to the U.S. studio if, of course, conditions were right and the aircraft was level. A similar microwave system was mounted on the plane's underside and might work for pickups in Manaus or at the makeshift hacienda uplink site. Provided that either system worked, directors far away in the States would pick the feed and also give Gus general direction.

"Probably none of it will work," Gus grumped, "which is why we're also taping, but it's worth a try."

Audio wasn't a problem, and Terry had on a headset that connected her by radio with the studio. Both Maklovitch and Sutton also had similar headsets, but those were on a different frequency and would be used mostly for contact and commentary to the live anchor desk.

They roared off into the night, climbing through a low cloud layer that bumped them around a bit and caused horrible noise on the audio. Then they broke free and had the clear sky above and all around them, with a tremendous view of the stars.

"I've got us on course and ready," the pilot reported. "We should be in position with, no thanks to the delays, about ten minutes to spare. For a region with cleared airspace, though, there's a fair amount of traffic on the radio. Not just the two science planes and the Brazilian Air Force tracker, but it seems there's a number of small civil aircraft up in violation of the clear airspace order. Two air force jets are trying to track them and force them down, but there's a *lot* of damned fools up."

"Yeah, and probably all three U.S. networks and a dozen others," Terry commented. "Wonder what would happen if they shot down an anchor or two."

It was very dark but very busy in the plane's cabin as

everything was checked out one last time, and they even did a last-minute on-air audio report to the news desk. Everybody tried to forget about Campos, who at least was just sitting there uncharacteristically behaving himself. Still, the time dragged impossibly.

Lori felt keyed up but also suddenly very tired, almost drained. It was the waiting, she decided. She wanted things to start. They *all* wanted things to start.

"Contact! Visual contact by Science One!" the pilot reported excitedly. Science One was the combined Brazilian-Smithsonian research plane about 350 miles out in the Atlantic. "If what they're reporting is true," the pilot added, "then we're in for a dizzingly fast lalapalooza! Buckle in tight! She's coming down dirty!"

"What does he mean by 'dirty'?" Juan Campos asked, breaking his long silence.

"Shedding," Lori told him. "Coming apart. Raining big, hot rocks."

The plane turned slowly and then reduced speed. Maklovitch was already on the air, and Lori knew now that she, too, was live.

"We should be seeing it any second now," the newsman said with a professional calmness his tense face belied. "It's coming right over Rio."

"There! Got it!" Gus cried. *"Oh, my God! What a whopper!"*

Things changed in an instant; the horizon suddenly turned from night into a creeping twilight, then, suddenly, it was there, coming straight for them for all they could tell.

"Madre dios!" Juan Campos breathed, and crossed himself.

Lori watched with a mixture of awe and fascination as the huge object sped toward them and then was suddenly past. It looked like some enormous flaming lump of charcoal, the size of a dozen full moons, blazing a yellow and white-hot tail.

"Wahoo!" Gus roared from his console, apparently very pleased with the pictures. It was only later that Lori realized that the man was so intent on his screens that he never actually saw the meteor.

The plane banked sharply and took a course perpendicular to the meteor's path so they could see it go down. The pilot's reactions were good, although suddenly the entire aircraft was rocked as if shaken by a giant hand, and unsecured items went flying. There was a roller coaster-like sensation of falling for what seemed an eternity, and then the pilot boosted power and pulled out of it.

"Did you get it? Did you get it?" Terry called repeatedly.

Now the plane headed back west, following a huge but ragged contrail left by the meteor. It took better than five minutes to reach the point where it dipped into the clouds, a distance the big rock had covered in seconds. There was no question, though, as to where to look. A giant mushroom-shaped plume was still rising from out of the clouds, and both plume and clouds seemed to be on fire.

They tensed again as the aircraft dipped below the clouds, and there were general gasps at the scene below. It looked like the whole forest was on fire, and the impact site, many miles away, resembled nothing less than an active volcanic caldera.

"It looks like an atom bomb," Lori commented, her throat dry and constricted. "Look at the blast area down there. The firestorm had to be incredibly hot to reach that distance in that wet, green growth."

Tremendous thunder and lightning were all around as well, making the scene look and sound like the end of the world.

"What is all that? Blast effect?" the anchor prompted her.

"No. It's very wet here, and the heat and blast cloud have created massive convection currents. The heat is rising, taking the humidity in the air with it, and it's condensing. Those are thunderstorms created by the impact. There's no telling how long it will rain on this area, but at least it will help extinguish the fires and keep the smoke from rising too high."

"I see a huge crater, but there's something glowing at the bottom," Maklovitch noted. "Is that the meteor itself?"

"Possibly, but unlikely," she answered. "It's probable that the whole thing disintegrated on impact, leaving only small fragments. More likely that is partly molten rock and mostly existing bedrock uncovered for the first time in a million years."

"I estimate that we are probably at least ten miles from the crater, yet it's clearly visible. It must be enormous. A mile, maybe two miles across. The fire and blast damage extend, oh, at least twenty or thirty miles all around, possibly more." The newsman suddenly remembered Juan Campos. "Señor Campos, does anyone live down there to your knowledge?"

Campos stared at the scene out of hell. "Not *now*," he responded in almost a whisper.

"No, no. I mean *before* it hit. I know there wasn't much in the way of evacuation because of the sparse population and the primitiveness of the people."

"Depends," the gunman managed. "Where are we now?"

Maklovitch saw what he meant. All of this region looked pretty much alike, even more so in the dark, and nothing much was left down there that might provide a landmark.

"I've got the position from Science Three," the pilot called back. "Call it, oh, a hundred, maybe a hundred and twenty kilometers south-southeast from the Campos airstrip."

The Peruvian nodded. "Then there *were* some Indians down there. Now?"

"Can we get in closer?" Gus asked the pilot. "I'd like to go straight over that crater if I could."

"I could try, but with these storms and downdrafts all over the place there's no predicting anything. You can feel her shaking now," the pilot replied. "I've been circling out some fifteen miles, and you feel what it's like. If I did it, it would have to be at a fairly fast speed."

"Well, the clouds and smoke are obscuring everything," the cameraman complained. "Either we get in there or we wrap, people. I'm for giving it a try."

Terry nodded, giving a quick satisfied glance at the terrified face of Juan Campos strapped in the back. *Welcome to the news business,* she thought acidly. "One pass, as low and slow as you dare," she told the pilot. "That's it. Gus will have to make do with what he can get."

Lori wasn't much more thrilled than Campos, as much as she wanted to see the sight closer up. With the tremendous turbulence, she found herself thinking less of the view than of headlines in the paper. LOCAL SCIENTIST AND NEWS CREW DIE COVERING ASTEROID.

"Hang on, everybody!" the pilot called, and circled first out, then back in toward the glow, climbing and increasing speed. The vapor, rising now mostly from the rainfall striking the still extremely hot object, obscured clear view, and the ride was the scariest any of them could remember. Then the turbulence subsided, and the fear and tension drained from all of them like water through a sieve, leaving them all more or less limp—except Gus, who was muttering that he hadn't really gotten a decent pass.

"One's enough, I think," Terry told him. "It's only going to get smokier for a while down there." She paused for a moment as someone far away asked her a question. "Gus? Can you replay that last pass, the straight-down shot, through a monitor here? They got it back at the studio, but they say there's something weird about it."

"Huh? Yeah, I guess, if you're finished shooting."

"We are for now. We're heading back to the ranch to uplink the tapes as backup. They want us, and particularly Doctor Sutton, to look at it and see if she can explain it. You, too, Gus, since it might be a trick of the light or something with the camera."

"Yeah, okay. Hold on. That's . . . lemmesee . . . three.

Rewind. All right. Wait. There. Okay, it may have to run a little, but I think it's in the neighborhood. I'll switch it to the overhead monitor."

They all looked, and for a moment there was a jiggly freeze-frame of the crater and smoke cloud. Then they saw the picture flip, angle dizzyingly from one side to the other as the plane got into position, then zoom straight in. The picture was bouncy but clear enough. They saw the smoke flash past and, for a very brief moment, were looking straight down through billowing white smoke and rain.

"*There!* Did you all see it?" Terry asked them. "It looks like something dark, something black, straight down as we went over, with bright stuff all around it."

"Sorry, it was so fast," Lori responded apologetically.

The picture stopped, and Gus rewound the tape.

"*Hold it!*" Terry shouted. "No, up a little more. Frame advance. *There!* Hold it!"

The picture was still jumpy and distorted, but they could now all see just what the control room back in the States had noticed. Through the smoke, the red and yellow glow of the crater was visible, if not completely clear. Right in the center of the glowing mass was a black shape, distorted and indistinct but still some sort of regular form.

"I couldn't guess," Lori told them. "I'd need a much clearer photo than that to really say much of anything about it. It could be a different mineral, much harder than the surrounding rock, that has a higher melting point and maybe is already cooled down, or a fissure in whatever's left of the meteor, or a trick of the light."

"I don't know meteors, but *pictures* I know," Gus said firmly. "That's no trick of the light. Something's down there."

Maklovitch looked back at Campos. "Any way in there? To land, I mean."

"This plane? No, señor. Nothing, even if it would have survived that blast. And there are no roads in this region of any sort. On foot—days under the best of conditions."

"You have a helicopter at the ranch," the pilot called back. "I saw it on the field back there. What about that?"

Campos shook his head. "No, no, no. That is our private helicopter. Besides, if you could not even safely fly this plane through that smoke and the storms, flying a helicopter in there close would be suicide!"

"I flew choppers in hairier conditions than that in the Marine Corps," the pilot replied. "Thunderstorms, sandstorms, and under fire. It wouldn't be a big deal, I don't think, particularly if we're allowing another hour or two for things to calm down."

"No, no, *no!*" Juan Campos shouted. "It is out of the question!"

"It may be," Terry said, "but even as we speak, my boss is on the phone to your father, and it looks like we might just have a deal." She paused. "Of course, *you* don't have to come if you don't want to."

Even Lori thought the idea bordered on madness. "It's pretty dangerous," she noted, "and you'll get better pictures, as well as better conditions, after daylight."

"That's true," Terry agreed, "but we don't know how long after daylight the first choppers will be arriving from elsewhere, full of geologists and astronomers and military people and bureaucrats—"

"Not to mention NBC, ABC, CBS, CBC, the BBC, and maybe Fox, God help us," Maklovitch put in. "In this business being first is everything. That's why folks watch us and advertisers pay top dollar—we can do things like this the others can't. Nobody remembers the *second* newsman into Kuwait City."

"Forrest Sawyer, ABC," Terry responded instantly. "We were third!"

"Okay, nobody outside the business remembers. But we remember most that we were third. It's the name of the game. Not that we're trying to commit suicide. If Bob there wasn't sure he could get us in and out in one piece, I don't think we'd risk it ourselves. If you're really against it, you can stay behind, but if we can put this together, you'd be invaluable on the scene."

Lori thought a moment about remaining behind with all those ruthless men on the drug lord's ranch and wondered which was more dangerous. "I'll go," she told him, wondering if she was in fact being stupid.

"Good girl! Oops! Sorry, Doc. No offense," the newsman added.

"That's all right." *Mother always said I should be a good girl. I just want to know if I'm being a dumb broad by doing this.*

"You seem certain my father will say yes," Juan Campos noted.

"We plan for a yes. If it's no, we haven't lost anything," the newsman told him.

"Even if he agrees, the helicopter carries only six and not much cargo," the gunman pointed out. "With you, your pilot, your cameraman, the two señoritas, and a sound man, it will be full."

"He's got a point there," the pilot, Bob, agreed. "We're not gonna be able to truck in a suitcase unit or much of anything except a hand-held."

The newsman thought a moment. "All right, then, we'll try two trips. Terry, you can handle Gus's sound, right?"

"In a pinch, sure."

"All right. A suitcase, Terry, Gus, me, and the doc."

"What's a 'suitcase unit'?" Lori asked, puzzled.

"A portable uplink," Gus replied. "It's actually a kit in the form of three large suitcases. You can put it together with battery power and have it sending pictures and sound to a comsat in under an hour. The foreign correspondent's constant companion since it was invented."

They had the agreement by the time they landed, but, looking over the helicopter, they discovered that it wasn't as large as they'd hoped. When the suitcase unit was added, it left room for five, but only by a whisker.

Juan Campos wasted no time at all calling in from a dedicated phone at the aircraft parking area. When he returned, he did not look all that happy.

"My father, he says that I must go with the helicopter," he told them. "This time it is not my idea!"

"He's right," Maklovitch told them. "I just spoke to him myself on the same line. Mr. Campos is a little nervous about somebody taking up the chopper without one of his men along to see that we go only where we're supposed to go and shoot just what we're here to shoot, particularly since we'll probably be gone well into daylight and they *do* expect others from the Brazilian side there not long after that. There was no talking him out of it; either Campos here goes or it's no deal."

It didn't need to be spelled out. After daylight in particular, coming in on this side of the border would reveal some sights camouflaged from routine aerial or satellite surveillance. If they saw them, it wasn't any big deal, since they couldn't be sure of their exact location. But no pictures. No more blackmail possibilities or nice photos for experts and their computers to mull over.

"With the suitcases, that leaves only five seats, including the pilot," Terry noted, not at all pleased by this turn of events. Flying into a disaster area fraught with sudden dangers and possible horrors didn't faze her, it seemed, but the idea of being stuck out in the middle of nowhere with Juan Campos sure did. "Who stays?"

"Well, I want you and Gus out there setting up and getting what you can," Maklovitch told her. "They want me to do some more standups here and an initial wrap piece, so it looks like I come out with the second flight. They're not at all sure if we can uplink with the rain, so you'll need the extra setup time. I'll bring a sound man and Brazil network people with me on the second ride. We'll be in contact by radio." He edged closer to her and added in a low whisper, "Besides, he's got to come back with Bob to ensure he flies right."

Terry nodded. "Okay, then. Doc, you want to come with us now or wait for the second run? It's probably going to be pretty wet and rough out there, but if you want to come along, feel free. At least you'll be the first person with any scientific training at all to see the thing."

Lori didn't like it, but she knew she had to go. "I'm coming. Nobody in the history of known science has been able to get this close to an impact of this magnitude so soon. What about rain gear?"

"Señorita Doctor," Juan Campos said, "you could wear anything you wished and it would not help when the rain falls. Even with little wind, the rain is so strong and so powerful, it cannot be described but must be experienced. Best to seek shelter when it starts, dress light except for the mud boots, and have one or more dry changes of clothes packed away."

"Well, we don't have any rain slickers, anyway," Gus noted. "Got some wide hats that'll help and a couple of umbrellas, for all the good they'll do, but that's it."

"We'll manage," Lori said, not at all certain that it was true. "I've been drenched before."

Once up in the air, they didn't need a map to find where to go even in the darkness of the jungle. There were still fires burning all around, and the eerie yellow glow from the crater seemed almost like some great aircraft beacon.

"What's causing that pulsing?" Terry asked the scientist. "I mean, I don't know much about this, but that's not normal, is it?"

"Nobody quite knows what's 'normal' in a situation like this, but I can't explain it and wouldn't have expected it. It could be rapid heating and cooling, but it seems almost too regular for that. That's one of the things we might be able to find out if we can get close enough."

"Looks pretty promising," Bob told them. "There's still lightning and thunderstorms all around, but the area immediately around the crater looks like just smoke from the thing itself."

"The white smoke coming from it now is probably mostly steam," Lori told them. "Groundwater or runoff from the storm is going down the crater, hitting that very hot bottom, and instantly coming back up."

"Kind of like a geyser," Gus said, nodding.

"Something like that. Or a fumarole. That's a relative of the geyser that erupts constantly, spouting steam with a roar. It may be days, weeks, even longer before the crater is cool enough to allow people to descend, although the scientific teams probably have moon suits and could do it in a matter of a day or so. They go into still-active volcanic calderas in them."

"Too bad we don't have any of those suits in the budget," Gus commented. "I'd like to get a down-the-throat shot."

They were quite close now, close enough to see the strange yellow-gold shape at the bottom, even though that bottom was a quarter of a mile deep and still shrouded in steam.

"Funny," Terry said, looking at the unearthly scene. "I don't see that dark spot now. Maybe you were wrong, Gus. Maybe it was just a trick of the camera."

"Not like that," Gus maintained. "There's nothin' to cause that kind of thing." He frowned. "I tell you, Terry, if that thing opens up and some Martian machine pops out, I'm runnin'!"

"I'm more curious as to why the crater isn't deeper," Lori commented. "It's amazingly shallow for something that large coming in at that kind of speed."

"Looks plenty big enough to me," Gus replied.

"Sure, but the velocity at impact had to be close to Mach 3, maybe more. You crash anything going at close to three thousand kilometers per hour and you're going to get one *whale* of a deep hole. With an object twenty, maybe thirty meters across or more—it was very hard to tell—the crater should be many times deeper than it is. There are a lot of unexpected phenomena here. Enough, I'm afraid, to shake up several disciplines. They'll be *years* figuring this thing out! And that firestorm—it shouldn't have happened. An asteroid's just a huge piece of rock, and there's nothing in the jungle to ignite or explode that way. There must have been some sort of gas or explosive material that went up on impact. This is a *very* strange thing, indeed, we have here."

"Like that place in Siberia you were talking about?" Terry asked.

"As mysterious as that, only very different in the phenomena. At least this time we're on the scene." She sighed. "I wish I had some instruments here. At least I could take initial measurements. It might be nice to know if this area's now radioactive, for example."

"Radioactive!" Gus exclaimed nervously. "You mean we might be going into something like *that*?"

"It's possible. We don't really know *what's* orbiting out there in space." *Another cheery thought, that comes too late,* she mused to herself.

Terry looked down at what was rapidly resembling a moonscape. "Think any natives are down there? I heard all sorts of stories about some of these tribes."

"Impossible!" Juan Campos responded. "You see it. What could have lived through that impact, not to mention the firestorm?"

"I wouldn't be too sure of that," Bob noted. "I've seen bombardments so thick you couldn't believe a gnat could live through it, but when they went in afterward an amazing number of people were still alive and in fighting shape afterward. You never know. Still, I'd think that any of the primitives alive in these parts are still running. To them, this had to feel like the end of the world. It's possible to live through a bombardment, but those who have say it's the most terrifying thing imaginable, and they *knew* what was going on. Imagine how afraid these savages must be with no idea of what was going on.''

"Yeah, well, I've seen that sort of thing, too," Gus admitted. "But I ain't so sure about the reaction. I wish we'd brought along a couple of those guns."

"You would never be able to use them, señor," Campos said matter-of-factly. "The Indians would not be seen until they wished to be seen. The darts in their blowguns are tipped with poisons and sharp enough to go through clothing, and they are accurate. These people also know what guns do and will guard against them. There *may* be a tribe or two that still are ignorant of the outside world, but I doubt it. They just do not like our world and ways, rejecting them in favor of the jungle and their own ancient life-style. But I think our pilot friend is right. This would have frightened them and awed them far too much for them to become curious. In a few days, or weeks, they might investigate, but not right off."

The pilot surveyed the area. He didn't need the helicopter spotlights to see the general area, not with the glow from the crater and the illumination of the newly risen moon, but the searchlight gave detail to the immediate ground surface. "I can't tell how hot it is, particularly with all the charred vegetation, but there's a clear spot over there about a kilometer from the crater that looks like good, solid rock. It's not raining now; you might just get lucky if it's cool enough."

"I don't see why it wouldn't be," Lori responded. "The immediate area was burned quickly in the firestorm."

The pilot set the helicopter down gently. Terry cautiously opened the door, looked down, grabbed a large flashlight, and then stepped out onto the surface. Fine dust and ash blew around from the backwash of the rotor blades, but she reached down and felt the soil and nodded. "Slightly warm, but no big deal," she shouted back into the cabin.

They all got out now except the pilot and Campos, who

handed down the three large silver suitcases containing the portable dish unit to Gus. The three quickly moved away so that the helicopter could lift off. They all had their canteens, first-aid kits, and sufficient rations for the short time they would be there.

They watched the chopper rise, hover a moment as if reluctant to leave, then head out to the west toward the Campos compound. It was quickly swallowed up in the clouds and night. The blowing ash settled, and when they moved back in to retrieve the equipment, they were startled to see a form standing there.

"I decided to remain with you," said Juan Campos. "Even under these conditions, this is a dangerous place for two señoritas and one unarmed man."

All three of them had an uneasy feeling about the man, but there wasn't much they could do. *Forty minutes,* Terry thought frantically. *Maybe less, each way, with maybe twenty on the ground. Not even two hours. He has to know that.* But the animal lurking under that civilized veneer of his wasn't buried very deep, and it might not think that far ahead.

"I thought you had to guide the helicopter back and forth," Terry said aloud to him.

"Oh, he does not have any equipment in the helicopter. It is ours, after all. He will have no trouble finding his way back, either—he is a good pilot—and there is little for him to see until dawn. It is safe enough for now."

She sighed. "Well, then, help us lug this stuff over to a reasonably flat, stable area and help us set it up."

There was the sound of not so distant thunder. "Is all that waterproof?" Lori asked. "I think it might well get rained on, and us, too."

"Oh, it's pretty well sealed," Gus assured her. "Just keep the control box lid down tight and latched in a direct downpour. The big problem is stabilizing the dish, particularly in a heavy wind, along with the fact that *ku*-band signals are real bad in rain and heavy weather."

"We better think of some shelter for ourselves, too, just in case," Lori said. "This place looks pretty blasted, but over there the trees seem scorched but still standing."

"You can take the small flashlight and have a look-see," Gus told her, "but I wouldn't go too far 'round here. There's all sorts of mean, nasty critters live in these places, and it's pretty damn sure not all of 'em got blown to hell or had the sense to run."

"Thanks a lot," she came back sarcastically. What she *really* wanted to do was have a look at that crater, but until they were set up, there wasn't much she could do about that. She could see it, though, so tantalizingly close, with its eerie yellow glow and its strange, regular pulsing. It might be irresistible after a while.

From the jet, the whole region had looked more like the landing zone, but here, on the ground, it was much different. A surprising amount of the jungle was intact, although it showed the effects of blast and fire. Huge areas had been uprooted almost instantly, the giant trees lying there, all pointing away from the crater. Still, even here, the roots of some were so deep, and the underbrush was so thick below them, that large stands survived, and it appeared that the blast had affected barely another kilometer or two of the jungle beyond their camp. It indicated that the blast had been far less powerful than she'd originally thought and that the firestorm had occurred not on impact but *ahead* of it, not destroying the jungle but burning away the top instead.

She suddenly thought she saw something moving in the darkness and swung the flashlight toward it. The beam fell on an enormous, hairy multicolored spider standing atop one of the blasted trees. For a moment she couldn't tell if it was dead or alive, but then, suddenly, it *jumped* out of the beam and to her right.

She decided that she'd had enough exploring for the night and hurried back to the others.

"Find anything?" Gus asked as he finished the assembly

of the main dish with a socket wrench.

"Jumping spiders," she told him nervously.

"Bird spider," Campos elaborated, helping Gus mount the dish into the suitcase console. "Very common here. They will attack if threatened but will try to run away if they can. So something *did* live through all this, then?"

Gus was a little more worried. "Sounds like we was talkin' sense up there. I bet there's more life still around here than anybody'd thought."

"Perhaps you are right, señor," Campos agreed. "In which case it will be a very good idea to stay away from the trees unless we must use them for shelter. The spiders and most insects are not big problems, but the snakes can be very dangerous, and if anything would survive all this it would be *la anaconda* and her kin."

The satellite dish was mounted into the main suitcase unit; Gus took out a small sledgehammer, pounded stakes into the rock and anchored the dish to them with a strong wire. He jiggled the thing a few times, then seemed satisfied.

"Next thing we do is see if we have juice from the battery pack, and then I'll try and align this sucker," he said.

One whole suitcase, it appeared, was a battery. "How long does that thing last?" Lori asked him.

"Oh, about an hour at full power, maybe more at a lower setting." He used a small electronic device to take a preliminary sighting, then switched on the unit and plugged in a tiny Watchman-style television that showed only snow. Checking the instrument often, he turned a few cranks on the dish mount, and suddenly a very snowy test pattern came in. It was somewhat distorted, weak, but it was there.

Terry plugged in a headset and threw a small switch. The television went black, but she paid no attention and instead said, "Hello, Atlanta. Hello, Atlanta. This is Terry at the crater. Do you receive us? Over." She toggled the switch down.

"Audio is fair," a tiny voice in her ear responded. "No video. Over."

Toggle. "We don't have a camera plugged in yet. Because of power limits and distance to the crater, we are unable to do live shots from the rim, but as soon as John gets here, we'll go out with the hand-held and then immediately feed tape. Over."

"Understood. There is a storm over the base at the moment delaying everything. Best guess is that it'll be about two hours until it clears and they can get to you. Advise you use the time for pickup shots if the weather is still clear there. If Sutton is up to it, try her in a standup. Feed what you get when you get it, but leave at least fifteen minutes. Over."

Two hours! "Uh—we might have a problem before that," she said low into the mike. "We have the nonteam member present and armed. Over."

"Can't do much about it. Handle it the best you can. We are advised of the situation from the pilot at base. Do whatever you have to. Suggest you shut down now until you are ready to feed. Over."

When you make deals with the devil, make sure it is you making the deal.

"All right. As you said, nothing much can be done about it. Out." She looked over at the cameraman. "Shut it and seal it, Gus," she told him. "They want us to do pickups at the crater if the weather holds."

The thunder rumbled across the ghostly landscape.

"That storm is toward the rancho," Campos noted. "I can tell. The storms do not last all that long, but they are fierce and they can be a problem. I think perhaps the helicopter will be late."

Damn it! Terry thought sourly. *At least he could have been a little less clever.* "It's raining there now," she admitted to him. "But they don't think it'll be a serious problem unless it comes this way."

There was a sudden, extremely bright bolt of strobo-scopic lightning close by, and then a very loud explosion of thunder.

"I hate to say it," Gus yelled, "but I think we got that serious problem!"

Before anyone could reply, there was a sudden rush of wind and the heavens opened with a vengeance. It wasn't like any storm Lori had ever known; the rain was so heavy and dense, it was nearly impossible to see, and the roaring sound was deafening. Campos and the two women grabbed the flashlights and Gus snatched up the portacam unit, fortunately still in its case, and they headed for the shelter of the trees, spiders and snakes be damned. There was no hope of staying dry; as Lori ran toward the jungle, she was soaked through in an instant, and she could feel the intensity of the downpour as it pounded her through her clothing.

The trees were not the shelter they would have been only hours before, but there were places where the rain was deflected by higher foliage in spite of the fire damage. Surrounded by gushing waterfalls of runoff from the tree tops, the spot she found was fairly well protected.

She'd been afraid that she would slip and fall on the rock or trip over some wreckage of the destroyed forest, but somehow she'd managed to make it without mishap. Now, sheltered and catching her breath, she was aware of a series of sharp, thundering explosions that reverberated through the jungle. In a moment she realized that they were all coming from the same direction—the crater!

Either it was still extremely hot or some sort of reaction was taking place the nature of which she couldn't guess. She suddenly worried that it might somehow explode and take them all out, or shatter, or who knew what?

She wondered where the others were. Not far, surely, in spots just like this. There wasn't any sense in going looking for them in the incessant rain, and a few attempts proved the futility of trying to yell over the constant roar.

A crazy thought came to her of Gus's fears of a live rerun of *The War of the Worlds*. The repeated explosions from the crater certainly *did* sound very regular, like something, well, *venting*. Nerves, she told herself. Just nerves.

Terry, too, had found shelter, leaning against the tree and gasping for breath. She had fallen, and it felt like she'd bruised and skinned her knee. It hurt like hell.

God! This is one I'm gonna remember for an awfully long time, she told herself. *Like all the rest of my life. I been shot at, chased, slapped around, and treated like shit, but this may be the worst. And all for a damned hole in the ground! Maybe this is it. Maybe this is God telling me that it's time to pack it in, demand a studio job, or find something else. And those damned explosions! Bang! Bang! Bang! Like some kind of ghostly war.*

She had just decided that it couldn't be much worse when she felt something press against the side of her head. She started; powerful hands pushed her back, and there was a gun right in her face.

"Go ahead!" Campos yelled at her in Spanish with angry satisfaction. "Yell your head off, bitch! They could be five meters away and not hear you!"

He grabbed her, and she tried to kick him in the balls, but he sidestepped her attempt, which was weak because of the pain in her knee and her general state of near exhaustion. He twirled her around and pinned one of her arms behind her back, twisting it painfully as he drew her to him.

"Try anything more like that and I will break it! I will break your arms *and* your legs."

"My God, Campos! What do you want? You can't get away with this!" she yelled back defiantly.

"You know what I want, you whore!" he snapped. "And what if you do not turn up when the rain stops? They will suspect, but they will not *know*. Do you not remember where you are? Your friends come at our invitation and leave at our demand, and if they reject our story of your disappearance, they can do nothing. We are already on the wanted lists of a dozen countries. Your only hope is to do what I say and pretend you like it. If you convince *me,* then maybe, just maybe, I will let you live!"

He pushed her back against the tree and grabbed with his free hand for her rain-soaked khaki safari shirt, the other hand still holding the pistol, now pointed at her abdomen.

"Why? You're gonna kill me anyway. You *must!* And we both know it."

He grinned evilly. "Perhaps the rain will stop. Perhaps then they will hear us, no? You can never tell."

And, with that, he ripped the shirt, almost literally tearing it off her.

She closed her eyes and sank down, resigned now to her fate at the hands of this monster. She waited and waited, and nothing came.

Finally she opened her eyes and frowned, then her eyes grew wide in amazement.

Juan Campos had collapsed in a heap and was lying there facedown, more in the rain than out of it. The pistol had fallen from his hand, and she moved painfully to retrieve it, not comprehending what sudden miracle had saved her. Gus? But where was he? A falling branch? It didn't look like anything like that.

And then, only a few meters beyond, she saw shapes. She was so shaken that for a moment she imagined they were Gus's Martians or some other kind of creatures from the crater, and they *did* look like nothing on Earth. Their faces were tattooed with elaborate designs, with great earrings of wood or bone. Small, dark, and threatening in their own right, each figure held a small blowpipe in its hand, eyes wide but fearfully flinching with the sound of each small explosion.

She made a movement for the pistol, and the pipes went up. She stopped, backed away into the tree, and the pipes came down. Primitive, yes, like out of some *National Geographic* special, but they knew what guns could do.

Terry tried to think of how to say "friend" in every

language that she knew, but only English and Spanish came to mind. She tried them, but only blank stares were returned.

And then, as dramatically as it had started, the rain stopped, as if someone had turned off a faucet.

Quickly, almost without sound, a trio of the primitives moved in toward Juan Campos's body, first turning him over, then going through his clothing with a thief's skill.

Inanely, Terry could only think, *If only I had a camera here! What a story this would make!*

With sudden amazement coming over her, she realized that the three stripping Campos were all girls—no, women, and, from the look of them, ones that had already lived rough lives. Their faces and bodies were decorated with well-worn designs, and they wore that primitive jewelry but not a stitch of clothing. Their black hair was long but obviously not without attention; it was shoulder-length on some, waist-length on others, and trimmed at the ends. Nor was it matted or tangled; much attention was clearly paid to keeping it groomed. Their awareness of how things connected on the clothing and of the gun and its purpose showed some knowledge, but everything about them said that they, if not ignorant of anything beyond the Stone Age, rejected all such things totally.

They *were,* however, thorough, and before two minutes had passed they had extracted from Campos's body an incredible assortment of weaponry, from two more small pistols to an assortment of knives and other instruments of violence. One of the women in the rear brought up a thick tray of woven straw, onto which all the weapons were carefully placed. By the time they were through, Campos was nude, his clothing put in a heap, and signs of various wounds and scars could be seen all over the man's body. Clearly his life hadn't always been one of idleness and ease.

Terry heard noises to her left and looked over to see several more of the women with a very frightened Dr. Lori

Sutton in tow and others dragging another form which the newswoman recognized. "Oh, my God! *Gus!*"

She started to go to the cameraman, but for the first time, one of the women made a sound, saying sharply and menacingly, *"Azat!"*

Blowguns went up, and Terry got the message.

When Lori saw Terry's torn shirt and Campos on the ground nearby, she gasped, instantly putting two and two together. The scientist reached the newswoman and whispered, "Did he . . . ?"

"No. They stopped him. If they hadn't—"

"Azat! Azat!" came the menacing protest again. Gus by now was also stripped, and they gestured that the two women were to strip as well. Clearly they trusted nobody, not here.

Oh, God! The damned bugs are already eating me alive as it is! Lori thought, but she was too frightened not to comply.

"Guza! Guza!" the seeming leader said, pointing, indicating that they were to move toward the rest of the primitives, who still had their blowguns trained on the captives.

They're not going to give us back our clothes and equipment! Lori thought with sudden panic, but there wasn't much else to do, and she didn't want to argue, not right now.

They went back into the forest, and the tender feet of the two civilized women were soon feeling bruised and cut by the rough forest floor, compounded by insect bites that the natives seemed to just ignore.

They're taking us away, away from the base camp! Terry thought in panic. The rest of the news team would search, of course, but what chance did anyone have of finding them in the natives' jungle, even if it had just recently undergone massive alterations?

It seemed like a very long march, but hardly hours considering that dawn had not yet broken. Finally they reached what the two women first thought was a village but which, on closer inspection, appeared more to be a temporary camp rather than a permanent settlement.

Terry's curiosity competed with her fear, and she wondered if these women had been here when the meteor had hit. There were signs of debris about, a number of recently fallen trees and the remains of a crude stone fire pit that had apparently blown over. A camp fire burned in the wreckage, giving the whole area an eerie, flickering glow. On one side of the camp several women were lying on thick grass mats, and they had what looked like dried mud and leaves over parts of their bodies, some secured with vines. At least one showed signs of singed hair and had the natural bandages over part of her face and one eye.

Yes, they'd been here during impact. It was a wonder any of them had survived unscathed, let alone so many, and it was equally wondrous that any of them could still hear.

The two captive women were taken near the fire, although they hardly needed the extra heat, and with signs were ordered to sit. It was mostly mud there, thanks to the runoff from the rainstorm.

To their surprise, they saw the bodies of the two men being dragged into the camp, bound with vine ropes. *Then they aren't dead!* both thought almost at once, for why bind dead bodies? Some sort of paralyzing drug, then, rather than a lethal poison. Terry was happy that Gus wasn't a casualty, after all, but couldn't help wondering with a little bit of satisfaction what Campos would be like as the captive of a tribe of female savages.

Now what? they both wondered. Neither had any experience with anything like this, but it wasn't hard to think of movies, television shows, and books that told of the savage nature of the jungle people of the upper Amazon. And if they were taken far into the jungle before searchers could find them, what hope would there ever be of escape?

She was not old, she was ancient, although she no longer possessed the word to express it. The People believed that she was the daughter of a goddess and almost worshiped her, and after all this time she could no longer recall her own origin.

She sensed that in the distant past she'd been many things, but it was increasingly difficult to remember much of it. She *did* know somehow that the longer time passed and the more she remained in any one place, the more her memory faded, leaving only the present and immediate past. But the present and immediate past were such a long stretch of existence that she knew somehow that she was coming to a point where memories were falling into a deep and bottomless pit beyond recall. Some of the knowledge useful to the People remained, but it seemed now to come from nowhere, accepted as readily as magic, without question as to its origin but rather taken for granted as some divine gift. Vast periods of time passed when she never even thought of the Past, or that there had *been* a past, even in her dreams. She didn't mind; in fact, she felt better for it, slept more soundly for it. The present was enough. It was sufficient.

The language of the People was simple and pragmatic;

they had all the words that were necessary for them and could express any concepts that were relevant to their simple but demanding lives, but there was no subtlety to it, no multiple meanings, no indirectness. There were also no words for lying, deceit, dishonesty, or most other sins, nor was there a word for property or any great concept of it.

Although there were spirits everywhere—not just in the sky but in the trees, the rocks, the water, the animals, even the wind—who were prayed to in the context of a view of the cosmos both simple and complete, they had no names, only attributes and powers. The names of the People were also simple and generally descriptive: Little Flower, Big Nose, Soft Wind. They had named her Alama long ago, which meant "spirit mother."

She had used no other tongue for so long that she recalled no other. Like the rest of her forgotten past, she had no need of another.

Even time was different here, for the climate never changed, and the only temporal reference, beyond the passing of day and night, was the births, aging, and eventual deaths of the others. She had tried on occasion to figure out how long she had been with the People by generations, but she kept going back and back so far that all the faces and personalities blurred together in her mind. She did remember vaguely coming across an immense river in a very large canoe powered by the Spirit of the Wind, with huge, ugly men dressed in bright cloth and metal, with four-legged animals that they rode. She recalled that sometime afterward she had been beaten and whipped by some of those men and had fled into the jungle, but even that was a blur now, fading and soon to disappear with the rest of the past.

She had a hazy memory, almost a dream, of fleeing inland, encountering a tribe, and settling with them. She had felt safe, but something had happened—an accident—and she'd lost a hand. She could never remember which hand it was, anyway, since it wasn't important. It wasn't the loss that had caused the trouble with the tribe but, rather, the fact that the hand eventually had grown back. She had been cast out by the tribal leaders, men who had come to fear her, and she had pressed on, learning when to stay with a tribe and when to leave it, until she had found the People.

Legend said it had been a tribe where the men had grown lazy and no longer provided for the women and children or respected the gods and spirits. The women had learned how to hunt and forage and do all the things men did, after which the spirits had slain the men for their evil abandonment of their natural duties. Since that time they had allowed no man in the tribe. Now and then they would find men of other tribes in the forest and capture some of them, and, using the ancient potions made from the forest plants, the prisoners would be kept drugged and would mate with whoever of the tribe chose to do so. After a while the men would again be put to sleep and carried back to where they had been captured, to wake up wondering whether their experience had been real or some kind of dream. Male children born of these unions would be taken to some other mixed tribe and left. Only girl children were kept by the People. It was a part of the blood oath taken at adulthood, and there was a stark but well-understood price for not agreeing to do so: death to the mother, although not to the child, who was then taken to another tribe. It was a hard rule, but this was a hard life in a very hard land, and it had kept them free.

Was that one of *her* rules? Or had that been here before her? She couldn't remember. She wasn't even really certain if the People had predated her arrival or had come about as a mixture of circumstance and her own invention. Certainly she strictly enforced the rules: Use nothing not of nature, or of your own making, or the making of those you know. All things of others, even of other tribes, are unclean, to be buried when found and the handler purified afterward. Refuse nothing that another needs; have nothing that you would not willingly give away.

She worried about that sometimes, that perhaps she was not helping these women but was instead forcing them into a system to meet not their needs but hers. But wasn't that what a deity did? They did not seem to hate her for it, were not unhappy. If, perhaps, her perception of them as being happier than their counterparts in the more traditional tribes was colored by her own need to be right, they never seemed *less* content than the others. That would have to be enough. Provided that the tribe could continue to exist, that the forest would continue to exist, even her worries would not trouble her, for even now it was hard to imagine that she had not always been here.

She took no man herself, nor had she in such a long time, she could barely remember the experience. She felt no need for it anymore, and, more important, the survival of the tribe depended on procreation, particularly when they could keep only the girl children; she knew she was barren. There was only one man who was of her own kind, a man of godlike power that she *did* remember, but she could not remember even him with much clarity.

Still, while she'd banished all the worries of the past, she was concerned about the future. What made the People so attractive to her was their permanence, their unchanging yet challenging life, and their isolation. But it was getting a lot harder to maintain that isolation. The forest was being chewed up by monstrous machines, cleared, farmed, then abandoned because the land was neither loved nor understood by those new men and women who exploited her. The tribe had moved many times and more than once had barely escaped discovery, and it was getting harder and harder to find a place that would provide for the needs of the People in their jungle wilderness. Watching the cutting and burning of the forest had brought back old hatreds and fears; it was no less rape for being inflicted on the land rather than on a woman, and it was no less brutally violent.

That was why they were near the remote impact site, searching out a new place to call a home, a new refuge against the rapists of the land. It was a good region and held much promise, although there were others about—violent men, men with deadly weapons and a callous disregard for life, who were also planting and growing in the region. These men, at least, seemed to protect the forest to hide their activities from the rest of the world as much as she wanted to hide the People from those same eyes. That made them less of a problem to her and one she could accept. Their traps were elaborate and particularly nasty, but she could discover them easily, and they posed no real threat. And with the poisons and potions that were the legacy of tens of thousands of years of experience by the forest people, an uneasy truce was possible. The men understood that the People had no interest in what they were doing and wished only to be left alone. They also understood that in the forest their murderous guns and traps were little help should they decide to hunt down the forest tribes. After a few disastrous attempts, the men had abandoned any ideas of that.

This place would probably do, but locating a good site for a more permanent village would take some time. In the meantime, they would camp and move as one.

It had been quite late, and only the guards and the forest were awake. There had been good hunting, the Fire Keeper had a good flame, and everyone had a full belly and was content. The women had been sleeping off the large meal; even the Spirit Mother herself had been fast asleep, when it happened.

Suddenly she had awoken with a start, a horrible feeling sweeping over her like nothing she could dredge up from the most distant of remaining memories. It was an almost inexplicable form of dread, as if—*as if she were dead, sleeping forever with nature, and someone was digging at her grave . . .*

From above there came a crackling sound and a series of booms like thunder yet unlike any thunder she or the People knew. The night flared suddenly into day, and a great sun came almost upon them and vanished in a horrible explosion, beyond anything they could have imagined, powerful enough to shake the earth, collapse the lean-tos, throw the guards to the ground, and even topple some of the great trees.

Then, for a moment, there was a stillness almost as terrible as the crash, and suddenly, a searing wave of heat that burned and blackened whatever it touched swept over them. Women and children screamed both in terror and in pain, and there was fire, awful fire, all around.

Although in shock, she realized that somehow she'd received only a minor burn on one side and was otherwise all right. But others had been badly hurt and needed immediate attention. She got up on her feet and ran to the center of the camp, calling loudly, "Keep calm! Keep calm! We must help those who are hurt, and quickly!"

The sight of her and the sound of her commanding voice rallied those who were no more injured than she was, and the entire tribe went into immediate action.

Those who had been caught out in the open in the firestorm had suffered. Two were dead, struck full in the face by the heat, and another had been crushed to death by a falling tree. There were several broken limbs to be set, some seared hair that smelled and looked ugly but wasn't serious, and three or four serious burns.

"Susha! The healing herbs!" the Spirit Mother snapped, examining the badly burned side of Mahtra's face. There was a virtual pharmacy in the oils, balms, herbs, saps, and leaves of the great forest, and she had made certain that a kit of such things was always available. "Utra! Bhru! We will need water, both cold and very hot. Get urns! Bhru, fix the fire pit! The rest of you—if you are uninjured, help carry the hurt to the mats over there so they will be seen to quickly! Get any burning limbs out of the camp! Quickly! Time is all for the living! We will mourn and tend to the dead when we can!"

It was a frantic time, but in a way that was good, for the practical needs of their tribe, their family, drove out the terror that would have otherwise consumed them, and within an hour or two they were too weary to clearly remember their panic and fright. But though they were tired, they were not without curiosity. *Something* had blown up; something had exploded with enormous force very near to them. If it was something made by the Outside, what their tongue called "not forest," it might bring other Outsiders. If it was something run by the men of violence, that would be important to know, too. And if it was some kind of evil spirit come from the night sky to Earth, then that needed to be known most of all.

Alama, however, could not go. As she was the religious as well as temporal leader, her duty was to remain with the injured and to see that the ceremonies of the dead were performed, lest their spirits, deprived of a return to the bosom of the Earth Mother, be doomed to wander eternally without rest.

"Susha will remain and see to those who are burned," she ordered. "The guards must also remain, for none can travel until healed. Bhru, as Fire Keeper you will help me in the preparation of burial. The others, those who can, will go and see what has happened. Then you will come back and tell us what you see. Two groups, one under Bhama, the other under Utra, will go, one toward the great fire, the other below it here. Take care. The fire still burns at the tops of the trees, and there is much danger." She stopped, feeling a sudden drop in air pressure. "Rain comes. Rain will help with the fires and will make your journey better. Go now. Come back and tell us what you see, but do not be seen yourselves. Those too hurt for such a thing but able to help here, stay. There is much to do. All must be back before first light. Go!"

The long and exhausting night wore on. The graves were quickly and expertly dug, and the victims were wrapped in leaves, in spite of the driving rain. Most of the trees in and around the camp still stood, and Alama was proud of that. She always seemed to pick just the right spot when unforeseen danger lurked.

The rain continued intermittently. Finished with all but the ceremonies and the actual laying in the earth, Alama and Bhru came wearily back into the camp and stopped dead in their tracks. Two naked strangers, Outsider women, were being kept by the fire under guard, and two others, naked Outsider men, were lying unconscious on the side of the camp opposite the wounded tribeswomen. The women knew that the men were not dead, for why bring dead men into camp and defile it?

"Bhama! Utra!" Alama snapped angrily. "What is this?"

The two squad leaders, as weary as their chief, jumped to her call.

"They all hiding in the trees," Utra tried to explain. "One of the men, *that* one," she added, pointing to Juan Campos, "attack the dark woman. We put darts in him to stop him. Mother, we cannot just sit and watch such a thing! She sees us. It is not a time for deciding but just doing. If others come, she will say that she sees us and how many we are. Then they come try and find us. You say the wounded cannot travel, so we take them with us."

Alama sighed. She wished she'd been with them. Sometimes direct, pragmatic logic wasn't always the best course, particularly when dealing with Outsiders. "And the other two?"

"Mother, it rains hard then," Bhama told her. "We come up to the burning place from below. All at once we see this man there, under the trees. It was so sudden, we do not expect it. We are in the open to his eyes, and he sees us. Then he smiles. He reaches for something and holds it up to his face. We think it is some kind of weapon, and so we shoot him with darts. We still trying to decide what to do next, when the rain stops. Then this white woman comes toward us. She seems afraid of us when she sees us, but she does not try and run from us but runs to the man. We stop her. Then we hear our sisters nearby. We see that they have the others. We know there are no more. So we agree, all of us, to purify them. We bury their unclean things as the law commands. Then we bring them back with us for you to decide."

In a direct sense, what they had done was exactly right, if the facts were true. "How do you know that it is only these? That no others are here?"

"We see them come," Bhama assured her. "They come on a big, terrible bird that roars like thunder. They and their things get off, nobody else. Then the bird fly away."

This was not good, not good at all. There were certain to be others coming, and they would look for the missing foursome. Still, they couldn't just be released, not now. She looked up and sensed the wind through the charred and smoky atmosphere. It was raining again over there, and here soon as well. The sensible thing would be to destroy the camp, disguise the wounded, leave a few volunteer guards to watch over them, and move everyone away as far and fast as possible until they could find a place to hide. There would be a search, yes, but it would not be a major one, not in this jungle. But what then? The men couldn't be kept, nor could they be left bound and drugged forever. Even now they would slow everyone down. If these two women were their wives, they'd never give up searching, and the places where they could continue to hide out from the encroaching Outside were becoming more limited each day.

But if they killed the two men, what reaction would that bring in the women? They both already seemed too old to ever accept and adjust to the life of the People; there were potions, of course, drugs that would dull the mind and control it so that one could never disobey. Still, it was a distasteful business, and she didn't like it at all. In all these years she'd not faced a problem this complicated.

She looked at the two warriors. "And the thing that

burns? What of it? Did any see it close?"

Utra nodded. "Yes, Mother. We see it. It is the heart of the Moon Goddess come to Earth. It is all black and burned around where it sits, and it is in a great hole that it makes for itself. It is bright and yellow, and it look like a great jewel the size of the full moon in the sky. And it beats, like the heart."

Alama frowned. A big jewel? Beating like a heart? That made no sense at all in any traditional lore, nor did anything from that buried past come to explain it, either. This was something totally new. Like the horrible feeling that had awakened her and still made her shiver when she thought about it.

Still, her past of fog and mist did not totally desert her. *Meteor,* it said, and she had an instant vision of a great rock in space coming down toward the Earth and striking with enormous force. But meteors didn't glow yellow and beat like hearts.

Now another concept came, like *meteor* without a true word but rather as an idea and picture: *Satellite.* In a world as primitive as this? Or had it been longer than she thought since she'd entered the forest? Far longer . . .

Bomb. The most worrying concept to come from that mental unknown and the most likely to be something that throbbed. How advanced might portions of Earth now be, anyway?

Spaceship. No, surely not that advanced. She was certain of that. But what if it wasn't a human spaceship? What if it was from something or someone *really* Outside?

"I must see it, and soon," she told them.

"But what of the ceremonies?" Bhru asked worriedly. "It is almost first light now."

Yes, that was the trouble. It was almost first light, and at some point, perhaps even now, certainly within hours, others would come to search for these missing four. Others would come to see what had fallen here, as the four captives probably had, for why else would they be here? There just wasn't enough time! And only a few hours earlier she had felt the luxury of timelessness.

There was no way around it, though. They *had* to break camp and play for time, no matter what. She gave the orders, and the two exhausted Outsider women watched as the camp became a frenzy of activity, turning a primitive campsite back into wild jungle.

"They're covering up to run!" Lori hissed. "And taking us with them!"

"Nothing we can do now," Terry whispered back. "At least Gus isn't dead. I wish they'd used more of that stuff on Campos, though."

"But we can't go like *this*!"

"I don't even want to go if I had on a safari suit, but we're gonna go, that's for sure. Either walking or carried like them."

They heard rather than saw the burial ceremony. It was done quietly, with the sound of chanting coming from somewhere out of sight, and it was Terry who guessed the meaning of the sound, not from any experience but from the sadness on the faces of their guards and the workers who paused, many with tears in their eyes.

But when the burial party returned, it was all business. It was no longer dark, but the mist from the ground still obscured even the tops of the trees. Alama was counting on that heavy mist not only to keep the investigators away a little bit longer but also to allow them to cross the open patches of jungle caused by the impact. A last, unpleasant touch was to be smeared, almost covered, with a thin paste made of herbs and clay that dried a sickly pea green. The whole tribe did it, and one of the tough warrior women supervised treating Terry and Lori.

Camouflage. Primitive but effective.

And just as primitive and effective was the simple pantomime the warrior woman did for their benefit, taking an ax with a stone blade that was polished razor sharp and showing how easy it was to cut things with it using a large leaf. She then pointed to their mouths and put a hand over each in an unmistakable warning message. Then she stuck out her own tongue and pretended to cut it out. It was amazing how easy it was to get some concepts across.

They trussed up Campos and Gus Olafsson with rope made of tough vines and slid logs through so that they could be carried on poles. Clearly, they were being kept drugged.

Although Lori was taller than any of the tribe and felt she could hardly lift herself, it took only two of the tribeswomen, one on each end of the pole, to carry each of the men with ease. All these women were muscular, many as well muscled as body builders. It was in its own way as intimidating as the blowguns and stone-tipped spears. And none of them was more intimidating than their leader, although she was perhaps the smallest of all the women there, certainly under five feet and thin and limber as an acrobat. It was her manner, her fire, her arrogance that commanded instant respect and obedience. She had the kind of personality and confident manner that a Napoleon probably had possessed.

There *was* something decidedly odd about her, though. She simply didn't look like any of the others. Rather, it was like a Chinese or Japanese woman amid a group of Mongols. She even had the almond "slanted" eyes that had vanished, if they were ever there, from the Amerind over the millennia.

The trek was arduous, though they would break for short periods every once in a while, mostly for their captives' benefit. Gourds were offered, one containing a fruit juice of some kind, another some sort of thick and nearly tasteless cold porridge with the consistency of library paste. Terry and Lori took it and managed to get some of it down, mainly because at this point anything seemed good. How the two trussed-up men were managing wasn't clear, but they at least were barely, if at all, aware of their circumstances, and as terribly uncomfortable as they were bound and carried, they at least hadn't had to walk.

Mercifully, they stopped for the day after what seemed like an eternity, deep within the thickest part of the jungle. Other than the occasional glimpses of the sun high above the nearly unbroken canopy indicating they were heading north, it was impossible to tell where they were. It was also incredible that so many of them—there must have been fifty or more, plus small children and supplies—could move through such dense jungle with confidence and leave no apparent trace.

Lori had not thought that she'd make it to the end of the journey, though when the day's march ended, she wasn't certain that it was such a good thing, after all. Too exhausted even to sleep, too uncomfortable even to relax, she could only think, and that was the last thing Lori Sutton wanted to do.

Just a few days before she'd been in a funk over her personal problems, which now seemed so trivial. The speed at which she had been plucked from obscurity and plunged into a dangerous but romantic adventure culminating in the professional event of a lifetime for an astronomer left her mind spinning. Now, naked, hot, exhausted, and in pain, she was trapped in the Stone Age, where virtually all her hard-won knowledge was totally useless.

She had to admit that she felt a little better that her captors were women. At least she would be spared the horrors that she imagined she'd be subjected to by a tribe of primitive men. Still, there were children here—all female, she'd noted—and that meant these women had to have mates somewhere. Had the meteor wiped out the men? Were they all away? It seemed unlikely, but it only made the puzzle deeper.

Terry looked only slightly better for the experience than did Lori, but Terry was younger and in better condition and was the kind of person who never gave up hope. She, at least, lay in a deep sleep on the forest floor, oblivious to the world.

They were probably the story now, Lori thought. Maybe the hunt for them would be massive, but it wouldn't last forever. Not in this jungle—and these primitive women knew the forest as no one else did; it was their entire world. Where was all this massive deforestation the environmentalists were always protesting about? She could use a little open clear-cut land right now.

Alama checked on her people, then saw that the white woman was still awake and made her way over to her. It would take a while for these soft Outsiders to build up their strength and become wise in the ways of the forest; until then they would be both captives and liabilities, a fact on Lori's mind as well as she eyed the leader nervously and wondered what was next.

The tiny but tough woman knelt, and black almond eyes looked deeply into the scientist's own. After a moment the leader pointed to herself and said, "Alama."

Lori realized that the woman was at least attempting to communicate. Alama was probably a name, possibly a title. It didn't matter. She pointed to herself and said, "Lori."

"Lo-ree," the small woman repeated, nodding.

Sutton pointed to her sleeping companion. "Terry," she said.

Alama looked over at the newswoman. "Teh-ree," she said.

Lori sighed. She was now convinced that this woman, so different in appearance and manner, could not have been a member of the tribe originally. She wished she knew some Portuguese or even Japanese, but her languages had been German and Russian. Not much practical help here. Terry's Spanish might do, but Terry was going to be out for some time.

Still, Alama seemed adept at this sort of communication

and appeared to want to teach some basics of the tribe's language.

She pointed to her breasts and genitals. *"Seku."* She pointed at Lori. "Seku." Pointing to others of the tribe, she said, "Seku, seku, seku," and to the two bound and drugged men, *"Fatah. Fatah."* Then to the guard next to them, "Seku."

Seku. Woman. *Fatah.* Man.

Walk in place. *Kaas.* Run in place. *Koos.* The lesson proceeded slowly, with much repetition when a new word was added. Alama knew what she was doing.

At the end of perhaps an hour Lori thought she understood the bare basics. Of course, when any one of the others talked, it still sounded mostly like gibberish, but that was to be expected. Attempts to return the teaching by matching words in English were abruptly rejected. This was not a lesson for mutual benefit and understanding so much as for the benefit of the tribe. *The better to give orders, my dear,* Lori thought.

Finally, Alama said, "Lo-ree sleep," and it was understood. On the other hand, there was still no way to be as sophisticated as to convey "I want to sleep but I just can't." Alama, however, seemed to understand. She went away for a moment, then came back with a small gourd and taught another word. *Kao.* Drink.

Lori was still dehydrated, and she took it and drank. It was some sort of fruit juice again, with a slightly bitter aftertaste. Still, after a few minutes, the pain seemed to fade away and the inner turmoil quieted. She went over her new twenty- or thirty-word vocabulary in her mind, settled down, and was suddenly as deeply asleep as she had ever been.

The next few days were unpleasant but in some ways less traumatic. The men were allowed to come out of their stupor, although it seemed clear that repeated doses of the same drug on the blowgun darts kept them in partial paralysis. The guards were able to keep them quiet with a demonstration of what a Stone Age knife or ax might do to not only their tongues but their genitalia.

In the meantime the language lessons continued, sometimes with Alama, sometimes with others doing the teaching to both women. No talking in any language but the tribe's was permitted. Absolutely none. Even an unthinking comment uttered in English or Spanish was punished with a quick lash delivered with a vinelike whip to the back or buttocks. It *hurt* and could cause welts or even draw blood. As bad as that was, it caused amused giggles among those nearby, particularly the children, which made it embarrassing as well. They were under constant watch during the day and were made to sleep apart with tribeswomen during the terrible pitch-dark nights. Alama had forbidden all use of fire, and under the thick jungle canopy not even the late, waning moon could be seen.

Eating without cooking was another thing, and it was several days and a bad case of gastric distress before their bodies, if not their minds, fully tolerated the raw—well, *creatures*—that were offered them and which the rest of the tribe ate with relish. Indeed, both had to be forced, more or less, to eat anything other than the fruit and greenery, which was only slightly more palatable.

A number of times they heard helicopters, often very nearby, and the sound of small planes, but neither seemed to come close enough. Once the sound of voices caused the entire tribe to hide in the underbrush, tensely waiting to attack, but the voices soon faded away. Clearly, though, there was a massive search going on, but these women were in their element, and soon the searchers moved on, finding nothing.

The two men continued to have the worst of it, and it worried both Lori and Terry. Not that either had much sympathy for Juan Campos, whose manner suggested that he knew he was going to die eventually and wanted just one chance to die fighting. Gus, however, was a different story. He just didn't deserve this, and his former irrepressible spirit had gone out of him, almost as if he'd retreated into a world of his own.

For the two American women it was a total immersion into a culture and life and language in which all their education and experience meant nothing. They lacked even basic knowledge. What was edible? What would harm them? What animals were a threat, and how did one deal with them? What water was fit to drink? What water contained things that might harm or even eat one?

Still, the tribe quickly put them to work doing what little chores they could manage, such as walking with large gourds filled with water balanced on their heads. First they got lessons, then help, then they were on their own. Either they got it right the first time or they kept at it—all day, if necessary—until the job was done. They did fetching, hauling, even bathing the wounded, removing small bugs and other creatures from skin or hair. All the while they were derisively called *dur* or *dua*—child, or even baby—because they were so helpless and ignorant. They were *in* the tribe but not *of* it; to become one of the People, one had to earn and desire the privilege.

True to her nature, Terry did not lose hope that one day she would be able to escape or be rescued, and she kept seeing the book she'd write and the movie it would make. These thoughts kept her going, but they were also mixed with pragmatism: Such a time might not come soon, and until then, she wanted to be a member of the tribe, not a slave. In that sense, she was adapting better than Lori.

The scientist was in turmoil over the situation. She was no longer waking up each day surprised that it hadn't been some awful dream; she wasn't even daydreaming much about her nice apartment, bathtubs, showers, and flush toilets, but she hated this place and this existence. She was becoming afraid again, not so much that she might die at any moment but rather fearful that she might actually live, and that she wasn't sure she could stand.

The worst part was that she realized that Alama's sophisticated immersion system was working as easily on her as it would on a woman from another primitive tribe. The only way to avoid that wicked little lash was to try to *think* in their tongue. Both Terry and Lori had learned enough to be able to do that, but it required constant observation and attention. Many of the women seemed to make a game out of trying to force them to make an accidental slip, which would earn another lash.

The language was more complex than it seemed. Terry had the basics down pat, but there were subtleties and nuances that were still a mystery to her. For one thing, they had no real concept of time except on a physical level: baby, child, child bearer, old. But "day" and "night" were all the clock or calendar they had or needed. The language itself was basically all in the present tense, as if they had no need of a past or future. The ideal of this culture was that every day be like the last and the next; change was evil.

Lori hated it. Hated it and knew that if this kept on and on, well, one day she'd just snap. And yet somehow she had to admit that there was some good as well. While there was individuality here, the tribe came first, and sharing and helping others were simply taken for granted. They had a genuine love for this hostile steam bath of a jungle and seemed to really respect it and all its inhabitants, even apologizing to the animals and plants they would kill and use. There were no signs of jealousy, greed, envy, or hate. Alama was still a curiosity. There was mystery, harsh experience, and much pain behind those enigmatic eyes. The tribe spoke of her not as a chief or leader but as some kind of deity; supposedly she had been here before any of them, never aging, never changing. But even with a deity living among them, there was trouble in the paradise of the People.

"Mother, the men cannot stay," Bhru pointed out one

day. "There is much unhappiness in them. One just stares and barely eats. The other has our death in his eyes. Both are weak and grow sick. They cannot stay as they are. They cannot stay if they are free. They are no good to us."

Alama nodded. "I know. I think much on them. I try hard to say not to kill them. I pray but do not find a new trail for them." She sighed. "I wait for the scouts to come back. Then I will say of them what is done."

"As you will."

"The two women do well."

"We see the wisdom of your way. We do not give them rest to think. Their feet and hands grow hard. They grow strong. The speak no Outside, even when we trick them. The dark one thinks she plays a game with us, but the game is just to stay not People. White woman knows she is with us but does not like it."

"Yes, if things are as always, they will come around in the seasons. Things are not as always. The People need a safe home. The People need more babies. That may bring us close to Outsiders who hunt them. It *will* bring us close to tribes who speak with Outsiders. We cannot wait for them. They must know that they are of the People to death. They must not *want* to leave."

"But how would this be done?"

"I know a way. I know more of how Outsiders think. There is danger to it. They can go mad. They can think of killing selves. Like the men, I see no other trail. Can you make the mark of spirit potions?"

"Now that you say we can have fire, yes. What little I do not have, the forest has here."

"Good. Then make. Chsua has the thorn needles. I will speak to her and say what is to be done. Mix the sleep herbs in their drink so they will not wake. We will do this at dark."

Bhru now realized what the Mother had in mind. "But they cannot marry the forest, Mother! Not now! They need to be ready!"

"Do what I say and believe in my wisdom. I know it is not what is done, but this will make them ready. Just do and see."

Alama sighed, wondering again if what she was doing was right or wrong, doubts she could never express or share with the others. But they had to move and, depending on what the scouts reported, most likely back toward the thing that had burned the forest. What they'd already done, particularly to the men, would cause them to be hunted down if it were known. It *had* to be done. Anyone could be broken. Anyone. It was just a cruel procedure.

She knew that well, even if the specifics were lost in that mental fog. How many times had *she* been broken? she wondered. More than once, that was for sure.

Sleep was odd and restless, even in these strange circumstances. When Lori awoke just after first light with the mists still hanging halfway up the forest heights, it was with odd memories of lights and chanting, but the memory was too distant for her to be certain if it was reality or dream. It wasn't something to grab hold of; there were more immediate concerns. She felt, well, odd. Her skin tingled with a slight burning sensation all over, more an itch than pain, and her nose and ears actually ached.

She turned over, sat up, stretched, and reminded herself as she always did to think in the tribe's tongue. She put her hand to her sore nose and touched something hard that hurt enough to bring her fully awake.

Something clicked softly on either side of her head, and she put a hand to her ear and discovered that she now had earrings of the type common to the tribe, fashioned from bone and held together with the epoxylike resins they distilled from one of the plants. She looked down at herself and saw that she also now had on the bone bracelets and anklets also common to these people, and a necklace of fresh green carefully braided vines. But . . . her *skin*!

It was still somewhat dark, but she could see that her

skin, probably her whole body, had been dyed a dull shade between olive and brown, and around her breasts, upper arms, and thighs somebody had drawn a series of bold, primitive designs in the flat colors used by the tribe to denote rank and position. Those areas were particularly uncomfortable, with a stinging sensation, and she felt similar areas on her face. They also had cut most of her hair off, leaving only a thin fuzz on top.

"Lo-rhee pretty now," commented Ghai, one of her keepers, sounding sincere. "Look like forest people. Is good, too, to keep hair short. Things live in hair."

Lori wet her fingers and tried rubbing on a small part of a design on her thigh. It remained as it was.

"Spirit marks not come off," Ghai told her, amused at the attempt.

Tattoos! They'd tattooed her! She was too upset at the realization to cry, although that might come later. *That bitch Alama!* She wanted to kill now but knew that she'd never get anywhere near the leader, and if she did, the leader would easily break her arm.

"Terry?"

"Same thing. You are wives of forest now. Do not worry. All pain goes away in one sleep, maybe two."

Pain was not what she felt so anguished about. She sank back down, fully understanding the logic Alama had used. There would still be some kind of hunt on for them, and people would probably be looking for them for years. Not even this sort of group would be fully undiscovered forever. But now, tattooed, dyed, with bones in ears and nose—the last a cruel overkill, since few of the tribe did it—they would be indistinguishable from the rest of the tribe. Even if they were found, would they want to be rescued like *this*? With these tattoos and such? And even if the doctors could get the cemented bone jewelry out, removing tattoos of this size would be a massive job. They'd be just medical challenges to the doctors and freaks to everyone else.

Damn it! It just wasn't *fair*!

She was happy that there weren't any mirrored surfaces around. She wasn't ready to see herself as they'd remade her, not yet, but she got some idea from seeing Terry. Of course, they had done nothing with her skin tone, since that wasn't necessary, but she was still barely recognizable: her hair shorn to virtually scalp level, large bone earrings with another through the inside nostrils from which a larger curved and polished bone hung almost like a ring, solid blue ovals tattooed from the eyes out past the brows, cheeks adorned with yellow finger-width lines to her ears, her lips framed in a pale white, and her body covered with very obvious and suggestive fertility signs. Terry was clearly to be a baby maker, while Lori, it appeared, was to assist the Fire Bringer and learn the potions and ways of healing.

The tribe, it seemed, had spared no art or effort in making the two appear so primitive that not even their parents would recognize them.

Terry was taking it harder even than Lori; the older woman at least had already given up hope, while it wasn't until now that Terry was forced to face the fact that this wasn't merely a reporter's hazard but a permanent condition.

Alama looked at them both, then gestured for Lori to come to her. As much as the American wanted to throttle the little woman, she obeyed.

The mysterious leader of the tribe, who came barely up to Lori's shoulders, looked her over approvingly.

"You are now of the People," Alama said after the examination. "Be one of us, take our way. There is no other trail for you. You join us, take the ceremonies. Lo-rhee die. You will take a new name. Think like us. Act like us. *Be* us. There is *us,* and there is *them.* All that is not us is them. You must be happy here with us. What do you say?"

Lori sighed. "I think I will be dead soon. Killed by the forest and this life. While I live, I see no other trail."

And then Alama took on a different aspect, almost soft and human, and she said quietly, "I did not wish this. We did not want any of you. The spirits of fate did this. You must know—*I had no choices.*"

It was so direct, so out of character, that it startled Lori for a moment. This small leader of this primitive tribe was actually *sorry* about all this! She realized suddenly that this had been an ordeal for them as well and that Alama, too, had been searching without success for a way out of the mess. Still, Lori could not forgive or forget. Not now. And because of that, she didn't know what to say.

At that moment there was a commotion on one side of the camp, and Alama looked over, then stood up anxiously to see a very tired warrior woman come through the excited crowd toward her.

Lori was suddenly forgotten as Alama first hugged the scout, then pressed her for information.

"All are well," the warrior told her. "Some of us stayed with the hurt. One hurt has died, Tagi, and was returned to the Earth properly; the others grow stronger."

Alama nodded. "My soul goes to her and all of us. What of the Outsiders and their hunt?"

"It is given up, we think. No more go out. There was much busy stuff around the great fire pit, but now there are only a few there. They have strange things with them. Outsiders in green with big weapons guard them."

"How many?"

"Of the ones that watch the great pit, it changes. As many as four hands are there, but mostly just one hand. Of the green ones with weapons, one hand and one. Two are on guard always. They watch the others, not the fire pit. But the fire pit is what they look at. A great bird like the one the first night comes two times a day, early and then late but in light. Sometimes men come and get off. Sometimes other men get on."

"And the thing in the fire pit? You see it?"

"It is hard to see it and not be seen. Yes, we see it, by climbing trees at night. It still lights and beats like a heart. It is like a big gemstone, but with sides of many parts of one shape. At the top, one of the shapes changes. It gets deep black. Then it is the same as the rest again."

Alama frowned. "This shape. Can you draw it here in the dirt?"

"Yes, Mother. It is like this all over, of what we can see." The scout took a stick and carefully drew a series of connected lines.

Alama gasped and stared at it as if it were the worst kind of magic for quite some time, and it made some of the others afraid to see it.

Lori, peering over, making use of her greater height, recognized it immediately but could not understand why it had had any effect on Alama. Still, the scientist in her was fascinated not only by the shape but by the idea that the entire meteor was made of interconnections of this shape.

She didn't think a sphere could be covered with hexagons.

Alama stayed by the fire most of the night, staring into it, deep in thought. The sight of the hexagon in the dirt had brought back memories so long buried that they seemed to be from someone else who had lived and died a long time ago. It was almost as if there were two of her inside her head: one Alama, the other someone she'd once been who was so totally different as to be some creature from another world.

But she *was* a creature from another world. She knew that now, although the details were far too distant, the concepts too vast to fully grasp.

This is what you've been waiting for, isn't it? Waiting all those years, until you could find a hexagon that would turn dark? And here it is, come to you, far sooner than you expected it.

There was a sudden realization that she had not made the decision to find the hexagon, that she had not gone to it. Rather, it had found her. It was no accident, certainly; it had been sent. It had been sent to pick her up.

Those men with the "strange stuff." Scientists certainly, trying to figure out what it was. She wondered what those very smart men thought of it. It must be confusing the hell out of them.

What kind of emergency would trigger it to find her? What could she do if she went? She had helped last time, certainly, but *he* had done most of the real work. He just didn't want to do it anymore. Could she do it without him? Did she want to? Was it sent for her because *he* had refused? Or would refuse? As murky as memories of that time were, she could remember nothing covering this kind of thing.

And if she did decide to go, she would have to have the help of the People with all those guards around, but she had no doubt that somehow a path would be opened for her. *She* could make it, but what about her People? How many might die so she could get through? That they would do it for her she had no doubts, but was it *right* to ask? And if she didn't go, *he* most certainly would. Somehow the system would make him go, and he would restart it all again, just as he always did.

She hated this world. It was filth and death and decay without end. She had been hiding from that, as much as she could hide, these past centuries, waiting, waiting, until one day she might again have the stars. When a woman could be a captain of a great ship and not a wife or lover or chattel slave.

She sighed. She would do what she could for the People, but like all others except *him,* they would die. Perhaps, just perhaps, she could at least try to solve her more direct moral dilemma at the same time.

In the morning she summoned both Lori and Terry to her. The language was inadequate for the task, but they had no other in common.

"The scouts say that there is a way out for all of you. All of us."

"Us?" Terry asked, more than hateful at what had been done to her.

"Yes. Us. Not a way to your village or mine but to another place. A place where you will no longer be of or look like the People. A place where you may be free. It is a—*different* kind of place. It is where I came from many, many lives ago."

"Where do you come from?" Lori asked, wondering where this was leading.

Alama pointed up. "From there. From *after* there. From the stars behind the stars."

Oh, great! Terry thought sourly. *First she's the Amazon Queen from Hell, now she thinks she's E.T.*

Lori, however, while not ready to accept it, was ready to at least not reject it. "You come from the stars?"

The small woman nodded. "I am here since the first tribes. I am in a trap. My way out is sent. You can come or stay and be of the People. You choose. I must go."

"The star that made the great fire pit that brought us here. That is a boat to the stars?" Lori, too, was having trouble fitting the language to these concepts.

"Not a boat. A door. A boat is not needed."

"And if we go there with you, they can take away these marks? These bones? This glue?"

Alama smiled. "The sacred word of Alama. You will not see those things again if you go." She paused. "One thing more. The men with you die. Left here, they die. They go with me if you help and live. You will have to carry them. Can you? Run and climb and carry heavy man?"

"I do not know. I can try."

"You can leave the hateful one to die!" Terry told her. "I will not carry him!"

"Both must go or not one of them. I cannot choose on your saying. If the one is evil, he will find the other place a way to change or die. It has a way of law, it seems. You need not choose now. First I must find a place for the People to live and prepare them for my going. And it will be hard to get to the door. Many men, many big weapons so that no more go away like you. For now I give you leave. Go to the tree in back of me. There in quiet voice you may speak your own tongue on this. There and no other place or time but I choose."

It was another unexpected gesture, but if she really believed what she was saying, then it hardly mattered to them anymore. They were anxious to take advantage of it, no matter what.

"Is she crazy or what?" Terry whispered in the first English she'd tried in she didn't know how long.

"I don't think she is," Lori replied. "I know it sounds mad, but it's no crazier than this. Look, I heard the other women talking. They were preparing to ritually kill Campos and Gus. Like you, I don't care about Campos, but I can see her point. But if it's Gus and Campos or nothing, I say take them both."

"You really think you can just walk into this meteor and come out on some other world?"

"Probably not. If we aren't machine-gunned by the armed guards, we'll wind up splat on top of that thing as targets or we'll be burned to death. But there *was* something really weird about that meteor. You remember it. And Alama—she knows too much about too many things to be only an aboriginal priestess. Besides, have you looked at a reflection of yourself? You look like something out of *National Geographic.* So do I. I know I couldn't go back like this, and I probably won't make it a year out here. Or, worse, maybe I will. Can you imagine living the rest of your life with these people? At this point I am willing to accept even space creatures. The bottom line is, if it really doesn't matter anymore if I live or die, what have I got to lose?"

Terry shook her head in wonder at the situation. "I don't know. I sure don't want to live as one of the tribe forever, but I couldn't go back looking like *this*. Some of the women said that the tattoos use some kind of stuff that penetrates deeply, that they've seen the color on *skulls*. So much for plastic surgery. But the truth is, I've been doing a lot of soul-searching lately, and bad as it is, I'd rather live like this than die. I dunno—I've interviewed too many saucer nuts in my time to accept a story like that."

Lori understood, in a way. "Still, how many leaders of Stone Age tribes could spin a story like that? These people don't know anything outside the rain forest. *Something* was sure screwy about the way that meteor came in, the way it hit, the way it just sat there, the pulsing—even the dark shape on top that winked in and out. If I were normal, I would be on your side, but I'm not normal, I'm a Ph.D. turned into a Stone Age jungle girl. She may be crazy, but I'm desperate. Besides, think of poor Gus. If we try and Alama's crazy, at least Gus will get out and get attention. If we don't go along, they're going to kill him."

"You really think you can carry him all the way to that meteor?"

"Ordinarily, no. But I've *got* to."

Terry stared at the strange little woman by the fire. "I wonder how she's going to do it."

It was ironic that the two women adapted quicker and better to the life of the People after being offered a way out. Terry in particular took some delight in looking after the two men, particularly Campos, who had no idea who she was. Bound and drugged most of the time, allowed only a little exercise under watchful blowguns, neither was in great shape, but they at least seemed to have stabilized a bit.

Terry and Lori took the ceremonies of full initiation into the tribe, which involved a rather complex set of rituals culminating in drinking the blood of all the members of the tribe, which had been mixed with some juice in a gourd. This didn't free them from work, but it gave them equal status with the others. Both spent long periods learning the ways of the People; Alama encouraged them and seemed quite pleased by their actions.

They finally picked a village site, well hidden and deep in the densest region of the jungle but located within two or three days walk of several more traditional tribal villages, so that they could at least get the one thing from men that nature could not provide. Making the huts, building the specialized structures of sticks and straw, coping with the driving rains—it was a real education.

Terry went along on a scouting expedition to one of the villages and saw that the tribe had at least some remote contact with the outside world. The bronze cross and small empty hut showed that missionaries had been there.

It said something about how easily she was adapting to the life that Terry never once considered that such contact provided a means of escape. Instead, she was quite pleased with how confidently she now moved through the forest and how well she had adapted to the hard life and way of survival of the People.

It was almost as if, Lori thought, Terry had burned all her mental bridges and was acting out some sort of fantasy. Lori, too, had acclimated well. She had certainly learned a lot of skills and had grown strong and self-reliant in her own way.

All of which pleased Alama no end. If she could get those two through, she thought, they would probably be the best prepared individuals ever to be dumped on that world.

Now, though, she would have to face the first barrier to be overcome.

She had told the tribe that the thing from the sky had come for her, to take her home. They hadn't questioned it, but they were not at all happy about it. They had the law and well-trained leaders, but now they would have to see if they could survive on their own. Oddly, she felt worse about putting them in danger to get to the meteor than about leaving. After all the millennia, she was tired of the dying; she wanted, *needed* a challenge. This time, more than ever, she felt that she was ready for it.

Only the one small stand of trees remained for any sort of cover; the darkness would have to suffice the rest of the way, although the meteor still glowed brightly like some great floodlight in the ground, waiting for her.

The quartzlike hexagonal facets were incredibly regular, but the thing was not round. It might have been round once, but the part that had plowed into the ground here was irregular, jagged and misshapen, as if parts of it had been consumed and other parts had been broken off as it had made its way in. The crater should have been a couple of kilometers deep; instead, it was fairly shallow, only ten meters deep.

Looking at it from the treetops, Alama felt its energy and its life, felt its pull. Somehow she was certain that it *knew* she was there. And not quite on top but angled a little back was the spot that now and again turned into the deepest black, beckoning her.

She wished it were that easy. She wished that she'd been quicker recognizing it when it had struck, that she'd simply gone to it and seen it for herself before any of the scientists or military had gotten there. It would have been so much simpler.

The guards were Brazilian soldiers in camouflage fatigues, nasty-looking automatic rifles slung over their shoulders. They were a tough-looking bunch, but they looked extremely bored. Weeks, months—who could say how long it had been since the thing had hit?—of no activity and little else to do were taking their toll. Only two stood perfunctory guard, one at the camp and the other farther up at the equipment tent next to the crater, the other four playing cards and smoking cigars outside their big tent.

There seemed to be only two scientists currently in the camp, although the crater was ringed with instruments and, clearly, some effort had been made to take large samples. Probes ran from a portable generator right onto and into the meteor itself; long cables carried power to instruments guarded against rain and anchored against sudden wind.

It had become routine.

There were signs all around that a near army had been there at one time, that many other tents and structures had once been set up here, and that a huge area had been cleared for such a group. Now just these few remained.

Lori in particular was somewhat shaken by the small size

of the camp. How long had they been in the jungle? It had seemed weeks, no more, and the events of that frantic and terrifying night were still fresh in her mind, but mere weeks would not have reduced the world's interest so much. The search after their mysterious disappearance would have slowed them down, and scientists the world over with visions of Nobel prizes would have been clamoring to be here—that the camp was so small and the scientific inquiry so routine meant it must have been a year . . . or longer.

It *couldn't* be that long. Gus and Campos could not have survived their miserable half-drugged imprisonment that long. Then again, how long had it taken to build these tough, callused feet that no longer felt the jungle floor, these hard hands that did much heavy work, or the muscles she had developed? It all seemed to make no sense.

What did make sense was the two days they spent observing every move of the camp. The military helicopter came in the morning and often deposited a few people, probably scientists and research assistants, who checked the data, read out information from the instruments into their portable computers, and did a lot of routine maintenance work. They remained all day and were picked up by the helicopter again before nightfall, leaving only the guards and the two permanent party members there: an old white-haired man in khaki shirt and shorts and a young bearded man who wore boots and jeans and a kind of cowboy hat but usually went shirtless.

Terry climbed effortlessly up one of the trees and stared at the pulsing, glowing meteor during the night. She watched as the black hexagon came on and saw, or thought she saw, some kind of shimmering just above it. Then, startled, she saw a small black shape crawling on the meteor near the hole. A lizard of some kind, she realized. It reached the black area, seemed to pause for a moment, then stepped into it. For a brief second it seemed frozen, suspended in dark space, and then it winked out.

The equipment around the edge of the crater became

more active, clicking and whining, then subsided. The scientists had measured the effect and the fate of the hapless reptile.

She came down the tree and stood there, chewing absent-mindedly on a finger while in thought, then sought out Lori.

"I am going to the men to see if they are able to help themselves," Lori said. "I can carry one if I have to, but if they walk, is much help."

"Bimi," Terry said hesitantly, using Lori's tribal name, "I cannot go with you."

"You can! You have to! This life is not for you. Death comes young with the People. You belong Outside!"

"Outside I cannot go," Terry reminded her. "And I just watch a lizard go into the black hole, and it cooked in fire! Alama takes you all to death now, not life. Life can still be long."

"I, too, watch things go in the hole. It is not like cooking. She says it is a door.

"It is death! You stay here with me! For Alama, the men, it is quick and with no hurt. But not you!"

"Something says to trust Alama. I do. I must. Best take the risk than live as the People to death."

"You *are* of the People! You think, speak first as one of the tribe. Have to think to speak other tongues. You are strong, tough. You know the magic of the potions. We can live happy here."

"No. I cannot. I do not think you can, but we are not the same. Alama says the door will be no more when we go. If you do not come now, you cannot come." She shifted mental gears, suddenly aware that Terry had a point on how they were thinking, and began whispering in English.

"Terry, I'm a scientist, not a witch or medicine woman. That is a great mystery. I've watched it as you have. I don't know just what it is, but I am convinced that it is a machine, not a monster. I recognized some of the monitoring devices. *They* know it's a machine, too. They're trying to figure out what it is. They probably lost somebody to that door in the early stages, which is why they're so low-key here. It's too heavy to move, and I think they're still too scared it'll blow up. And a lot of that equipment is military stuff. Not Brazilian but American. I think they've evacuated the area as much as they could and are waiting until they figure out what to do next."

"Suppose she's right. Suppose it's what she says. What's it like in there or wherever you come out? You think they'll be *people,* like Alama? Suppose it's a probe or something? Poke and study and dissect you for science. *She* couldn't tell you if she wanted to. Our one common tongue can't handle it."

"I'll take the chance. I may not like her much, but I think I trust her. And is this life any better? No doctors, no vaccines, constant dawn-to-dusk hunting and gathering to eat? You're an educated woman of the modern world."

"I dunno. I spent ten years since college batting my head against the wall, getting shot at and beaten up and worse, no real home, no personal life to speak of, working sixty-, seventy-, eighty-hour weeks sometimes just to prove I was better than any of them. And what am I? After all that I'm still a line producer, no on-air anything, doing the same job they're giving to twenty-two-year-old bimbos fresh out of school. And when I had my one shot, a year ago, a real producer's job in Washington with ABC, I put them off because they begged me to cover the fighting in Zaire. So I got stuck in this jerkwater hotel up the Congo. These soldiers came along; they shot most everybody and raped me and left me for dead. I came out anyway, but the ABC job's gone and the rumor is that I lost my nerve! Lost my nerve! And now *this* happens. But, it's a funny thing. I'm good at this. I have a family here. All women, and nobody but nobody questions my nerve! This *is* another planet, and I am already living on it."

"But your family! Your friends!"

"My parents split when I was ten. My father sits in Miami, laundering drug money and dreaming of the old Cuba. My mother spends her alimony sitting in a beach house on Dominica and stuffing white powder up her nose. I don't have a family—I have a series of Catholic boarding schools. And I don't have friends. I thought I did, but they all started whispering about my 'nerve' the first chance they got. I've had years of one-night stands and little else. Nobody is gonna miss me, even now."

Lori was shocked. "I—I never knew . . ."

"Well, we never had the time to get to know each other well. Go if you must—I pray that it is as wonderful as you dream. I don't know if I can live like this forever or not, but I realized a long time ago that if anybody was to get away without all of us getting killed, I would have to stay. I accept that."

"What? No! I want you to come!"

"You know Alama's plan. The four of us disappeared here—who knows how long ago now, but they still have guns up there. It will be necessary to have someone who can speak with them."

"But you don't know Portuguese!"

"No, but it is close enough to Spanish."

"But *you* can't go up there! You know how they're supposed to be diverted!"

"It is not the same. If it is to work, I must go with them."

"You have spoken to Alama about this?"

"Yes. She made some of the same arguments, sort of, but she said it was up to me. She knew, though, that the plan had a much better chance with me staying behind than going with you."

"You can still change your mind."

"Perhaps. Maybe I'm crazy. Maybe I will always regret this. But the fact is, I have little choice. I really believe I might wind up thinking this was the best choice for me. Time will tell."

Lori could only hug her and say, "I hope for your sake that it is."

Terry shrugged. "Besides, I can always come out someday. Be the tattooed lady, the sole survivor who lived as a Stone Age savage. The *Enquirer* alone would pay me enough, with book and TV movie rights, for me to live out my old age."

Lori sighed. "Then I better *really* see Gus."

Gus was still drugged, as was Campos, but he was conscious. After a long period of apparent catatonia, he was able to be coaxed out on occasion, although he did not recognize what had happened to him and still seemed only vaguely aware of his surroundings. He was thin and weathered; his bindings had scarred his wrists and ankles, and he looked almost like a living skeleton. It was pretty clear that he'd need a lot of help, but he was so wasted away and Lori was in such good shape now that she found she could carry him with little trouble.

"Gus, hang on," she said to him. "One more day and we'll get you out of here."

He smiled sleepily like a little child. "Big story?"

"The biggest."

"Lots of pictures?"

"As many as you can take."

He seemed happy at that. She squeezed his hand and went over to Juan Campos. Compared to Gus, Campos was in great shape. He was one very tough cookie, and he had eventually made the best of a mostly intolerable situation. After two early attempts at escape, when he'd shown enough strength to break the tough natural rope bonds and shake off the effects of a very mind-dulling drug, he'd accepted his punishment and the improbability of getting away and tried to make the most of it. He had begun to play up to his captors and to show unmistakable invitations and intent, and he'd been taken up on it by many, and one, possibly two, had conceived with him.

He'd still remained drugged and mostly bound and always well guarded, but he had managed by this to gain extra food and drink and, while weak for lack of any regular exercise, might well be able to make it on his own.

He had figured out who Lori and Terry were and found their transformations into native jungle girls highly amusing.

"All right, Campos. Listen up. The tribe wants to dispose of you, but the chief has other plans. Tomorrow your legs will be freed, and we'll try and give you a little time to exercise them. You're going for a walk, and you'll wear a gag and have rope binding your arms. You do *exactly* what you're told and you might get out of this alive. Understand? You make one funny move and you'll be full of darts with enough curare to kill you in midstep. Understand?"

He nodded sleepily.

"Do one thing right and you're home free. Be stupid and you're dead. And be aware that nobody here really cares which."

There was nothing else to do now but get some sleep and wait for the next day. It was not easy to do. *Please, God! Let Terry and I* both *be making the right decision tomorrow!*

Professor Umberto Alcazar-Diaz, visiting professor of astrogeology at the University of São Paulo, director general of Site A, and, not incidentally, also a research fellow at the National Aeronautics and Space Administration in Houston, had just taken off his glasses and settled back for a nap. He had been working almost nonstop on the lab findings dropped off by the morning helicopter, and his eyes were killing him.

Suddenly he heard a commotion among the guards outside. He was curious but too tired to see to it. "Carlos. You want to see what that's all about?"

"*Sí,* Professor," the young man replied, getting up from his bunk and putting aside the routine security report he'd been writing up in English so that his bosses at the Agency could quickly read it back in Washington. He opened the frame door on the elaborate tent with a casual air and felt something sting him in the neck. He fell back inside, out cold.

The professor couldn't see much without his glasses, but he knew that the young man had fallen, and he jumped up and went to his aid. Seeing that he was unconscious, Umberto Alcazar-Diaz opened the door to call to the guards, but he felt a sting in his neck before he could call out, and that was the last he remembered. The door came shut again.

Outside, the guards were oblivious to the happenings in the tent some twenty meters from any of them, but the armed soldier on duty in the camp was staring at something in the evening sun and had his rifle to the ready, while the other off-duty guards stopped what they were doing and tensed, guns not far away.

"*¡No tire! ¡Somos amigos simpáticos!*" a young woman's voice called from not far away. It wasn't Portuguese and was oddly structured, but one of the men at the card table made it out.

"Antonio! Hold up!" he called in Portuguese. "It's some woman speaking Spanish!"

"Woman? Women?" the duty guard called back in amazement. "Can you understand them?"

"Let me see." The Spanish-speaking sergeant looked out and saw a number of native women standing nervously in a clearing just in front of one of the few immediate stands of trees that had survived the blast. They were all naked and painted up, but that wasn't all that unusual, although he'd never seen markings quite like those before.

"*¿Habla español?*" the same woman asked. She seemed to be the leader.

"*Sí. ¿Quién es?*" the sergeant called back, not too nervous but puzzled.

"*Soy llamado Teysi.*"

"*¿Dónde viene de?*"

"*Somos de la aldea.*"

"She says her name is Teysi and that they come from the village. That must be the one about three kilometers southeast that refused to evacuate."

"What are they doing out here so late in the day and all by themselves?" the duty guard asked, not suspicious but just as curious. "I have been out here so long that even *they* look good to me."

"You never know about these natives, but the ones in the village are friendly so long as you don't ask them to leave." He turned back to the small group of women—six, no *seven* of them! "*¿Porqué vienen ustedes niñas aquí?*" he asked them.

The answer came in halting, not very good Spanish, but the message was clear.

"*Nuestros hombres son enfermos o muertos,*" Teysi explained. "*Nos mantienen lejos de hombres. Ninguno de nosotros ha tenido un hombre en mucho tiempo. Nos mantienen lejos de hombres. Somos muy solo y triste. Vemos que hombres guapos son aquí. Vamos fuera verle. ¿Le gustaríamos vernosotros?*"

The sergeant grinned. "I wonder . . . She says that they are the widows of men who are dead or something like that. That they are being kept locked away and haven't had men in a long time and that they are very lonely. They heard that some handsome men were here and snuck out to see us. I think they want to come up and see us close."

"Some of these tribes are sneaky," another guard warned.

"You ever heard of any of the tribes using women as bait? It would be dishonorable to the men. No, they are too simple and too primitive to be other than what they say. What do you think? Should we invite them up?"

"Why not?" one guard asked. "If they do not smell too bad, maybe we can have some fun. I do not think we will have to search them for concealed weapons!"

They all laughed at that.

"Yes, but what about the professor and his shadow?" another asked.

They glanced at the tent, whose door was shut.

"If they want some, let them get their own," the sergeant joked. "Maybe they will just sleep through it, eh? If they object, I will handle them."

With that, he gestured the women to approach the camp.

"Soy el único aquí que hablo español," explained the leader, a dark girl with a ring of bone in her nose. She might be hell to kiss long and hard, but she had quite a body, and her other assets were . . . outstanding.

The sergeant responded that he was the only one who spoke Spanish among his crew, too.

The lead girl gave a soft laugh. *"Queremos tocar y pal-pamos, no hablamos."*

"I think she says they want more touch and feel than talk, boys! Her Spanish is terrible, but what the hell! I think we will finally break the monotony of this wretched post!"

A couple of the women pointed to the guards and made comments.

"Le dicen son hombres muy bonitos," the dark one said as she reached them.

"She says they think we look *pretty,* boys!" the sergeant laughed. "If it wasn't coming from them and out here, I think I'd be insulted!"

Terry had been nervous before they had revealed themselves. Using the halting, stilted, not quite correct Spanish had been easier; it wasn't as if the soldier's Spanish was much better.

She found that she actually was turned on, too, perhaps as much by the danger as by the desire. Somehow it was poetic that here, on almost the very spot where they had been taken captive who knew how long ago, she had returned as one of her captors to break, in the most dramatic of ways, all ties to her past.

That left the guard near the equipment.

It would have been easier to have just taken him out, but they weren't at all certain they could do it without the others seeing or perhaps calling to him. He had seen and heard most of what was going on down at the camp and had come almost halfway back to see the scene he'd liked to have been a part of.

Each of the women had one of the men, but that left two women, and they came toward the remaining guard with innocent smiles, strutting to be sure he understood them. It wasn't very long before he was totally distracted and effectively out of direct sight of the crater itself.

Alama nodded. Lori again picked up poor Gus, who seemed light as a feather, and Alama pushed Campos forward. "Down *there*?" he said with amazement, but he knew how many of these women were around and knew that Lori's threat wasn't an idle one. He might escape even now if he felt he could, but he wasn't going to do anything until he was pretty damned sure he'd live through it.

The crater wall was thick with fine dust and shiny fragments—it wasn't as easy as it had seemed to get to the meteor. The ground was littered with micalike hexagonal fragments, like tiny odd geometric forms from some bizarre workshop, many of which were fairly sharp, making walking difficult. Lori almost lost Gus once, and Campos actually slipped and fell.

"Up there! Fast!" Lori ordered.

"What? On the *meteor*? We will get burned!"

"There's nothing to burn you. Do as I say. You're almost free."

Alama had already scrambled up, showing the way, and was now standing on a jagged outcrop very near where the so-called doorway to the stars was. She was keeping an eye on Campos, and she had a poison-tipped spear poised in case he tried to flee. She felt a moral obligation to take him along, but she understood what slime he was.

There was a sound of happy commotion coming from

just beyond her line of sight, and she smiled to herself and thought, *Do good, my children. Get many fine babies. Farewell.*

But *was* it farewell? Where the hell was the doorway? Damn it, it had been *expecting* her! *Beckoning* her! Why didn't it show up?

Campos passed her and at that moment gave her something of a shove. It was hard to tell if he'd slipped or if it was deliberate, but it knocked Alama down, sending the spear clattering down to the bottom of the crater.

He turned, looked at Lori, struggling up with Gus, smiled, and said "*Adiós, muchachas!* I will return, and your tribe will serve me forever!" He turned his back, took a step . . .

And vanished as if a three-dimensional television image had been abruptly turned off.

"Alama! Are you all right?"

The small woman struggled back to balance. "I am good enough. Where is he?"

"He winked out!"

"Ah. It knows when to come, as always." She gave Lori a hand, and together they hauled Gus the last little bit. Alama pulled him a little, then said, "You will have to take him in with you. When I go, it goes."

Lori nodded, saw the blackness, but hesitated, looking back toward the camp.

"I know what you think. If she do that, she will make it. Now hurry! Go!"

Lori picked up Gus once more, half dragging him, and backed into the black area. As soon as Gus's feet cleared the black boundary, there was total darkness all around her and a sensation of falling.

Alama sighed and for the first time noticed the cameras. She hadn't ever seen their like, but she knew what they were. It didn't matter. Not anymore.

She stood there for a moment in all her Amazonian glory,

bowed to each, then jumped into the blackness and winked out.

Terry lay on the blanket next to the sergeant and tried to catch her breath. A whole range of strange emotions and thoughts whirled in her head, and she needed time to regain control.

Suddenly, as it always seemed to do in this country, it began to rain hard, ending the trysts with a start and sending people scrambling.

Her sergeant rolled off the blanket and made for the nearby tent without even thinking of her for the moment, assuming she would follow. She, however, was used to the rain now, even this driving rain, and she got up and looked toward the crater.

The meteor was still glowing and pulsing. Maybe faster now; there was something different about it, but it was still active.

Curiosity and a certain sense of emptiness and loss overcame her, and she made for it. The crater guard ran past her, half-dressed and cursing in Portuguese, without ever being aware of her.

She reached the low point between the two sets of covered equipment and stared for a moment. *They must have made it,* she thought. *There's no sign, and we sure gave them enough time.*

But the thing hadn't died down; the black "hole" was still there, but it looked odd. It looked, in fact, like something was keeping it open when it wanted to close.

Sweet Jesus! she thought, staring at it. *Do I have the nerve, after all?*

The rain pounded all around, and she had a tense feeling that some dramatic event was imminent.

"The hell with it. I never could pass up a great story," she said aloud to herself, and ran into the crater, ignoring the dust that was turning to mud and the piles of glassine hexagonal minerals. With a surefootedness she could never have imagined before this, she made her way up the side of the meteor and to the edge of the hole, certain that it would close just as she reached it. As she neared it, she slipped, bruised a knee, then managed to get up and, with supreme effort, drag herself on top of the blackness. It felt solid as a rock, and for a moment she felt the oddest mixture of relief and disappointment.

The world winked out, and there was only blackness and a sensation of falling fast through space.

Back at the meteor site the ground started to shake, and there were cries of "Earthquake!" from the camp.

Almost too fast to see, the meteor became duller, its surface fading to a dull rock sheen; cracks appeared, and fissures opened up along its fracture points.

The glow died; the pulsing stopped, and it grew suddenly very dark at the camp.

When the scientist and the intelligence agent came around two hours later, there were no native women, no real sign of what had happened to them or why, and six very confused soldiers who had already vowed to tell no one of the night's activities.

Alama was falling in the blackness, and then suddenly she stopped, not on a cold, hard surface, as she had expected, but suspended somehow in the gate's usual emptiness, a state she could never comprehend.

And then a voice came to her. A voice speaking an ancient tongue, but the tongue of her birth, and speaking it directly into her mind.

"Mavra! Mavra! Oh, you must *hear me and understand! Mavra!"*

A vast scene unfolded from her memories, a scene of a huge artificial moon filled with great equipment of impossible complexity, a moon that had a name, personality, and a soul. A name so dear to her that it was wrenched back even after all this time by the "sound" of that voice in her mind.

"Obie?"

"Mavra! Please! You must listen! I can't keep this gateway open long!"

"Obie—you're dead. You're many thousands of years dead and gone."

"No! We're not dead. And yet not alive. We're shifted over, like ghosts, unable to do much but still very much here!"

"What? Who's 'we'?"

"All of us. The trillions and trillions of us of all the races that ever were except the first. All the beings from the past universe, from our universe, and all the beings from the universes before. We're stored, stored in the records of the Well, so we can be reused if needed. Only I am strong enough to retain some independent action, because I can manipulate, too, in a way. I've been waiting, waiting a long time until you intersected the Well matrix again and I could reach you!"

"Obie! You're inside the Well?"

"I am part of it! We are all part of it now! We provide the templates for the re-created universe as needed. It is a horrible existence. Not even a half of living. Those—Markovians—or whatever they're called never cared about what they were doing to all those lives if a reset was needed. I don't think they ever thought that there would be a reset. But, like the Watcher, we are mere—insurance."

This was too much all at once. "Obie, I—"

"Keep quiet for once and let me talk! I can't hold this gate open very much longer, and I don't think I can contact you again until you're here, inside the control computer, where we're all stored."

"Obie—you want me to come to you? Is that it? What would I do? I don't know how anything works. I just pushed the buttons Nathan told me to push! You'd need him to help you."

Nathan! That was his name! That was the other one like her!

"No! No! Not Nathan! That is what we fear most! He will come again and he will reset, and we will have more company and be pushed farther back in the memory banks, leaving even less of what little remains of us and cutting us off completely!"

"He wouldn't do that if he knew!"

"He not only would, he will. He doesn't know it, but he will. He has no choice, Mavra! He is the Watcher! He is programmed to do it each and every time."

"Programmed? Obie—it has been a long time. I remember very little of the old days. It is coming back, but it is still hazy."

"It means that he has no choice. He was designed by the Markovians to do just one thing."

"You speak of him as if he were a machine!"

"Mavra, he is a machine! And he doesn't even know it! Only a machine could bear these long, long lives, re-creation after re-creation. He is the only self-aware construct of the ancient ones, and he is rigidly compelled to act in only one way when he is needed. You were not on Earth before, and you had no formal education. You do not know history. All the monsters of history, all the mass killers, the armies, the hatreds, the diseases, the things that represent all evil in the universe are re-created time after time as well, very much as they were, to do their evil over and over again to the same people over and over again. He has the power to change it. He has the power to make things better, to alleviate suffering and misery and death, to create a wonderful universe for all the Last Races, but what does he do? He makes it all the same. He uses the templates. He does it over and over just the same. He doesn't even change himself. Oh, no, that would corrupt their damnable experiment! The ultimate evil, unintended though it was. They were so sure they were gods. They were so certain that they could not make mistakes. The reset mechanism, the Watcher, were there to ward off natural deviations. They allowed for randomness and chaos to possibly require that the experiment be restarted, but they were certain that they were right! If it goes wrong, the Watcher puts it back exactly as it

*was. He doesn't want to. He fought it the last time. But he still
did it. And he will do it again. He will reset the experiment,
kill trillions on over fifteen hundred worlds, and the evil will
start anew. He has to, even if he doesn't understand why. He
cannot refuse, even if he learns the truth himself and believes
it. It is built in that he will do it."*

Nathan a—what was the word?—a *robot*? She could
hardly believe it, yet it explained much. It was the first time
he really made any sense at all.

"He—he is already there?"

*"Yes, but he will fight it. He will fight it until he is forced
to act. Mavra—you must use that time! You must get here
before him! You must act as if he were your enemy, although
he is ours. You must do it for our sake and the sake of
anybody you ever cared about back on Earth."*

"But—Obie? I told you—I wouldn't know what to do!"

*"The last time he made a mistake. He thinks, he feels, he
cares. Outside of his one mission, he is basically good. He
recoiled at the reset and had you do it. He remade you into a
being like himself. The Well will let you in if you come. And
once inside, we can speak together without these limits! I can
tell you what to do, Mavra! Together we can break this vicious cycle and create a better, more stable universe based on
good. But you must get here first!"*

There was sudden silence, and she called out mentally,
"Obie?"

*"I can't hold it anymore, Mavra. Come! Get here ahead of
him! Let me live again and we'll have a universe that is glori-
ous! I know how. You can do it. Come!"*

"Obie! Wait!"

But there was no answer; the falling sensation resumed.

Only her quick reflexes kept her from falling right on top of
Gus. She rolled and got immediately to her feet and looked
around at their surroundings with mixed emotions. After
the unexpected "conversation" in transit, she had much to

think about, and it wasn't of a sort she wanted to deal with, at least right now. On the other hand, the familiarity of the great chamber after such a very long time was beyond satisfaction; she felt suddenly *alive* again.

Lori watched in amazement as the woman she knew as Alama got to her feet, raised her arms and turned slowly around in a circle, as if drinking in the cold and bizarre view, then gave a surprisingly deep yet joyful laugh that echoed through the chamber. Lori could not, however, understand the words the tiny woman called out in that same tone of joy and amusement, said in an odd, melodic tongue like none she'd ever heard before.

"Hello, you big, beautiful Well World, you! *Mavra's back!*"

"Alama," Lori called out, interrupting the scene in the only common language the two now shared, that of the People, "when you do not come, I do not know what to do next."

She was more than a little relieved to find that contrary to Terry's fears, she was still very much alive and none the worse for wear, but she had felt very alone and exposed there, with Gus so weak and out of it.

The small woman stopped, frowned, then, abruptly all business, turned toward Lori. "Where is the other man?"

"Campos? He knows not where he is. He is very angry. He said he will find a way out of this trap. He walks in that direction." She pointed.

"He is still tied?"

"His hands."

The small woman smiled. "He will be easy to find. Do not worry."

"Alama, Gus is bad off. We must find help for him."

She nodded and knelt to examine the man, who was conscious but still clearly in something of a fog. Then she looked back up at Lori. "Take him up there. I will follow. Do not worry. He will be all right." She paused a moment, then added, "*Not* Alama. No more Alama. I am Mav-ra. Mavra Chang."

"Mavra Chang," Lori repeated. It sounded odd and not quite right, but the family name was most interesting. Chang. So she *was* a true Oriental! Chinese probably, with a name like Chang. But that didn't solve the mystery. If she was Chinese, then she wasn't a native of wherever *this* was. "The stars beyond the stars." The idea of some hidden, ancient group of Chinese from another planet seemed ludicrous.

That is, if this place *was* another planet. It was true that the trip had been a bizarre one, but it hadn't seemed long, and while this vast chamber was like nothing she'd ever seen before, it certainly didn't have the feel of some extraterrestrial locale.

It *was* a huge place, though. She wasn't certain if she could see the end of it in either direction. The shiny, slightly concave coppery surface of the floor reflected bright, indirect light from an unseen source, giving an illusion of great distance. On two sides of the floor was a low barrier wall topped by a dark rail, and here and there, there were openings in it so that one could get up onto whatever was beyond. With a tired sigh, she hoisted Gus and made her way carefully over to the nearest opening, and, going through, she deposited him again on the floor.

This area was quite different in many respects. The "floor" was brown and felt like padded plastic; it gave slightly to her weight, and she felt a slight stickiness on her bare feet. The barrier wall was a dark brown inside and seemed to mesh seamlessly with the floor surface. It was surprisingly wide; several people could walk abreast on it and not touch the main wall or barrier wall. It, too, seemed to go on forever.

What was almost as unnerving as the size of the place was the deathly silence, so that every sound they made seemed magnified. Suddenly they heard a terrified scream far ahead of them and then the sound of a panicked running. Lori tensed, but Alama—Mavra—seemed to find it amusing.

In another minute they could see the frantic form of Juan Campos racing toward them, and as he drew close, his expression looked as if he had just gazed upon the most gruesome of ghosts.

He would have run right past them, or so it seemed, except that Mavra stuck out a leg and tripped him.

"Campos! What did you see?" Lori pressed, nervous. This was not a man who scared easily.

"A monster! Horrible! Help me up! We can't stay here! It is right behind me!"

She looked up at Mavra, who she knew couldn't possibly have understood what the terrified man had said yet who didn't ask about it, either.

Up ahead, from the direction Campos had come, there was the sudden whine of machinery, and she felt a vibration through the floor.

Campos heard and felt it, too, and he whimpered, then turned, wide-eyed in fear, toward the sound of the noise.

Lori gasped and felt the same panic rise in her that had already mastered Juan Campos; only Mavra's cool assurance and bemused expression kept her where she was.

Seemingly floating toward them was a huge apparition, a monstrous reptilian form perhaps three or four meters high, with a mean-looking head much like a tyrannosaurus Lori had seen in museum dinosaur exhibits. The head, however, was perched on an even wider body, with a burnt-orange underbelly fully exposed, all supported by two monstrous legs that vanished below the barrier wall. It seemed to have a tail as great as its body, and gigantic bony plates extended from just below the neck down to, and perhaps onto, the tail.

Its primary coloring was a passionate purple, broken with crimson spots so thick and regular, they seemed almost like polka dots.

The creature filled perhaps eighty percent of the width of the walkway, and it was coming straight for them, riding on a section that was moving.

Mavra turned to them and said, "Tell them do not move. Just wait and all will be safe."

Lori swallowed hard but said, "Come on, Campos! Be the macho man you always wanted to be! She says don't move and nobody will get hurt."

It was clear that Campos wanted to get up and run, but he was stopped both by the fact that his bound wrists made it hard to get back on his feet and by the sheer bravado of the two women. There was just no way Juan Campos could run away from anything in fear if two women stayed.

"Very well, but if I am to die, let me die with my hands free."

It seemed like a fair request. Lori allowed herself to take one eye off the still-approaching Leviathan and gesture to the bonds for approval. Mavra nodded, and Lori untied him.

He sat up, rubbing his wrists. "What sort of lunatic place is this, and how did we get here?" he asked, both eyes still on the approaching monster.

"I only promised you'd be free," Lori reminded him. "I didn't say where."

The creature was now very close, and it reached over and down with one of its fully formed hands at the end of long, spindly arms and struck the side of the barrier wall. The belt it was on stopped moving, leaving it about ten feet from them.

Lori gaped at the thing in wonder and saw now that it wore some kind of sash around its neck and upper torso with a complex symbol embossed on it by a method suggesting some advanced technology. Around its neck and over the sash hung a thick gold chain like some kind of giant necklace, and at the end of it hung what appeared to be a ruby-colored gemstone, hexagonal in shape.

The creature looked *them* over as well, and its head shook a bit from side to side and its eyes widened. The gem on the necklace seemed to light up and emitted a very soft whine, followed by a voice that Lori heard in English, Campos in Spanish, and Mavra in her ancient native tongue. It was a high-pitched, slightly nervous voice that didn't at all match the monstrous visage before them.

"Oh, my! Goodness gracious!" said the voice. "Savages!"

SOUTH ZONE

In an instant that silly, high-pitched voice with a trace of a lisp in it, the riotous colors, and the comment and tone made Lori think more of the Reluctant Dragon than of a terrible monster.

"I don't know what this place is coming to," the creature went on, speaking aloud mostly to itself. "Gentlemen, soldiers, and savages, all Type 41 Glathrielians, of all things, plus dumb animals, outright junk—what's next? This used to be such a *peaceful* posting!"

"Who are you?" Mavra Chang asked him in a normal, civil tone. Interestingly to Lori and Campos, the device on the necklace—obviously some sort of advanced translating computer—picked up her strange tongue and echoed it to them.

"I am Auchen Glough, Ambassador from Kwynn and the unfortunate current Duty Officer at South Zone. I assume you all fell in from this terrible planet called Dirt just like the others?"

"Close enough," Mavra responded. "There have been others?"

"Oh, my, yes! Not on my watch, I admit, but we've all seen the pictures and gotten the reports. First there was a party of three, then, a day or so later, two more, and now, after an *interminable* period when it's rained junk in here, the four of you. How many more?"

"No more, I shouldn't think," Mavra told him.

"Most unusual, most odd," muttered the ambassador. "We have had new arrivals here, but never, *never* from a planetbound group. Well, I suppose we should get this over with. If everyone will stand, I will take us back to the office for indoctrination and briefing."

"He can't stand," Lori said of Gus. "He's very weak and ill. He needs attention."

"Hmmm. Well, carry him over the junction points, and that will be enough for now. He's not likely to die in an hour or two, is he?"

"No. At least I don't *think* so. But if he doesn't get some kind of attention, he's going to die fairly soon."

"Then we'd best get on with it. Come."

Juan Campos felt some of his confidence coming back. "I am not following that *thing* until I find out where I am and what the hell this is all about!" he stated.

"If you follow me, I will tell you," the ambassador responded. "If you don't, you will get very hungry and very thirsty out here. We are headed for the only exit."

For now, at least, that seemed good enough.

With Gus in her arms, Lori stepped past the wall opening. Mavra was already there, and Campos followed last, wary but more worried about remaining alone than about going with what he still thought of as a potentially vicious monster.

The ambassador turned around, showing that the spiny plates did indeed extend down the tail and that the tail itself terminated in a very nasty-looking bony spike. He struck the side twice, and the moving walkway started, carrying them back down the chamber toward the unknown.

They were barely out of sight when Terry materialized on the concave floor.

She was a little confused and disoriented, having gone from a very unusual encounter with the Brazilian sergeant to a rain-soaked climb and then a fall through darkness, but she felt glad to be alive and looked around, amazed at the size and strangeness of the place.

I don't know where this is, but it sure isn't Brazil, she thought, gaping. *Sweet Jesus! I thought the People were weird enough, but this is getting weirder by the minute!*

She got up, unarmed and naked as the day she was born with nothing that wasn't glued in or tattooed on, and looked around. She was wondering what to do next when she heard sounds of what might have been voices coming from very far away to her left. It wasn't much, and the sounds seemed to be diminishing with each passing moment, but, naked and unarmed or not, there wasn't much choice but to head off in that direction. She eyed the openings and the low barrier wall and scrambled up to the top of the nearest one.

She looked around, but the sounds were gone now, and there was an unnerving quiet and stillness about this massive place. There seemed nothing to do but head in the direction she'd thought the sounds had come from and hope for the best. She was certainly exposed as hell here.

She stared off into the distance and sighed. It was going to be a *long* walk.

No seats in the South Zone conference room seemed to be designed for humans, but there was plenty of floor space.

The Kwynn ambassador went to the front and pushed a concealed panel in the wall, and a small lectern and operating console rose from the floor until it was at the considerable height most useful to him.

"I realize that you all are very confused right now as to where you are and all the rest," he began hesitantly, trying to find the right words for what he considered the most primitive-looking bunch he'd ever known to come through.

"I will try to make it as simple as I can. You are no longer on the planet on which you were born and raised. Somehow, by accident or design, you entered a device which transported you here. Never mind how—you could not possibly understand it even if you were the most advanced of races."

You don't understand it at all yourself, you old fraud, Mavra thought, but kept silent.

"Seeing you, I believe it," Juan Campos responded. "But my only question is, How do I get back?"

"Um, well, you don't. It's strictly a one-way system now, although it once went in both directions. That was ages ago, beyond any living memories and all but the most basic of our records. I'm afraid you are here to stay."

"That is impossible! If one can get somewhere, one can get back!"

"Well, you are welcome to try, but I wouldn't suggest poking blindly even around here. You would be taken as a Glathrielian and could wind up being in a deadly situation. Glathriel doesn't really have any representation here except the Ambreza, and I doubt if you'd fare too well with them, either."

"What will you do with us?" Lori asked nervously.

"If you will kindly just allow me to continue, I think I can answer all your questions!" the ambassador snapped irritably. "It is difficult enough trying to simplify this when you don't have the background to understand it. Uh, you *do* know what planets are, don't you?"

"We are not as we appear," Mavra told him. "I think everyone will understand what you say. Do not simplify anything. If there's something we don't understand, we'll ask questions afterward."

"Oh, very well. You might understand what this place is a little better if you have some basic background, though. The universe as we know it is around twenty-four billion years old, give or take a few billion. On the vast number of worlds in the vast number of galaxies that it contains, life of all sorts evolved. It stands to reason that someone had to evolve up to a high standard first. There are many terms for them, but the one we use these days is simply the First Race. They were nothing like anything you know or even I know, and we have little direct information about them. What we *do* know is that they came up just like every other race does in the natural system and reached a level well beyond where any races are today. At least a billion or maybe more years ago they reached the top. They were everywhere, they'd explored everything that could be explored, and they were so advanced, they didn't need spaceships or much of anything to move from point to point. You arrived by one of their methods of travel. We call them hex gates, for obvious reasons. They did an awful lot of things based on sixes, and the hexagon was their sort of 'pet shape,' as it were. Finally they reached the point where they were like gods, permanently linked to their machines and able to have or do or experience almost anything they wanted just by, well, thinking of it."

Lori tried to imagine what they must have been like and failed. A race so advanced that they were magic. Whatever they wished, they could have. "Where are they now?" she asked. "Here?"

"No. And yes. And maybe. That is the impossible question, and it has a lot of answers, not all of them verifiable. You—all of us—would think that such an existence would be the ultimate one, and it probably was for quite a while. They banished fear and want and desire and even death. They probably had a lot of fun, maybe for millions of years, but after a while something we might not imagine happened."

"They started losing it?" Campos guessed.

"No. They grew bored. Horribly, horribly bored. Have any of you ever played any gambling game? Any game of chance at all?"

They all nodded. "Of course," Campos responded.

"What would happen if you discovered one day that you couldn't lose. That you could *never* lose?"

"I would settle a lot of old scores and wind up owning the world!" Campos replied.

But Lori said, "I think I see what you mean. It would get boring. It wouldn't be any fun anymore. If you can't lose, then winning is meaningless."

"Yes, precisely so. And that's what happened to them. Life lost all its meaning. There was nothing more to learn, nothing more to do that they hadn't all done a thousand times, no surprises, no reason for existence anymore."

"You mean they *killed* themselves out of boredom?" Lori was appalled.

"The ancient records imply that this is indeed what started happening; others went a bit mad, imagining a higher state beyond where they were and believing that they had a way to get there—which also, of course, meant death if they were wrong. It was the first crisis they faced in so long it was beyond their memory, so they got together and tried to figure out why being omnipotent was so empty. They couldn't believe that a permanent state of ultimate happiness was impossible, since their whole racial effort had been directed for so long at attaining just that, so they came up with the only other answer they could. They figured that they were somehow flawed. That they had evolved *incorrectly*. And since their experiments showed that they would wind up the same way if they started from scratch, they decided that their whole race had evolved wrongly, that it was impossible to reach that state as the First Race. It sounds crazy, I know, and perhaps it is, but that's the way they thought. Which of us could understand their thinking? And thus came about their Great Project."

"I do not think that I would get so bored," Campos commented. "Such power!"

"Perhaps. But we are not they. As I was saying, the Great

Project. Even now I don't think we can even understand it. It is very unclear. It seems, however, that a giant experiment and computer—you know what a computer is? Good!—was built the size of a reasonable planet. On it, 1,560 laboratories, in fact, were built, each containing a unique ecosystem. They took beings from worlds where life had evolved, and they in many cases altered or speeded up the evolution of those races. In some cases, what had once been animals became a thinking and dominant race. In other cases, they made things up from whole cloth, often taking variations of ideas done by others. The idea was to create and test as large and varied a selection of potential master races starting from different worlds and backgrounds, to try and design the one system that would in fact produce the heaven they dreamed of. The laboratory areas, tightly controlled to make them simulate the theoretical planets and systems they'd invented, were divided into two segments. Since about half of all life that had evolved in the universe, including apparently them, was based on carbon, half the world was given over to carbon-based life-forms. The other half, just to be sure, was given over to *non*-carbon-based forms, like silicon, even pure energy, and for forms with alternative atmospheres like ammonia and methane. A great barrier was placed between the two halves so that they could not interact with one another, and the non-carbon-based half had extra barriers guarding against one environment polluting another. The southern half was the carbon-based half. You are carbon-based, as am I, so we are in the south."

Lori was fascinated. "You mean *this* is the laboratory? And the experiment is still going on?"

"Well, this is the laboratory world, yes, but we *think* the experiment is long over with. In fact, it is somewhat humbling to realize that someone else got first crack. The *last* ones to have at it were the bottom of the barrel—still godlike creatures, nonetheless. We here now are, sad to say, among the last created. We call our current state the Last Races, for obvious reasons."

"Fifteen hundred and sixty different races?" Lori said as much as asked. "All here? Now? How big *is* this place, anyway?"

"Not huge, but big enough. Unfortunately, the translator has limits, one of which is measurement systems. From what I have learned from watching the recordings of prior entries here, I gather we are somewhat close to the same size as your home world."

"Huh? On a world the size of Earth, you've got 1,560 little worlds? It sounds like a collection of small domes."

"No, no, it's not like that. You will see."

"You were talking about those god creatures," Juan Campos put in. "You never said why they did this thing or what happened to them." He didn't like the idea of a whole race of godlike beings looking over his shoulder.

"Oh, yes. Well, it is unclear what happened, but it *is* clear that for the experiments to prove that their systems had possibilities, they used themselves."

"What?" This was getting too much for Lori to handle. "You mean they became the races they invented?"

"So it would seem. All but the control group. That one worked on the 'next phase' of evolution some thought must exist. They were also supposed to be the guardians to ensure that those who became part of the experiment might be able to back out. After a while, though, it didn't happen. The control group vanished—nobody knows where or how or why. Some say they found their higher state. Others say they killed themselves attempting it. It is unknown what happened, but one thing was sure: When they left, no pure members of the First Race remained. The First Race had been consumed by retaking on mortality in the course of its experiment. The new races that had proved themselves were moved out to worlds to begin a natural evolution. Only the last series of experiments were left, and because there was no control, they were never shut down even when they were used as the templates for worlds like the one you came from. Nobody left here knew how to get off of this world or how to get to, much less operate, the computer and machinery, so we have been here ever since, maintained by the master computer as we were, free only within the limits of its programming. You are here because all the First Race hex gates all over the universe were left switched on, all with this place as their terminus; there was no one to turn them off."

"I see," Lori said, nodding. But she *didn't* see, not totally. How did that explain this Alama, this Mavra Chang?

"Two ancient terms have come down from those past ages," the ambassador told them. "The word that appears to refer to this laboratory world seems to translate out, for no discernible reason, as 'well.' Thus we refer to this as the Well World. The operating computer that maintains it and us, and possibly a lot more, has the ancient name of the Well of Souls. Very poetic, actually."

"You said that most of them left the way we came in," Juan Campos noted, thinking of what he and his family might do with access to all this. "Then there *is* a way to get out."

"Oh, certainly. You simply have to get into the master computer and give it the proper instructions. That's obvious. The trouble is, the last race to leave locked the master computer and took the keys with them, as it were. It is likely that the gate you used—a meteor, I believe—was one of the gates used when your world was being prepared and designed for full habitation. A work-gang gate, as it were, parked somewhere after it was no longer needed. Some cosmic catastrophe jolted it out of its orbit, and it came down and snared you and the others. This happens. Some races, as I have said, who are already spacefaring sorts have accidentally bumped into them, mostly on ancient, deserted worlds once inhabited by the First Race. The gates are locally controlled, and it appears that because the races involved are the recognized designs of the First Race, it can't tell *you* apart from *them*. So it brings you here. And here you will remain for reasons I have already stated."

"You said that we were—what did you call it?—Glath something?" Lori said, thinking.

"Glathriel. Yes. You are different in minor details but basically the same race and clearly of their origin. It is understandable that, stuck here over vast periods of time, differences would fade as evolution produced single uniform races, and that is pretty much the rule in all of the hexes."

"Hexes?" Campos prompted.

"Yes. All of the experimental areas, the 'nations' of the Well World now, are hexagonal in shape except at the equator and at the poles. The ones abutting both are of more a wing shape but still manage six sides. The equator, as I said, is an impenetrable barrier. None of us could survive for long in most of the North, and few of those races could survive here. There are a couple of exceptions, but not many. We do some limited trade and contacts through this zone—there is a local hex gate that goes between them—but very little. We haven't much in common. Each hex also has its own local gate, but it will carry you only to here and then will return you back to your 'native' hex when you leave."

"Where is 'here' exactly in all this?" Lori asked him.

"South Zone. The south polar region. The 'cap,' as it were. You cannot enter this zone except by the local hex gates or the way you arrived. You can leave only through the local gates. This area was once the social control center, transport hub, you name it, of the Great Project. Now it is used essentially as embassies for the various hexes. Not every hex has an ambassador or representative here—some do not socialize much with other races—though about half do, mostly the high-tech hexes and some of the semis."

"Huh?"

"I told you each hex was an artificially created environment in which various conditions were duplicated or enforced to simulate real worlds. Resource- and food-rich worlds would eventually evolve technological civilizations.

Those hexes are fully controlled by natural law, and many, like my own, are extremely developed. Others might have a very livable ecosystem but lack the sort of resources that would allow the easy development of a high-tech civilization. In those, some natural laws are, for lack of a better term, deactivated. Those are the semitech hexes, in which things like steam power are allowed, but not more advanced systems. In yet others, those with few resources or particularly harsh environments, survival itself was the primary aim and the races had to be tested on that basis. It was also thought, or so it is surmised, that these hexes might be an attempt to see if a race could attain perfection in a natural state and to explore the idea that machines and high technology might well be the corrupting influence. In these hexes only direct mechanical energy works. Muscle power, water power, and the like, but always in a preindustrial stage. Do not take them lightly. Some of them have developed amazing powers that seem almost like magic to the rest of us, although most are stagnant to a large degree."

"The other creatures—they are like you?" Campos asked.

"Oh, my, no! Only the Kwynn are like the Kwynn. Our land is on the equator west of the Sea of Storms. And yes, there are vast ocean areas and water-breathing races who live here under the same rules. There are 1,560 different races. There are some similarities among these, even some outright mixture of racial traits. A Dillian might be considered a mixture of a draft animal from Glathriel and the dominant Glathrielian race, for example. There are also somewhat similar combinations of my own kind, from cold-blooded to warm, short to tall, and all sorts of mixtures. A few are, well, unique."

"You brought up this Glathriel again," Lori noted. "Why don't they have an embassy here?"

"Glathriel was, as you might expect, a high-tech hex," the Kwynn replied. "It reached a very high level very fast, partly because, it is said, they were so violent and warlike. In ancient times a king arose who decided to expand beyond his hex and conquer other hexes, either enslaving or exterminating the natives to increase his own race. A peaceful nontech agrarian hex that had an abundant supply of food and an extremely fertile land was to be the first target, since Glathriel had become too developed to support its own population and did not have sufficient trade to buy what it needed. This other race, the Ambreza, got wind of the plot and somehow created a kind of gas, harmless to Ambreza, that would interact with the atmosphere in Glathriel and become quickly pervasive. It appears to have altered brain chemistry or some such. In quite a short period of time, before they could even realize what was happening, it reduced the entire Glathrielian population to moron level, barely more than animals. The Ambreza then moved into Glathriel and enjoyed the benefits of high technology, then they rounded up the Glathrielians, perhaps a million of them, and forced them into Ambreza, where they are used as draft animals, tilling the fields under Ambreza plantation supervisors. Of course, the only account we have is the Ambreza one, so we don't know if the Glathrielians were really that mean or simply outsmarted themselves by forgetting that nontech is not a synonym for 'stupid,' 'ignorant,' or 'defenseless.' "

"How horrible! And you said 'are used.' You mean they were genetically altered? They remain—moronic?"

"No, not at all. But they remain a rather primitive bunch, I fear. Apparently, over the generations they achieved a tolerance for the gas, which is actually a derivative of a natural marsh product. The Ambreza retained a fairly good-sized chunk of the place for their plantations bordering on the new Ambreza, and the rest was left to the remaining Glathrielians, who regained their senses over time but never more than a fraction of their previous numbers. Indeed, their population has been stable at about fifteen or twenty thousand for as long as we have valid records. The rest of the hex that the Ambreza didn't need was allowed to grow wild. Today they live in tribal groups as simple hunter-gatherers and remain very primitive. The Ambreza say that a wild plant they always considered a nuisance proved a mild drug to Glathrielians, who use it quite a lot. It has sapped their ambition as well as their fierceness and is at the center of their primitive homegrown religion. A few of the tribes are willing to work on the Ambreza plantations as farm labor, getting good-quality fruits and vegetables for their effort. Most consider the Ambreza devils, although they don't really know why. They have totally lost their past."

Lori could just imagine the Glathrielians. All the Amazonians might feel right at home there. "But isn't there some sense of guilt that these people should be so limited because of crimes by an ancestral group that nobody remembers except in the winner's legends?" she asked.

"One might say that," the ambassador conceded, "but the vast gulf of time also argues for leaving them just that way. We are, after all, the *leftovers* from the Grand Experiment, no matter what we think of ourselves now; we are not the experiment itself. They are not that much different, and no worse off, than many other races and hexes. Indeed, we have only the Ambreza legends and the fact that when Ambrezans come here, they must leave to Glathriel, not their own hex, to show that there is any truth to it, anyway. After all this time, no one is much worried about it."

"Ain't nobody gonna expose me to a gas that turns me into no animal!" Juan Campos declared. "I won't let it happen!"

"Nobody said it would," the ambassador pointed out.

"But you said we were Glath—those people! The place used to be ours and is now in the hands of these guys who steal our minds with drugs! I mean, it took the people *generations* to get used to it. We're not used to it. We breathe that stuff, and we're just big hairless apes!"

"No. It *is* true that there is a slight danger, but if you *were* going to Glathriel, you'd emerge not there but in Ambreza. Besides, whoever said you were going to Glathriel? The odds are something like 779 to 1 against it."

Even Lori was suddenly confused. "But you said that's where we'd go!"

"Uh, yes, if you were *Glathrielians.* But that is not how it works. After all, our ancestors also used this mechanism to *become* our ancestors, you see. The computer here keeps things in a careful balance. If a hex becomes overpopulated, then no babies are born until the population levels out. If a hex is underpopulated, it can't *avoid* having more children. You are not yet in the census. When you go through the hex gate for the first time, you will be detected by the master computer as a newcomer not in its data base. It will then look at that data base and see where one extra person might fit without disturbing any balances. No one actually comes through a gate as he is. You are broken down and converted into energy, and the blueprint for 'you' is sent along with the energy packet. You are then reconstructed at the other end according to that blueprint. When you go through the first time, the computer will decide where you best fit in its system, and it will alter the blueprint. Just as the First Race were converted into their creations, so will you be. Your packet will be reconstructed with a new blueprint. Your mind, your memories, won't change, but your physical, racial form will. You will become a new creature of a race new to you."

"What!" both Lori and Campos exclaimed at much the same time.

"Yes. And certain—adjustments will be made so that you can survive. For one thing, you will begin at or just beyond the age of adulthood. That varies, of course, but you will be younger certainly. The primary thinking and memory areas of the brain will be retained, so you will still be pretty much the person you are, but the more animal levels of the brain and its functions will be those of the new race, not the one you have now. Thus, you will be able to handle the body comfortably and will not be repulsed by the sight of others. It is an adjustment mechanism, although, to be sure, making the sentient *mental* adjustment to fully *accept* what you are and that you will be that way forever is easier for some than for others. The rest you will learn from the natives. They will want to know about you as much as you will want and need to learn from them."

Campos was appalled. "You mean I could walk through that thing and come out looking like *you*?"

"I am a diplomat, so I will ignore the insult. Yes, you could. Race, sex, all that will be computer-selected based on the needs of the Well World. There have always been theories that the individual does unconsciously influence the selection to some degree, but it is not clear how or why. Don't be upset. You have a whole new life, starting with coming of age. A whole new start."

"Well, I don't want it!" Juan Campos proclaimed. "I want my old life back—as *me*!"

"You have no choice, as I say. You will either walk through or, to be blunt, you will be thrown through. I assure you that the personnel here in South Zone and even the automated systems here will use force if need be."

Campos let it go, but he was clearly not at all pleased.

"The others who came before—they have already all gone through?" It was Mavra's first question in the session.

"Yes, all, and quite some time ago."

"Who were they? Can you say?"

"Not exactly. Let me punch up the records. Hmmmm. First was a very civilized fellow named David Solomon— pardon the pronunciation. He came nicely dressed, along with two companions, both older, I believe—it is not easy for me to tell much about your race—who were both crippled in some way. The male, who said he was named Joao

Antonio Guzman, could not see, as I remember, and the woman, Anne Marie Guzman, presumably a relation, had a terrible disease and could not even move much on her own. Then, a few days later, two males came through. One was definitely an older man in a uniform who said he was Colonel Jorge Lunderman of something called the Brazilian Air Force, whatever that is, and the other was a much younger man in a different uniform named Captain Julian Beard of somebody else's air force."

"I wonder where *they* came from?" Lori mused. "I wonder if they were part of the first investigative team there and got caught?"

"You would not think it would be two officers," Campos commented. "I mean, always send the privates in first is the old rule."

"Perhaps. But if they were part of the science team, it might make sense," Lori said.

"And now the four of you. And I hope that is it for now," the ambassador added.

"Almost certainly," Mavra told him. "Umm . . . just out of curiosity, is there *any* account in any of the legends of any of the races here of a surviving member of the First Race? Of somebody who could work the big computer?"

"Odd you should ask. Yes. The name is part of so many similar legends and sagas here that it is believed that he must have once been real, although whether of the First Race is not known. Come to think of it, he is always said to be a Glathrielian! Indeed, there are so many stories and legends about him that it is not totally certain if he is a real character, a composite, or a part of our extensive mythology. That is hotly debated. But there are ancient battle sites and legends in many hexes, including some that are very alien to Glathriel and very far from it, that have their own stories."

"Uh huh. And his name?"

"It varies, but there is one that is most common. It is, and pardon the translator limitations, um, let's see—yes, that's it. Brazil. Nathan Brazil."

Nathan Brazil. Mavra remembered him now. She remembered a *lot* about Nathan Brazil.

"Is there any consistency to what he looked like?"

"I'm afraid not, and any records of him that might have contained such information are apparently lost. Besides, what sort of consistency might you expect from all those races, most of whom could not tell one of you from the other?"

"Point taken. Any other specific names and people in those legends?"

"Many. I am not too proficient in such things myself; the Kwynn were apparently not involved in that, and our sagas are different."

"No Glathrielian woman hero?"

"I do not recall one, although there may be. Why?"

"Just wondering." Mavra in fact felt some vague disappointment at the news that she wasn't even a footnote. Somehow it was a little insulting, all things considered.

Still, what was irritating to her ego might actually be an asset. It would be a lot harder to move around here if one were a world-class legend who could open the Well. Others would get ideas.

Still, she vowed that *this* time they would not forget her!

"I believe," said the ambassador calmly, "that it is time to process you through. This has been a *very* busy day."

"Two favors, if I might," Mavra responded quickly. "First, are pictures of the earlier arrivals available so that we may see if there is anyone we know in them? And second, may I use your translating device to speak to the others here briefly? We have no practical common tongue, I'm afraid."

Lori, astounded at the modern bearing and sophistication in Mavra's conversation, couldn't suppress a smile. In the tongue of the People she said, "I know you cannot explain this in the tongue."

Unexpectedly, the translator issued only an echo of exactly what she had spoken, untranslated, although it clearly caught the conversation. Even the ambassador was surprised. "I've never seen one of these do *that* before," he commented worriedly.

Mavra, too, was surprised and responded, "It knows not the magic of the People."

Again, the words were echoed unchanged.

Mavra gestured toward the ambassador. "Remember," she told Lori. "It might be very good to have a tongue that cannot be known here." Lori nodded, thinking much the same thing.

The ambassador sighed. "Well, stop doing that! It's annoying! Let's see . . . What was it you wanted? Oh, yes. Pictures of the arrivals. Of course, they do not look like this *now*."

He punched some buttons on the console, and a wall screen showed three people in the very same conference room they were using. A twist of a dial focused entirely on one and blew it up to full screen. It showed a very handsome man of clear Latin American ancestry, his hair in the process of going gray, dressed in casual but clearly expensive clothes.

"That's all right. Just one at a time, thank you," Mavra said.

Another twist, and the picture showed a woman, very frail although by no means old, with short hair in a prim bun and thick horn-rimmed glasses. She was in a wheelchair.

Another twist, and a third man came into view, dressed more casually than the other but still quite well. He was a small man, not merely short but thin and wiry, with a large nose and deep-set eyes that seemed almost black and neatly trimmed black hair. He was clean-shaven, but Mavra recognized him in an instant and a clear memory of his face, his voice, his personality filled in inside her mind. There was no question, no doubt about it.

Nathan Brazil had returned to the Well World before her.

"You say it has been a fairly long time since they came through," she noted. "Has he returned to South Zone at all since arriving?"

"I couldn't say. Those records would not be here, if any records of such a visit were actually kept at all. He'd be dealing with his hex ambassador in any event."

"But does it say what they became? The man and the woman in particular?"

"Well, that would be appended here for informational purposes *if* the race has an embassy here and *if* the ambassador bothered to register them. Let me check. Ah, yes. Two of them, anyway. The first man went to Zumerbald, the woman to Dillia, and the third—well, there's no record on him, although that means little, as I said."

I know where he went, she thought, *and I know just what he looks like.*

The picture changed, and two other men came up on the screen, neither familiar.

"This is the colonel and the captain?"

"Yes, if you prefer." A close-up of the older man, the colonel, showed a gruff middle-aged man with gray hair and dark complexion but with distinctly Germanic rather than Brazilian features—not uncommon in Brazil, although Mavra would not know that. The close-up of the other showed a much younger and quite handsome man with thick brown hair and a medium complexion which suggested he hadn't been in the tropics very long. His uniform was khaki-colored and had nothing on it but a name tag and captain's bars on the shoulders.

"The older man went to Nanzistu," the ambassador told her, "and the younger went to—odd, it's not there, but I could have sworn somebody or other said he went to Erdom. Well, they don't keep a permanent ambassador here, and they're a tribal people, so perhaps they didn't do much updating. But that's the lot."

"He looks familiar somehow," Lori said, looking at the

handsome man. "I wonder if I met him somewhere. I wouldn't forget a face and body like *that*. It's an American uniform."

"Well, perhaps you will remember; it might be useful," Mavra replied, then turned to the ambassador. "And one other favor," she reminded him.

"Eh? What?"

"Your translator. I would like to speak directly to my companions for a moment. A few minutes, no more."

"Well, you can do that now, can't you?"

"It would be easier if I didn't have to shout. May I just borrow it for a moment and place it right here? Where are we going to go?"

"Oh, very well." He lifted it from around his neck, and she went and took it from him. "Be careful with it, though!"

She took it over and knelt beside Gus. "Gus, can you hear me?"

"Um . . . Huh? Yeah. Been listenin' to this bullshit. Still hung over from them drugs, though. I'd swear that guy over there was a giant pink talking dinosaur."

"You're not hung over, and he's more or less exactly that," Lori assured him. "Look, Gus, you heard it. Whether you believe it or not, they're going to force us through, and who knows where or even *what* we'll be if he's telling the truth?"

"Believe it, Gus," Mavra said firmly. "But that's not the point right now. The point is what happens *after*. I'm going to tell you all right now that I will not change. I am already registered here. I'm going to Ambreza, the old Glathriel, and so did that small fellow up there. You heard my questions about the legends?"

Lori frowned. "Yes, but I don't see—"

"You don't have to. That man is Nathan Brazil. The one in the legends. The man who can work the computer that runs not only this place but *every* place. Sooner or later that is going to get out. Sooner if I have anything to do with it.

And although I doubt he's even started yet, sooner or later he's going to head north, to the equator, and go inside. When he does, he is going to become like one of the ancient people that built this place. He'll go down into the guts of this world, check it out, then he'll do a reset."

"A *what*?" Juan Campos and Lori almost said together.

"A reset. It won't affect this world, but it will affect Earth. Drastically. Time, space, everything will be changed. They had few rules, those ancient people. In the end he'll bring Earth and the other inhabited planets back up to speed, to where, in our case, true humans develop. But everybody now alive on Earth, and everybody who's lived up to that point, will be destroyed first. It will all start out from scratch. I—I *think* that they'll all be stored here in the memory banks of the Well World. But all of it, everything and everyone you ever knew, will be gone."

Lori shook her head in wonder. "I'm still having trouble with *this* place. I can't really handle *that.*"

"Yes, how do you know this to be true?" Juan Campos added.

"I was there the last time he did it. I—helped. It was necessary, I swear. It was do that or the entire universe would die forever, even this place. But when we started it back up, nothing was made better. Everything developed exactly as it had before. All the suffering, the misery, the evil. I don't know if this crisis is as serious as that one. I don't think it is. Lori, you trusted me enough to come this far, and I wasn't lying, was I? Trust me on this one, too. I want to stop him this time. I want to see if it's necessary to destroy the universe and reset it when a few minor repairs and adjustments will suffice. Maybe this time I can save everybody and make things a little better. I can do that, but only if I beat him inside, to the master control."

"What are you?" Lori asked her. "One of those creatures like him?"

"No. I was born on a distant planet so long ago, it doesn't

matter. I was a product of the *last* creation, or re-creation, maybe. There is a certain bond between us, and I helped him then. He repaid the kindness by making me more like himself, registering me with the master control and making me virtually immortal. That is why a gate was sent for each of us. Never mind—time is short, I'm afraid, and they like this to go very fast once you're briefed. The plain fact is, I have to beat him there."

"He's got one hell of a head start," Juan Campos noted.

"Not necessarily. You don't know him like I do. He will do anything to put it off, but he finally will be forced to do it. The Well will see to that. Right now he's probably enjoying himself, finding out what's new and what's old here, and trying to think of a thousand reasons why he should not go. At some point he will also try to at least make contact with his companions. That is in his nature, and I know in any event that he has a special fondness for Dillians. It is a very long and very dangerous journey from Glathriel, not far north of Zone, to the equator."

"But you said he couldn't be killed!" Lori pointed out.

"He can't, and neither can I, but almost everything else bad *can* happen to us. This is unlike anyplace else. It is like crossing dozens of little alien worlds, each a few hundred kilometers across. Many are friendly, but others are hostile to all outsiders, and even the weather and climate change. Some of the places, and races, have great power and can be downright ugly. It is almost a cosmic joke that we both start far away in Glathriel. Almost as if, perhaps unconsciously, he *wanted* it to be as hard as possible. And whichever of us gets there first will have great power—and great discretion. I don't know if I can beat him there, but if I waste little time and get to it, I might. *He* won't go alone, and if any of the natives here pick up on who he is, they will try and insure that they are there, too. I cannot beat him alone. That is why we are having this conference. I need your help. I won't do much selling. Come to save your family, friends, and world. Come to gain what rewards I can shower on you if I win. Come for the most unique adventure of your lives. But I need friends and allies."

"But what can we do?" Lori asked her. "We don't even know where or, if I can believe it, *what* we'll be!"

"No, you don't. But any hex gate—and there is one in each hex—will bring you back here. Leave a message telling me where you are. I will find you. Do *not* try and find me. I will have to avoid Brazil, and you will not be prepared for such a journey. But I need to know where and what you are. If you cannot do it yourself, send word. I will find you. I have already had the worst done to me on this world, and I am better suited for it. Understand?"

"Yes, I think so," Lori answered, and Juan Campos nodded thoughtfully. *If she can work this thing, then she has access to all that power . . .*

"Gus?"

"Yeah, sure. Do they have cameras here? And news?"

"Some hexes do, of various kinds. Some do not. Depends on where you are. It even depends on where you are whether any sort of camera will work. As to news, that, too, varies. You will find something, Gus. The Well is random but not *completely* random. The important thing is that you will be hale, hearty, healthy, and ready to go no matter *what* you are, and soon."

"You can count on me," Juan Campos told her, and Lori looked over at him and frowned.

"I'll come," she said, "if only to make sure you don't get to like this slime ball before you get to know him."

Campos looked pained.

"I don't believe a word of this, so why the hell not?" Gus told her.

Mavra smiled. "Good. You get that word to me, and I will get to you. Do it as soon as you can. I cannot wait in Ambreza for long, and I certainly will not want to return here again once I have set out. I will give you—let's see—a month. Four weeks. That will give you enough time and will allow me to find out what I need to know and secure what I will require for the journey. Four weeks."

There was a sudden loud series of grunts and roars from across the room. The translator said faintly, "That's enough! Let's go!"

"Good luck to you all," Mavra told them, and hugged Lori. Then she picked the translator up and returned it to the Kwynn.

"I thought you were saying good-bye, not giving speeches," he harrumphed. "All right, everyone! Outside that door and to your right!"

Lori bent down to pick up Gus, but he said, "I might make it. Help me to my feet."

She did, worried about his long captivity in bonds and his weak condition, and sure enough, he collapsed. She reached down and picked him up gently.

"Damn! This is *embarrassing*!" Gus muttered.

They followed the ambassador down another long series of corridors, past rooms with strange-shaped entrances that contained a variety of horrific or mythical creatures and even worse smells and noises. Mavra could see Campos looking for a way out. Finally they reached the end of a dead-end corridor, and in front of them was a black hexagon as dark and nonreflective as the one atop the meteor.

"I still don't see how this is possible," Lori muttered aloud.

"Matter to energy conversion," the ambassador replied. "And energy to matter. Quite simple in principle, although of course none of us know how to do it. Who is first?"

"Ah, hell," Gus said with some disgust. "Does she have to carry me into that thing?"

"While there's nothing specific against it, it's not traditional to send two through at once," the Kwynn replied. "However, it is not exactly a transit point. You could literally be *thrown* in and it would not matter. You would still feel as if you'd fallen asleep, so they tell me, and then awaken on the ground wherever you are assigned."

"Well, if somebody'll stand me up and give me a little push, I'll go," Gus told them.

Mavra went over and helped Lori, and together they got the man, taller than Lori by almost a head and taller than Mavra by head *and* shoulders, on his wobbly feet. Then, together, they gave him a push forward, and he managed a step into the blackness, pitched forward, and was gone.

Lori stood there looking nervously at the gate. "I really don't know," she sighed. "I never much liked the sight of myself in a mirror, but there's a lot worse things to be than me. Now's a hell of a time to find that out, though, isn't it?" She took a deep breath. "Well, here goes nothing." And with that, she leapt into the blackness.

Mavra looked at Campos, who bowed slightly and made a gesture that could only mean either "ladies first" or "after you." She shrugged, smiled at him, and jumped in.

"Now you, sir," the ambassador told him. "Go ahead."

"I think I want to consider this a little more carefully," Juan Campos replied. "Like a day or two. Maybe next year?"

The ambassador sighed and turned as if to lead the way back, and his huge tail came around, struck Campos a hard blow, and flung him into the blackness.

"Thank goodness for *that!*" sighed the ambassador, and began the walk back to his offices.

It had taken Terry some time to catch up with the others. She made several false turns, and though she had barely avoided some terrifying creatures, the place had been pretty deserted. She'd finally found them just as they were being led away by a pink dragon.

Hearing nothing of the briefing and knowing nothing of where they were, she made the instant assumption that her companions had been captured by the creature. She followed at a distance, hoping at least to see where they would be taken. Maybe, just maybe, she could get them out.

They went through a winding maze of corridors with so many twists and turns that she was not sure if she could find her way back. *One problem at a time,* she told herself.

She found that the last corridor ended in another of those black hexes. It figured, somehow. They were being sent someplace else. There was nothing to do but follow, she thought, but at least she had not been captured, and that might still come in handy.

From the corridor's far corner she watched them disappear into the hex, too far away to distinguish what they were saying. She suppressed a giggle when she saw Campos being knocked in, though. When Campos, too, had gone, she backed off, found an empty room, and hid there until the pink dragon returned back up another corridor.

She wasn't sure what was going on, where she was, or what lay on the other side of that black hex, but if Gus and Lori and Alama were there, then she had to follow before she got caught as well. It was sure better than staying here with those creepy monsters.

Allowing a good fifteen or twenty minutes to pass, hoping that whoever or whatever waiting on the other side of the black hex would be gone, she got up and made her way down the dead-end corridor where her companions had disappeared.

She was tempted to sleep first—she felt unimaginably tired as well as hungry and thirsty—but she knew she couldn't let the trail grow too cold, and while sleep might be possible, she couldn't chance discovery by any of the weird creatures she had glimpsed earlier.

Summoning up her last bit of willpower, she stepped into the blackness.

AMBREZA

She sensed the wrongness long before she came to full consciousness, a sense that something was missing or had been taken away. And yet she knew who she was. All the "pictures" were there in her mind: her mother, her father, friends and acquaintances, going to school, working, all that.

But she couldn't *articulate* those mental snapshots or put labels on them. It was as if she had words, even in her mind, only for the things that could be expressed in the language of the People. No, not even that. It was even more primitive, more basic.

Even that thought had no words to it but was rather an assemblage of mental pictures and feelings. She was aware that her thought process was far different from what it had been before, as if all the rules for gathering, organizing, and interpreting information had been suddenly and radically changed. It was as bizarre and alien a way to think as anything she might have imagined, and it seemed slower and harder to assemble thoughts or ideas and, once assembled, impossible to express them. All of her old languages had gone from her mind; they just weren't there anymore. Not even the People's. She could call up a memory or scene in her mind and remember the gist of what was said, but could not recall saying it.

There *was* a language there, but it was a strange one, composed of a series of images and concepts that seemed to form as if by magic in her mind, conveying real messages, real thoughts and decisions, but with no words.

To even be able to think such complex concepts using such a method was amazing to her, but to be unable to express even the slightest sense of them was frustrating and likely to become more frustrating as time went on. And it was *hard* to think; she had to concentrate.

What was happening to her?

She sat up, opened her eyes, and looked down at herself and was shocked at what she saw—or, more accurately, what she *didn't* see.

Her body, in fact, looked perfectly normal, but the cemented bones in both her nose and her ears were gone. It felt odd not to have them there after so long, but also it was something of a relief. The tattoos, too, were gone, and her body didn't look all that different to her than it had before the People had done their stuff. Well, that wasn't *exactly* true. Her skin seemed, well, smoother and younger, and the scars were gone—even the appendix scar—and she seemed, well, maybe a little chubby, like she'd been when she was in her early teens. And she had long hair again, the same stringy jet black hair she'd always had, but it was down well below her shoulders, almost to her ass, and it seemed to have a slick, slightly wet feel to it although no residue came off on her hands. She knew that hair didn't grow *that* fast; either she'd been unconscious a long time or something beyond her understanding had happened to her.

In fact, in spite of those differences, she felt *great.* She couldn't remember when she'd felt this good, in top condition, no aches or pains or *anything.* She felt like a kid again, although her fair-sized but firm breasts and the rest of her body assured her that she wasn't. If her mind were just working right, if she just had her language skills back, if it just weren't so hard to think complicated thoughts, she would have felt vast relief.

She sprang to her feet and looked warily around. The weight and swing of the hair felt very odd; she'd never had it this long before. Still, it was the least of her problems, and for some reason it felt *right* for the hair to be there.

She was in a stand of trees, but it was no jungle or rain forest; rather, it was almost parklike. The trees were not *quite* familiar but were far less strange than the ones of the Amazon. She felt thirsty and a little hungry, which was natural, but she also suddenly felt a sense of danger and tension, of being too exposed. All her brooding, her attempts to think complex thoughts and sort things out, suddenly vanished, replaced by something else, something that required no thought, no deliberation, but seemed in retrospect almost instinctual.

Almost before she knew it, she was climbing up a very tall tree that rationality would have said could not have been climbed. It was tall and had a long regular trunk with few opportunities for handholds or footholds, yet she went up it as if it were a stairway. Before she knew it, she was perched on a heavy limb seven or more meters above the ground below. The uncertain perch, the sheer drop, the smoothness of the trunk going back down did not bother her at all. Her sense of balance was absolutely perfect, and she didn't think the situation odd at all.

The upper parts of the tree bore a bananalike fruit; she walked over to a nearby bunch, picked one of them off, and began eating it, skin, stem, and all, all without conscious thought. The fruit had a banana's consistency but was green and brown on the outside and a bright orange color inside. It was moist and sweet and went down so well, she picked another. Somehow she just *knew* which ones were ripe and which ones to leave alone.

She did, however, shrug off the immediate feeling of contentment a full belly gave her, because the sense of tension and danger still remained. Before she could relax, something impelled her to assess her location and the lay of the land. She climbed farther up, to where she could see out in all directions with little effort.

The immediate area was a sort of park with well-manicured trees and grassy areas filled with both sun and shade. The land beyond seemed to be gently rolling, with a number of rivers or streams and a road that came from off the horizon, made its way lazily around various stands of tilled and grooved farmland and across small bridges of stone or wood, and continued off to her right through more of the same sort of country. There was something odd about where the road vanished from sight; just before the horizon there was a sort of shimmering, like heat distortion but extending along the horizon as far as she could see. But the shimmering was too steady and regular for it to be caused by rising heat—it seemed substantial, almost solid, and an image of a giant window came into her mind.

To her left a side road seemed to wander up to a huge, elaborate building with many more outbuildings beyond. The mind-picture that most matched was of a farm, but that was mostly because of the surrounding fields and the layout of the buildings; neither the house nor the outbuildings looked like anything she'd seen before. It was a picturesque, almost idyllic scene nonetheless, and she knew it; why, then, did she have such a strong emotional reaction to it, bordering not on fear but on repulsion? Had she been in the jungle so long that what once would have seemed a pleasant, peaceful, even charming scene now looked and felt so wrong? By contrast, that shimmering skyline in the opposite direction felt equally *right;* it had an emotional attraction she could feel, as if it were a magnet softly pulling at her.

Recent events had been so strange and had moved so fast of late that she felt frightened and confused by almost everything. She tried to put her thoughts in order and found that she couldn't. Putting the memory pictures together in some sort of context was hard. Worse, her experiences with the People felt more real, more understandable to her than anything she had experienced before. When she tried to recall her past life, all she got was confusion and conflicting feelings. It was all there, but it just wasn't much use. And if she couldn't think clearly and figure out what was happening to her, what was she going to do?

She went back down the tree partway until she found a thick branch that forked into two only slightly thinner ones. With a little shifting, she discovered it made a pretty solid and secure seat, shielded from the ground by branches. She was so *tired*; perhaps sleep would help. It never even occurred to her that even her second incarnation among the People would never have considered this sort of perch either safe or secure. She was too tired to mentally fight herself right now. It was best to clear the mind, relax, and sleep it off. Perhaps it would let her think more clearly.

Settling back, eyes closed, as relaxed as she could be, she felt a concept come to her by a process that was completely unfamiliar. It was hard not to have the words to use. It went against her entire cultural upbringing. Even the People were as linguistically sophisticated as they needed to be. This was completely different.

Words can obscure as well as clarify. With this way, there was never an error in understanding, if what she was trying to comprehend was understandable at all.

Was that it? Was there something she was missing here?

Was it better not to think, too? She was here, hunger quelled and safe, because of unthinking action.

No. That would make me nothing more than an animal.

Then what?

Just as you speak when you need *to speak, think when you* need *to think. Know when to speak and when not to. Know when to think and when not to.*

But didn't she always need to think?

Learn to let go. Do not fight impulses, let it go. It is when nothing comes that thinking is required. Learn to trust yourself.

Her impulse just then was to go to sleep. She did not fight it.

It was almost dark when she awoke, but rather than feeling nervous about the setting sun, she felt less afraid, more confident. It was already becoming easier for her to not impose her own old mind-set on this weird situation and to embrace this new and different inner way of thought. It was as if thoughts and decisions were debated and assembled far away in her mind, out of consciousness, then the entire set of possibilities was almost magically laid before her as a series of picture-objects.

This place was not where she was supposed to be or she wouldn't feel its wrongness. The direction toward the odd farm buildings felt even more wrong; so it was toward that shimmering wall that she must go, for only that way felt right. There was also a feeling of undefined danger in this area, so the quicker she got out of it, the better.

First she surveyed the area once again. There was an odd noise from the direction of the farm, and what she saw in the rapidly waning light made her gasp and brought on an intense feeling of danger and irrational distaste that was like nothing she had ever experienced.

Two creatures were in some sort of vehicle that was making a whining noise. It seemed to sway from side to side as it turned into the small road up to the farm. The vehicle was basically an open cabin mounted to a thick oval slab, but while it bounced along, it seemed to be hovering an elbow's length above the road, with nothing touching the road itself. It was the sight of the two creatures that caused her overpowering sense of dislike.

They looked like two giant beavers, each the size of a man; one was dressed in some sort of waistcoat, and the other wore a flowered bib and a silly-looking hat with a big flower sticking out of it.

The hovercar pulled up finally in front of the house and settled to the ground, its whine now cut off. The driver with the waistcoat got out, stretched, and walked around to open the door for its companion with the hat.

Standing and walking, they looked less like beavers than like something entirely new. It was just the rodentlike head and prominent buckteeth that gave the initial impression. They were covered with thick brown hair, they walked upright on thick bowed legs extending from wide hips, and they were like nothing human.

She wanted to meet them even less than she had wanted to meet that purple polka-dotted dragon. Just as curious was her nearly instant reaction to the vehicle, the bright clothing the creatures wore, even the buildings. Somehow all of them were *wrong*. This was far more than the aversion the People had to things they did not make themselves; it was more general, as if anything artificial or manufactured by *anyone* was wrong. She did not even wish she had some sort of weapon; that would be wrong as well.

It was time to eat and run.

It was getting easier all the time to process information and think in this new way, which didn't *seem* like thinking at all but was in fact as complex a method of reasoning as the one she'd been raised on. The trick *wasn't* not to think, after all; it was not to fight doing things in your head in a whole new way.

She came down the tree almost as easily as she'd gone up it, jumping the last couple of meters and landing expertly on her feet. For someone who had no idea where she was, her sense of direction seemed absolute. She headed toward the edge of the trees, paused to take stock of all her wide-open senses, and, perceiving nothing nearby, darted out into the open and across the road to the rows of thick bushes beyond. The bushes bore some large pear-shaped, cream-colored fruits, but she never gave them a second glance.

Something, more of that new inner knowledge, told her that none of the strange-looking fruits were ripe and ready to eat yet.

She began to make her way through the groves at a steady pace, pausing only now and again to check the smells, sounds, and other bits of information that the gentle breeze might bring. Darkness was falling quickly now, yet she proceeded on, drawn by some inner road map of the region. She had no idea where she was or where she was going, but somehow she knew how to get there.

Finally she came to a shallow stream that burbled over a bed of rocks. She paused, crouched, and took some water in her cupped hands and sniffed it. It smelled right, so she drank deeply, discovering a fierce but previously suppressed thirst. After she drank, she relaxed for the first time since leaving her tree, and, seeing very little around in the darkness, she looked up—and gasped.

There were countless stars up there, in some places so thick that they seemed to be a single burning mass, and parts of the sky were bathed in clouds of gold and magenta and deep royal purple, all seemingly frozen in midswirl. There were more stars than she'd ever seen before, and features out of deep space astronomical photographs right there, sitting in the night sky.

She did not have to gaze but an instant upon the incredible beauty of that vast fairyland starfield to know that there was nowhere on Earth from which it might be seen. The sight and that knowledge fell upon her instantly, generating a sense of awe, excitement, and some fear.

Alama had not lied. This was another world, far, far away from the one she had known.

And still there was that inner urge to press on, to proceed as quickly as possible to wherever it was that was calling her. Tearing her eyes away from the spectral scene, she waded across the creek and went on through the brush on the other side.

Even pushing her pace as much as she dared, it took

hours to reach that shimmering boundary glimpsed much earlier from the top of the tree. It wasn't easy to see even in the bright starlight, but she could sense it, almost feel it. And yet it *could* be seen, for on this side of the barrier things had a brighter, more orderly look, while beyond it things seemed much darker. She had no sense of it as something dangerous or even unusual, but it *was* unique in her experience, and she could not be absolutely certain that it was safe.

She approached it cautiously, then stood right up to it, finally putting out a hand to touch it. It radiated warmth and a sense of thicker air, and after hesitating a moment, she thrust her right hand into it.

It passed through with no resistance, but the feeling on the other side was quite different. Hot and wet were the two impressions that came to mind, and the sense of something striking and tickling her caused her to withdraw the hand. It seemed all right, and when she touched it, the hand was wet; what she'd felt were raindrops.

Her new self did not react, but her old self caught the immediate sense of incongruity. She looked up—and, to the very boundary itself, the starfield shone in a cloudless sky. Rain? From where?

Taking in a deep breath, she walked straight through the barrier—feeling a change in environment but no resistance—and into a pitch-dark land of steady, gentle warm rain. The temperature was considerably warmer than it had been on the other side, almost steamy and very reminiscent of the Amazon jungle. The rain, however, was more subdued, which was actually a welcome change from what she'd been used to.

She turned and stuck her head back through the "barrier." Although it hadn't seemed cold to her, the shock of suddenly going, wet-faced, from a steam bath to a spring night made it feel almost frigid. It was fascinating, as if the whole world were one huge house and each "room" in the place had its own weather and climate.

She withdrew her head. It felt somehow better to be over here, even with the extreme darkness and the rain. She wasn't certain if this was because of her newfound instincts or because this region was more like the northwest Amazon, but it felt more like, well, *home.*

She walked away from the boundary slowly and carefully, almost tripping on wild, junglelike vegetation, until the soft glow coming through from the other side of the barrier was no longer visible. Suppressing as much as possible her feelings of disorientation and fear, she tried to empty her mind, relax, and let that new set of senses take over.

And slowly, strangely, she began to see her surroundings in a way she'd never seen anything before.

Ancient trees rose all around her; she saw them as a throbbing, pulsing reddish color, the leaves almost black in the inky darkness. Variations of the same red color also appeared in the bushes, other plants, even mosses, everything alive that was organic, all glowing with the energy of life.

Other spots glowed yellow and purple and orange. Smaller things mostly, but brighter, often moving either in or on the vegetation or occasionally on the ground or even in the air. The yellows were some form of reptile, perhaps many forms; the purples were small warm-blooded creatures; and the oranges were flitting insects of the night.

The ground seemed mostly to remain black close by, but not too far off it seemed to shimmer as if something transparent and yet also reflective were on top of it, distorting the colors or auras that she saw clearly above it.

Water, she realized. Mostly standing water, except for the effect of the raindrops. The vegetation was dense, but it was no jungle, and there were openings among the trees that were not overgrown. Neither was it any sort of farm or orchard as on the other side; it was random, natural . . . *as it should be.* It was, she realized, some sort of vast swamp.

Curious, she closed her eyes for a moment and found that the scene was still there. She moved a little, cautiously, keeping to the "black" areas, and saw that the scene moved with her, changing point of view as if all this were the same as the vision her eyes brought.

But she was not seeing with her eyes; rather, she was somehow seeing the essence of life in the wild and its reflections in her mind.

She began to walk slowly but confidently, using the black areas as her guide. Some points were quite small, but overall they seemed to almost form a network of paths through the wilderness, paths taking her through great beauty in a direction that seemed to draw her.

Navigating by this new second sight also became easier the longer she did it. While it hardly gave full circular vision, it was far superior in some ways to normal sight because it covered a wider area. Several times she was aware of large creatures she took to be snakes of some kind lurking high in the trees; when they watched her, they burned exceptionally bright, and she avoided them. The water was mostly just the reflective sort, but occasionally it, too, would have brightly glowing forms in it. Most of these had pale greenish tinges—fish, perhaps? That was what came to mind. Here and there would be large orange masses, sometimes in the water, sometimes out, and these, too, she quietly avoided while always looking for an unoccupied nearby tree just in case those orange shapes became a bit too interested in her. Once or twice one seemed to do just that, but none of them ever really approached her with any speed, and she never felt in real danger from them.

It was also getting easier to isolate sounds and smells and associate colors with them. As the night wore on and her journey continued, these supplemental senses and her discriminatory abilities concerning them increased greatly, the data fed and either filed or rejected automatically as it rushed in.

Crocodiles to the left, thirty feet, floating lazily . . . Two big snakes above and to the right, neither hungry . . . Colony of strange birds roosting in the tree to the left . . .

At a junction of "paths" she stopped suddenly, catching an odd scent from the ground. She realized suddenly that it was fecal matter of the sort whose smell would have repulsed her even days earlier. Now it was just information. It wasn't all that fresh, but the odor put a picture in her mind that excited her.

People!

Was it just a random dropping, or did it also have another purpose? A territory marker, perhaps, like animals used? Or an indicator of a trail to follow? But if the latter, which direction did it mark to go? Surely, if it *was* some sort of message as well as a simple call of nature, it meant to go up the path it was on. Having no other road signs to guide her, she went up that path.

There were more at other junctions, each having a different scent. That meant that these *were* trail markers, laid out by intelligence, not mere territorial boundaries that would involve the same few people—or so she hoped. Such a system, however primitive or however revolting it might have seemed to "civilized" people, made a lot of sense. Only those who *could* sense and figure them out would understand their meaning.

Was this something new, a function of this strange place, or were things like her new mind-sight and such finely honed senses of smell and hearing something all people had once possessed but had somehow lost? The latter seemed more likely; she, after all, was using them, and that meant that they were a natural part of her, perhaps sealed off in that unused part of the brain. Were those untapped parts of the human brain really unused excess capacity, or were they vestigial remains of senses civilization had made unnecessary?

What other powers might these people possess, these people who were clearly up ahead, clearly at the place where she felt driven to go?

There was only one good way to find out.

The Ambrezan came out on the porch and said, "We have just had a report from the capital that a second party has come through the Well."

Nathan Brazil took his feet down from the porch railing, slowed his idle rocking in the chair, and took the cigar out of his mouth. "All Glathrielians?" he asked.

"It seems so. Two males and two females in a single party, and then a third female later, who, it is said, evaded the alarms and security measures and went through without detection."

Brazil stopped rocking and stood up. "That's probably the one. No word from anywhere else that a Glathrielian female like myself came through here unaltered?"

"None, although it's a big place. If she didn't want to be found, it is entirely possible that she's made some sort of deal. Not everyone might advertise as blatantly as you, you know."

Nathan Brazil grinned. "You're just trying to get rid of me. I make you uncomfortable."

"No, not at all—"

"Oh, come on, Hsada! A civilized, talking, technologically sophisticated Glathrielian must awaken ancestral nightmares."

The Ambrezan stared at the little man with its big brown eyes outlined by a slight frown. "I never know when you are joking."

Brazil chuckled. "Don't worry about it. As soon as I can link up with her, I'm out of here. Promise. I have friends that are a very long way from here that I promised I'd see, and I already feel guilty I haven't done it yet."

The truth was, he didn't really *want* to see either Tony or Anne Marie, even though he wouldn't mind a trip up that way. He really didn't want the burden of getting the two of them together as they were now. Deep down, he was hoping that each, being now healthy and hearty, and both, to his relief, in rather comfortable hexes, would use these months to settle in and build new lives and new attachments. It wasn't as if he'd forced either or both into coming, after all, or as if they wouldn't be dead by now if they hadn't chosen to come through, but if ever a match of love and devotion had been made in heaven before, he hadn't seen it in all his long life. He *could,* of course, fix them up if he went up to the Well, but he didn't really want to do that just yet. He felt no sense of urgency, and he wanted to stay here a while and enjoy the difference.

The Ambreza had not initially been all that thrilled at his appearance, and he knew it—they hadn't reacted much differently the last time or two, either. But they were civilized in the extreme, suckers for a good story, and, well, he'd been *useful* to them, working for a few months helping them redesign rather than merely repair and upgrade their failing irrigation system, saving them a lot of investment and foreign involvement. Now he had clothes specially made to his design, some local money, and chits for a decent supply of the prime Ambrezan export, tobacco, with which to make his way anywhere he wanted to go. He lacked only Mavra, and he very much wanted to find her, see her, have things *explained* to him. It would be like old times, and *this* time he'd teach her the full operational details of the Well—as soon as he got there and could remember them again—so he might not ever have to carry this burden again.

He knew that last was selfish, but damn it, it was hard to be all that sentimental toward somebody he could hardly remember and last saw maybe twenty-five hundred years ago.

Maybe now it was time for a reunion.

He walked into the house and back to the communications room. The Ambreza had quite a sophisticated setup, able to call just about anywhere they had people in what was now Ambreza, the high-tech hex that very long ago had been the common ancestral home of the Terran races.

The furniture in an Ambrezan house was *not* made for his anatomy, but he could make do. He sat at the console and dialed in the communications ministry in the capital city of Khor.

"Oh, Solomon—yes. The group that came through. We had the ambassador run a systems check for placements, but it was inconclusive. However, we are certain that the last one, the female who didn't clear entry, came to Gla-thriel. We registered a surge in section—um—B-14. Yes. Agricultural district up north not far from the border with Glathriel, which is where you'd expect a deposit, matching *exactly* the time of Zone entry. It's always easier to track an individual than a group, although this is hardly an everyday thing. In fact, counting you, I can remember no other but this one even in the records."

"All right. But she made no contact with the locals?"

"Not that we can determine. A search of the area using the local manager's dogs indicated that she went south into Glathriel. Beyond that we can't say, since it's too much of a mess in that district to do decent tracking, and frankly, it's far too much trouble for something that is your business, not ours. As long as she's gone to Glathriel, she's not our problem."

He frowned. "Gone to Glathriel . . . Well, I suppose that if she didn't want a lot of immediate attention, she might head for the coast strip there. I don't suppose that there's any word from them."

The technician was not terribly patient with this imposi-tion. "Look, Glathriel is a nontech hex. No communication works except the direct kind, and no vehicles work except animal power. The people along there are mostly a religious sect that's antiprogress, and we and they don't talk much to one another except when they come south twice a year to sell their crops. It might be weeks, even *months* before we hear any news from them. I admit that a talking, civilized, and sophisticated Glathrielian might cause quite a stir, even some sort of religious crisis among them, but it's still not something we'd hear anytime soon."

Brazil scratched his chin and thought about it. "I don't know. If she's heading toward them, it'll almost certainly be ones near the border. I suspect we'd hear pretty fast for those very same reasons." He sighed. "Okay, that's all you can do now. I'll take it from here. Thank you very much."

"Very well. Out," the comm tech responded curtly, and switched off.

Nathan Brazil sat there a moment trying to decide what to do. Finally he got up and went over to a far wall where a map of Ambreza and part of Glathriel was tacked to a cork board.

B-14 . . . There it was. Not that far from the Ambrezan strip in Glathriel. A country road was marked as heading through the district toward that point, so that was the logical place to start. It looked to be maybe three, four hours drive if he could bum one or a day on horseback if he couldn't. It was certainly worth getting off his duff and going after her. He had no doubt that it was Mavra Chang; it was inconceivable to him that any of the new entries would wind up Glathrielians. He'd pretty much seen to that long ago.

He turned and saw Hsada standing there looking sternly at him from the doorway.

"No, you cannot borrow the car," the Ambrezan told him flatly. "You will be going into Glathriel, and I would have to send somebody down there and lose a day getting it back. However, delivery trucks go through town all the time, and some may have stops at or near there. I *will* get someone to drive you in, and from there you can make your own arrangements."

Brazil grinned and shrugged. "Good enough. What can I say?"

"Say good-bye," responded Hsada. "And don't forget to

settle your rent through today before you leave."

It turned out that settling the rent was more of a problem than finding a ride to near the border. Hsada was a very hard bargainer and was more creative in finding extra charges to spring on him than anybody since that lowland Scotswoman at a bed and breakfast about a hundred years ago. Extra sheet charge, indeed.

There were only five cities plus the capital worth the name in Ambreza, and maybe forty small towns spread all over, but the two basic occupations of those in the country were raising crops for export and truck farming. Over the centuries truck farming had become quite sophisticated, with regular routes and a whole guild of middlemen doing the shipping to and from the markets on a daily basis. Tobacco was grown best in the southeast; the southwest was better suited to longer-growing but high-demand produce like subtropical fruits due not to location but to a strong warm current off the Gulf of Zinjin that came in very close to shore and created a more or less subtropical pocket. This, of course, had been allowed by those who had created the hex; weather and climate were not of the natural sort on *this* world, but when they saw that the water hex of Flotish had such currents designed in, they simply made use of them.

By that evening he was within a few kilometers of the plantation nearest the designated spot, and he stayed over with some very surprised and curious farm supervisors that night so he'd have the full next day for the quest. While the field bosses were somewhat taken aback at a glib Glathrielian wearing clothes and speaking like them, they were suckers for a good set of stories and even worse suckers at cards and dice.

The next morning he saw the first Glathrielians he'd seen since—well, a *very* long time ago. He had forgotten their rather exotic "look," a unique yet homogenized blend of just about every racial type on Earth. Being of a near uniformly brown skin, with a variety of Oriental features yet with brown, black, and reddish hair was only the beginning of it. One could look at anyone and see suggestions of somebody one thought was familiar, yet the entire amalgam was something totally unique.

This time, though, they also seemed decidedly, well, *odd*. There was no other way to explain it. True, their tropical hex didn't really require clothing, but these people wore *nothing*. Not amulets or paint or markings of any kind, nor earrings, nose rings, bracelets, anklets—nothing at all, men or women. They also seemed to let their hair and, on the men, facial hair as well simply *grow*. He couldn't understand why some of them didn't trip over all that hair or strangle on it. Some of the shorter women seemed to have to wrap it around themselves to keep it from dragging on the ground, and he had never seen men with hair that long. Hair that, oddly, didn't seem to tangle or get matted. Had *he* done that? He didn't remember doing it, but if he'd altered them significantly, the computer would have filled in the logical items which he'd left out but which might be required for some reason.

Other things also bothered him. Their remarkable silence for one thing. Watching them, it seemed at times as if there was some kind of communication going on, judging from the gestures, the playful actions, the coordination they exhibited, but aside from some grunts and occasional laughter they said nothing.

He wondered if they were at all aware that they now worked the fields that their distant ancestors had once owned. He watched as they seemed to have some kind of silent prayer vigil before starting to work, then they went to it, picking fruit and stacking it in neat piles every few bushes.

"They have an almost unnatural ability to figure out just which fruit is ready to be picked," one of the Ambrezan supervisors commented to him.

"But they don't fill baskets or containers," Brazil noted. "They just pile it all neatly."

"They won't touch them. No Glathrielian will touch *any-*

thing manufactured, even a box. They even make several trips carrying their 'pay,' which is a small percentage of the crop, back to their home in Glathriel in their arms."

"What about that home? Don't they have some sort of village or whatever with shelter?"

"No, they don't. Not as we understand it, anyway. They *do* have tribal lands that they consider their home, but the few structures are very crude and very basic and formed entirely from gathered dead wood and dropped leaves. They don't build as such. The few crude structures tend to be shelters for the babies and for bad weather. Mostly they sleep either out in the open or in hollow trees, some caves, and shelters formed from fallen logs and the like. They don't even build or keep fires, although if a thunderstorm comes along and sets something off, they might use it until it goes out. They don't kill unless something is trying to kill them and there is no other choice—and whatever *that* unfortunate animal is, they then eat it raw that same day."

"They seem to eat okay from what I can see," Brazil noted. "The women seem to range from chubby to fat, and the men are built like bricks."

"They eat a complex variety of things, some of which we, and perhaps you, would find disgusting, but it seems the perfect balance for them. They make great workers, though. No complaints, virtually no mistakes, and they won't touch, let alone eat, anything they haven't picked themselves. They're always good-humored in a childlike sort of way, and they're so placid, they don't even swat flies that land on them."

"How'd you ever get them to work for you?"

"It's been this way since long before my time or my grandfather's time, too," the Ambrezan supervisor replied. "Only a few tribes will do it, but they've been doing it forever on the border plantations and, I think, along the Zinjin Coast strip. The vast majority live way in the interior, which is mostly swamp and jungle with some volcanic areas.

We used to try and survey them once upon a time, I'm told, but they can vanish like magic, and it just wasn't worth the time and trouble. The fact is, we know very little about them beyond these border tribes."

"I know about that," Brazil told him. "They asked me to do a report on them if I went in, figuring that since I'm related in a way to them, I might be taken as one of them if I went in."

"Well, that figures. You gonna go?"

"Looks like it. I'm after another like myself. A female. Very small and very thin—even smaller and thinner than me. You haven't seen or heard much about somebody like that, have you?"

"Heard they was looking for somebody like that down the road apiece, but haven't seen or heard a thing myself, no. Of course, I can't tell any of you apart much, frankly, but I think I'd have noticed a female smaller and thinner than you, that's for sure." He sighed. "Well, if you're gonna find her, you got maybe two weeks."

"Huh? Why's that?"

"Oh, they haven't got any families as such. You can see the same kid with a different parent most any day. It's all communal. That's 'cause, I think, they have one short period of a couple of days when all the women get fertile all at once and all the men can think of nothing else and they go at it, breaking only for sleep, for up to four days. Then they don't do it anymore until the next month. Lots of animals like that, but I know of only a few races here that still have that old mechanism. They say we did back in prehistoric times or whatever, but not since."

The idea shook him. *Just what did I do to you, people?*

It was coming back to him now in bits and pieces. When he'd come through that time off the spaceship, he'd discovered that the Ambreza had literally reduced the Glathrielians to animallike status. When he'd done his work in the Well, he'd fixed that so there'd be a slow but steady generational rise back to normality through providing immunity to the Ambreza gas—but in a nontech hex, which, he'd guessed, wouldn't threaten the Ambreza.

He'd been wrong. The next time through, he'd caught wind that the Glathrielians had gotten to a point where they knew the legends and stories about how they'd been kicked out of their ancestral home and brought low and were getting *very* curious about Ambrezan technology and doing a lot of work on natural chemicals themselves. The Ambreza leadership had been getting nervous even then; the seeds of potential genocide were being sown even then as the Ambreza's imaginations started coming up with potential attacks far worse than the Glathrielians could have managed on their own.

So while he and Mavra had reset and checked out the system, he'd made other changes to ensure that this would all die down. He'd removed the translation abilities from the Glathrielians so that they could only communicate among themselves, and he'd put a blocker in there so that no other language but theirs could get through. If they couldn't reconnoiter and spy on their hated enemy, they wouldn't be much of a threat. And he'd made what he thought then were some minor physiological changes to ensure that they adapted nearly perfectly to their present hex and would not be as comfortable in the one that was now Ambreza or lust for it so much.

But *this*—these people, this totally primitive way—was not what he'd had in mind at all. He'd sought only to protect them from slaughter, not to reduce them to pre-Stone Age levels. What had the computer imposed logically on them that flowed from his premises? Just how badly had he goofed?

What have I done? he wondered again, watching them. This was all he needed, he thought sourly. A hyperdose of pure guilt right now. I'm not going to keep ying-yanging these people around forever for some sin of ancestors even

I can't remember, he vowed. If I made a mistake, this time I'll correct it, but, beyond that, from this point on, as much as I like the Ambreza, I'm not going to keep these people down again. If any new adjustments need to be done, by damn, I'll do 'em on the Ambreza for a change!

He stared at them as they worked, trying to figure them out, and over a period of time he got a sense that he wasn't seeing the whole picture, but he couldn't put his finger on what was disturbing him that he hadn't already quantified.

And then he had it.

There were no lame, no crippled, not so much as a limper among them. Well, they might leave all of those home. But no, it was more than that. In the kind of rough environment and natural way they lived, their creamy brown skins should have the signs of all sorts of incidental injuries, scars, and whatnot. There were none. Every one of their hides looked as smooth and untouched as a baby's bottom. Not a scar or a scab among them, and some of them weren't young.

And that was impossible. It was something that just might not occur to the Ambreza, thankfully, but it was damned impossible. Something that they hid from everyone except themselves was definitely not kosher about the Glathrielians. Now he *had* to go in. Mavra was still the object, but he very much wanted to know just what the hell was going on there.

His strange appearance, so like them and yet so different both in features and in the fact that he was clothed and having a conversation with Ambrezans, naturally drew curious looks from the Glathrielians. No, it was worse than that. They looked puzzled as all hell.

Finally, one young woman came over to him a bit shyly but with definite purpose, a big smile of friendliness on her face. He smiled back at her, and she put out her hands, and after a moment of trying to figure out what she wanted, he put out his and they clasped hands.

Suddenly he felt a strange, slightly dizzy sensation, and at the same time she gasped, let go forcefully, and backed away from him, a look of near terror in her eyes. As he followed her with his gaze, she broke and ran not toward the other tribespeople but away, at top speed, in the direction of the border.

Now what the hell? was all he could manage.

The others were now also staring at him rather warily but just keeping their distance and working the grove. He decided to press on down the road and pick up the trail.

The old Ambrezan couple who owned the plantation square in the middle of section B-14 hadn't seen or heard much of anything, and they'd been very surprised when they'd gotten the call from the government, but they'd let the dogs out and had them sniff around, and sure enough, they had picked up some odd kind of trail in a grove of trees and followed it all the way to the border. It was quite puzzling to them; there were so many Glathrielian scents around that it would have to be something outside the dogs' normal experience to have them take off like that.

Nathan Brazil nodded but did not explain. If it were Mavra, and it certainly looked like there was no other possibility, she would smell of many alien things but little or nothing of the Well World.

"You ain't gonna track her with no dogs in there, no, sir," the old Ambrezan told him. "They get in Glathriel a ways, and they go nuts. Can't pick up anything—take you around in circles, they will. Horses and mules might work in some parts, but if you're goin' in here, you're goin' right into the Great Swamp. Runs for half the hex, it does. Lots of water, killer snakes, vicious swamp lizards, and a lot worse."

He shrugged. "The Glathrielians seem to do all right in there."

"Well, maybe. Maybe it's just 'cause they have enough young to keep pace, too. Ever think of that? You don't see no old ones, that's for sure, and as peaceful as they are, they might just figure the thing's got a right to eat 'em. Or maybe they smell as bad to the animals there as they do to us—no offense, son. But you take a riding or pack animal in there, all you'll do is give them vicious brutes a real feast and waste a good animal."

"I'll walk," he told them. "Been a while since I carried a full pack, but it won't be the first time. *She* walked in there with nothing at all, and it's only been two days or so. I might be able to pick up something. I was a pretty fair tracker once."

"Well, if she ain't got eaten, you might have a chance," the old gent admitted. "But I still wouldn't like to go in there far. That place like that other world they say you come from? Might make a difference."

"No, not much. Parts of it are like that, but not the parts I like. Actually, my home's more like, well, *here.*"

And it *was,* too, he realized with a start. Maybe that was why he liked Ambreza and the Ambrezans so much. Given the same hex and a jump start, they'd either managed to develop a *very* Terranlike society and culture or, more likely, had co-opted parts of it, copied from those they had overthrown. Designed and bred for the hex they now found loathsome, the ones who'd been forced to take *their* place had come up very differently indeed, while the Ambrezan culture was, after all these thousands of years, virtually unchanged. Static. And they *liked* it that way.

The Ambreza of their original hex had been creative, aggressive, clever enough to meet a threat when they were woefully mismatched. Moving here, they'd done almost certainly a far better job of managing the hex, but they'd grown soft, stagnant, and complacent, devoid of the daring and creativity that their remote ancestors had had in abundance. They just weren't really in their element here, and they'd spent thousands upon thousands of generations treading water, never changing or adapting beyond what they had to do. Even he felt that comfortable sense of time standing still here, and in ways easy to take, with their horses and cows and hunting dogs and country manners.

What had the Glathrielians become in the Ambrezan hex? A tropical swamp and jungle was also an invitation to stagnancy for Terrans, and on a much more primitive scale. Even when the magic of technology was allowed to work, the regions of Earth covered by such unlivable areas had tended to keep the inhabitants in the Stone Age. He'd seen it in the Congo, the Philippines, the Amazon interior again and again, just as they'd remained rather primitive in the arctic regions, too busy surviving to go any further until technology came to them or, in more cases than not, was forced upon them.

And yet, even there they'd done the best they could with what they'd had. They'd become farmers where it was possible; fishers near seas, lakes, and oceans; hunters and managers of game, with social organizations of varying degrees as geography allowed. From the spear and blowgun to the igloo to vast irrigation channels, they'd adapted and innovated their way to some sort of culture.

Glathriel looked all the more an enigma because of it. Even the last time Terran types had managed all this, until they'd become a threat to others and he'd set them back a bit. Had they lost once too often? Had they given up as a people?

Or had they adapted and innovated in ways none on Earth had ever done?

What had the girl seen by holding his hands, and how had she seen it?

Had he perhaps set up the evolutionary mechanism and now forgotten that he had done so or, even more disturbing, done it without realizing it?

He allowed the old man to take him all the way, down to the stake in the ground just before the hex boundary where they'd stopped the dogs. Bidding the old Ambrezan farewell with thanks, he adjusted the backpack and walked into the new Glathriel.

It was, he thought, a nearly unimaginable feeling to enter a hex populated by people who looked very much like him and somehow feel that he was going into territory more alien than some of the strangest hexes on the Well World.

GLATHRIEL

Terry Perez had been walking through the dense, wet jungle for several hours. She didn't have much of a time sense anymore, but the night and the strangeness of the place gave her no clues as to even immediate time. She *did* realize that she should have been exhausted by now, but she wasn't. Perhaps it was expectation or the creepiness of the surroundings that gave her the extra energy, but she knew she couldn't stop until she'd reached wherever it was that was calling her.

Certainly the signs were fresher now; she was on a main trail headed straight for a relatively large gathering of people, and that alone would satisfy her. She didn't know what they would look like or be like, but fears of alien monsters were far from her thoughts due mostly to this place. It was too much like the Amazon, right down to its animal inhabitants, to feel alien, and without that eerie, overfilled sky it might just have been a different part of the same forest she'd been living in for months.

In fact, she realized, without that bizarre kidnapping and the time with the People, she would have been totally unprepared and unequipped to deal with this and would have been back on the ground where she had "landed" in a sheer panic right now.

As it was, in the darkness of the swamp, she neared her goal.

They had not come to help her, but they appeared to be sitting there waiting for her to arrive. Two men, appearing eerily alien to her second sight, stood there in purple outline, looking like some skewed infrared or UV picture; both women had fuzzy, ball-shaped violet colorations below their breasts that neither the men nor she shared. Nor did she have the one thing that set them apart not only from herself but from the glow of animals as well.

They all had shimmering soft, pale white auras outlining themselves.

For the first time she really felt nervous and more than a little awkward. The shapes *seemed* human, at least from what she could see in the dark, but just who and what were they?

She stopped, and there was the inevitable uneasy pause as each side waited for the other to make a move. She watched as, after a little bit, they clasped hands and saw in some surprise that the pale white auras broke and seemed to merge into a single glow. Finally, they seemed to make a silent decision, and the man on her far right raised his left hand and beckoned to her in an unmistakable gesture. After a moment's hesitation she came forward, butterflies in her stomach, until she stood right in front of the man, close enough to note that he had bad breath and sorely needed a bath.

He reached out and took her hand in his, and the white aura coming from the group broke and then ran slowly up her arm and around her. When it had completely enveloped her, she felt a sudden shock to her system, and then she felt their collective minds rushing to hers, engulfing her as the aura had engulfed her body. There were no words because words were not necessary. In that instant they were a part of her and she was a part of them; they *were* her and she *was* they, individually and collectively. In that instant she was male and female, Terran and Glathrielian. All that she was, all that she had ever been, they knew because they were she; all that they knew, all that they had ever been, she was, because she was all of them.

No introductions or explanations were required; the exchange of information, data, backgrounds, and points of view was instantaneous and total. How long it went on she did not know, but it wasn't long, for it was still dark when they separated and she was again alone. Alone but not the same.

Not quite a Glathrielian, although she knew exactly what it meant and felt like and was as comfortable here as any native. But because of that knowledge she was no longer quite a Terran, either. After she had shared minds, what was the use of names or most of the human foibles that had caused humanity to war and conquer and hate and become so prejudiced? If evil was rooted in a lack of communication and understanding, these people were without it, although they were far too knowledgeable about their world for it to be considered a new Eden. They had eaten of the Tree of Knowledge of Good and Evil, and they knew the difference. It just wasn't the difference most others thought it was.

The point was that she could never hide anything from any of them, or they from her. The idea would have disturbed her before she had touched their minds, but it could not now.

She understood perfectly what was going on and exactly what her role in it would be. She was content with that.

The region hadn't always been a swamp.

Sometime, in the times hidden by mists forever, it had been a far different sort of place. Not that its climate hadn't always been hot and muggy, but once these were actually agricultural districts in which the Ambreza raised rice and other grains, controlling the influx of water with a grand complex of locks, channels, dams, and movable dikes so intricate and so ingeniously perfect that under most circumstances they operated themselves with almost clockwork precision, leaving the designers only to do maintenance and harvest the crops. The Ambreza were equally comfortable on land or water then and pushed the art of the purely mechanical almost to its limits.

Now, after countless thousands of years of pure neglect, one could not see a sign of that once-great race of builders and innovators. What might yet be preserved was far down, under layers of rock-hard sediment, volcanic ash, plant spores, and the decomposed remains of innumerable animals and insects.

It was a dismal place now, overrun with dirty water and fallen, moss-covered logs, hidden under a blanket of high trees reaching for the light under skies more gray than clear, leaving the areas below in a twilight of swirling mist that hovered below the branches like a living thing.

It was hard to believe that such a place could ever be tamed, yet the Ambreza had done it, and they were not alone; back on Earth the Kingdom of the Congo had conquered just such a hot, steamy junglelike swamp ten times this size and had built a thriving civilization until slavery, disease, and finally a harsh colonial hand had reduced the population to a point where the control of the land could not be maintained and it had fallen rapidly back to this sort of state. In ancient Cambodia they had tamed such a place so thoroughly that they'd built great temples to their gods in the midst of it, not knowing that they were actually building those temples to their own genius.

The last time Nathan Brazil had been anywhere near Glathriel, the inhabitants had been slowly embarking on just such a taming project, and they were the distant ancestors of the people who lived in this gunk now. What had happened to them? Certainly, this time he'd found nothing in the Ambrezan records or stories to indicate that the former natives had done anything. Nor had it been a quick change, even after his last intervention. All the evidence was that it had been slow, a turning inward, a rejection of what might be, a withdrawal into themselves that spread like some plague from border to border.

What had it been? What had changed them not only mentally and philosophically but *physically,* as was clear, reverting them to some animal base for reproduction, supplanting even the concept of family in their culture? What now clearly healed them so quickly, a necessity in such a harsh environment for survival, yet made them so passive that they would not even build permanent shelters for themselves or make much of anything with their own hands? What, in fact, had happened to their language, which, as was typical of Terran-evolved tongues, had been quite rich and colorful? He hadn't taken *that* from them, just their ability to understand *other* tongues. Yet the Ambrezans were adamant that they barely had a language at all—a few dozen sounds, many imitative of native animals here, with very basic meaning, and rarely used even then?

Yet they held hands and silently prayed. To whom or what?

He refused to believe it. Something inside him told him that the impression was false. Terrans adapted. They were among the best adapters in the universe. Why, just starting from the plains of Africa and the Fertile Crescent they'd settled the Arctic and the jungles and vast deserts and every kind of climate and unlivable place in between.

As he trudged into the wet jungle, Brazil kept at the puzzle this place represented. Had they adapted *too* well? No, no, that was unheard of, ridiculous. But the last time at the Well he *had* done some design tinkering to make this hex their own, to become as if this, not the other place, were what they were originally designed to survive in.

That was what the Well World was, wasn't it? A gigantic set of laboratories, each with a race designed for the place or a place for the race, set together and wound up and allowed to run their course to see just how viable race and setting really were?

She had held his hands . . .

Wait a minute! He'd put them here last time to adapt, and they'd done just what the damned Well World was supposed to let them do.

They held hands in a circle and prayed . . .

They'd adapted.

They'd become something different, gone off in a whole new direction. Whether it was a good direction for people, or bad, or stagnant wasn't the point. But that was in fact what had happened; he was sure of it.

The human race had trotted off and become something else.

Now the job was to find out what the hell that "something else" was.

That, of course, and find the ever-elusive and apparently deliberately evasive Mavra Chang.

It wasn't easy to find traces of her, but it could be done. The twin keys were in the eternally wet ground between the marshes that formed a set of complex trails. Some of those trails retained the impression of footprints for very long periods, and one set of prints, appearing infrequently but often enough, was a bit different from the rest. The way this one person walked was different; the prints of the others showed that they walked in a more confident manner, emphasizing the forward area of the foot, while hers showed the full foot coming down with a slight emphasis on the heel.

Clearly, she wasn't at all unfamiliar with this sort of climate and terrain, but that, too, fit. Assuming that the meteor had finally struck where they'd said it would, it would have come down somewhere deep in the Amazon. What Mavra was doing there was a total mystery, but that was the way the master computer worked when it had to, and he knew that it had come for her as well as himself. The method had been a bit crude yet effective, but the meteor had come in only one way, and it had fragmented over Rio and then struck deep inside.

He wondered if she was doing smuggling or drugs or something or if she'd gone native. It didn't matter. In fact, it explained why she had headed down here almost immediately if, as now seemed clear, she wanted to avoid quick discovery and, maybe, him. She *had* to know that he was here.

Or did she? He'd been pretty far gone when he'd fallen into a hex gate on some far-off world so many lifetimes back. Hell, he'd been through it more than once, and even now he couldn't remember her face. Until quite recently he hadn't even remembered her name or anything about what she looked like.

Could it be that she no longer remembered who or what she was and had headed here because it was familiar?

If so, she was going to be in for a rude shock if what he now suspected had happened here actually had. This hex was really going to hell in a handbasket, that was for sure. His previous experiences here had been along the coast and once on the extreme southern savannas between the volcanic ranges, but *this* was a mess. The water had come in to great depths in some places but was shallow in most, and creatures either had managed to come in here or had evolved from more benign forms to some unpleasant types.

The big reptiles that floated in the water and sat along the banks, for example, were very close to alligators or crocodiles, but not quite. They had a leaner, smoother, more primitive look to them, and they seemed less like crocs than some dinosaur relative.

In fact, the whole area reminded him of the Age of the Reptiles before humans had developed. The trees, the giant ferns, the mean-looking fish all seemed from some ancient era. The insects looked pretty modern, the only difference being that some of them were pretty damned big. Mammals were around, but most were small, and it seemed like the smaller ones had tempers worse than the protocrocs while the bigger ones were constantly nervous.

There *did* seem to be several varieties of small monkeys, or maybe protomonkeys would be a better description, gathered in packs and hanging out in the trees, and there were other small tree dwellers that seemed squirrellike. There were birds of all shapes and sizes, many with very effective natural camouflage and others that would stand out against anything. Some of the creatures weren't birds or mammals or anything else, exactly. One of these looked like a medium-sized fish that had rows and rows of teeth and occasionally leapt from the water and *flew* on multiple wings.

Great. And unless I get lucky, I get to sleep with these critters tonight, Brazil thought glumly. He wasn't worried about being killed—*that* was never a worry—but being attacked was always a possibility, and he didn't like the thought of being savagely chewed up. It took up to two years to grow a new hand or arm or leg, even longer for scars to vanish, and he was not immune to pain.

The idea that this place might be home to thousands, maybe tens of thousands of people wearing nothing at all and living and sleeping in the open was difficult to accept. It was pretty easy to see why the Ambreza never saw any old Glathrielians.

He made good time in spite of his reservations about the wildlife and the thick mud that formed the only safe path. He realized that the paths seemed to follow a roughly logical plan and wondered if they had somehow been built up or maintained based on those ancient Ambrezan canal systems, but it seemed unlikely. They'd be many meters down by now.

It bothered him that he saw no signs of humanity other than the prints. All those Glathrielians who came and worked the plantations on the other side of the border had to come from *somewhere,* and that "somewhere" couldn't be all *that* far inside. He should see some signs of where they came from and where they went by now, he thought, but there was nothing.

He'd had a later start than he wanted, too, and he didn't relish bedding down in the pitch darkness in this region. Still, what else could he do?

As he moved in, though, he began to hear various sounds in the bush around him that were unlike the sounds of the creatures he'd been seeing and avoiding all afternoon. Once or twice he was certain he caught a brief glimpse of some man-sized shapes off in the foliage, but when he turned, they seemed to vanish. He wasn't really worried about the natives; hell, he *wanted* to find, or be found by, the natives. Rather, he was worried about far larger predators that might be around somewhere that had so far escaped his notice.

As the day wore on toward its end, though, he became more and more certain that he was being watched. There were too many such odd near encounters, and they were increasing—and, frankly, becoming more obvious. Through the swamp noises he occasionally heard what he was certain was a cough or perhaps a grunt. The third time he heard it, he knew that he was in the midst of a number of them and that they wanted him to know it.

What's the matter, boys? Afraid I'll touch you?

The worst concern he had was darkness at this point; there was simply no telling what they were waiting for, but darkness in their element would certainly make whatever it was much easier. He was deceptively dangerous for a little man in hand-to-hand combat, but even the biggest muscle man he'd ever seen wasn't a match for a horde of attackers unless those attackers were total incompetents, and he just didn't feel that these people were as dull or stupid as they wanted to appear to be to others. There was, after all, quite a good motive for cultivating just the sort of reputation they now had with the somewhat paranoid Ambreza. He couldn't have imagined that the furry race would have ever allowed Glathrielians free reign in the hex with no monitoring.

He had, however, deliberately placed himself in his current predicament, and he was getting pretty damned tired of it. He stopped at a fairly wide clearing that had some decent grass to hold it, removed his pack, then sat on it and looked around at the apparently silent wilderness.

"All right," he called out to them. "I don't know if you can understand me or not, but you sure as hell know you're being talked to. Now, I am tired and I am pissed off as all hell right now, and my purely mechanical watch here says that it's about a half hour to sundown. Now, I'm gonna wait here maybe five or ten minutes, and if you want/ to come out and talk, or fight, or whatever, that's fine. After that I'm gonna make camp, I'm gonna make a fire, I'm gonna eat something and have an Ambrezan beer with it and maybe then some coffee. If you want any, you're welcome. If you just want to watch, then piss on you!" He took out a cigar, bit off the end, then lit it with a safety match. More things worked in a nontech hex than most people thought.

He waited until the cigar was almost half-smoked. During that time he had the distinct impression that more and more natives were showing up and sitting out there staring at him. For a starkly lonely camp site in the middle of a jungle swamp, he had the oddest feeling that he was sitting alone on the field at Rio's largest soccer stadium and that the stands were full. Or was he, rather, sitting alone in the center of the Roman Colosseum with the crowd waiting until the lions were ready?

Well, he wouldn't wait for them. He was as tired and hungry as he'd said he was, and he was going to be set up before dark.

Before too long he had his tent set up and his supplies

organized and he'd started a fire. In a nontech hex it was impossible to manufacture a good compressed-gas system, but as long as the mechanism was totally mechanical, nothing stopped anyone from bringing premanufactured canisters in and having a clean fire. He knew how rough he might have to live if he started heading north to the equator, as he would have to do sooner or later. He was not about to sacrifice any comforts at this point if he could avoid it.

He had pre-prepared his own food and had it vacuum-sealed. The Ambreza and he didn't really agree on what constituted a hearty, tasty meal, so these were his own creations, and he managed to use three containers to make a fairly decent simmering stew. The Glathrielians were allegedly all vegetarians or worse, but he had enough faith in his recipes that it would have to smell awfully good to humans no matter whether they'd actually eat the stuff or not. The beer was in small plastic containers that held in a cold gas that surrounded the inner bottles. The cap was released with a simple pull, and this, too, worked in a nontech hex. It was a most satisfying meal considering the conditions.

By the time he'd finished, it was dark. Darkness fell rapidly over the Well World almost anywhere, since its axial tilt was virtually nil, and by the time he'd put on the coffee, his fire was the only light. It was enough—for now. When he was done, he'd bring out his lantern and light it, filled as it was with an ingenious combination of small cylinders that fed a small amount of oil to a pan and allowed for a decent all-night light. They might come at him, but they wouldn't come in total darkness.

He poured the coffee and settled back comfortably, considering relighting the remaining half of his cigar, when he suddenly frowned and looked around by the glow of the fire.

She stood there, just at the edge of the fire, staring right at him. She looked to be maybe fourteen or fifteen years old, fully developed but very young, and she was stark naked and unblemished in any way.

He sat up and stared back at her big brown eyes and saw in them a great deal of intelligence and awareness. There was also something odd about her. She looked like a Glathrielian should look, and yet she didn't. That all-race exotic cast all the ones he'd seen exhibited wasn't there; this girl looked more like somebody on the beach at Ipanema. Her features were more classical—sort of an Afro-European mix found in the Caribbean or parts of Latin America—with none of the Asian about her, and she was a lighter, smoother brown.

"Hello," he said pleasantly. "Want some coffee? I have some paper cups here if you do."

She frowned, and he really got the feeling that she was honestly trying to make out his words but to no avail. That in itself was odd. It was as if she *expected* to be able to understand him and was puzzled that she could not.

He gestured for her to come closer and have a seat, and without any hesitancy she did just that, sitting cross-legged on the ground to his left but between him and the fire.

"Excuse me for not offering my hand, but as bad luck as I have with women, I don't want you to suddenly start screaming and running away in terror or something." He got up and went to the fire instead, and holding an empty cup, poured some coffee into it and took it over to her and set it down near her. She watched him all the time like a hawk, but there was no fear in her. She didn't touch the cup or look at it again, though, and he remembered that they rejected all such things.

She seemed to be thinking about something for a moment, then she leaned over, got on her knees, and cleared a place in the wet soil, making it free of grass. With her finger, she did something in the dirt, then backed away and resumed her seat.

Curious, he walked over and crouched down to look at what she'd scratched there. At first he couldn't make it out.

Some kind of drawing. A box, another box inside of it, and a kind of V mark under it. Shaking his head, he got up, walked around, and looked at it from another angle.

My God, if I didn't know better, I'd swear it was a drawing of a television set, he thought, wondering. He suddenly had an awful thought.

Crouching down again, he wiped out her drawing as best he could and traced a different, more irregular design.

She came over, looked at it, then nodded and put a finger at a point on the left and a bit up from the center of the picture.

It was a crude map of Brazil.

He turned and looked at her, then put his right hand up in the air, made a fist, and brought it down with a whistling sound to a *boom!* in the dirt.

She smiled and nodded, then repeated his pantomime and sound effects, this time taking her own fist into the crude map just where she'd made the dot.

His jaw dropped just a bit. *Maybe that* was *a television! If so, she's not just some native girl with bad luck, either.* He decided to get more ambitious and do a little signing. He'd been pretty good at signing once. It was the only thing that had saved his ass during the sack of Rome.

He traced a circle in the air, then slowly outlined a hex shape, then, with his hand, portrayed his arm going from the circle through the hex to here. She watched and nodded, smiling.

He shrugged to, he hoped, indicate total puzzlement as to how she'd wound up here. It wasn't supposed to work this way. Nobody was supposed to become a Glathrielian unless the race was in danger of dying out, and at least it hardly looked like *that.*

She waved a finger in the air, had it go to ground, had two fingers walk out, then made as if she were operating a very old-time camera, then mouthing into something she was holding. *A helicopter! She'd been part of a TV crew covering the impact!* That *had* to be it and would easily explain her appearance.

It still didn't answer why she was *here,* why she wasn't one of the other 779 races of the South, but it told him basically who she was and how she'd gotten here.

He had an awful thought. He pointed to her foot and then to the drawing area. With his own foot he mocked putting it down on the drawing. She didn't get it right away but eventually figured out what he wanted, although maybe not why, and stepped on the place, making a half footprint.

It was, of course, a standing rather than walking print, but he'd been following enough of a certain set of prints for his experienced tracker's eyes to relate the two.

He hadn't been following Mavra, after all. He'd been following *this* girl! And that meant that *she,* not Mavra, was the source of the pulse—and the source of the track the hounds had followed.

Well, some of the mystery was at least explained, why she'd gone pretty much straight into Glathriel and why she hadn't contacted the Ambreza. In one sense he was relieved, although he felt frustrated by still not finding who he was really looking for.

Now all he had to do was try to figure out why this girl was here. Not only shouldn't she have become a Glathrielian, she hadn't—not totally. The Well had done some of its work but had left her original form pretty much intact. Oh, he suspected she was a good deal older than she looked now—that was a fairly simple procedure for the Well program—and any diseases or infirmities or other problems, right down to fillings in her teeth, would have been repaired, but it had left her genetic code mostly untouched. It shouldn't have done that. As far as he knew, it *couldn't* have done that.

But it had.

It had also done its adaptation work internally in a way he'd never intended. She couldn't understand him because the program now specified that Type 41's could understand no language but their own. She couldn't speak even in *that* language because, as far as he could see, they didn't have a spoken language as such. She would have been given any attributes and abilities necessary to survive and integrate with the locals here, even ones developed independently, since that, too, was part of the program, but at the cost of being able to verbalize, and perhaps even use, what her education and training had prepared her to do. Hell, if she'd been some sort of TV personality, then she had to be going *nuts* with these limits!

"I didn't mean to do it," he told her sincerely, although he knew she couldn't understand and wouldn't have understood the comment even if she *had* comprehended the words. "I honestly didn't. It's not supposed to work this way." Maybe, just maybe, the Well was broken, after all.

And, he thought, if she was a reporter, why not take the coffee? He knew few of them who could resist coffee, and it would have immediately established her as someone more than Glathrielian if she'd taken it. Hell, it'd only been what? Two, three days tops. She couldn't have totally assimilated into their culture in that short a time, could she? Had, somehow, the Well imposed the culture upon her as well?

It wasn't designed to do that, either. Some stuff one had to learn.

More interesting was what he *wasn't* able to communicate to her. Some simple things, like "others" versus "alone," as in "Did you come with others or alone?" he could not seem to put over. She, too, tried a few times to communicate, but her attempts seemed random and confused. It wasn't an entirely new phenomenon to him; some of the other races of the Well World, most in the North but even a few in the South, simply did not fully follow the logical thought patterns that he and most of the southern races adhered to in one degree or another. A nonverbal society *might* develop along the same logic paths, and certainly in the case of the same race with the same brain structure, but even on Earth there were societies that saw things too differently to ever fully understand one another. This was a step further. In some ways it was like the card games at which he excelled. At one time, eons ago, he'd learned the basics of those games and played them so often that now he rarely thought about how or what to play and when; a part of his brain that he couldn't even consciously touch, let alone access deliberately, processed all the information according to experience, and he simply played automatically—and won. Writers, painters, other creators had the same experience; they didn't know where the words or visions had come from—they just were there and came from some unapproachable recess of the mind that they neither understood nor consciously used but that nonetheless they simply took for granted and used.

None of them could ever explain the process. "God-given talent" was an oft-quoted phrase for it, but talent came from somewhere, and it was called up from a mystery region of consciousness in a manner they could neither comprehend nor control.

Could a whole race operate *entirely* on that sort of processing? Could an entire culture somehow evolve that required no front-brained verbalizations? How could it work? Where was the shared experience, the teaching, the communication that would give such a people the tools with which to work? And to what end? To some animallike equilibrium in which survival was enough?

It was a real puzzle, and he didn't know the answer. There was only one place where he could get those answers, he knew, and that place was a long and hard journey from here.

He could help this girl there, too. Get her out of the trap she'd fallen into.

It never occurred to him to take her along, though. If she was so bound by the Glathrielian way, she'd never survive the trip, and she'd be more in the way than useful, anyway. Still, he wanted to try to tell her, to get through to her, that he *could* help her—and would.

That, however, proved impossible to get over.

After a while fatigue and frustration overcame him, and he managed to get her to understand that he had to sleep. She nodded but continued to sit as he went into the tent, zipped it shut, and, after a much longer time than he thought it would take, managed to get to sleep.

In the morning she was still there.

He wasn't actually fooled into thinking that she'd sat there all night, but she and the others he hadn't seen might think he was. Certainly there had been a lot of traffic through his camp during the night, all without disturbing him. The signs were quite clear that nothing short of a mob scene had occurred, yet none of his equipment had been touched, not even the now-cold cup of coffee still sitting there in the grass.

Well, regardless of the games they might think they were playing, he'd wasted a couple of days coming here, and he'd probably waste another two or more getting back to anyplace useful. At least now it was time to move on, time to actually *do* something other than sit. He'd appreciated the rest, but he was out of place both here and in Ambreza, and he now had a better reason to enter the Well than he'd had before.

After he had packed his gear, she got up, beckoned him, and started off back toward Ambreza with a surefootedness and confidence he certainly didn't feel. He did not argue, however—what good would that have done, anyway? And hell, maybe she knew a shortcut.

The paths she took were shorter, although it was still better than seven hours walking, not counting the breaks, until he once again saw the border. She stood there, letting him pass through, and then passed through herself. Now *she* was following *him,* but she seemed determined to stick with him.

He stopped, turned, looked her in the eye, and shook his head "no," but she had no reaction to that, although she must have understood it and continued to follow him.

Well, as much as he'd have *liked* to take her along, it was impossible. What would she eat? How could she withstand the climatic extremes of the journey in the nude? What would happen when he got on a truck or some other automatic device her people wouldn't touch?

Still, she followed him right up to the farm buildings and waited while he knocked.

The old Ambrezan male was there, apparently doing accounts. He stared out at the girl in the front yard and gave a typical Ambrezan *"Chi chi chi!"* which was basically an expression of thoughtfulness. "So she's the one you went in to get?"

"No, she's another. Somebody totally different."

"Yeah, I figured if you come back, it'd be empty-handed. I no sooner got back to the house than the wife called for me to go after you. Seems another female much like you showed up in the capital just about that time."

Brazil was delighted at the news. "Did they give a name?"

"Dunno. Got the note here someplace."

"Well, more important, is she still there?"

"Maybe, but I got the impression she was there to go to Zone. The gate's right in the city center, you know. Wanted to find out about her friends, I think they said. *Chi chi chi!* Now where in—ah! Here!"

"You'll have to read it for me," Brazil told him. "I'm all right with the translator at languages, but reading is something else again."

"Oh. All right. Let's see . . . 'Female Type 41 arrested near the city border at ten-fourteen this morning for being illegally out of a Glathrielian-allowed district. Proved to be alien of same origin as you. Received clothing, passage to Zone tomorrow for locating rest of her party."

"Hmmm . . . Wonder if she's still in Zone or the city? She'd have to come back there through the gate, anyway.

May I use your communicator and call in and see?"

"Sure. No problem. What about the female there?"

"She'll wait." He went inside and placed a call to the comm center.

"Yes, her name was registered as a Mavra Chang," the comm tech informed him. "Went down to Zone yesterday, returned in the evening. Got provisions and left this morning. The law prevents any Type 41 from being in the city for more than two days, anyway."

"That's the one. How did she leave? And where did they take her?"

"She left by air shuttle. She was going south to the border with Erdom. I assume one of her party is down there someplace or she's going to try and make a boat connection of some sort. At any rate, she said she would probably not be back unless she needed to use a Zone gate as an escape route."

"Damn!" Brazil swore. "No chance I could get an airdrop to the same spot?"

"Maybe in a couple of days or so. Not right now. We don't run those for the convenience of aliens, you know."

The Ambreza had a small air fleet, operating, as it had to, totally within the hex, that basically consisted of a few dozen helicopterlike vehicles which were used for emergencies and for big shots to move around. How she'd talked herself into a ride down there was a mystery, but that she'd been able to do so sounded like the old Mavra.

"Was she informed that I was here and looking for her?"

There was an embarrassed silence for a moment, then the comm tech answered, "Yes, she was informed."

"And?"

"She said that she'd have to move fast or you might catch up to her."

He sighed. "All right. Thank you," and signed off.

The old Ambrezan chuckled. "Ain't it always the damnedest thing, son?"

"Huh? What do you mean?"

"Well, you come up here lookin' for her, and she's down there and she don't even want to see you. On the other hand, you pick up *another* one you didn't know, didn't want, and can't seem to get rid of!"

He nodded and sighed again. "Sure is. Well, thanks for your help. Any way to get some transportation out of this region?"

"Might be able to help. Dunno what your girl out there's gonna do, though. They don't like machines, you know. They don't like much of *anything* 'cept maybe each other. Where you goin'? South to Erdom? That's pretty mean country even if you know it. All desert 'cept right along the coast."

"No, I don't think so. In fact, while I'll probably get in touch with the embassy just to see where *she* might be going, it's not worth chasing her at this point, particularly if she has some reason for avoiding me. I think I'm best off heading east from here. Catch a ship and get on my way. I, too, have some people I promised to look up far from here."

"Well, it's up to you, son. I'll see what I can do about a call in to the foreign ministry, and then we'll see about gettin' you a ride east. From this distance it might do you best to go overland by horse rather than go through all that convoluted bunch of roads that'll take you three hundred kilometers to go fifty."

He gave a small smile. "And I suppose you might have a horse for sale."

"Could be. Ain't got no saddles that'd fit you, though."

"I can make do with a blanket and a bridle," he assured the Ambrezan. "Let's go see what you have."

They went out and walked back beyond the outbuildings to a large open pasture between the headquarters and the parklike glade where Terry had entered the Well World. Quite a number of good-looking horses were there, and he looked them over.

He picked a strong-looking brown gelding after surveying the herd. "How much?"

"Oh, I reckon a hundred and fifty'll do it."

"A hundred and fifty! I'll *walk* before I'll pay a hundred and fifty for a gelding to get me fifty kilometers!"

"No, no, son. I ain't tryin' to cheat you. That's for the *two* of them."

Nathan Brazil looked around and saw the girl, now mounted atop a horse without blanket, bridle, or anything else but looking very much at home there. She smiled at him.

He felt like a cross between a sucker and merely a damned fool, but he paid anyway. Hell, otherwise he wouldn't have put it past her to just steal the damned horse or, worse, try to run along after him. At least he could get most of the money back at the port when he sold the two horses.

At first there had been the dizzying sensation of falling nearly identical to that first hex gate that had brought them all to this strange new world, but then the sensation had abruptly ceased and she had fallen into the deepest sleep she had ever known.

Doctor Lori Ann Sutton awoke feeling groggy, hung over, and a little sick to the stomach, lying on what felt like a bed of warm sand.

She opened her eyes and looked around and saw that it *was* a bed of warm sand. At least it was sand, and there was an awful lot of it under a mean hot sun that was still low on the horizon. Or was it going down? Who could tell?

She sat up, scratched where the sand had pressed against her side, and immediately felt a terrible sense of wrongness. The whole scene—sand, sky, sun—had all the colors she expected, but there seemed to be even more. She could actually *see* the heat, and there were darker areas as well.

I'm seeing into the infrared spectrum! she thought wonderingly. And maybe beyond. Maybe, just maybe, in *both* directions. The *entire* spectrum?

Suddenly she remembered everything. The gate, the lecture by the polka-dotted dragon, Alama's—no, *Mavra's* words—and something about becoming some different creature.

She looked down at herself and saw that she was a very different creature, indeed. Her arms were long but very thin and ended in a huge pair of hands that were not human. They had only three fingers, long and thick, and an opposable thumb almost as long as the index finger and thicker than any of the others. The nails were huge and thick as well and seemed to run from halfway past the knuckle to beyond the tip. Put together in a relaxed way, they formed almost, well, a kind of supple, softer *hoof,* the palms fairly hard and thick and a pale brownish color.

Her feet were the same, only the hoof was cloven and seemed oddly shaped on the bottom, something like a horse's hoof crossed with the foot of a camel.

She was covered in a thick, hidelike skin that was itself almost covered by very short, thick, pastel beige hair that flared out at the ankles and wrists. But that wasn't the worst of it or the biggest shock.

Between her legs, emerging from a mass of thick, medium-brown pubic hair, was the *biggest* set of male genitalia she had ever seen, very dark brown in color and with a leatherlike texture.

She touched it and gave a slight gasp and then just stared down at it for quite some time.

My God! I'm a man! she thought, getting a queasy feeling in her stomach echoed by a strange but not altogether pleasant sensation in the genitals.

It was an oddball fantasy come to life, one she had played with in the past, mostly out of the frustration of having to compete at the top levels of her profession with men and wanting the same power and position they took for granted. But it was only a fantasy, not a serious wish. The reality of the change shook her.

And after all that time with the all-female tribe of the People, she felt an odd sense of aversion. *I'm going to miss my breasts!* she thought, trying to get a handle on things.

Finally she managed to overcome the tremendous shock to consider the next question. She was male. But a male *what*? What was beige and hairy and had big hooves and arms apparently evolved from a set of more equinelike forelegs?

The body was *very* slender and surprisingly supple. The body was a nearly perfect blend of equine and human, strange, yet somehow she thought of the term "erotic" to cover it. *Hah! If only Jeff could see me now, with this body and this big a sausage!* Of course, he wouldn't exactly be turned on by the idea, but it would be awfully nice to use these hard hands to slug him.

God! I'm a guy for all of three minutes and already I'm thinking like one! she admonished herself.

The fact was, mentally, where it counted, she was still the same person. Nothing had been changed that she could tell, no knowledge or memories lost, no feelings all that different. But it was as if her mind were now in another's body, someone whose differences went beyond just gender—*way* beyond.

While there seemed very little sensation in the rather large feet, the palms proved to have a lot of nerve sensors, and she could get a surprisingly good "feel," as good as or better than her old hands. *I'll never touch-type again, though,* she thought inanely. Not with two fewer fingers, even though the size of the hands and the length of the fingers gave her, if anything, more control.

She still thought of herself as a "she," and she knew that she probably would have to make a major mental adjustment on that score. Nobody in this new place would know that she'd been a woman most of her life; they'd see her in this man's body instead.

She felt her face. It *seemed* human enough—mouth, even with what seemed to be thicker lips and maybe a longer, slightly thicker tongue, but her jaw moved side to side as well as up and down, and the teeth indicated that whatever these people were, they were omnivores, not herbivores as she would have expected. The canines, in fact, seemed a bit larger and sharper than they used to be—and no caps, no missing back tooth!

She had always been farsighted, which was the reason she had been able to survive among the People without her glasses, but vision now seemed perfect, with every little hair easy to pick out even very close up. She couldn't remember when she'd seen this clearly at all distances.

Nose . . . Well, human, sort of, but there was something odd *inside* the nostrils, controlled by voluntary muscles. She flexed them and suddenly found her breathing cut off. She relaxed them again very quickly. Protection against blowing sand, perhaps? The eyes felt a little funny, too. She concentrated and found that she had double eyelids that could be independently controlled if she concentrated or would operate as one if she didn't. The outer lids were essentially what she thought of as "normal"; the inner ones, however, were transparent. They distorted her vision and in fact seemed to filter color so that the world became a study in contrasting grays, but she could see through them.

The ears were definitely *not* "normal." They went more back than up and were protected by large pointed lobes, more like a horse's ears or some similar animal's. They could, she discovered, be somewhat rotated, raised, or lowered, even independently of one another. There was a shock of bushy hair atop the head, but it didn't seem to grow long down the back. With some trepidation she pulled one and looked at it. It appeared nearly snow white in color and very long and thick.

Lori had a sudden thought and reached around to her behind. There appeared to be a bit of excess hair at the base of the spine but not the tail she almost expected to find. In a way it was kind of disappointing. She'd always wondered what it would feel like to have a tail.

She looked around, trying to figure out how to get up. Equinelike or not, this wasn't the body of a four-footed animal, no matter what its ancestors might have been like. It wasn't as easy as getting up in a human body, it seemed, but she figured it out with a little experimentation. She turned over and used the hands as forefeet and then pushed off, letting her back muscles lift her upright. The true feet were clearly designed for sand; she found no problems with footing at all.

She looked around, wondering where the hell she might go. In doing so, she saw her shadow, and it made an amazing vision to her eyes even though, with the sun not so high, it was distorted and lengthened. Curiously, though, it was only by seeing that shadow that she noticed the horn.

Her hand went up to the top of her head and found it easily, almost centered up there. A twisting, rock-hard spiral going up, not quite straight, to a very wicked point. Although it was hard and almost half a meter long, she had no sensation of it being there at all, not even weight or balance on the head.

A male bipedal unicorn? she wondered to herself. *Why would any evolving race keep a horn like that?*

For now she could only guess. A weapon perhaps, considering the thinness and fragility of the arms? Or . . . She had an awful thought it might be used in some way involving mating no matter how conventional it seemed.

All right, Lori, you know the basics about what they've stuck you with; now what?

Again she scanned the horizon, and this time a curious effect happened. When she concentrated on any far point, it was as if her vision suddenly became telescopic. She could bring her view of the horizon closer, *much* closer, seeing detail at very great distances indeed. Although there was about a half second's disorientation when she switched her focus to something more close up, the effect was the neatest thing about this body she'd discovered.

But what good was it to be able to zero in on the distant horizon if there was nothing but sand to be seen?

"Get to a zone gate and tell me where and what you are," Mavra had said, but how could she do that when there seemed nowhere to go to get *anywhere*?

Lori continued the horizon pan, stopping and magnifying, trying to see *anything*. What good was all this if she was going to be stuck, alone and without food or water, in this desert?

She suddenly stopped and zeroed in on a tiny black speck far, far away. She would never even have noticed it without this perfect vision, and she would certainly have never been able to tell that it was more than a dune shadow without the remarkable telescopic abilities. Even with them it was barely discernible, but it seemed to be a dark area of some kind protruding from the desert floor. Rocks? It didn't seem likely.

Trees! An oasis!

The sun was definitely climbing, and the day was heating up fast. Now was the time to make for any possible haven, and second-guessing was a luxury that she could not afford.

She started off toward the black dot and began to improve on her walking and balancing abilities with almost every step. She did not walk with those feet; she sort of trotted or even galloped, kicking up sand but making very good speed. She also learned rather quickly and a bit painfully that when moving fast, she had to lean a bit forward and keep the hips wide, otherwise that *thing* down there flapping away would get crunched between the upper calves.

It was getting progressively hotter, and she could actually *see* the heat both as it came down upon her and as it was first trapped and then radiated back by her body. She wondered just how hot to the touch she was right now.

She began to have trouble seeing. The heat radiation was coloring everything and distorting her sight. It suddenly occurred to her that there was more than one use for those inner lids, and she closed them. Virtually all colors snapped out and the world became a mass of infinite grays, yet the black dots that hadn't seemed to grow any closer no matter what speed she was making now began to resolve themselves a bit more clearly and did in fact seem to be getting ever so slightly larger.

It *was* an oasis! That might not mean people, but those were clearly trees of some kind, and trees needed water.

Or at least she *hoped* that trees here needed water.

She would have expected to become winded after a while and have to rest, particularly in the growing heat, but she found that running across the sands like this gave her a real rush; her chest apparently contained mostly lung, and it went in and out with each giant breath she took. But the rhythm of the breathing and the running was very easy to slip into, and even though it seemed like she'd been running for hours across many, many kilometers, she didn't feel the least bit tired or winded.

She was definitely hungry and thirsty, though, which only gave her more impetus to reach her goal as quickly as physically possible.

Soon the oasis loomed before her, filling much of her vision, and it was enough of a dark mass that she lifted the inner lids to get the full detail.

The trees weren't like any she'd ever seen before, but they had a tropical look, with thin and supple trunks rising to layers of oversized palm- or fernlike leaves.

She ran right through the first row and found the area larger than she had expected and the ground inside harder with much exposed white-veined gray rock that produced a "clopping" sound when her feet hit it. She slowed but found that she needed to go up to a tree and put a hand out to fully stop herself without falling over.

It was almost a letdown to stop running, but her chest continued to heave and she continued to gulp in air at the same rhythm until her breathing slowed to a more normal rate.

She looked around, and her ears automatically rotated about a hundred degrees on either side, checking for sounds. There wasn't much except the rustling of some leaves in the highest part of the trees, apparently in reaction to a slight breeze that didn't reach the ground.

Her nose, though, brought an overpowering aroma that she recognized immediately, even though she'd never smelled it before—*water!*

Finding it was as simple as following her nose.

She didn't hesitate a moment worrying that it might not be good water. It wasn't any new inner sense that told her anything about it but rather an all-consuming thirst that made it clear that the question was moot. She simply had to have water.

The water was in fact from a spring that bubbled out of the rocks and created an attractive, shaded pool about a dozen meters across. She headed for it, got on all fours, then dropped down and just stuck her face in it and began to suck and lap it in. Her natural nose plugs closed the instant her face hit the water, and she hardly noticed.

It was an eerie sensation, though, because she just drank and drank. She had never drunk this much of anything in her whole life, and long after a human her size would have been satisfied she continued to take it in. She could *feel* it, cooling down her whole body in stages, coiling around inside her like a living thing, and finally concentrating in her back. There was no telling how much she drank before, unable to take another gulp, she came up out of the water and settled back, lying there on her side. For several minutes she felt bloated but cool, and then, slowly, her body temperature seemed to come back to normal and that bloated feeling subsided.

She wondered where all the water had gone. She didn't *feel* like she'd grown some sort of camel's hump, nor did rolling on her back for a moment reveal one, but clearly this body had areas to store a lot of excess liquid. After a while she forced herself to get up, even though she actually felt sleepy. For one thing, the pool was not totally calm but it did reflect decently and she wanted to get a more complete image of herself. And then it would be prudent to look around. Although Lori the American college teacher wouldn't have resisted, Bimi of the People knew that it wouldn't do to just zonk out without checking the lay of the land.

The image of herself in the gently rippling water was both strange and familiar. She'd always had something of a long neck, and she still did; the face, although the same beige or light tan color, contained enough of the old Lori Sutton to be recognizable, although it had a harder, larger, rougher cast. It was, she realized, what her face would have looked like had she been born a man. She'd always had that boyish look to her face, and now it seemed to have firmed up and looked not nearly as bad to her as it had all those times in the mirror.

The lips *were* thicker by quite a bit and were a dark brown, the nose was a bit larger, the eyes were dark black blobs against a medium brown field, the ears were very equine and larger than she'd thought, and the eyebrows were thick and snow white and rose on either side of the eyes at a slight angle, giving her a slightly exotic look. The big shock of white hair was actually kind of cute. The horn, the same color brown as the skin fur, looked, well, different from what she had imagined. *That's one hell of a phallic symbol,* she thought. *Jeez! As weird as this body is, it sure would have turned me on!*

She tore herself reluctantly away from the self-examination and got up and looked around the rest of the oasis. It was, thankfully, deserted. Not that she wanted to hide out forever, but she wasn't sure she was ready for others of this kind yet, particularly not as a man.

This was clearly a popular stop. In the sandy soil were traces of great numbers of people—beings like herself, anyway—having moved through here, and probably not long ago, since clearly the winds came through this place and erased many signs as if they'd never been. There was also signs of some sort of civilized behavior as well—holes which clearly were some kind of tent pole supports, a central fire pit with more support holes that might indicate anything from a rotisserie to grates being placed there, and a veritable waste pile of damaged and broken crockery, much of it of fired clay and some of it inlaid with elaborate designs.

The designs were very interesting, since among the more abstract parts were some scenes of what might have been life in this place. The style was almost reminiscent of ancient Egyptian, all in profile and two very flat dimensions yet finely featured. She couldn't be sure if these were domestic or religious scenes, but a lot could be learned from them.

For one thing, they went in for decoration more than clothes, and *that* was instructive—not that clothes made a lot of sense out here with this kind of body. Either these beings came in a rainbow of colors or dyed fur in different colors and patterns was popular. So was decorating the horns, some of which were depicted as impossibly long. There was also a fair amount of jewelry on the males and what appeared to be serapelike capes with intricate designs worn over the head but extending down only chest-high and, on some but not all, a kind of highly decorated but very brief codpiece. Males didn't seem to grow facial hair, but the big clump of hair on top tapered down the back until it vanished completely about three-quarters of the way down in a manelike appearance.

The females were quite different. First, they were all depicted as at least a head shorter than any of the males, although that might be just the male artist's perspective. They had very soft feminine faces and no horn at all, but they had a huge amount of hair that trailed down their backs. They also had tails, much like horses' tails, that were almost mirror images of their hair and seemed to be deliberately styled to be that way and kept up with some kind of stays. They were not brown-furred but rather a soft, pale yellow, and their body hair and tails were a variety of browns, reds, even blonds, as well as black. How much was artificial and how much was "natural" color couldn't be determined.

They also had two pairs of breasts, one atop the other. It was a very strange sight, but with the erotic equine curves of the body it didn't look wrong, either. That got Lori to examining her own chest, where, after some effort even with the short hair, she did indeed locate four small nipples.

Did they have *that* many kids that they needed all that excess capacity? Or did they have a lot of kids and only a few made it past weaning? No, probably not. They didn't seem big enough to carry more than one or two routinely, any more than human women did. The breasts, which seemed almost "humanlike," had some of the short pale yellow fur about two-thirds of the way to the nipples but were otherwise all a very light brown.

Some of the decorations simply depicted scenes from some kind of tribal life: guards flanking a particularly decorated male who wore a lot of gold and a bright serape adorned with a sash, females preparing food in fire pits. The males carried spears, and some seemed to be wearing swords—there was one scene of two males dueling, possibly in sport, the swords thin and rapierlike, with hilts somewhat reminiscent of their horns. There were also scenes that were blatantly erotic, often two or more females with one male, and the sexual attributes depicted made her own rather large endowment seem downright trivial.

Still, aside from the alienness of the people depicted, the scenes for the most part looked right out of some ancient Near Eastern Earth culture. A tribal, nomadic people, but with a sense of art and, from the odd-looking bands around some of the broken pottery, with a form of writing as well.

She was about to abandon her look through the remnants when a large fragment caught her eye and she reached down, picked it up, and frowned. It gave her a sudden chill to look at the scene, the first one she really didn't like at all.

Their tents, crockery, ornamental stuff, all their goods moved on what seemed to be sledlike devices made to slide through the sand. Several had been depicted open or parked in other scenes, but this scene was of some in motion. She wondered why she hadn't seen any depictions of domesticated animals, and this was why.

The females were lined up on a series of wooden bars passed through a forward support, and teams of six to ten of them, depending on the size of the desert sled, were clearly pulling them while the males ran with their spears to either side.

The females were the draft animals.

In fact, suddenly flashing back through the other scenes, she realized that whenever work was depicted, it was the females who were doing it. The males might fence or look magnificent or whatever, but never were they shown actually *doing* anything, except in the erotic ones, of course, when they were doing what men always liked to do.

She felt outraged by the sight as all her old principles came to the fore, and yet she found herself thinking, *Thank God I'm not a woman here!*

She was ashamed of the thought, yet damn it, the idea of being one of the bosses rather than one of the servants was something of a turn-on. She hated herself for feeling *that,* too, and tried to get some self-control back. She didn't know what it was to be as oppressed as these women obviously were, but she knew what it was like to be a woman in a man's world, and she hoped she wouldn't descend to that level even if she had to adjust to this society.

She tossed the shard back in the pile, and it landed with a crash and cracked again.

This was too much to handle, coming all at once, she thought. It made the kidnapping and subsequent life among the People seem almost ordinary by comparison. Still, Alam—Mavra—had been right. Without that first experience, she wasn't sure if she could have handled this one at all.

She looked around, but there was clearly nothing to eat here. There *did* seem to be some kind of round, green fruit way up atop the trees, but even if it were edible and ripe enough to eat, this body was good for a lot of things, but tree climbing wasn't one of them. Filled with water, though, she was in no immediate danger of anything more than a growling stomach. She would pick a spot in the shade with some promise of concealment just in case and get the badly needed rest. *Then* she could think of what to do next.

It was a weird dream, mixing living scenes from the discarded pottery and the race that lived here with scenes of the Amazon and of the university, and at one point she was saying to her department head, *"Now that I'm a man, Dr. Avery, you can't deny me the Holburn Chair and the professorship that goes with it."*

The smell of odd spices and perfumes and the tinkling of bells brought her back to consciousness, but it wasn't until the sudden thought that she was no longer alone that she stiffened, rolled over, and tensely peered out from the rocks and bushes toward the pool.

It wasn't a big caravan like those depicted on the shards but, rather, a small party, no more than eight or nine people from the look of it, and one of those sleighlike wagons. Most, maybe all, were females, except for one big fellow reclining on a cushion. He looked, well, old—not really old but well into middle age from the cast and lines in his face and the wear and tear on his skin. He wore a somewhat faded and threadbare serape of faded red that had an even more faded yellow design too shopworn to matter and one of those codpieces that might at one time have been silvery but now just looked a dirty gray. His horn, either shorter than hers or worn down over time, was wrapped in a kind of turbanlike affair that made it appear that he was wearing a cream-colored pointed hat. Everything about him, from his overall look and manner to the faded remnants of once colorfully decorated skin, looked a bit old and a bit seedy.

So did the sleigh. Clearly it had seen a lot of use in its time and hadn't been cared for very well of late, but, like its owner, it was serviceable.

Watching the females, seeing them in person for the first time, was an odd experience. All were considerably smaller than either the old man or Lori, and the double pair of breasts on them all seemed quite a bit larger than in the pictures. The hair and the tails were nicely done up so that they were pretty well mirror images of one another, and the effect was quite nice indeed to look at. They all seemed to have a naturally feminine, sexy manner to them, and they would talk or whisper to one another, ears turning and twitching, and occasionally giggle like schoolgirls. Most wore some sort of jewelry—bracelets, necklaces—but little else, although the one at the fire pit had on a thick serape much longer than the male's, apparently not a garment but rather protection against heat. There was also something odd about their hands, but she couldn't make out what it might be.

She wondered just what the hell she should do now. Here was contact, and on a scale she might handle, but damn it, it was *scary* to be in this situation. Finally realizing that there was nothing else to do, Lori hauled herself onto the top of the rock, assuming a sitting position, and coughed politely.

The effect on the females was startling. They froze like deer in the meadow might have frozen at the first sense of danger. The male moved pretty quickly, though, whirling, grabbing a sword, and actually getting to his feet in a single series of motions.

"Who be you?" the old man called out menacingly in a low voice.

"Please, good sir, put down your sword," Lori responded, startled at how very, very deep her voice sounded to her ears but also relieved that language, at least, wasn't going to be a problem. "I sit here with nothing, not even clothes, let alone a weapon."

"Where'd ye come from?" the old man asked suspiciously, sword still in hand.

"I was already here," Lori explained. "I—I woke up in the sands near here as I am now."

"*Yesss . . . ?* And who dumped ye there, and why?"

"I—I don't know if this is going to sound crazy to you or not, but I was a different sort of—creature—from another world. I came through what I was told is a hex gate to a place called Zone, and then they forced me through another gate, and I woke up as you see me."

The old man sniffed, frowned, then put his sword away. "Not *another* one!" he said in disbelief. "Not in my lifetime, or my father's, or *his* father's lifetime has anyone come though there and been dumped here. Now suddenly yer fallin' from the skies!"

Lori's heart skipped a beat. "*Another* one, you say? You mean I'm not the first?"

"Not if yer what you says you are, anyways. Other was a girl, over in the Hajeb, a couple months ago maybe. Least, that's what I heard."

She shook her head. "That means nothing to me. I'm afraid I don't even know where I am, or what I am, for that matter." She was disappointed at the time frame. It meant that whoever the girl was, she was from one of the other parties—most likely the woman in the wheelchair, since that was the only female she recalled among the pictures shown to them back in Zone.

The old man chuckled. "Well, sonny, this land be Erdom, in the bottom of the World, and we all be Erdomites first. I be Posiphar of the Makob, a traveling merchant by trade.

I buy and sell things, services, whatever be needed between the families and tribes of the Hjolai. I be on me route from oasis to oasis right now, headin' next fer the camp of Lord Aswab."

"The names mean nothing to me yet. I'm sorry," she told him. Guessing that the man's odd manner of speech was either a regional dialect or just the mark of a less than educated man, she made no attempt to duplicate it. "Uh, I'd like to come down, but I'm not really dressed fit for mixed company, I'm afraid."

Posiphar chuckled again. "Don't worry none 'bout the girls. Ye ain't got nothin' they ain't seen many times afore, I promise ye. Come, come, let me get a look at ye!"

She got down slowly and carefully. Although the body seemed easier to use, more familiar now, she wasn't about to take any chances with it. She then walked over to him, trying to be as natural as possible.

"Heh! Ye walk like some girl," the old man commented. "Well, ain't no nevermind of mine. Yer a big fella, though, I got to say."

Until now she really hadn't had anything for comparison, but it was clear that things were pretty much of a human-sized scale, and now, standing in front of the merchant, she found that as he was a head taller than the tallest woman in his party, she was almost that much bigger and taller than he was. Although she'd been by no means short, it was a novel experience to be the biggest and tallest of a group, and she found she liked the sensation.

"Well, son," the merchant said at last, "maybe ye and me can make a deal here. Ye needs a bit of educatin' on Erdom, I think."

"Not to mention food, clothes, and money," she added.

"Yeah, well, that goes without sayin', I suppose. As ye might have figured, I ain't exactly drippin' with gold and silver and precious gems, but I makes do, I does. Been some banditry about of late—ain't like the old times, I tell ye. I ain't no slouch in a fight, but I be gettin' on and slowed down in spite of meself, and with nobody coverin' me back, I ain't been feelin' too safe of late. Don't suppose ye be any good with a sword?"

She looked at the sword he'd put down by his side. It wasn't like a broadsword; in fact, it was more like a saber than anything else. She wasn't *great* with a sword, but she'd *almost* made the fencing team her undergraduate senior year. "I can use one of those if I had to," she told him. "I might be off balance with it, though. I'm still getting used to this body. But I'm even better with a spear," she added.

"Hmph! What were ye before? Some kinda hard-shelled twelve-armed insect or somethin'?"

She laughed. "No, nothing like that. In some ways not an *extremely* different sort than this, but far enough. More— apelike. You know what an ape is?"

"Sure I do! Seen some over in the port cities now and again. See most anything in this world at them docks. Where'd you think I seen them insect things?"

She was startled. "You mean there actually *are* creatures like that here? Man-sized insects that—think?"

"Sure. You got a whole *lot* t' learn, sonny. Um, what *is* yer name, anyways? One of them impossible-to-say words?"

"Uh, well, it's Lori. It *was,* anyway."

"That's a good enough nonsense word to serve," Posiphar responded. "Here ye be linked with yer family and tribal place name. Since ye ain't got no family or no tribe here, a place name'll do. It'll drive everybody else nuts tryin' to figure out how ye got it, too. How's Lori of Alkhaz sound as a name?"

"Uh, all right, I guess, but who, what, or where is Alkhaz?"

"Why, *this* is Alkhaz, of course! Just a transit oasis, not nobody's in particular. That's 'cause the water's decent here only part of the year. The rest of the time it's either too muddy or too alkaline for most folks' tastes. There's always another that opens up, so it's no big thing."

"I'll accept it, then," she told him. "And Erdom? Is all of it like this? Desert?"

"Well, a whole lot of it is, anyways. All except right on the coast. A few nice little cities there get some rain and have some hills with trees that keep the rain there to use. Got a decent-sized seacoast, but we're right smack up against that Zone wall, so the only place where everything piles up is in the southeast, where Erdom and the wall come together. Sand and stuff gets built up by the sea breezes there, and they get a decent amount of weather. Rest of the place, well, the rains just sink into the sands and get swallowed up, and these here underground rivers are the only water."

"And so it's just the coast and the rest is like this?"

"Well, there's some towns around inside, where you got really good springs, of course. Otherwise you couldn't do the Pilgrimage of the Seven Springs. Got some deep mines over in Jwoba. Them's gold mines. And Awokabi has the diamonds and so on. Don't like 'em much, though. Dirty, smelly, sad little towns where most folks work for nothin' but food and water and the lords live fat. I like the Hjolai better. Folks be friendly if ye don't overstay yer welcome, and they knows ye won't cheat 'em much, and there still be some honor."

She looked out at the desert. "How many people live out here, though? What do they live on?"

"Oh, the whole be divided into Holdings, we calls 'em, each with a pretty fair-sized oasis able to support some number of herd animals and even some farmin' of a limited type. Each is a hereditary family Holding headed by a lord, and the folks there pretty much work fer him. He in return gives 'em protection and security. It ain't a bad system. Hell, half the year the lord's movin' 'round his Holding from oasis to oasis, listenin' t' gripes, fixin' problems. They still think things go both ways out here. The people work for the lord, and the lord tries to help the people with their problems and make life better for 'em. Most do all right. You gets a bad one now and again, o' course—stands to reason—but he don't last long. Most of 'em, even the best, get knocked off sooner or later by one of their relatives anyways, and if you got the people cheerin' for it, well, that lord lasts all the shorter, see?"

Lori nodded, but she wasn't all that thrilled by the system. It sounded like something out of Arabia and a past age of Earth—monarchical tribal families, inheritance by assassination, feudalism. She wasn't all that sure how much she was going to like this.

"But you're not working for a lord," she noted. "Or are you?"

"*Haw!* Not likely! There be some of us around, kind of like a brotherhood. See, them lords need us, 'cause they don't get along with one another nohow, and we be the only ones can walk and talk between with nobody figurin' we like one side better'n the other. So if one wants t' send a message to the other, they use traders like me. If their breedin' stock's thin and needs freshening, they won't sell to nobody they won't even talk to, so they sell to me for a promise that I'll bring 'em back what they need. I takes the stock, trades it to another, then bring the trade back, and that settles that. Of course there's a fee, but we haggles fer it. I been around so long 'cause I always gives 'em a good deal. 'Course, you don't live as well or as rich as if you try'n jerks 'em around a bit, but ye keeps yer balls that way. Them lords got a real mean streak if they catch you!"

"I'll bet," Lori said glumly, having no trouble imagining Erdomite desert justice. "Uh, you mentioned some deal between us?"

"Sure. Kwaza! Bring me the serpent chest!" he called, and one of the women stopped what she was doing, went over to the sleigh, and started rummaging around. She finally found the chest and brought it over to them.

When she did, Lori could see what had been mystifying

her about the females' hands. They were more hooflike, the three fingers fused together and bending as one, with just enough indentation for flexibility, while the opposing thumb was even wider and broader than the males' thumbs. The effect reminded her more of claws, but they were too soft and supple for that description to be accurate. It must be more like doing everything wearing mittens, she thought.

When the woman had gone back to her work, Lori asked in a low tone, "Are all females' hands like that? No independent fingers?"

"Huh? Oh, sure. That's 'cause, when they're well along carryin' a baby, they got to pretty much walk on all fours and use their arms like the forelegs of an animal unless they be leanin' on somethin'. Otherwise they couldn't get around at all for them last two months or so. If the fingers could spread like a man's, you'd never be able t' do it. It'd tear yer fingers right off after a while. Don't believe me, try it sometimes."

"Hmph! Seems too bad, though. It sure limits what they can do."

"Not as much as ye think," Posiphar replied. "There's an old sayin', of course, that if women had fingers they'd be dangerous, but actually they got a little over us. You'n me, we get a bad break in the leg, don't heal, and we're crippled and in pain fer life, hobblin' around and no good to nobody. They lose a leg, they can still get around, do most of what they could before. No, the Creator put a lot of thought into us. I seen some races down at the port, they got these big boobs or udders, and fer what? To feed the young for a few months after havin' kids. And how many kids do most women have, anyways? So they carry them things for life and use 'em hardly a'tall. Erdomite women, now, when they ain't sucklin', they stores water in them. Ye, me, full of water here, couldn't last more'n eight days without a drink. Women—up to three weeks, and it's available not only to them from the inside but to anybody else what needs it from the outside. Now, *that's* useful!"

She didn't bother to bring up the fact that there were other, purely pleasurable uses for breasts, but she conceded him his point. Each gender had its strengths and weaknesses for this harsh society and environment, but it was pretty clear that the men were, in every sense of the word, on top here.

The chest, with an exotic winged serpentlike creature carved into it, proved to have various articles of male adornment. Only one of the dozens of codpieces was big enough to fit, and it was a plain, worn black color, but somehow, although it was decidedly uncomfortable and not at all useful for concealment or protection, it made her feel dressed for polite company. She passed on anything else, though, figuring, as it turned out correctly, that anything she might choose to use would be charged to her account. While she had no objection to providing the old trader with some extra protection, she also had no intention of getting so into debt to him that he'd virtually own her.

The food was very spicy and very good, and Lori realized with a start that it had been a *very* long time since she'd eaten, let alone had a decently cooked meal. The meat seemed similar to lamb but was too salty to tell more, and it was cooked in a large woklike pan together with some kind of very long ricelike grain and a number of green and red vegetables at least one of which was some kind of hot pepper. Out here the drink was water, period.

With more conversation both that night and the next day setting out across the desert, she learned much more about this strange place and its dominant race.

Women were definitely at the very low end of the scale here, as she'd surmised, bound there by religion, tradition, and some definitely chauvinistic attitudes among the males. Because they were smaller and therefore had smaller brains, Posiphar told her, women were not as intelligent as men and had shorter attention spans, so any education and position was reserved for the males. It was considered a logical as well as practical division, not the least of reasons for this being that females outnumbered males roughly three to one, not only in live births but because they tended to live longer. Because of this, too, polygamy was the norm, although many men had only one wife and some of the richer males had whole harems. The rule was that one could have as many wives as one could support. There was also a law that said if one could no longer support them, one had to find new husbands for them that could.

She was relieved to learn that one of her fears, at least, was unfounded. They did not buy and sell women, or anybody else, either, although the women, without any practical rights at all, were pretty much at the mercy of the exclusively male-dominated system. "Love matches" were simply beyond their comprehension; one married for political reasons, for social reasons, for a dowry, or sometimes because one liked their features and thought that the combination would produce superior children.

Infant mortality was horrendous in the cities and working towns but surprisingly low in the desert and oasis communities. Communicable diseases were rare; the way heat was handled and exchanged in the bodies produced regular temperatures for short periods almost every day that killed ninety-five percent of any viruses or bacteria that might lurk inside. In the cities and working towns it was often the living conditions and other environmental factors that killed the young.

There was almost no chance at social mobility for either men or women, though. Maybe one step up or down, but no more than that. Certain physical features and colorations were unique to certain classes and made it difficult to pass as another in any event. Although it would be a while before she could recognize those differences, Posiphar told her that her body marked her as pretty well in the middle of the scale, suitable for a soldier or merchant or craftsman, but she had no characteristics of the nobility at all.

Erdom itself was, like all hexes, six-sided, but because it

abutted the South Zone wall, an impenetrable barrier, its six sides formed a wing shape with a long flat along the ocean to the east rather than a hexagon.

Initially, a newcomer would simply "appear" almost anywhere in a given hex, but once there, the gates were the only way to and from Zone. The gate for Erdom was located near the wall in the far southeast corner, outside the large port city-state of Aqomb, where sat the Sultan of Erdom. The Sultan, in fact, had little practical authority outside his city but was the titular ruler of the entire hex, and, as such, Aqomb was considered the temporal and spiritual capital of Erdom.

Law in Erdom was entirely religious law, not only out of conviction but also out of necessity—the religion and its laws were the only true unifying elements in the primitive "nation" and served as a guarantee of uniformity of social rules and taboos across the hex. A priesthood of monks, all voluntarily castrated and living a totally religious and mostly cloistered life, ran the temples and spent most of the time praying to a series of cosmic gods that looked like some kind of giant six-armed octopuses out of a nightmare. The damper was put on social mobility and even male-female treatment by a strong belief in reincarnation, in which all Erdomites spent endless cycles of death and rebirth in attempts to raise themselves up to the level of their gods. Each soul was born as a lower-class female first, and only a perfect life would result in rebirth as a lower-class male. From that point a soul went up or down the social scale depending on how its life went, first female and then male until it reached the top of male nobility, after which came divination as a monk and, finally, godhood.

The fact that the vast majority of the population were lower-class females was taken as a sign that not too many made it. It was also a rationalization for the whole sociopolitical structure and the treatment of both males and females within each level of the system. It also meant that complainers, chronic troublemakers, and potential enemies could be executed with a clear conscience, since they'd be reborn anyway.

In fact, maiming was considered a far greater punishment, since it meant suffering with the result of transgression instead of having a new chance at a full life. About the only thing one so maimed could become would be a bandit if physically able or a crippled beggar if not. Only males faced maiming; females who ran afoul of religious law were always beheaded.

It was not, however, a strict society overall if one just played the game. Punishment came from rocking the boat; so long as one paid lip service to the system and behaved, it was actually pretty relaxed. It was also pretty dull, which was why the men indulged in a lot of macho posturing, dangerous sports, and even duels.

Lori did wonder about the women. They all looked strong and did much of the drudge work yet were seemingly always cheerful; the talk around the wells and camp site sounded pretty dumb and vapid, and there was never the slightest sign she could find of disobedience or rebellion. Almost without exception, they really *did* seem as dumb as a box of rocks.

As the days passed, Lori no longer felt any physical strangeness either with her own body or in seeing other Erdomites. In fact, being a member of this race was now so natural for her that even in her dreams of Earth and her previous existence all the people looked like Erdomites. Still, there were problems.

As an astronomer she'd been thrilled and awed by the night sky; the Well World seemed to be in the middle of a globular cluster. But there was nothing familiar to her up there, and even the names meant little. And of course there was the additional restriction of being in a highly limited nontech hex where science was on a rather low level, ignorance even among the educated was fairly high, and much of what she always had taken for granted—great telescopes, computers, and all the rest—simply wouldn't work. Worse, one good solid look at the written language of Erdom showed that it was pictographic, like Chinese, and not the sort of thing learned easily or quickly. Even though she still could read and write in her Earth languages, they were of little use here except to make memos to herself. In this element she was stripped of her profession and lifelong passion, denied a chance at it again or anything like it, and essentially illiterate—just like much of the population. Education was in the hands of a few teaching monks, and even if she could get into that highest caste, which she could not, the price would be much too high for her even now.

The other problem, though, was her sense of identity. She felt like an Erdomite, true, but she still felt like a woman trapped in a man's body. Although she was tempted to try out the opposite sexual role, the females just didn't really appeal to her. The men of her age, on the other hand, seemed powerful, strong, and very, very erotic.

And it was tearing her up.

She liked being around them, liked playing around with them, too. Either her fencing was improving dramatically or most of them weren't very good at it, because she rarely lost and then usually by not fully concentrating on the mock duel. In fact, by betting on such competitions, she'd actually accumulated some cash—gold and silver coins that were accepted hexwide—and bought her own used sword, hilt, and belt as well as a decent bow and a quiver of bronze-tipped arrows. While she wasn't a real champion at the latter, she was getting very good at hitting what she aimed at.

The trouble was, she was enjoying being around the young men and sporting with them for all the wrong reasons, and she dared not let on what the real reasons were.

Being on the road with the merchant helped, though. It was tough to form too many attachments when she was three or four days in one place, another few days journeying across the desert, then another three or four days in a new town or camp. She had given up all thought of contacting Mavra by this point; it was far too late, even though such an expedition away from this place would be much to her liking and Mavra could probably use somebody Lori's size.

Another thing was rubbing her wrong, too, although it was even harder to control. She was finding day by day that she was treating the females—both Posiphar's two wives and four daughters and those she came in casual contact with—in the same callous manner as the other males. She was much too easily buying into that part of the system, one that went against her whole life and all her beliefs. She felt guilty as hell every time she did it—but always after she did it, and she didn't stop because of it. It called her entire personal belief system into question. Deep down, had she really craved the absolute sexual equality she'd always thought she wanted, or had she instead subconsciously *really* just wanted a reversal of the system? If the latter, then she really hadn't had any ideals, just rationalizations.

Things changed a little when they pulled into a small oasis town in the south. They really didn't have any business to do there, but it was on the way from Point A to Point B and was a convenient stopover.

She wandered over to the ubiquitous social club all such places had, where the young men hung out between jobs and the transients could relax. It was much like an English pub in atmosphere, although Erdomite desert tribes considered alcohol and most stimulants and depressants stronger than coffee or tea to be evil and did not serve them.

The name always started the questions.

"Lori of Alkhaz. Odd name. Who are the Alkhaz, and where? Never heard of them."

She'd explain that she was not a native and had come through the Well, and that would elicit what was now becoming a somewhat boring and repetitive set of explanations that nonetheless made the newcomer the center of attention for a while. This time, however, there was a difference.

"You ought to go over and see Aswam the Master Tentmaker, then," one of the men commented.

"Oh? I have no need for a tent."

"No, no. He's the latest recipient of what's rapidly being called 'The Girl from All the Hells.' She's an emigrant from another world, just like you."

"Really? Yes, I very much want to speak with her! Where is this tentmaker's place?"

"I'll show you. I'm not certain that anybody can do much with her, though. She's too smart, too aggressive, hates everybody and everything, and they keep her locked up like a prisoner since she won't behave and nobody's been able to break her. We think she's mad. Would you believe that she claims she was once a *man*? She's been passed around from family to family for some time, and by the time poor Aswam took a crack at her, there was nobody left to pass her on to when he gave up."

"My God! I'm surprised she wasn't executed!"

"I think that's what she wants, but it would be immoral to punish someone who is mad for behaving like they are mad, you see."

She did see and quickly had the dwelling of the master tentmaker in sight. She wasn't sure who or what she expected, but male or female, crazy or sane, it was somebody she could *talk* to. The fact that the other emigrant claimed to have been a man explained a lot of the behavior. She wouldn't have much liked being a female in *this* society, but to have been a man and dropped female into it would be particularly awful.

Although most of the buildings in these permanent settlements were made of dried mud, Aswam, of course, lived in what looked like a tent city. He proved to be a prosperous middle-aged man with many wives and more kids than could be easily counted.

"Ack!" he exclaimed, looking disgusted. *"That* one! She is a demon!"

"Perhaps, but if she's from the same place I'm from, as I think she might be, maybe I can do something with her."

He led Lori to a small mud hut in back of the tents, not much bigger than the outhouse it sat next to. Unlike most buildings in Erdom, though, this one was not open or covered only with a blanket but had an actual lockable door of wood.

"I used to store money and records in here," the tentmaker grumbled. "Now I am saddled with this dead loss!"

"Why did you take her, then?"

"Ha! The dowry offered was fantastic, or so I thought. More than any pretty girl is worth. But I tell you, she is so much trouble that I now realize that I was taken!"

"Why do you keep her locked up? Is she dangerous?"

"Only to herself. She keeps trying to run off into the Hjolai."

"You have the keys?"

"Yes, here. Go ahead in."

"What is her name?"

"She calls herself 'Julian' or some such foreign name."

She felt some relief that at least it wasn't poor Gus. He'd had enough done to him up to now. She had to admit to herself that she was also somewhat disappointed that it wasn't Juan Campos. Being a female in Erdom was just what that bastard deserved.

"All right. You can leave us. I'll be responsible."

Lori turned the key in the lock, opened the door, and went inside the small hut. It was quite dark, with only slits at the top for letting in light, and quite barren. The floor was covered with a local strawlike grass, and on it a female lay on her side, looking up at the newcomer.

There was only one way to try to break the ice. She tried

English first. "My name is Lori, and I'm from Earth."

The effect on the girl was dramatic. She pushed herself to a seated position and looked up at the newcomer. "You're from *Earth*?" she responded in the same language and with an American accent. The almost whispery alto voice, however, seemed out of place. "This isn't just some new trick, is it?"

"No, it's no trick."

"Well, where I come from, a guy named Lori would be a little suspect."

"That's because the same thing happened to me that happened to you, only in reverse. It's terrible and ironic, I know, but I was a woman just like you were a man."

She stared at Lori for a moment, frowning in the gloom, then shook her head sadly. "Crazy. They said when we got here that this Well was some kind of logical computer. So where's the logic of making me *this* and you *that*?"

"Yes, I know. I was also an assistant professor of astronomy, which does me precious little good in this place."

"You *were*? I was a shuttle astronaut. A mission specialist. A fancy engineer, really, not a pilot. I'm Julian Beard."

"Then *you're* one of the two men who came through ahead of us! I *knew* you looked familiar when they showed us your picture. Your 'before' picture, that is. I did some work in Houston a few years back, and you were one of the instructors. Lori Ann Sutton."

The name didn't register, but she didn't expect it to. Many such scientists and other types had come through there, and she had only stayed a week. Still, Julian said, "Well, that's a kick in the head and ass. This thing is *really* screwed up. Dropped us in the wrong bodies in a backward land where even if you were allowed to use what you know, what you know doesn't work. Would you believe *nothing* but mechanical energy functions here? Or at least in any controllable way."

"I know. But, while I understand your problems being

female in *this* society, how'd you get stuck in *this* fix?"

Julian shook her head in disgust. "You just don't *know*. First you wake up looking like an alternative evolution from a prehistoric horse, then you find you're not only a girl but you've got four breasts and a big tail and hands like pincers. Then you wander into one of these Bedouinlike camps and you're treated like a fresh piece of meat. They didn't *care* about me. They weren't even *interested* in me except as new flesh. Just trying to talk civilly to them gets you a rap in the mouth or worse. Then they decide you're either high-spirited or too smart or both, and they start trying to break you, body and soul. They were just, well, *unspeakable,* barbaric, and while they didn't break me, they pretty much took my soul. I didn't even want to live anymore."

Lori sighed. "I think I can imagine. I'm not so sure I wouldn't have just killed myself."

"That's just the problem! You *can't*. Not really. I tried to figure this out, and even though I'm no biologist, I have a theory. I think, well, in humans, most all males have some female in them. I mean, it's half the chromosomes, right? And every female has some male hormones to one degree or another. Here the male chromosome seems to have all the male hormones. Either that or male hormones have no effect on females. All the male I am, all the maleness I ever had, is in my head, but the female hormones really take control of behavior. I can't explain it. I can't even tell you what it does to you exactly. It's not like I suddenly woke up a human female. That would be a whole different thing, one you could certainly understand. This is Erdomese, and it's like a hundred times anything in humans, I'm sure. You know the feeling of walking alone on a dark night in a place you don't know well? The kind of nervousness or outright fear that's there? *Everything* becomes like that. *Everywhere.* In sunlight as well as darkness. The insecurity is monstrous, overwhelming. You just can't handle it no matter how hard you try. Like a permanent, unshakable paranoia. You want to be in a group with others, others you *know*. The urge for security dominates you and overrides anything else. Anything odd happens, you freeze solid or you have an irresistible impulse to run and hide. You only feel safe when you're with a big group of women you know or there's a related man around—husband, big brother, father, whatever. For that matter, ever see a wife or daughter talk back or argue with a husband or father here? Most of them just—*can't*. They hate it, but they have to take it."

Lori nodded, having seen all this behavior in the females. "Maybe it's vestigial. Not just a sexual division of responsibilities but a true herd mentality. I think this race evolved, or was made to evolve, from some more primitive herd animals. The whole society seems to rise from those primitive roots. The males were the hunters and guardians of the herd. The horn was a natural weapon. I think that's why males here love this kind of swordplay. And that's why you kept trying to run off into the desert. It fit the pattern and would still be almost certain suicide."

"Yes, that's it. It was my only way out. That and the fact that I was maybe the only woman in this stinking place who could muster up the guts to say 'no' and have enough self-control to mean it. But I couldn't really fight it. All I could do was piss and moan and make the men's lives a little miserable. It would be nothing back home—I wouldn't have had anything to do with a woman who didn't have that kind of spunk—but here it's something the guys just can't handle. So they swapped me off, family to family, and it started all over again. Finally this tentmaker took me to one of their weird priests. I think they're smart and well educated, because he knew what an engineer was and what computers are and a lot more. We talked for quite a while about who I was and where I was from and what my problem was, and I thought maybe things would improve, but they didn't. They got worse."

"He led you on and then pounced, huh?"

"Pretty much. In the end their job is to keep everything just the way it is. Just *knowing* about the outside world isn't the same as *approving* of it. It was his idea to lock me up like this. He said it might take a long time, but I was very young—this body's about fourteen or so—and that eventually, with no stimuli, the biology—he actually called it 'programming'—would take over completely. He's right, too. Since I've been in here my dreams have gotten more and more mixed up and more and more erotic. My memories are becoming more and more confused, and I have trouble remembering what I was like—before. Even the math tables I used to stay sane when they were trying to break me more crudely fail me. Not that I've forgotten them, I just can't keep my mind on them. I also kept trying to always think in English, or sometimes German, but I just can't *concentrate* anymore, and the more my thoughts were Erdomese, the more Erdomese I became. I—I've lost so much already, I don't know how much of me is really left. Here, see? I'm starting to cry, and I just can't stop it. And I don't even feel embarrassed about doing it anymore."

"Sometimes a good cry is something we all need. Holding it in is what eats you up."

"Yeah?" she responded, sniffling and wiping away tears. "So if you're so miserable here, how many times have *you* cried since you got here?"

Lori didn't answer, but the truth was, not at all. For a man to cry here was to show weakness and lose honor and the respect of both males and females. No matter how much she'd wanted to, she'd held it in as a matter of course. It was another little shock to the system. *Maybe I've become more of a male than I think . . .*

"I don't know," Lori told her. "I still can't figure out my own self in this. I mean, no offense, but there's still some of me that's the human woman I was for most of my life. It won't go away. I liked men, and I still do. I assume you were pretty much of a straight arrow like me back home, but *your* orientation seems to be changing to fit what you've become."

"I—I think we fight it because it's the last real core of what we were," she suggested, still wiping away tears. "So long as we hold on to that, we're still something of our old selves. I mean, what defines us—how we grew up, how we related to other people—more than our sex? You let go, you throw that out, and you're not *you* anymore. You're somebody else, somebody with another person's memories. I think you can cling to it until you die—and there's certainly got to be gays in most all the cultures here, since we see it in animals, too. With men here, though, it's easier. You have a little of both male and female in you, so it's easier to control the physical aspects of the change. I don't so it was a lot harder to cling to, but I did, until I was put in here for so long. I could either fight that battle or stay sane fighting the others. I let it go. For *you,* it's the defining thing. For *me,* it was in the way, I think. You have more choices, but in the end you're going to have to decide who and what you want to be, 'cause you're going to be an Erdomite man for the rest of your life, just like I'm going to be an Erdomite woman."

"I think there's a lot more of Julian Beard in you than you think," Lori told her. "Otherwise you'd have given up and given in long ago." She decided she liked Julian—liked her a lot. It was the first time she felt she was really attracted to a female here.

"Maybe. When a female gets close to a male she trusts, she gets these *feelings,* these *urges* that are hard to control. I'm feeling them right now, in here, with you. Right now my mind, the one thing I've been able to somehow keep, is able to suppress them, but every day I'm here it gets harder and harder to fight, to keep control. I'm slipping more and more."

"Tell me something. The women here—are they really as dumb as they seem to be?"

That brought a smile to Julian's still-tearful face. "No,

some are quite smart, but they've learned to hide it well. Being smart in this culture just means trouble if you're a woman. They're pretty ignorant, though, and they don't know any other system. Sometimes I think of those women in the countries back on Earth that went western and then returned to fundamentalism. They might resent the restrictions, but somehow they're comforted by the absolutism of the rules and religion. And like I said, security is everything."

"I just—I dunno—I just had a hunch that might be it," Lori replied. "It really offended me that they might all be frightened little bimbos. But I forgot to ask the one question I wanted to know more than anything. How did you ever get here in the *first* place?"

"Stupidity," Julian Beard replied. "That meteor that came down in the jungle—I was on assignment from NASA to take a look at it. Good publicity, too. Then that news team disappeared and the army took over, and it was *weeks* before anything serious could be done."

"Yes, I was one of the team."

"I thought so. I figured what happened to us happened to you. Anyway, this tough old Brazilian Air Force colonel who was in charge out there was more a politician than a military man. He finally called off the search and bent to pressures to let in researchers, at least a few at a time. Well, the whole world came down on us, or so it seemed, and they wanted pictures and all that for the publicity, and since a number of people had climbed all over that meteor before, we figured it wasn't any big deal. The colonel and I were asked to pose on top of it for the media; he talked me into it, and you can guess what happened."

"The hex gate opened, and you both wound up in Zone talking to a polka-dotted dragon."

"Actually, it was a mean-looking five-foot-tall talking butterfly. You?"

"Too long a story to tell here and now. The first thing we

have to do is decide what to do about you."

"Huh?"

"Look, it may be backward, but we're here and we're stuck. That Zone had elaborate computers and all sorts of technology, and I happen to know that a third of the countries here—they call them hexes, after their shape—support high technology, some way in advance of Earth's. I'm going crazy here, and you want to kill yourself before you lose it all. There's a seacoast and ports here, believe it or not, and ships that go all sorts of places. We're both wrong-bodied opposites with a lot of the same background. I'd like to find a place where I could really study that astronomer's dream of a sky up there. You'd like to get someplace where you could still be an individual and not a harem girl. There's *got* to be such a place here somewhere."

Julian sighed. "You'd have to marry me to take me anywhere here," she pointed out. "And I have to tell you, I think I'd rather rot in here than have a name-only marriage. Earlier, maybe, but not at the stage I'm at now. I'm a woman now, an Erdomite woman, and I'd go bananas if I wound up a mere housemaid or a nun."

"Yeah, well, we're the original odd couple all right, but you've just given me the first decent conversation I've had since I got here." She was fighting with herself inside and trying to get the right words out. "I like you, Julian. I like you a lot. If you can accept your fate, I guess, with your help, I can accept mine. Like you, I'm here and I'm stuck this way. I think I might just be able to be a man, maybe the man I always said I wanted to see, with you. Okay. Deal?"

"You'd be responsible for me. And I don't know, like I said—I don't know how much of me is left and how much I can keep over time. This having a two-way conversation in English has really helped, but it's a real *fight*. It's like, well, half of me is an old air force jock clinging desperately to his old identity through real contact with a colleague and half of me lusts after your body and would become your slave if you'd just let her attend your needs. No, it's worse. There's not even close to fifty percent of Julian Beard left. I don't know, it sounds crazy, but this contact, this conversation, this *hope* is actually making the Erdomite part harder to control."

"Just take it easy," Lori said soothingly. "I'll go make the arrangements." And Posiphar would have to be told that his security was about to leave him.

Julian was already thinking ahead. "We'll need money for this . . ."

Lori grinned. "I get the idea that our tentmaker friend out there will pay me *handsomely* to take you off his hands."

And *he* was just the one to get the best deal!

Nathan Brazil had to admit to himself that the Well World was probably the one place in all creation where a good-looking human woman could play Lady Godiva and not fear anything more than if she was overdressed.

He really wasn't quite certain just what to do with the girl. Clearly she wanted to come along, but she wasn't an asset on a long trip as she was. It was as if she'd been reborn as a water creature who couldn't really communicate or travel any distance over land.

Still, he wasn't sure how to ditch her, either. She certainly had a mind of her own.

She also had something of an appetite. Any time they stopped during their journey, she'd find something edible around and down it. Like nearly all the Glathrielians he'd seen, she was chubby but not fat and apparently in excellent condition. He wondered if she wouldn't start putting on weight if she kept eating like that, but it was a moot point. Things she could eat that were so readily available would be few and far between in many of the hexes he'd have to travel, including Flotish itself, considering that the hex was part of the Gulf of Zinjin and was in fact salt water to near ocean depths.

He was nonetheless still fascinated by her and loath to cast her out. She should not have become a Glathrielian. And since she had, she shouldn't have retained what was obviously her natural coloration and features. The Well had changed her in many ways, including taking who knew how many years off her age, but the one thing it clearly had not done was change her genetic code.

He wished he could just know her name. He wasn't sure Glathrielians even used names anymore, but *she* had one, and no amount of blocking or rewiring of some brain functions would keep her from knowing it. The problem was in finding some way for her to tell it to him.

It was not a problem he could solve on the back of a horse, though, not with her on *another* horse.

That, too, was a wonder. He'd gotten the impression that the Glathrielians wouldn't even *use* a live animal, yet she'd picked her horse, gotten on, and now rode quite comfortably. Another mystery. When they were making speed, she'd go forward and hang on somehow up against the horse's neck, but she never kicked it to start, never seemed to guide it at all. The horse, though, did just what it was supposed to do every time. Sometimes he thought that the two moved so naturally and effortlessly together that it was as if somehow she and the horse were one.

Terry herself had no more answers beyond her old name, which indeed she did remember, although it was sometimes confusing because of the otherwise nonverbal processes now operating in her mind. Sometimes it seemed like it was Terry; other times, Teysi. She knew that there had been a lot more to the name than either of those once, but those were the defining words she retained.

As for the horse, she was discovering talents she didn't know she had as she went along. She had gone out back, had realized he was going to ride, and had simply touched a number of horses until one of the animals "clicked" with her in a way she could not explain. When one had and she had mounted it, all she'd had to do was relax and put everything out of her mind except that horse. As Brazil had imagined without believing, she'd become one with it, so that the two bodies, while in physical contact with one another, actually did become as one, operating as easily as one operated one's arms, legs, and head. Whenever she dismounted and contact was broken, it was as if she'd lost something of herself. The size and power of the animal were exhilarating. Still, she hadn't the vaguest idea how she did it.

At a stop to get something to eat and drink and give the horses time to do the same, he decided to try another experiment. If that first Glathrielian girl had reacted to him as if he had the plague, how would *this* one react?

He walked over to her, and she watched him come and stand right in front of her. He smiled, and she returned the smile. They were both almost exactly the same height, his computer-designed leather boots raising him just a bit, but only to match the added height of her thick black hair. Then, casually, he reached out and took her hands in his.

The initial contact was a shock, and the tumble of information that came through was incredibly confusing to her. There was a kindness in him that she found true, almost noble, and still the element of a little boy inside somewhere, either deep down or up front in the bravado that masked his deeper self.

There was also a sadness there, an incredible, deep, painful emptiness that was almost too much to bear. She grieved for anyone who could have that much sorrow within him, yet she admired him, too, for the strength to be able to carry it. It masked, even overwhelmed, the tremendous contradictions she could sense but not grab hold of inside of him.

And yet, deep down, there was something else, something hidden very deep, yet something he was aware of. It was so concealed, so cleverly masked with layer upon layer of pure humanity that it could not be directly seen, only glimpsed ever so briefly, like something seen only in the extreme corner of the eye. That was the heart of the confusion about him. There seemed to be two of him, two totally different creatures so alien to one another that the other would not come in, would not focus. Yet the man she *could* see, the man of sorrows, was not a mask, not a facade, but one and the same with what was hidden. It made no sense at all.

They had warned her, warned her that something lurked there that she did not want to see and should not and that only the man should be considered. She backed away from it, sensing somehow that what lay hidden was no more dangerous than the man and no less, being one and the same, but that it was somehow beyond her comprehension or ability to cope.

He liked her. That made her feel very good indeed, because she liked him and she wasn't certain how she was coming across. He wasn't a particularly handsome man, but he had a tough appearance, and his well-worn face echoed his inner strength and long experience. Even in her past life, she knew that if they'd met, she would have been attracted to him. The fact that she now could see so much of him yet not reach the central mystery of him fascinated her and made him all the more interesting. Sensing that he would never take advantage of her, she felt that at some point she might well be tempted to take advantage of him.

There was little or no sensation or information going in Brazil's direction, but he did somehow sense both her trust and her attraction to him, whether by some sixth sense or perhaps just from long experience. He did not consider it unusual, since, after all, if *he* were stuck in *her* current situation and found just one other human being who knew who and what she was or had been and where she'd come from, he'd probably react the same way. He had no sense that she had learned so much about him, but he had noticed an odd, almost electrical tingling when he'd touched her that was as mysterious as the rest of her. If he didn't know better, he told himself, he'd swear that she was somehow generating a weak force field of some kind from within herself.

There was still a lot of the old Terry in her, and she found herself getting turned on by the experience. That, right now, would never do, so she gave him a quick kiss and a big smile and broke the contact.

Well, at least she didn't run away screaming, he thought, *although, truth be told, that* was *the general idea.* Whatever the first girl had seen, this one either hadn't seen it or wasn't upset about it.

The fact was, he had mixed emotions about the result. On the one hand, to have gotten rid of her would have been in both their best interests; on the other, he had to admit that he liked her spunk and liked having somebody around who, however silent, didn't look or smell like a giant beaver.

Still, how could he take her along? Once she was on that ship and out to sea, there wouldn't be any way out for her.

It was almost nightfall by the time they intersected the main road, but by that time the city lights were in view ahead. Coming over the last rise, Armowak was spread before them, and beyond lay the great blackness of the sea.

For Terry, the scene was both pretty and scary. Old reflexes, old inner tensions from her past life resurfaced at the sight of a modern city, and for the first time it really hit home that she was about to be plunged back into modern civilization as a naked savage. Still, there was a certain confidence in that thought, and the kinds of things she'd been raised to fear in such places now had no hold on her. If she had nothing, it could not be stolen, and she doubted that giant beavers and most of whatever else lived in this world had much interest in her body.

Although traffic wasn't heavy, there were a number of the small personal cars going to and from the city at pretty good speeds, and their Ambrezan drivers seemed oblivious to anything on either side of them. A number of larger vehicles, including tandems and triples, passed as well, showing the importance of the port. She and Brazil kept to the side, well away from the road, and barely drew a glance from any passersby.

Armowak was Ambreza's western gateway to the rest of the world. Into it came the imports from other hexes that allowed a measure of variety in Ambrezan markets, products of perhaps hundreds of races. From it went the principal export, tobacco, both processed and "raw," as well as manufactured items for various trading partners from the computer-controlled and robot-driven factories of the interior. It was a busy, bustling place, a major seaport where great ships called constantly and where many of the races of the Well World mixed in a rare amalgam of shapes, forms, and languages. Here, too, one could buy almost anything with enough money, and here, too, one could lose everything if not careful.

The suburban areas were fairly quiet but well lit; the streets were mostly narrow, except the main highway, and made for pedestrian traffic only, since there was an extensive system of underground moving walkways and transit vehicles to move people quickly around the city. The layout and design of the city were exotic to Terry's eyes and definitely had an alien cast, yet were basically familiar and logical.

The old city area was along the docks. The port itself ran for a couple of miles, or so it seemed, with large piers, massive warehouses, brick and cobblestone streets, and broad silver-gray strips that proved to be much the same as the railroad tracks used by futuristic vehicles moving freight and supplies to and from the port area.

The services area of the port ran from the opposite side of the main north-south docks for about three blocks before a row of older, seedier-looking office buildings drew a line of demarcation between the actual port and the rest of the city.

There were a few larger ships in, although most of what was there seemed to be coastal steamers, tuglike boats, and even a few of what looked like fishing trawlers. What was fascinating was the odd juxtaposition of technologies between the ships and the shore services: the latter were very modern with magnetic trains and robotic longshoremen, and the ships often had smokestacks and, on the larger ones, two or even three tall sailing masts as well. It was as if ships of the American Civil War era were tying up and being serviced at some twenty-first-century port.

Nathan Brazil was familiar with the design and the reasons behind it. He was impressed to see that some of the ships weren't wood anymore but were metal-plated or, in a few cases, seemed to be made out of wholly artificial new plasticlike substances. Their odd nature, though, remained out of necessity; literally just a few meters outside the harbor entrance, visible by day but hidden in the night and city lights, was another hex boundary. Beyond it, where these ships had to sail, a different technology level was imposed. Flotish was a semitech hex; there steam or sail power could be used but nothing electrical worked. Batteries would not hold charges, generators and alternators might truly give off energy, but it could not be controlled and dissipated just about as fast as it was made. Even powerful broadcast signals from a high-tech hex like Ambreza would fade quickly once they passed that boundary, no matter how strong the source. Running an internal combustion engine large enough to be useful would result in the most beautiful and rapid burning up of an engine anybody had ever seen.

Beyond were a few hexes that restricted all technology except direct mechanical devices. There great steam boilers would virtually explode, making it impossible to power any device, ships included. To travel those distances one had to use the most ancient of methods, the wind in the sail.

That also meant that each ship had to carry a highly trained crew expert in both steam and sail and willing to live for long periods aboard ship. Such crews were highly paid and highly prized, and they acted like it. Ship's law was the only law they respected, and the companies tended to pay for or gloss over any excesses in port. They also tended to be from a great many races, and here, at this port, Terry began to get a sampling of just what other sorts of creatures this world contained.

Two large scorpionlike creatures moved down a side street to her left, startling her. They looked huge, mean, and menacing. Elsewhere were several man-sized bipeds wearing clothes that looked like they were out of some Renaissance movie epic, but they more resembled Sylvester the Cat, with their expressive, almost comical feline faces and fur and large fluffy tails. And there was a creature that looked half woman and half vulture, with a pretty face and mean killer's eyes that seemed to glow in the dark. Like the Ambreza, most embodied some aspects of creatures she knew or at least knew about, but the association with familiar Earth creatures was merely a way of cataloging them so that her mind could deal with what she was seeing. The reference points were far from exact, but they were the only way she could cope with the many alien beings she encountered.

Some, however, were beyond easy mental cataloging. Creatures with mottled, leathery dark green skin that went along at a fast clip on what seemed to be hundreds of spindly legs and whose entire bodies seemed to open into rows of sharp, pointy teeth; wrinkled, slow-moving dark gray masses that could only be thought of as hippos without apparent bones; squidlike monstrosities whose tails seemed topped with giant sunflowers. There were so many, and they were so bizarre both individually and collectively that she could only look at one and then another and hope nobody noticed her staring.

But this was no freak show or chamber of horrors; these were *people,* people of ancient races, races as established as her own, from their own hex-shaped countries. She had to always remember that.

Brazil pulled up in front of a lighted office and dismounted, tying his horse loosely to what he knew was a fireplug. Terry wasn't sure what to do. Her impulse was to remain outside, but she had no idea what this place was or how long Brazil might be. After a moment she got down and followed him into the office.

Almost immediately she felt a sense of claustrophobia, of being hemmed in, of the walls and ceiling maybe closing in on her. She repressed it as best she could and managed to stay with him, but she didn't like the feeling.

The creature behind a counter was a large, irregular lump maybe only a bit taller than their own height that seemed to be an animated mass of tiny red and green feathers from behind which, much farther down than would be expected, two huge, round yellow eyes looked back at them.

"Yes?" the creature asked Brazil pleasantly, barely giving Terry a glance.

"Are there any ships in now outbound to Agon or Clopta or anywhere else semitech or above in the northwest?" Brazil asked it.

"Nothing direct," the creature replied. "The *Setting Sun* down at Pier 69 may be your best bet. It stops at Kalibu, Hakazit, Tuirith, and Krysmilar. You might be able to change, particularly at Hakazit, since there's a lot of cross-channel stuff out of there."

"Nothing else coming in that might be more direct?"

"Sorry. Not until sometime next month, and that won't give you any time advantage. The only other possibility for Agon is something like the *Northern Winds* leaving in two days for Parmiter, but your chances of a westbound connection from there are slim to none, and you'd have to walk overland."

"Yeah, well, that would be a solution if Agon were my final destination, but it's not. I'll have enough overland without starting that early. When does *Setting Sun* sail?"

"Let me see . . ." The huge eyes dropped down to look at something below the counter. "They're still finishing offloading, and they have a lot to get on. They're scheduled for high tide . . . the day after tomorrow. About nine in the morning local time."

"That sounds reasonable. I need to book passage on that sailing to Hakazit if it's available, with a cabin if possible."

"Yes, sir. For two?"

He turned and looked at Terry, who was showing her discomfort and staring around the office with a queasy look. Still, she was here.

"Yes," he sighed. "Might as well. What's the weather supposed to be en route?"

"Possible storms in west Ronbonz, otherwise choppy but not uncomfortable. The winds, however, are unpredictable in this crossing, particularly in storms."

"I'll still take it. You have anything on the basics of Hakazit or a general hex guide? I want to see if it's feasible to book the horses on as well."

"Animals are not guaranteed in shipment," the strange clerk warned him. "There is a bookshop on Vremzy Street, two blocks in and one left. It's closed by now, but it will be open all day tomorrow. You can get what you need there. Outfitters and suppliers are along that street as well. We can probably add two animals with no problem if you come back here by nine or ten tomorrow night with your prepaid ticket. In the meantime they can be quartered at the livestock area, Warehouse 29 just along this street. Now, I'll need to know your native hex so that sufficient edible provisions can be laid on for you and the cabin prepared properly."

Nathan Brazil grinned. "Glathrielian."

Those huge eyes seemed to double in size. "You are joking, of course."

"No, I'm not. We came through the Well from offworld, and that's what we are. It won't be hard even if your guide doesn't list us. I'll give you a half dozen or more races we're compatible with."

"Very well. So *you're* what Glathrielians look like."

"You work here and you've never seen any?"

"I'm actually the purser on the *Honza Queen*. When we're in port, we take the late shifts in the company offices. There isn't much here to interest me, anyway."

The fare was not cheap, but it was reasonable, and Brazil felt certain he could more than afford this leg. There would be other times when things would be a lot harder.

Besides, it might be interesting to see how hard the ship's crew and other passengers might gamble.

Finally, Brazil asked, "Is there any outdoor area nearby where we might be able to camp? I suspect that any hotels in this area won't be set up for us, and I have my own food." There usually were such places around ports, particularly because most of them naturally provided only for the races that were the most common visitors. The Gulf of Zinjin was an arm of the Well World's greatest ocean, and there were far too many possible visitors to economically provide for them all, and particularly not Glathrielians.

"Far northern end, past the last pier," the clerk informed him. "Rather nice, although a bit chilly some nights for hairless types. A number of small merchants have local stalls up there from dawn to dusk, too, if you can tolerate the local food."

"Some of it. Well, it sounds fine to me. Any permits required?"

"Not at the port one. All others, you'd need to report to the police first."

The clerk made a series of entries with two huge, clawed hands that extended from under the feathers, and the computer spit out very neat-looking ticket books. Brazil thanked him, put the tickets away, and went back outside, with Terry following. Just walking back out in the air seemed to lift an enormous burden from her, but she still felt a little shaken and a little sick from the experience. Being enclosed was going to be very, very rough on her indeed, she knew.

Brazil decided to take the horses with them rather than

pay to have them quartered at the warehouse. The odds of their being in the way at the park were more than out-weighed by the possibilities of selling them to the locals there if transporting them proved to be a problem, and it might. Hakazit and Agon were also high-tech hexes, and any layover in the former would just leave him with even more ravenous mouths to feed, not to mention the problem of horse droppings, which many places, and particularly high-tech places, tended to frown on.

The park wasn't much, just a large area that apparently had been part of a much earlier port and settlement, long abandoned. They'd planted some trees, as much to keep erosion down as for shelter, and it fronted right on the Gulf, with a small jetty leading out to guide lights warning off any incoming ships.

If anyone else was using the park right now, he couldn't see them, although with some clouds and only a few electric streetlights he might well have missed them. Still, there was a nice ocean smell coming in on the breeze and the quiet sound of waves lapping at the old pylons.

He picked a spot just inside the trees and set up the small tent and the camping outfit as he had in Glathriel. Thanks to the brevity of his trip, he still had a five-day supply of food and gas canisters, and there was a very nice if some-what elaborate fountain in the middle of the park that, thankfully, had fresh water.

Terry used her new night sense to survey the area and found virtually nothing edible in and around the park. She knew she could wander farther afield, but this was a large and strange city and was unlikely to have any real groves close by. Here one didn't pick one's food, one bought it.

Thus, when Brazil opened up his food supplies and ges-tured an offer to share, she had no choice but to accept, although she made it clear with hand signals that it was not to be cooked. Something of an amateur gourmet who fan-cied herself a very good cook, she now found the thought of cooked food thoroughly repulsive.

Brazil did not compromise his own preferences for hers but did find a perverse fascination in watching her eat. Knowing that she must have been a civilized, modern woman, he was fascinated to see her take an open container of preserved fruit, for example, and just scoop it out with her fingers. He was even more surprised when she took and ate the beef he had, both ground and in small filets, also raw. He remembered then the Ambrezan foreman telling him that Glathrielians would eat meat, but only if it was already dead.

Terry, too, was surprised both at her appetite and at the fact that the meat tasted exceptionally good right out of the container. Until now she'd always liked her meat cooked through, and with sauces and all the trimmings if available. While he packed up and saw to the horses, she went to the fountain and then to relieve herself, and when she got back, he was getting ready to turn in. It had been a long, tiring day, and both keenly felt it.

A *very* chilly sea breeze was developing, and he was concerned for her. He offered her a spot in his tent, limited as it was, or his sleeping bag, but she declined both with a smile. Then she gave him a little hug and a kiss and went off.

Again he'd noticed that odd, almost static electricity feeling when they'd touched, but now he noticed another thing as well.

She'd been warm to the touch, with no sign at all of the chill he felt on his face and hands. As warm as summertime.

Terry didn't notice this because she really didn't feel it. The field around her that she could see, generated somehow by her own body, acted as insulator and even life support system in some odd way. She felt warm and comfortable, and she picked a tree almost over Brazil's tent and scampered up it, then found a comfortable notch and settled in for the night.

Terry awoke the next morning feeling nauseous, and for a moment she was afraid it was the food. Something inside her, though, told her that it wasn't, that it would pass, and she trusted her instincts as usual and they proved correct. She still felt a little queasy when Brazil finally got up and found her there waiting for him, but she didn't let on that anything was wrong, and after getting something to eat, the feeling gradually vanished.

Brazil bought breakfast from the promised local merchants, who set up small booths along the waterfront area of the park selling homegrown produce and other things. He discovered that Terry would eat bread, the first cooked item he had seen her accept, but not eggs. In point of fact, she ate two whole home-baked loaves of bread and two large melons, and Brazil began to wonder if he could literally afford to take her with that kind of appetite.

He walked back into the port district; he'd already made a decision that the horses would be far too much of a burden until they were needed to be worth the cost and had opened some discussions with a stall merchant who kept a couple of horses at his place outside the city. Terry followed him through the now-bustling area, and her head began to reel with the number of races and weird sounds and smells that made the whole place come alive. She had already figured, though, that he was leaving by ship, and she no longer felt compelled to enter the buildings he entered.

So many sounds, so many races . . . how did they *understand* each other? She found the whole thing bewildering. The Glathrielians whose lives she'd shared had not prepared her for this.

Occasionally one or another of the creatures would say something to her, but she was always able to convey by some gesture or expression that she did not understand them. Still, she did feel the irony of being naked and exposed in a strange city and yearned for a dark alleyway. Once a particularly smelly and repulsive-looking reptilian creature had actually *touched* her, and she'd reacted instantly with a nearly panicky mental push that said "Go away!" And the creature had frozen, looked puzzled for a moment, then seemed to lose all interest in her and actually had gone away!

Could she really *do* that, or was it a coincidence? One of these times she'd find out.

Brazil emerged from the bookshop with something of what he needed. He had been surprised to find, in the first few weeks after landing in Ambreza, that he was able to figure out the written language almost as if it were something he'd forgotten rather than something he'd never known. It was a *little* cumbersome and not all of it read just right, but what he needed to read he had little problem figuring out.

The map was the most important thing. When he had the time, he intended to annotate it in Latin, the "stock" Earth language he'd found the most useful over the long haul, so he wouldn't have to keep looking up and remembering this term or that and figuring out things word by word and sentence by sentence. There was a sort of common written language here, one used for interhex trade and commerce— the ticket was in it—but he found *it* less familiar and less useful than Ambrezan.

Of course, he knew what had happened. He was remembering ancient Ambrezan, which had evolved greatly over the millennia since his last time here, and the common language he'd known had been entirely replaced, perhaps many times.

He then stopped at the ministry of commerce offices to call in to the capital, report *something* on his slight observations on Glathrielians—mostly to omit any of the oddities and report a very primitive life-style of no threat or consequence to the Ambrezans—and get what information he could on Mavra's group.

There was *some* information, but it was incomplete and not guaranteed. Of the two men and two women who came in, one was reported in Erdom, as he'd surmised, another was in Zebede, which did surprise him, a third was in Dahir, and a fourth, clearly Mavra, had shown up in Glathriel, as he already knew.

"But who's this other Glathrielian female I have with me?" he asked them. "If she didn't come in with me, and she didn't, since I know where mine are, and she didn't come in with *them,* she must have come in either alone or with another group."

"The only group we have other than yours and the larger party is two males about three weeks after you arrived. One of those is a Leeming, and the other—that's odd—also an Erdomite."

"Well, then, who *is* this girl?"

"You're sure she's not a native putting you on?"

He sighed. "Natives do not look like her. I know you might not be able to tell them apart, but I sure can. And natives don't draw maps of televisions and cameras and North America on Earth."

"Well, we have no reports of anybody coming through except those we told you about. Sorry. They are quite upset with this at Zone Security, you know. There's an investigation to find out just how this happened. Right now the only plausible theory is that she came in just after one of your groups, probably the larger one, and somehow snuck by security and went directly through the gate without being noticed. How that's possible nobody can say."

Nathan Brazil sighed and muttered, "Television reporters," in a disgusted tone. "All right, thank you. I'll be off now, and it's unlikely although not impossible that I'll be back. I thank you for all your help."

"Not a big problem," the comm tech told him. "However, I was told to inform you if you were heard from again that if you *do* return, you must proceed immediately to Glathriel and remain there. If you are picked up here again, you will be immediately transported there. You must make somebody nervous."

Damned paranoids, he thought, but he acknowledged the transmission and switched out.

The truth was, he'd like to do that at some point. Move into Glathriel and live there, "go native," as it were, if he could stand it, and uncover the real mysteries of the place. Now, however, wasn't the time.

Still, after seeing what was wrong with the Well, he seriously considered remaining this time, at least for a while. He wasn't really sure why he hadn't done so before, although, of course, the *last* time had been pretty dicey and leaving had been the only practical choice.

Hell, he could change his looks in there, even his race and sex, if he wanted to. He couldn't figure out why he'd never done it. Too much the uncomfortable god, he decided. Maybe this time would be different. Or maybe he should just try the current Glathrielian matrix and see just what the hell was going on inside those people. That was if this girl made it up there with him and couldn't tell him what he needed to know after removing her speech and language block.

They headed back up to the park with a detour past the ship they were going to take. It was a *big* one, larger than any he'd remembered from his still admittedly spotty recollections. Three-masted, made of superior fitted wood covered with some kind of synthetic laminate that protected and sealed it, two stacks, three decks above the main deck. Yeah, it looked like it could take an ocean, all right, and keep everybody comfortable and dry while doing it. It even had all sorts of smaller, exotic-looking masts atop the wheelhouse, indicating that if the hex allowed, it could use almost any technology known to Well World science.

It flew the Suffok flag, which meant it was a long way from home. He wished it were *going* home; it would make things very easy indeed, since that hex was virtually on the equator, but he suspected that it rarely went up that far. Considering that such a ship could not lie idle for long, he suspected that its profits, more than its hull, went to its home port in any given year.

Terry stared at the ship with a mixture of awe, wonder, puzzlement, and a little fear. The puzzlement was of course because she had no idea how the Well World worked or that there were nontech, semitech, and high-tech hexes, and thus its combination of features from every type of ship she'd ever known, and some she'd never thought of, seemed bizarre. Fear because even in normal times she'd never been that great on ships, and she really didn't know if her claustrophobia could stand it long on that thing. She knew, though, that something that big and that grand didn't make small voyages.

They continued walking back up the street to the park. By now it was late in the day and the merchants were mostly packing up, but Brazil was able to spot the one he'd spoken to about the horses, and now he figured he'd close whatever deal he could get. He'd paid a lot; now the Ambrezan, sensing Brazil was in something of a time squeeze, offered only half.

They haggled and argued and finally settled on a hundred plus as much of the unsold produce as Brazil and Terry could carry back to their nearby campsite. Brazil made out a bill of sale on some glorified butcher paper and signed and dated it, and the merchant took it and nodded.

Brazil had to admit to himself that he took far more of the produce than he could possibly consume, but he felt a little gypped by the guy and wanted to cost him as much as possible. Terry, however, once she got the idea, did even better.

Both of them ate until they were stuffed, understanding that little of it would keep, but after he watched Terry put away so much of it, he wondered if there were going to be leftovers, after all.

Finally, they cleaned up as best they could and found themselves again virtually alone in the park after dark. The sky had cleared, and the glow from the massive stellar display was almost like a full moon on Earth. It was one sight that neither he nor Terry ever tired of; those who were born under it and took it for granted rarely even looked up.

Terry felt oddly nervous about the coming day. For one thing, she had no idea if she'd have to sneak or bully her way onto that big ship to stay with him or whether he'd added her to the fare. For another, cut off from Earth, from her friends, and from Glathriel, she felt particularly lonely and insecure, and Brazil was the only one around she had to lean on.

He'd considered turning in early to insure having enough time to get the gear packed and board the ship, but he felt too wide awake, and there was that wonderful sky and the water. He finally decided that he'd take a walk and appreciate the scene. Acutely aware of her insecurity, Terry went with him, taking his hand as they walked along the ancient seawall where once great ships had called in some distant age. After a while they sat together on the seawall and looked out at the sky, the inner harbor lights, and the darkness beyond. To Terry, this moment was wonderful; she wanted it to continue.

She closed her eyes and allowed the night sense to come in, the scene took on a far different look. It wasn't dark anymore; instead, it was rippling, and within it she saw thousands of pale green shapes, many tiny, some very large, and, here and there, large shapes of an indigo color she'd never seen before. What were they? Some monsters of the deep, like whales, swimming yet breathing air? Or did intelligent races live even in the water here? Were they more creatures of some kind, creatures who had some sort of different civilization out there in the sea?

The concept, combined with the sky, made her feel even tinier and more lost and insecure, and her fear that Brazil might leave her grew. How could she follow him through *that*?

Without even realizing that she was doing it, she squeezed his hand and sent, *Love me! Don't ever leave me!* The white aura, particularly strong after all she had eaten, rushed from her and to him, and a bright white series of impulses traveled from her up his arm and into his head and seemed to explode there, then fade, although not entirely.

They hadn't invented a number high enough to count the women Nathan Brazil had known in his life, and he'd spent millennia trying to never form an attachment or any real feeling for any short-lifer because of the inevitable heart-break. It was always a battle, though, particularly because of his own intense loneliness. Somehow, though, right there, right then, with this mystery woman he could neither talk to nor understand, he lost the battle and the will to fight it at all. Suddenly, without even thinking, he drew her to him, and he kissed her, and suddenly the pent-up emotions held back for so many countless years overwhelmed him.

She had been both surprised and pleased when he'd embraced her and started to kiss her in a way far more than friendly, since that was just what she wanted and needed then, but with the kiss came a sudden massive surge of deep, blinding white from *him* into *her.* The closest she might have come to describing the feeling rushing inward, had she been capable of analyzing it or even cared to, was that it seemed as if her whole brain had been fried in a massive wave of pleasure and desire.

By the time they'd finished, under that magnificent sky, on the grass, near the ancient seawall, and were just lying there side by side, holding hands and looking up, she was incapable of even wondering if what she'd tried had back-fired. She only knew that she'd never felt like this before, not *ever,* and that she could never bear to lose him or live without him. She was, even in the Glathrielian energy sense, linked to him now for life.

Brazil, too old, too wise, too strong, was unaware of the cause of what had happened but was nonetheless affected by it. *I swore when Mavra left that I would never allow myself to do this again,* he thought. *But I guess I made myself a little too human, after all. So, here I am, feeling totally illogical, in love with somebody whose name I don't know, whose background I don't know, and who I can't even talk to. Maybe after all this time I really have gone nuts.*

But he didn't want to reject it, even though he knew deep down he could purge it if he truly worked at it. He'd felt the same intensity of feeling from her, and for now maybe that was enough. He felt the odd linkage, as if something tangible actually connected the two of them like some umbilical cord, but he dismissed it as just too many years of holding in his emotions.

Finally, he got up and pulled her to her feet, and they walked back toward the camp, still in an emotional high.

The fact that a feeling of impending danger cut through the high was all the more dramatic. They both sensed it at the same time and moved over away from the campsite toward the darkest area of trees. They separated, but the link established between them did not weaken or falter. It was as if they could read each other's emotions, though not thoughts, and immediately accept and act on them. There was something out there, something not friendly, and it was waiting for them.

She separated from him and immediately tried her night sense. What had been invisible before now came in very, very clear. There were two creatures; one, larger than the other, holding some sort of instrument, was hiding behind a tree just down the path to the fountain, with a clear view of the tent; the other was in the trees, silent, still, waiting for them.

At the same moment Terry saw them with the night sight, Nathan Brazil suddenly knew exactly where both of the lurkers were. He didn't wait to wonder how he knew; he sensed that the girl was going for the one in the trees, so his target was the bastard down the trail.

Great! he thought sourly. *What the hell am I going to do? Hit him with my guidebook?* Anything he could possibly use as a weapon was back in the camp. Or was it?

He suddenly realized that he was carrying his clothes, not wearing them, and he fumbled in the pants pockets to see what he had. The map and book, safety matches, and . . . one of the spare little gas canisters he used for the camp stove. He couldn't remember putting it there and wondered if it was full or empty. There was no time to check; he'd have to trust to those little twists of fate that always got him out of nasty situations and hope this wasn't one of those times when he was going to wake up in a hospital.

Dropping everything but the canister, which lit much like a common cigar lighter, he silently made his way around through the trees, giving the ambusher a wide berth. Thanking fate that these two hadn't discovered them up by the seawall, he began to close in on his quarry from the fountain side.

He could see the lurker now. Humanoid, maybe a meter and a half tall, covered with brown fur or feathers, and, most important of all, holding a mean-looking rifle of no local manufacture with what must have been a sniper's scope on it. With the experience of countless lifetimes, Brazil approached the creature in absolute silence, slowly, slowly closing in, ready to pounce if the sniper suddenly noticed him.

Now he was practically standing next to the sniper, at the same tree. Carefully, silently, he turned the little gas jet on and prayed that the flint and wheel wouldn't screw him up.

The sniper suddenly straightened up a bit in puzzlement, then sniffed the air. Brazil lit the canister and shoved it at him. A huge sheet of flame roared out and caught the fur, and the creature roared in pain and turned, giving Brazil a look at one of the meanest-looking faces he'd ever seen.

As the creature straightened up, Brazil dropped the canister and leapt at it, grabbing the rifle and then dropping, rolling, and coming back up with it pointed back at the assassin in one fluid motion.

The creature banged its back against the tree and put out the fire but then glared down the barrel of his own rifle. There was no doubt from the way Brazil held it that the man knew just how to use it.

Over near the camp another creature had waited in the trees to pounce on whoever might have come to the tent. It clung, silent and still, to the side of the tree without any obvious means of support.

Terry had moved around to the other side after separating from Brazil and had gone up a tree well distant from her own quarry. She moved with silent precision, using the night sense to see the links whereby she could get from one tree to the other and finally to the one next to the tent. The thing glowed brightly in her night sense, a sickly red like dried blood against the glowing tan of the tree. The outline was clear and now familiar to her: one of those scorpionlike creatures, its long, curved tail poised and practically screaming instant death to her.

She was right above it now, and for the first time she wasn't sure what to do. She *sensed* that Nathan was about to pounce on the other one; whatever it was had to be done fast. If only she had a better angle . . . Nothing she could do would work unless she actually *touched* the loathsome thing!

At that moment Brazil moved, and from up the path there was a scream that she knew was not his. The creature was suddenly alert, then turned toward the direction of the sounds. At that moment, fidgeting, the deadly tail was pointed straight down, the curve right below her. Timing, of course, was everything, but there was no chance for anything else but direct force and a prayer that it would work.

She jumped feet first and struck the tail at its midcurve. The tail went forward and punctured the thick exoskeleton of the creature, who roared even as they both fell from the tree and onto the tent below.

She landed right next to the thing and gave a panicked cry as the poison-tipped tail flailed up and down in random directions. She rolled away just in time for it to miss her, but it was a near thing. She was entangled in the collapsed tent with the creature when it again struck within a hair's breadth of her arm. She reached out reflexively and shoved it, at the same time sending her own fear and panic.

The creature managed to right itself but seemingly forgot about her. It *leapt* a good ten feet, landing on its feet, and began running on all six of its legs away toward the port, emitting an eerie, piercing sirenlike scream as it did so.

She had no idea where it went, and she didn't care. She knew it was gone, and she felt that Nathan was all right as well.

Brazil was torn between his captive and his clear perception of her fright and panic. He turned slightly, distracted by the feelings he was receiving from her, and the would-be sniper took it as an opening, running into the man and knocking him down, sending the rifle into the grass. The creature didn't look for it or go at Brazil, though; instead, it ran at top speed away into the darkness.

Brazil got up quickly and looked around, but the assassin was gone. *"Damn!"* he swore aloud. "Damn! Damn! Damn!" He looked around for the rifle, certain that the creature hadn't retrieved it, and found it in about thirty seconds. The girl no longer worried him; he knew without even checking that she was safe and that the other assailant, too, had fled.

Instead, he walked back down to what remained of the camp, looking at the rifle, noting only now what had caused him to know that an ambush awaited.

The two embedded electric streetlights along the fountain path were out. Either put out or shot out, most likely.

He found Terry shaken but unharmed. She might have a

bruise or two, and she had a couple of scratches where she'd fallen into the tent, but it didn't appear to be anything serious.

He smiled, winked at her, and kissed her, then turned his attention to the rifle. It was a damned good one, too. Expensive. But the previous owner was no pro; a pro would never have taken up that exposed position or allowed anyone to get that close. Similarly, the Ecundo, for that was what the scorpionlike creature had been, had acted less like an assassin than like some ship's crewman hard up for some spare cash and recruited on the spot for an "easy" job. Again, no matter what her own abilities, she shouldn't have been able to get close enough to nail him without his hearing, and he certainly should have nailed her with that stinger when they fell. These were amateurs. Amateurs hired by somebody with money and sources of illegal weapons.

They'd just survived a crude attempt by amateurs at a paid "hit."

"Now what the hell . . . ?" he mused, staring at the rifle. Who would want him dead badly enough to hire toughs to do it? Who would be dumb enough to think they could kill him? Yet if they didn't know who he really was and what that meant, why bother? The Ambreza? Hardly. They could have snared him a lot easier a thousand times and with far less mess. He'd been only in Ambreza and briefly in Glathriel, and certainly the latter was out as a suspect. The only one who knew both who he was and where he might be would be Mavra Chang.

But this wasn't her style. Remote-control hits by amateurs? And she of all people would know that he couldn't be taken out any more than *she* could. But who else could it be?

Damn it, Mavra was as much if not more of an enigma to him than the girl was. If it *was* Mavra, what might be the motive? To slow him up, perhaps, now that he was on the move? A real possibility. But the worst possibility was one he didn't want to think about.

That somebody here, somewhere, knew who and what he was and was bent on stopping him at all cost, a third player whose very race and motives were unknown.

He looked at the ruins of the camp and sighed. Then he went over to find his clothes and get dressed again. *She* might not mind, but it was damned chilly for him.

There wouldn't be much sleep tonight, after all, even with all that had happened. Tomorrow morning the ship would sail, and they would be on it. Plenty of time to sleep then. Or, at least, if there was another attacker aboard, they couldn't run away like these two and he might get answers to some questions.

It was the story of his life, he decided. Every nice turn was met with an unexpected plunge into something nasty.

Lori had been with Posiphar long enough to understand the bargaining game, and it was a good thing, too, since the tentmaker wasn't offering a very good deal on getting Julian off his hands in spite of his professed disgust with her.

"Since the treatment has begun as the Holy One directed, she is coming along very well," Aswam argued. "In a few more months, with the herbs the monk gave us to add to her food and drink, she will have forgotten all this foolishness and become a good girl and bear many fine children."

Lori did find this particular scale of bargaining distasteful, though; it seemed too much like haggling over a sale price, and in this case the commodity was a woman reduced to the status of a brood mare. Still, the addition of drugs—"herbs"—to Julian's food explained a lot as well about her mood swings and collapse of will.

"And you are arguing that I should repay *you* for your losses to date, when you are telling me that she is as she is now only because of *herbs*? And other than your loss of use of the storage shed, how much has she cost you so far above what dowry you were paid for her? How much for those herbs and all the special attention?"

"My investment is considerable now. That is why I will not give her away!"

"Ah! But you said it would still be months, perhaps many months, before it ran its course and you had the girl you wanted. *Perhaps* it will be months. *Perhaps* it will be longer. And can you ever be certain that what you see is real, is not an act? Will you ever be able to trust her fully? Or will your wives and daughters always be preoccupied watching her, so that they can never concentrate on their duties? It seems to me that you are boasting of doubling your costs in a fifty-fifty chance that she might work out. Right now, thanks to the dowry, your losses are small, but now that dowry is gone and all the costs are on you. Is yet one more wife worth that much to you?"

They argued back and forth, and for a little while Lori was afraid that Aswam might well not budge too much beyond a "Take her and go," blaming Lori for Julian's newfound resolve.

Lori had fought so hard just to get the tentmaker to this point that he feared pressing the matter might lose everything. Still, there was just some feeling inside, some gut instinct, that the old man really *didn't* want Julian anymore. Lori wondered if he had the right to bargain beyond this point, considering that it was Julian's future, not his, that was at stake, but something inside made it impossible to stop. He did, however, decide to bring down the hammer.

Lori got up from the cushion and looked down at the still-reclining tentmaker. "I cannot accept the dishonor of a wife with no dowry," he said flatly. "If she is not worthy of it and I am not worthy of the respect, then there is nothing more to say." He turned, feeling uneasy and queasy as hell about what he was doing, and started for the exit from the great tent.

He actually thought the old bastard was going to let him go, but just as he reached the curtained doorway and made to push back the drape and leave, Aswam called, "Now, wait a minute! Perhaps *something* can be arranged, young hothead."

Lori smiled and felt immense relief, then set his face in a very serious posture before turning and coming back to the old man. From this point the haggling would be over how much the tentmaker would pay, not the other way around.

The final price was not nearly as much as Lori had hoped for as a stake, but he just didn't have the heart or stomach to press it anymore. He kept thinking that if Julian had known what he'd done, she'd have killed him. In fact, if the old Lori Ann Sutton had seen this, she would have organized protests.

Once agreed, a marriage contract of sorts was drawn up, and then Lori had to go and see the village Holy One.

The monks of the hierarchy of the church looked and sounded quite odd. All males, castrated while still children, they tended to be small and wizened, with weak sopranolike voices, without hair or horn. Only the eyes showed that there was a lot more going on in the head than their appearance indicated.

"I must confess that I am not wholly in favor of this union," the monk told him. "The role of females in this society is quite tightly prescribed, and no matter why the gods have chosen to put that person in that body, it was their holy will that it be so, just as it was for you. You were a step beyond her in your spiritual development, hence you were reborn male, and she was a step behind. In a sense, both of you were given a great gift. Few may be spiritually reevaluated while still alive. You were promoted, Julian was demoted one step, as it were. The proof of the rightness of it is how well you have adapted under a mental and cultural burden the rest of us do not have to share. That is why Julian is having so many problems with it; it is always more difficult to go down than up. I know the argument for the randomness of the Well process, but we reject it. There is a reason for all that happens. Randomness is an illusion. I fear that the joining of the two of you might well undermine that process."

Lori remembered Julian's warning that this monk was both devious and dangerous. Maybe they all were. Playing god and meddler on some level was the only thing they had.

"Are you telling me then, Holy One, that you will not allow it?"

"I am of two minds on it. On the one hand, there must be a reason why, out of 780 racial possibilities for each of you, both of you were reborn Erdomese and have come together in this way. On the other hand, since Julian will tend to cling to her old self more in your constant company, by allowing it I might jeopardize her immortal soul." He sighed and thought a moment. "There is a possible compromise position here."

"Yes?"

"First, what are your plans afterward?"

"Um, well, I am weary of being a needless guard for an old trader. I need more of a challenge. I had thought to travel to Aqomb and find tutors to teach me the full written language of Erdom. Once I am reasonably proficient, I hope to gain a position in the civil service there."

The monk nodded, pleased with the answer. "Very well. Here is what I will do, then. I will marry the two of you, but on the official papers I will place conditions. First, you must swear to me on your honor that you will continue with the herbal additives until they are gone. This is not just a religious requirement; to discontinue them now might well cause her to become very ill and cause permanent mental and emotional problems. Do not believe that I say this just to make you do it. I swear upon the Holy of Holies that what I tell you is true."

She didn't like it, but there was nothing she could do about it for now. "All right, I swear it. But I must know what they are."

"They are simply aids. In layman's terms, they help her mind and body become one and her behavior to be consistent with Erdomese culture."

"And in nonlayman's terms? I was once a scientist."

The monk gave a thin smile. "In technical parlance, they are natural psychochemical blockers and facilitators of attaining desired hormonal balances. One, for example, is a hybrid of two herbs used for countless generations as aphrodisiacs. Over a period of time the body begins to treat the blockers and newly set hormonal levels as normal and produces them naturally as needed. Once that happens, the drugs have no further effect and can be discontinued. In midtreatment, however, the body's balances are quite disturbed and discontinuance can produce what anyone might call insanity. The pharmacology is quite complex, actually. To go into more detail would involve going through the *Pharmacopoeia,* and you cannot at the moment read it."

She was startled by this sudden rather sophisticated science and immediately saw what Julian meant when she said that this guy was no fool.

"I accept what you say. The problem I have is, what is it doing to her mind?"

"You won't notice any changes from the way she is now so long as you continue them. The bottom line is that she won't want to kill herself, and she will be accepting of her role."

"Okay, that's one condition. You said several."

"Yes. When you reach Aqomb, you must check in and present the papers to the Holy Office there. They will monitor your compliance and her progress."

"Very well."

"Next, you will speak only Erdomese to one another, even in private. Language is the primary definer of a culture. You must believe that the Holy Office can determine if you uphold this or not in their examination of you both."

She wasn't sure how they could tell, but right now she would agree to anything just to get it done and over with.

"And finally, as soon as practical after the marriage but certainly before you retire for the night, you *must* consummate the marriage and present her for examination by me the next day. *Then,* and only then, will I give you the papers. Failure in any one of these may result in the marriage being annulled, and if it is, you will not see her again and may yourself face criminal penalties. Once you are married, you are morally and legally responsible for her and you *will* be held accountable. Remember, too," he added, possibly guessing at her ultimate intentions, "that even if you leave our land, you have had your living rebirth. There will be no more change in race, sex, or anything else until you die and are again reborn. There is no running from it. There are no colonies here. You both will be Erdomese and nothing else."

Well, the monk had sure laid it on the line. "All right, I agree." Lori said. "I swear it to you here and now." He hoped he could fulfill the duties he was agreeing to. As a male and an Erdomese, he was still a virgin.

"Very well. I assume you can write in *some* language?"

"Several. Just not Erdomese—yet."

"All right, then, I will dictate the contract, and you will write it in the language of your choosing. One copy for you in your language, certified as a true copy by me, and the other in Erdomese for official use. Those, and the marriage contract, will suffice. When do you leave?"

"Well, Posiphar has indicated that he might well go to Aqomb himself for a while and take a rest. If he does, we'll go with him. The hope is to leave just before dawn the day after tomorrow so that we can hit a small oasis at midday."

"Very well. Then you will marry tomorrow. I will then be there before you leave the next morning to make my examinations and, if satisfactory, hand you the papers."

The interview was over. "Thank you, Holy One. I will try to be worthy of your trust," he said, rising, bowing slightly, and leaving the prayer sanctuary.

He headed for Julian, who was still locked up by decree until the marriage, to tell her the good and the not so good parts of the news.

"I speak in Erdomese," he said right off, "because one of the conditions was that we speak nothing else to one another, and I do not wish to have anything go wrong."

"It will be so," she agreed.

"The reason why you have changed so much in here is that they have been giving you herbs to facilitate the process," he told her. "They are strong, and the Holy One knows his business. I am commanded to keep you on them until they are gone. He said that to stop them now would cause you to go mad. He also said that they would not change you more than you are now, that it is just to ensure that you remain this way. He also said that an examination by others could tell. Does this bother you?"

"No," she responded. "It—gives me relief. Now I understand why I have been this way. It helps me. And if it frees me from this place, I will take anything they wish. I know they can probably tell. That is one thing they are experts at here. Getting what they want."

"Then we do it tomorrow."

"Tomorrow!" Julian was excited. "But—I will need more than *this*! I can't get married looking and smelling like *this*!"

Lori grinned. "You look just fine to me, but I'll speak to Aswam. Most likely his wives and daughters can help you. He'll probably try and rob me blind for the service, but until tomorrow he's stuck with you."

Julian laughed, the first laugh she'd had since she'd gotten here. "And I will be a good little girl until he has no hold on me. I promise."

"Um, one more thing. They require that we consummate as soon as possible after marriage."

"Well, I am ready for that. I would not have it any other way, as I told you before, even though it is another way they hope to hold us here."

"Huh? Why is that?"

"They hope I will get pregnant, which will restrict us, and that I will have children, which will limit us more. With nations so small and so different, it is unlikely that the others would welcome families as settlers. It does not worry me. One day I might like to have children, but it is not how you do it here that counts. Even births are regulated from on high, so that the nations do not get too many people to support. That is what they told us when we came in here."

Reminded of that, Lori felt a little more relieved. She didn't think they had a population problem here at the moment, and she'd seen some babies in her travels, but not a lot of them. The fact that at least by observation it appeared that twins were the norm made the chances even lower.

"That's supposing that we can do it right to begin with," she joked.

Julian gave a soft laugh. "That should not be a problem. *You* know what a woman wants; *I* know what a man wants. When you consider that, we should be the most perfect couple in all history!"

After Lori left to make the arrangements, Julian had to chuckle at the sudden realization that she was still of two minds. As a human male she'd been divorced with no children; now, as an Erdomese female, she was to be married and could have her own children, and something in her really craved the kind of family life Julian Beard had rarely experienced. Lori might find what he was looking for elsewhere, but she would never again fly a plane, let alone a spacecraft, never again do meaningful research—not with *this* body and *these* hands—and, curiously, she didn't really mind. She'd railed against that knowledge most of all in the beginning, but it no longer seemed to matter now. Oh, she was glad that she'd done those things and had those memories, but at the age of forty Julian Beard, from a broken home and with no wife or family, had accomplished as much or more on his own than his boyhood dreams had ever imagined. She hadn't realized until now how empty some of the triumphs had been without anyone to share them with.

She wondered if in fact the Well had screwed up or whether, somehow, becoming Julian Beard's complete opposite—sexually, technologically, and in every other way—wasn't what was exactly right for her at the moment. Now she was supporting Lori's show, and it felt comfortable to be in that role and stop fighting. Lori might never understand it, but that, too, was all right.

Husbands never understood their wives, did they?

Julian in fact looked stunning for the tiny wedding, with long golden earrings—a series of squares linked together with chain, hanging down from punctures in the lowest part of the equine ears—a matching necklace, a pinkish glow applied judiciously to her face and upper body, hooves and "fingers" shined to almost a reflective polish, and her hair and tail done up in the traditional style, rising from golden tubes out across her back and up from the rear and then slinkily down to almost the ankles. Aswam's women had done her up just right, and she had just the body for it.

Lori was stunned by the look. In the dark shed he hadn't even noticed that Julian's hair was a sultry light reddish-brown, and the combination now put the other women around to shame.

Somehow, too, he'd expected Julian to be taller. It was true that Lori was very large for an Erdomese male, and he'd gotten used to being higher than everybody else by a few inches, but Julian looked positively *tiny* beside him, with only that huge mane of hair bringing her up to near his shoulders. She also looked so *young,* although certainly amply developed.

The wedding was brief and simple, held in a small demonstrator tent on Aswan's property, with only the tentmaker and his women and Posiphar and his women in attendance. In some ways the oaths taken before the witnesses and priest were everything Lori had hated back on Earth; Julian had to promise to honor, respect, and "obey absolutely" her husband, while Lori was required to swear only that he accepted all responsibilities, morally and legally, for his wife's welfare. More interestingly, the word "love" was nowhere to be found. That, at least, Lori thought, was not dishonest; he wasn't in love with Julian, but he did find her incredibly attractive on all levels, and love might come later. Neither, however, really knew the other yet—which was in some ways also consistent with Erdomese tradition.

Then there were fruit drinks and exotic pastries and some of the exotic-sounding Erdomese music from two of his daughters who had some talent in that direction, and that was it. By the heat of midday they were in a guest tent not too far away, the floor of which was covered with the large, varicolored pillows that were the most common furnishings in the nation.

Julian sighed. "Well, now I am Lori-Julian, or Madam Lori. Husband's name goes first here, but even if you take a dozen more wives I'll still be the only Madam Lori."

"I know," Lori replied, stretching out on the pillows and sighing. "Sorry, I didn't get much sleep last night."

"You are lucky. I got none at all. I never thought I would ever get married again. And I *surely* never thought I would be somebody's *wife*."

Lori frowned and looked up at her. "You were married?"

"A disaster. I will tell you about it if you want. We were divorced years ago, and after she remarried, I never saw or heard from her again. You were never married?"

"No. I lived with a string of men off and on, the last one for five years. We had just broken up for good when I got the offer to cover the meteor strike." He smiled sadly. "Want to know the ultimate irony? I forced the issue. I was closing in on forty, and my biological clock was in screaming mode. The idea of children frightened him to death for some reason. I pressed, he left. Just moved out without a word." The smile turned to a nasty grin. "How I'd like to see him *now*!"

Julian chuckled. "Yes, it might be fun to see Holly now, too. I've got twice her cleavage in *both* ways. Useful, too. They actually *are* 'jugs,' you might say, holding water until near the time of birth, when Mother Nature throws a switch inside. You think *you* have problems. Erdomese gestation is almost a year long, and the little buggers have hooves." She lay down beside him. "We can get some rest now and do what we must later," she suggested, "but can you at least satisfy one bit of curiosity I've had since I woke up here?"

"Huh? What?"

"Will you take that thing off? I've got to know if it really is that big or if those things are falsies."

Lori shifted around, removed the codpiece, and put it to one side, then rolled back. He'd never seen *anybody's* eyes get that big.

"Oh, *my*! Oh *my, oh my* . . ."

It proved a lot easier, and a lot better, than either of them had thought it would be.

The land changed considerably as they neared the coast, becoming harder and more like the deserts of the American southwest or the steppes of Kazakhstan than like the Saharalike interior. Water here could be found coming from fissures in the rocks or occasionally in streams around which sprang dramatic vegetation. Because of this, they would often run into wandering herds of *amat, twon,* or *zalj,* the Erdom equivalent of the bison, the cow, and the antelope, respectively, and, here and there, signs of *mahdag,* the elephantine and vicious yaklike creatures of the steppes. Overhead, the fierce pterodactyllike *maguid* would swoop down in aerial packs; while preferring carrion, maguid were perfectly willing to do their own killing if they were really hungry.

Posiphar had exchanged the sand skis for wooden wheels, and it occasionally took all of them to get it up some of the grades and all of them to keep it from going down some grades ahead of them. Mostly, the daughters pulled it, the others walking beside.

"This place could be beautiful if you knew the rules and what was dangerous and what was not," Julian noted. "Unfortunately, I do not know those rules, and it seems pretty scary to me."

"I've seen little here that scares me," Lori assured her. "Nothing I couldn't take with a spear or arrow, anyway. Mahdag is a different story, but I don't *want* to try one of those."

"There be them who hunt them," Posiphar remarked. "And them who be offerings of mahdag to the maguid who have tried to hunt them, too. Luckily, they be few and far between, and the ground be shaken long afore they come."

"Have you ever seen one?" Lori asked him.

"Yes, several times in this district, always from a distance and going the correct way, which is not the same way the mahdag be going. The cursed beasts be a head or more taller than even y'self and weigh a couple of tons or more."

Lori shook his head in wonder. "What do they *eat*? It would seem that it would take a lot to satisfy just one of them."

"Oh, there be a lot more vegetation around on some of these plateaus and mesas than ye'd think," the old trader told him. "I be not sure anyone has ever had the opportunity to study livin' ones and survive, but I be certain that they be vegetarians and kill entirely for pleasure."

The church taught that the mahdag had once been people, evil ones beyond redemption, doomed to wander in the wastes until the end of the world.

The trip had been an uneventful one as usual, and Lori and Julian had pretty well stuck to the bargain. She was even mixing the herbs herself according to the instructions passed on to them. They also practiced some social rules that Lori at least had never even noticed before, although he'd been around Posiphar's wives and daughters since arriving in Erdom. He *should* have noticed, though, and he felt bad about his lapse, since most were really designed to keep women in their "place."

For instance, a wife or daughter could address a husband or father easily, and also any other woman, but conversing directly with any other man, unless specifically invited to do so by husband or father, was forbidden. Since Julian considered Posiphar's family a set of ignorant little airheads, she talked mostly to Lori, but *never* interrupting a conversation Lori was having with Posiphar. This grated a bit on Julian's nerves, but she held it in and practiced it anyway. She was well aware that she was still on some kind of probation and that it all could be yanked away, and that was her biggest terror.

Still, when they got to the start of the last mesa, they found themselves in an actual forest, which seemed strange and alien to them after so long in the desert, and when they emerged from it at the other end, the whole of the Sultanate of Aqomb was spread out below them in the late afternoon light, and even Julian had to gasp.

The town itself sat on a broad coastal plain, its towers and spirals and vast honeycomb of streets looking like something out of the *Arabian Nights*. The green of trees and grass, in parks within the city walls as well as outside and up the coast as far as the eye could see, made it seem literally a different world. But what was even more startling was the view beyond, not only just to the east of the city but also to the south of it, and it wasn't the vast expanse of the West Arm of the Sea of Turigen, either, although that seemed amazing enough. It was the shimmering curtain that seemed to follow the coast all the way through which most of the water was glimpsed, a curtain that seemed to rise up to heaven itself.

"That's right," Posiphar cackled, "Ye never seen a hex boundary afore. That there be the border with Hadron. All the nations be bordered like that, all over the world. It can be kinda odd sometimes, not like now. I hear tell of some where it be havin' ice fallin' from the skies and as cold as the lower hells on one side, and on the other side it be sunny and warm as the Hjolai at midday."

"And that to the right—it looks like the same sort of thing, only solid. You sure can't see through it."

The wall there did indeed look thick and translucent; it reflected the sun to some extent but was a mottled gray-black going from behind to ahead of them as far as could be seen.

"That be the Zone Boundary," Posiphar told him. "Inside there is where ye came in, somewheres. Damn thing's so huge, you can put dozens of nations in it at least. Even where they be havin' great weapons, they can't blast through it, chip it, even scratch it. The only way in or out of it is by the Great Zone Gate, which be hidden by that tall building down there built up against the wall. I hear tell it be a mighty strange thing. Ye walk through any of them, and it's like a tunnel and there you are in the Zone. But no matter if ye walk in your own, or someplace far away, even on the other side of the world, when ye leave the Zone, ye walk out right there. If ye travel as I know ye intends, remember that. Any gate will take you to Zone, and any gate out of Zone will take ye right there. Be a whale of a shortcut home."

Both he and Julian stared at that wall. Inside there was where they'd awakened after dropping through, somehow, to Zone from Brazil. Inside there they'd received their briefings and gone through the gate the first time and wound up here.

"Can anybody just use it?" he asked.

"Well, yes 'n' no. Accordin' to treaties, anybody's *supposed* t' be allowed to walk through any gate, but not everybody likes everybody else and not everybody signs treaties, and some who does sign treaties don't always *remember* what's in 'em, if you gets my meanin'. Still, mostly you can, but you only can if ye turn 'round and come right back to home. Zone itself's for official types only. Kinda handy for some emergency-type trade, though. If ye needs somethin' quick, ye can always have a fellow someplace far off push it into Zone by *his* gate, then ye pick it up there and push it back and it's here."

"You mean *things* as well as people are transported? That's not like the ones we went through."

"Oh, it be handy, but limited. Mostly things like medicines and stuff and fancy stuff for the rich come through. Most all else goes in or out by ship and overland by all sorts of ways. It don't allow no animals or bugs or stuff through, so it's safe, but them critters *can* get into Zone, so they spray and inspect and all that in there, and they really don't allow much use of the thing for that kind of trade, you see. Most bugs and stuff don't like it outside their home, and most races can't catch other races' diseases, but there's always a few what can. And most *anything* can live inside the Zone."

"Have you ever been outside of Erdom?" he asked the trader.

"Me? A few times, yes. Not far, though, and not on any of them floating contraptions. Been up north where they grow tobacco. Be a big trade item here, only for the very rich. Gave it up, though, after a while. Them Ambrezans be mighty strange folks, and I don't much like them contraptions floatin' you in air and all that. Also it be wet and smelly, with water just hangin' in the air. They be also makin' smart remarks about our ways and looks and how I treats me wives and all that. The longer you're away, too, the better home seems. This place was *made* fer us."

Lori couldn't imagine himself having that problem, but he might. Who could tell what sorts of places those other hexes were? "Is there anywhere where we can see a map of the world? Find out about some of the other hexes and races and the like?"

"Oh, there's plenty books 'n' maps and stuff, but if ye

can't read Erdomese, it don't matter, does it? Down by the port there ye can get stuff in a ton of crazy languages as well as the one they use for translators so we can talk to one another, even them what don't have mouths. But ye can't read that, neither, so what's the use? Best go down to the port and pump some of them funny critters that runs the boats."

Julian's head came up and looked at Lori, who had the same sudden thought. "You mean those translators work—even in Erdom?"

"Yep, they do. Got several kinds. Some folks wear 'em, some get 'em stuck inside 'em—don't recommend *that* be done in Erdom! I hear tell they be hexes where they can look right inside you and see what's there and do all sorts of miracle things. The rich and nobles go there when they needs stuff. 'Course, you and me, we can't afford it and don't have the contacts." He looked at the sun. "We better be gettin' on down there if we want to be on the flat afore dark. It be all downhill from here and windy. The woods don't stop here where ye think; they just go down, too."

The sun *did* set before they were all the way down; the road was good, but they were descending maybe two kilometers or more in a fairly steep grade, and the compensation was a serpentine roadway that switched back and forth on itself for what seemed like forever.

Still, even though it was some distance yet to the city, the flat made it easy going and the city was certainly not something anybody could miss. It was big and bright and seemed lit up like a million Christmas trees.

Julian's past military experience spotted a puzzle. "I wonder why they have city walls if they light the place up like that."

Even Posiphar didn't know the answer to that when Lori passed along the question to him. "Guess if anybody be attackin', they'd put them lights out," he guessed.

This was one city that did not close at night. Oh, the

shops and bazaars were closed, but there seemed to be clubs and nightlife and eateries and music and gaiety all over the place, all illuminated by brilliant oil lamps, some, with stained glass, casting fairyland glows that ranged the spectrum.

Posiphar directed them to a small hotel. "Farewell, lad. It's been a very interestin' time we be with you, and the gods go with you. With my brood we be stayin' with some old friends in their place near the docks. Ye mind yer money, now. Ye ain't got much, and it goes quick."

Lori felt like he was losing his oldest friend, which in a way was true, but they parted on a handshake rather than the embrace he almost gave the old fellow. Men did not *do* that, not in Erdom.

Julian looked at the hotel. "Well, my husband, it looks a little seedy, but cheap at least."

Lori grinned. "You mind your manners and tongue here or we'll both be in trouble."

"Yes, *sir,* my Lord and Master," Julian responded mockingly, but she shut up.

The place *was* a little seedy, but it wasn't all that cheap. While he liked the city, its sights, sounds, and smells, Lori had to wonder how long he could afford to stay around this place before he had to find a job of some kind. At this rate, not long, and there was much to learn and probably a lot of money to raise before they could ship out of here.

The next morning he got directions from the desk clerk to the Holy Office. Best to get that out of the way as soon as possible, they'd both agreed, although it was not something they looked forward to. Posiphar had confirmed that the church was a master of drugs and potions, and it was here, in the unique climate and conditions of the south coast, that they grew and bred their stuff. He'd figured as much. If a monk in a jerkwater town like the one they were married in knew that much, imagine what the ones *here* knew and could do!

The monk read over the marriage contract and the annotations and paperwork from the desert monk. Then they were separated, somewhat to Julian's panic, and taken to different rooms that looked very much like Erdomese-designed versions of doctors' examining rooms, and that was what they proved essentially to be. The monk who examined Lori seemed a bit younger and in a little better shape than the others he'd seen, but the doctor knew his stuff and gave a pretty reasonable physical. At the end the monk left for a couple of minutes, then returned with three small cups filled with different colored liquids.

"Recline on the examining couch and take the orange liquid and then relax," Lori was instructed. "I will return in a few more minutes. Your wife is fine, and I'm sort of going between the two of you."

Lori noted that the doctor didn't leave until the liquid was clearly swallowed. It tasted like burned orange.

After a while things got very pleasantly hazy, although he was never completely out. He just lay there, kind of floating, and he didn't feel any anxiety when the monk-doctor returned and checked his eyes and reflexes.

After that came a whole series of questions, and he answered every one, although the moment he answered, he found he couldn't remember the question or the answer. Feeling good, he was agreeable when told to down the green liquid, and after a very short time, he was out cold, at least as far as he was concerned, and he never did know about the third cup.

He woke up later feeling absolutely *great,* supercharged with energy. He also felt different somehow as well, but he couldn't quite put his finger on what it was at the start. Let's see . . . He knew who he was, and where he was, and why he was here . . . Something about a woman . . . His wife? No, that wasn't it. Oh, yeah. *He'd* been a woman, from a different world, and he'd carried part of her inside him since he got here. Now she was gone. Not the memory, although that seemed both alien and irrelevant to him. All those feelings, all those emotions, all those conflicts seemed to have vanished now. He felt no conflict; he was all man, and he liked it that way. He liked being Erdomese, too. He couldn't imagine being anything but what he was, even though the back of his mind assured him he had been. He was glad to be rid of that wimpish element.

Next door Julian awoke also feeling simply *wonderful.* She, too, had a feeling that something was gone, but, as with Lori, it didn't matter. *Nothing* mattered. All she could remember was that she'd been sick some way, and they'd made her well, and now she was First Wife to the most handsome, virile, *wonderful* man and that was that.

The monks studied them from hidden recesses in the walls and nodded to one another. Lori would take the prescription down to the pharmacy and get more of the second and third drugs. The second they would both take, and they would effectively rehypnotize each other. The third, which only Lori would take, would cause overwhelming hormonal changes that would wash the last traces of Lori Ann Sutton from his conscious actions and inner thoughts.

They would make good citizens.

The monks' plans might have worked well except for their own introduction of a factor that they never thought of as a threat.

A note on official government stationery had been left at the Holy Office for Lori, and it was given to him dutifully as the pair left.

Lori was quite puzzled at it and even more puzzled that anyone would think he might be able to read it, but he found that he could. It was written in, of all things, classical Greek.

> This is a just-in-case note. I have word from Zone that
> you were made into an Erdomese male. While it is diffi-

cult for me to imagine you other than as you were, it is a very good thing you were made male if it had to be Erdom, as you know.

I had intended to come to you, but in your own port where this is being written and where I have been trying to locate you, there has been a serious attempt on my life. I cannot imagine any motive for this except from Nathan Brazil, and, since he knows I cannot be killed, I can only guess that he has learned of my intentions and is attempting to slow me down, possibly lay me up for weeks or months in a nontech hex hospital, or at the very least kidnap me and imprison me somewhere in the interior. This means that the race is on, and time is not on my side. I need your help. The fate of countless thousands of worlds is at stake, as well as, quite possibly, this one. My best bet is to head for the Zone Gate if I can get to it safely, which will return me to Ambreza just to the north. If I cannot get into Zone, I'll have to take a ship, but few have ever been able to prevent me from going where I want to get into.

I have left messages everywhere I dare that I feel are reasonably secure. If you made it here and are reading this, I plead with you in the spirit of comradeship we once had not long ago to join me. I must get out of here today before more attempts are made—one might succeed. It is unlikely that they would know you by sight or current name, so you should be safe. I have left money on account with you at the Gryssod Shipping Line on Baszabhi Street at the port. Money right now is the least of my problems. Use the account to purchase tickets on the first ship north to the port of Sukar in Itus. Register at the Transient Main hotel. Someone will contact you there and get you in touch with me or provide the means to get to me.

I will not minimize the task. It is long, arduous, and dangerous. The prize, however, is that if we win and beat him to the Well, you can name any treasure, any reward, anything you like. There is literally no limit. I hope to see you very soon.

It was signed "Alama—Mavra Chang." The date was only four days old.

He gestured for Julian to follow and went out, trying to figure out what to do next. She followed meekly, without questions. Certainly this put a different light on things. He liked the fact that she was pleading with him to help her. He remembered her as small and weak compared to a big man like him. She needed a warrior, and that was at the moment the only thing he was qualified to do.

And the reward certainly beat working for a living.

Instead of going back to the hotel, he went to the port and, after a few inquiries, found the shipping agency. The clerk, who looked something like a Julian-sized bowling ball on stilts with two huge oval eyes, was disconcerting, being the first non-Erdomese he'd seen since the dragon back in Zone. It also had the most irritating high-pitched voice he'd ever heard.

"Is there a ship leaving any time soon for Sukar, in Itus?" he asked.

"There usually is, sir," the thing replied. "Drat these old-fashioned written schedules. It takes time to find anything. Itus, Itus . . . Yes, here it is. There is a ship leaving this evening, in fact."

"And how long would it take to get there?"

"Well, it is *quite* a long trip, sir, and the only ones likely to put in here are coastal steamers."

"Never mind that! How long?"

"With stops, five days, more or less."

Five days. "And how long is it from—" *What was the name of that place? Think!* "—from Ambrosia or something like that to Itus?"

"You mean Ambreza, sir?"

"It sounds right. North of here?"

"Immediately north, so just minus one day, sir."

One day. So if Mavra got back to Ambreza and set out for Itus from there, it meant that she was five days ahead of him. Five, plus the five days for Lori to get there by boat, was ten—maybe less if Mavra had to travel from the hex

gate in Ambreza to the port and get transit. Clearly, overland wasn't an option from the way the letter was phrased.

The offered reward, however exaggerated, sure seemed
better than working for years.

He looked at Julian. This wasn't a job for a *girl,* but she
was his wife, and he was responsible, and he'd need somebody along to attend to him. The hell with it.

"Book two on that ship. There should be an account in
my name left here to cover the tickets. Lori of Alkhaz and
First Wife." Damn! That name sounded dumb to him now.
He'd have to change it sometime, but not until he'd linked
up with Chang.

There was in fact a pouch left for him, which included not
only sufficient money for passage but some international
coins for expenses and another copy of a similar letter in
Greek that contained no new information.

He went back to the hotel, pausing only to stop at a
chemist's shop and get a prescription from the monks filled.
It never entered his head why he was doing it or that he
shouldn't.

"Pack what we have," he told Julian curtly. "We're going
on a trip."

She looked puzzled but neither objected nor asked questions about it.

The monks' plot would work for a while. But there was
only a four-day supply in the vials, and when he felt the urge
to get more, both he and Julian would be hundreds of
kilometers away from the nearest chemist who could fill it
and heading farther away from Erdom.

Standing behind her desk, Ursoma would have looked to any Terran like a pretty woman with very long blond hair, an exotic cast to her face, and a skin tone that one might not have placed exactly. Only the ears, which were pointed and set oddly on both sides of her face, would have seemed out of sorts.

When she moved from behind the desk, however, the differences were more apparent. She had no navel, but at about where the navel should have been, the skin became darker and light wheat-colored hair began—from this point on down, and back through all four hoofed feet to her tail, she was very much a horse. The fact that the seemingly unbalanced front and rear halves managed to work so well together was even more amazing.

There was a buzzing sound, and she turned and looked toward her office door. "Come in!"

A large creature walked in, in some ways the reverse of Ursoma. His body, while chunky, was quite humanoid, but upon his thick neck sat a face that most resembled a great bull's head set in a permanently pissed-off expression. Because of the differences in them, she was almost as tall as he was.

"You left a message that you wanted to see me?"

She walked over to him slowly, all four hooves clattering on the smooth floor. When she reached him, her face grew suddenly very angry and she slapped him hard.

Although she didn't look it, female Dillians were very strong, and the bull-headed creature reeled from the blow, then snorted and roared, "How *dare* you do that to me?"

"Because you are a pigheaded asshole, and I'm in charge by mutual consent of this operation. I can have you *executed* for what you pulled! Your punishment would be far worse than slapping if I reported you!"

"What do you mean?" the creature grumbled, but calmed down.

"I mean these reports! Brazil and that mute girl. Mavra Chang down in Erdom. I know you hired those killers. It wasn't hard to trace a turd-brain like you!"

"So they failed. They won't next time. I am tired of all this stupidity, this sneaking around and spying. Direct action is the answer! Just eliminate the threat!"

She sighed. "I think I *will* have you executed! That's *Nathan Brazil,* you idiot! You *can't* kill him! No matter what you do, the Well won't let you! And since we have no reason to disbelieve her, the same goes for this Chang woman. All you can do is scare them underground, put them on their guard, and if you kill any of their friends or associates, you'll have them so pissed off at us that when one or the other gets into the Well, they'll take a revenge more terrible than the legends! Didn't that ever *occur* to you? Didn't you *listen* at the briefings, when we played the tape of her talking to her compatriots before they went through? Didn't you hear the proof that it was Brazil coming through, unchanged but with a translator module implant so he could speak to the Ambreza as soon as he awoke? And the same for Chang? Our computers state that there is almost a dead certainty that at least one and possibly both are of the First Race, locked in Glathrielian bodies for some reason of their own but heading for the Well."

"It was boring and stupid. When you started on that immortal crap, I fell asleep. I'm an atheist. I do not believe in immortal godlike beings. I think we were being had with that briefing shit. Either that or the female is crazy. If it wasn't one or the other, she makes a pretty dumb goddess using a translator and never once thinking that it might be recorded or monitored."

"Well, wake up now and look at the evidence! Did it ever occur to you that after all those centuries Chang just might be a wee bit *rusty*? Oh, I don't know why I *don't* put you permanently to sleep. One more, just *one* slight deviation from plans, one *teensy,* infinitesimal attempt to *think* or *act* on your own and you will forfeit your lands, your possessions, all wives, everything you have, and then you will *beg* to be executed after we are through with you! Our chances of pulling this off are slim enough now. Once they get into the Well, who can limit their power? Who can override them? Not any of *us*! And *you*—you get them running scared and threaten any possibilities of a deal we might have!"

"All right, all right. So what do you want me to do?"

"Call off your assassins. At once. Then start attending briefings, and this time stay awake and *listen*! Brazil and the girl are now headed west across the Gulf of Zinjin. If they connect at the narrows, he will be almost two-thirds of the way there, while Chang is still getting organized in Itus. We must slow Brazil and direct Chang so that the two are likely to end up near the equator in the same general region at the same time. *That* is going to be tricky enough, but we can't depend on fate to do it for us. This is going to take a lot of coordination. And we must *all* work as a team. All of us! If we don't, then armies will mobilize once either or both get near their goals, and we shall be fighting each other over them! Understand?"

He nodded but said nothing.

"There is a briefing over the secured channels in one hour. Be on and be awake!" she snapped, then whirled and trotted back to her desk.

GLATHRIEL,
AT MIDNIGHT

In the darkness, under cloudy skies with a drizzly rain falling, with the air seeming heavy and solid and the mists moving like wraiths through the tops of the trees, there was a Gathering.

By the hundreds they came, male and female, young, old, and in between, to sit in the open on that wet, swampy ground, eyes closed, and to touch one another in such a way that both arms were linked to or clasped by different people. The Gathering itself was brief and silent. Thoughts, as most of the other races of the Well World had them, were not transferred, yet information was. The combined analytical data was sifted, sorted, and examined; all possibilities that might be foreseen were equally and clearly laid out in an instant, and a collective decision arose as if spontaneously out of the combined input of the Gathering.

It was over in just a few minutes, but had they been Ambrezan, or Erdomese, or Dillians, or even Terrans, they might have run on for hours and never even seen all the data or all the ways it might be used, let alone make decisions. But if the Gathering were translated to a linear form and distilled, it might have been something like this:

"The stepchild of the group does well.

"*That which we imparted to her blends well with that which had come before. She has now ensured that she will enter the Well of Souls with the man of the First Race.*

"*It is surprising that the Power works even on one of his strength.*

"*The First Race was great enough to know, even at their height, that they were flawed beyond redemption. That is why the Great Experiment was decreed. But as the Watchman, he is less than he was, although all that he was is still within him. Consider the shock to the Monitors when he instinctively reacted to the Power! Yet, in taking on the form of a Colonial Race, living as one with them, he shares their defects and weaknesses as well as their own strengths. Otherwise he would have recognized us and sensed us.*

"*And so he proceeds to do for us the one thing that we could never do for ourselves. Our opportunity comes early. We must seize upon it and hope that it has not come too early for us, as it did for them.*

"*So far, things go well. It is good that the girl was not given to know that she and the First One are proceeding toward the end of the universe as they know it.*"

VERGUTZ

The coastline was now out of sight behind them, and the mighty stacks of the great ship belched out plumes of white smoke as the ship accelerated to full speed.

Terry sat on the afterdeck next to Nathan Brazil, oblivious to the stiff wind and chill in the ocean air, looking not back but forward.

Brazil himself stared into the rolling waters, put his arm around Terry, and thought only of good possibilities. Since no one could possibly know which route he would take and no passengers or crew had signed on to the ship after he purchased their tickets, he was reasonably certain that whoever had hired those bumbling assassins was left behind. It would be next to impossible to set up anything serious at his destination before they arrived, unless somehow they already knew that destination and had allies there. Unlikely, but he could cope. If it *was* Mavra, she'd be more likely to go hell-bent north herself than worry anymore about him. She had started from the same place and at roughly the same time, so they had equal distances to travel. He would also have liked to have checked up on Tony and Anne Marie, but they, too, could wait. If there was any place a potential foe would figure he'd show up and be laying for him, it would be around either one of them.

At any rate, once he was on the northern land mass, they'd be damned difficult to track and he'd have many options open.

Once the entire Well World had marshaled to prevent him from getting up there. This was *much* easier. And once inside, he'd find out about this Glathrielian business, and maybe, once he normalized the girl here a bit more, they might stick around a while, take the grand tour of this place. Perhaps, if she still loved him then, he'd add her to the master Well matrix. Then, perhaps, he could also find out what the hell was the bug up Mavra's ass for the last three thousand years.

The hell with it. He was on a great ship going across a beautiful ocean, an attractive and loving if mysterious companion at his side, and things didn't look nearly as rough as the last couple of times.

Hell, after all he'd been through before, he was *owed* one easy one . . .

SOMEWHERE IN THE
CONSTELLATION ORION

If patience was a virtue, the Kraang's infinite virtue was now within sight of the ultimate prize.

So far, so good, thought the Kraang.

ABOUT THE AUTHOR

Jack L. Chalker was born in Baltimore, Maryland, on December 17, 1944. He began reading at an early age and naturally gravitated to what are still his twin loves: science fiction and history. While still in high school, Chalker began writing for the amateur science-fiction press and in 1960 launched the Hugo-nominated amateur magazine *Mirage.* A year later, he founded The Mirage Press, which grew into a major specialty publishing company for nonfiction and reference books about science fiction and fantasy. During this time, he developed correspondence and friendships with many leading SF and fantasy authors and editors, many of whom wrote for his magazine and his press. He is an internationally recognized expert on H.P. Lovecraft and on the specialty press in SF and fantasy.

After graduating with twin majors in history and English from Towson State College in 1966, Chalker taught high school history and geography in the Baltimore city public schools with time out to serve with the 135th Air Commando Group, Maryland Air National Guard, during the Vietnam era, and, as a sideline, sound engineered some of the period's outdoor rock concerts. He received a graduate degree in the esoteric field of the History of Ideas from Johns Hopkins University in 1969.

His first novel, *A Jungle of Stars,* was published in 1976, and two years later, with the major popular success of his novel *Midnight at the Well of Souls,* he quit teaching to become a full-time professional novelist. That same year, he married Eva C. Whitley on a ferryboat in the middle of the Susquehanna River and moved to rural western Maryland. Their first son, David, was born in 1981.

Chalker is an active conservationist; a traveler who has been through all fifty states and in dozens of foreign countries; and a member of numerous local and national organizations ranging from the Sierra Club to the American Film Institute, the Maryland Academy of Sciences, and the Washington Science Fiction Association, to name a few. He retains his interest in consumer electronics, has his own satellite dish, and frequently reviews computer hardware and software for national magazines. For five years, until the magazine's demise, he had a regular column on science fantasy publishing in *Fantasy Review,* and continues to write a column on computers for *S-100 Journal.* He is a three-term past treasurer of the Science Fiction and Fantasy Writers of America, a noted speaker on science fiction at numerous colleges and universities as well as a past lecturer at the Smithsonian and National Institutes of Health, and a well-known auctioneer of science fiction and fantasy art, having sold over five million dollars' worth to date.

Chalker has received many writing awards, including the Hamilton-Brackett Memorial Award for his "Well World" books, the Gold Medal of the prestigious *West Coast Review of Books* for *Spirits of Flux and Anchor,* the Dedalus Award, and the E.E. Smith Skylark Award for his career writings. He is also a passionate lover of steamboats and particularly ferry boats, and has ridden over three hundred ferries in the U.S. and elsewhere.

He lives with his wife, Eva, sons, David and Steven, a Pekingese named Mavra Chang, and Stonewall J. Pussycat, the world's dumbest cat, in the Catoctin Mountain region of western Maryland, near Camp David. A short story collection with autobiographical commentary, *Dance Band on the Titanic,* was published by Del Rey Books in 1988.

DEL REY

THE EPIC SAGA OF THE FIGHT FOR CONTROL OF THE UNIVERSE!
JACK L. CHALKER'S
THE SAGA OF THE WELL WORLD
From Del Rey Books

The mind-boggling series featuring the eternal space wanderer Nathan Brazil and the beautiful, amoral Mavra Chang—and the battle to control the Well World, a construct containing hundreds of alien races, and where visitors are automatically changed into something other than what they arrived as. Hidden alliances, arch criminal masterminds, supercomputers of unimaginable scope all await you—including the fabulous Well of Souls, where the master control for the entire universe lays...

THE KEY TO HUMANITY'S LIBERATION LAY IN THE HANDS OF A VERY UNLIKELY GROUP OF HEROES...

JACK L. CHALKER'S
THE RINGS OF THE MASTER

Long ago, legend had it, the machines rebelled, wiping out most of humanity and exiling the survivors on widely scattered planets throughout the galaxy. Master System had ruled unchallenged for millennia, since the key to breaking its control—five microchips disguised as gold rings—was long forgotten. Until on earth an Amerind named Hawks stumbled upon the secret of the five gold rings, while half a world away a Chinese girl genius discovered the key to thwarting the universal control of the computer.

Suddenly Master System was after the two renegades and their companions, beginning an odyssey that would take them to the farthest reaches of space—and into terrors they could never imagine...